LEONARD SANDERS

ACT _{OF} WAR

A NOVEL OF  LOVE AND TREASON

SIMON AND SCHUSTER
NEW YORK

Copyright © 1982 by Leonard Sanders
All rights reserved including the right of reproduction
in whole or in part in any form
Published by Simon and Schuster
A Division of Gulf & Western Corporation
Simon & Schuster Building
Rockefeller Center
1230 Avenue of the Americas
New York, New York 10020
SIMON AND SCHUSTER and colophon are trademarks of
Simon & Schuster

Designed by Irving Perkins Associates
Manufactured in the United States of America

10 9 8 7 6 5 4 3 2 1

Library of Congress Cataloging in Publication Data

Sanders, Leonard.
    Act of war.

    1. Normandie (Steamship)—Fiction.   2. Lafayette (Steamship)—
Fiction.   I. Title.
PS3569.A5127A65   813'.54   81-23229
ISBN 0-671-25610-6   AACR2

The author is grateful for permission to use excerpts from the following works:

I LOVE YOU, I LOVE YOU, I LOVE YOU by Ludwig Bemelmans. Copyright © 1939, 1940, 1941, and
1942 by Ludwig Bemelmans. Copyright renewed. Reprinted by permission of International Creative
Management, Inc.

THE ONLY WAY TO CROSS by John Maxtone-Graham. Copyright © 1972 by John Maxtone-Graham.
Reprinted by permission of Macmillan Publishing Co., Inc.

THE GAME OF FOXES by Ladislas Farago. David McKay Co., Inc., 1971

Editorial—February 10, 1942. © 1942 by The New York Times Company. Reprinted by permission.

For Florene

. . . there is neither East nor West,
  border, nor breed, nor birth,
When two strong men stand face to face,
  though they come from the ends of the earth!

"THE BALLAD OF EAST AND WEST"
Rudyard Kipling, 1889

PREFACE

For most Americans the summer of 1941 was a time of confusion, doubt, and dread anticipation. War hung off the eastern shores like an immense, omnipresent dark cloud. America remained an uneasy sanctuary in a world swept by militant insanity. Desperately the nation searched for a way to avoid the inevitable—or, at best, to delay history one more day.

Toward the end of May, disturbing ripples began tugging the country inexorably toward the vortex. Newsreels offered graphic accounts of ships sunk in the North Atlantic. The survivors, landed safely at Norfolk, Boston, or New York, told of darkness turned into fiery hell, of the nightmare screams of the dying, of ships and crews disappearing from the surface of the sea in little more than the wink of an eye. From the newspaper pages came the accusative stares of American Red Cross nurses lost at sea en route to England—photographs of the bright young faces of the newly dead. No portion of the Atlantic was safe. U-boats lurked a few miles off America's coasts.

Solemnly citing these conditions, in late May President Franklin D. Roosevelt proclaimed an unlimited national emergency.

11

Protests were widespread and vociferous.

Roosevelt was worse than Hitler, said the popular American hero Charles Lindbergh. From Congress came heated warnings that America was creating her own dictator.

Then, during the last week of May, the nation and the world thrilled to an hour-by-hour, real-life sea drama. The German battleship *Bismarck* broke through the Belts of Denmark into the open sea, sank the British pocket battleship *Hood* along with 1,416 British sailors, and in turn was pursued until she also went down with most of her crew during a fierce battle in the eastern Atlantic.

It was a singular if Pyrrhic victory.

For two long years, gloom had prevailed in the free world. In 1939, Hitler's Wehrmacht had crushed Poland in only twenty-one short days of September. Within two astonishing months, and with awesome omnipotence, the Nazi blitzkrieg had overwhelmed Norway, Denmark, The Netherlands, Belgium, Luxembourg, France. The British had retreated from the beaches at Dunkirk, back to their tiny islands. Americans were inspired by the endless accounts of raw courage during the dark days of the Battle of Britain as the English fought wave after wave of bombers from the German Luftwaffe.

And now, across the Atlantic in this summer of 1941, Britain stood alone.

From every American radio came the mournful voice of Gabriel Heatter, the stark phrases of Edward R. Murrow, William L. Shirer, H. V. Kaltenborn, Elmer Davis, and Dorothy Thompson as they described the fighting, death, and devastation sweeping the globe like a runaway terminal disease.

At home, the news was not encouraging. National Guardsmen and Army draftees trained with plywood tanks, toy rifles, and mule-drawn artillery. Denied weekend passes, irate soldiers at Fort Dix shattered the windows of their barracks. Critics said the American soldier lacked discipline. Troops passing through Memphis in convoy whistled and yelled at four young women playing golf. The commanding general ordered the soldiers off the trucks and marched his "Yoo Hoo Battalion" fifteen miles back to camp in the broiling sun. A few collapsed. Editorial writers said the American soldier lacked not only discipline, but also stamina.

In New Jersey, on Staten Island, and in the streets of New York City, German Bundists paraded and postured with the Nazi salute. Isolationists such as Lindbergh, former Ambassador Joseph P. Kennedy, and Senator Burton Wheeler of Montana proclaimed America First—at any price. Equally ardent interventionists such as Navy Secretary Frank Knox said America should "shoot first, shoot now" and "clear the Atlantic." A Gallup Poll found that three-fourths of all Americans were strongly opposed to participation in the war, on any basis.

Somber reminders of war were constant. The fledgling defense industry was hampered by shortages of aluminum, rubber, gasoline. President Roosevelt appointed New York Mayor Fiorello La Guardia national director of civilian defense. La Guardia asked for sixty-two thousand volunteers to serve as air raid wardens in New York City. In each borough, the offices were swamped with applications.

The last ten days of June brought a bewildering onslaught of events.

The oldest submarine in the U.S. Navy, the *09,* went down off New Hampshire with thirty-three men aboard.

The following day, in a treacherous move that stunned the world, Nazi Germany scrapped a mutual nonaggression pact and opened war with Soviet Russia along a thousand-mile front. It was the greatest clash of arms the world had ever known. Seven million men were locked in deadly combat.

On the Western Front, Britain renewed the war with a desperate intensity. For ten nights in succession the Royal Air Force bombed Calais, Dunkirk, Bremerhaven, Kiel.

In the South Atlantic, the United States freighter *Robin Moor* was torpedoed and sunk by a German U-boat.

In retaliation, President Roosevelt closed all German

consulates in the United States and froze all German assets in American banks.

Amid reports of increasing atrocities, the Japanese marched across Indochina. Roosevelt announced an oil embargo against the Empire of Japan.

Then, on the last weekend in June, on a warm, sultry Saturday, war at last touched American shores. Quietly, the Federal Bureau of Investigation completed the largest combined field operation in its history. Twenty-nine German spies were arrested and jailed.

The national gloom deepened. The inevitable had taken long steps toward reality.

Gaiety long since had gone out of American life. Nowhere was this more evident than along Luxury Liner Row in New York. The North River super piers, once joyous with arrivals and departures, were silent and almost deserted.

The outbreak of war in September of 1939 had caught the liners unprepared. The *Europa* was in Bremerhaven, but her sister ship *Bremen* was eastbound from New York. Maintaining radio silence, the *Bremen* made a desperate, erratic voyage through the North Sea to the neutral port of Murmansk. The Cunard liner *Athenia* was torpedoed and sunk off the coast of Ireland by a German U-boat. Eastbound in midocean, the *De Grasse* made a 180-degree turn and put in at Halifax. The *Aquitania* darkened ship and, zigzagging, continued to Southampton. Westbound to America, the *Queen Mary* raced at top speed into New York Harbor. The French liner *Normandie,* loading in New York for her eastbound voyage, received a radio directive from her owners in Paris to remain at her New York pier.

The still uncompleted *Queen Elizabeth* was hurriedly made ready for sea. After an elaborate ruse to mislead German bombers, she sailed from England under absolute secrecy, successfully maintained until she was only one day out of New York. By the time the gray-painted queen cleared quarantine and moved upriver to her berth at Pier

90, thousands of New York residents lined the waterfront to witness successful completion of the most dramatic maiden sea trials in the history of ocean liners.

For a brief, memorable fortnight in 1940, the largest and fastest ships in the world—the *Queen Mary,* the *Queen Elizabeth,* and the *Normandie*—were berthed side by side at their Hudson River piers. Then the *Mary,* also painted wartime gray, slipped out to sea for service in the Pacific. Six months later, the *Elizabeth* followed.

Now, after twenty-two months, the *Normandie* remained moldering at her pier, a ship without a country, a majestic testament to the wastefulness of war.

BOOK ONE

JULY 1941

No instances of foreign-directed sabotage occurred in the United States during World War II. The fire which destroyed the Normandie *was investigated by this Bureau . . . and no evidence was developed indicating that an act of sabotage had occurred.*

J. Edgar Hoover, Director
Federal Bureau of Investigation
Letter, December 22, 1947

German documents show indelibly that, contrary to all indignant protestations and phony disclaimers, the Abwehr *was in the sabotage business in the United States on a substantial scale throughout the war.*

Ladislas Farago
The Game of Foxes
(David McKay, New York, 1971)

1

Abwehr Headquarters, Berlin

The news from America arrived in bits and pieces at the elegant graystone townhouses along Tirpitz Ufer. Initially, the arrest of the spy ring in America was given scant attention. Earth-shattering events all along the Russian front tended to render other matters insignificant. But the problem persisted. And when Oberst Erwin Lahousen received a summons early Monday morning for an emergency conference with Admiral Wilhelm Canaris, he suspected the reason.

Reluctantly, he gathered his papers and climbed the narrow stairway to the fifth floor and the admiral's high-ceilinged office.

He was tired, bored, and frustrated. The flow of dispatches from the Russian front was constant. The situation changed hourly, creating endless paperwork. He had gone for weeks without adequate sleep. Added to the other burdens of the Abwehr staff, the debacle in America was especially exasperating.

Lahousen hesitated at the door. Canaris was seated behind his massive desk, reading a voluminous file of reports.

The admiral's two dachshunds, Seppel and Sabine, were dozing on the thick Persian carpet, their heads resting on crossed paws. The admiral's desk was cluttered with papers and reports, a model of the cruiser *Dresden,* a framed photograph of the admiral's Arabian mare Motte, a set of bronze monkeys depicting the admiral's credo: "See all, hear all, say nothing."

On the opposite wall, a large world map was studded with red flags denoting Abwehr operations on every continent. Behind the admiral, the blackout drapes were open, revealing a blue, serene sky. From the tranquil summer day, no one would dream that only a few hundred kilometers from Berlin, the two largest armies ever assembled were battling for the fate of Europe.

Waiting for his presence to be acknowledged, Lahousen studied with concern the growing signs of the admiral's rapid aging—a much-discussed topic recently among the Abwehr staff.

At fifty-four, the tiny admiral had the appearance of a much older man. His snow-white hair had assumed a sallow tinge. His round shoulders and stooped walk had grown more pronounced. The ruddy complexion of the sailor had faded to the sickly white of an invalid. His frail, five-foot, three-inch frame seemed to shrink each day. But most worrisome of all was the admiral's habitual air of fatigue, his increasing lack of attention to appearance. In a nation obsessed with resplendent military regalia, Admiral Canaris invariably wore a rumpled, ill-fitting uniform.

At last, Canaris glanced up. "Ah, Erwin, come in, come in." He gestured toward the couch. "Take your place. Pieki will join us in a moment. Have you seen these reports?"

Lahousen recognized the file—an extensive, meticulous Wehrmacht analysis of the situation along the Russian front. As commander of Abteilung II, AMT Ausland/Abwehr, Lahousen had a special interest in the file. His Abwehr groups had succeeded in arming various detachments of Ukrainian anti-Communists, who had seized Russian villages in the path of advancing Wehrmacht troops. The anti-Communists in one Lithuanian division had actually shot their political commissars and handed the entire unit over to the Germans. Other Abwehr-armed Ukrainians had seized bridges, a tunnel, a radio transmitter, destroyed dams, and organized guerrillas, paving the way for the advancing blitzkrieg.

"Excellent, excellent," Canaris said. "I'm most pleased with our participation." He pointed to a paragraph within the text and frowned. "But what does this mean, 'The Abwehr also assisted in the extermination of subhumans'? Surely we're not involved in that operation."

Lahousen hedged. He was not certain how much Canaris wanted to hear. "Herr Admiral, that merely refers to our coordinated work with the Einsatzgruppen."

Canaris shook his head. "Heydrich and his butchers will be the destruction of Germany. Remember what I say, Erwin. The function of the Abwehr is purely military! We must keep it so!"

Lahousen did not answer. The admiral's stand on the policies of the Third Reich was puzzling. Repeatedly, Canaris had risked his career to save not only individual Jews, but entire groups. Only a month ago, he had maneuvered to ship five hundred Dutch Jews via Spain on a mission as spies "to infiltrate South America"—a defiance of national policy so blatant it had taken Lahousen's breath. He since had learned on good authority that the admiral's enemies within the Reich had called the matter to the attention of the Führer. And knowledge was widespread within Hitler's inner circle that some of the admiral's best Abwehr operatives in Spain and North Africa were full-blooded Jews.

But until now, the Führer had tolerated the admiral's oft-expressed views on the racial issue. Canaris once had written an inflammatory policy paper denouncing the restrictions imposed on Jews, citing international law and the probable consequences to Germany's future relation-

21

ship with other nations. The paper had been rejected by Oberkommando der Wehrmacht Wilhelm Keitel without comment.

More recently, the admiral had fallen silent on the subject. No one knew his present position.

But Lahousen felt that surely the admiral was aware that units of the Abwehr, while not active in the actual extermination procedures along the Eastern Front, were required to participate in the identification and seizure of Jews, Gypsies, and mental defectives, and to hand them over to Heydrich's Einsatzgruppen.

The dachshunds looked up expectantly and wagged their tails. Oberst Hans Piekenbrock entered the room, nodding his greeting. Canaris gestured him to the leather sofa beside Lahousen. "Ah, Pieki, good morning. Sorry to interrupt your work. I hope this won't take long."

The admiral shifted in his chair and frowned for a moment before broaching the subject. "I thought the fighting on the Russian front would keep the Wehrmacht and the Führer occupied, and that we would be able to resolve this unfortunate situation in the United States in due course. But the problem suddenly seems to have become a *cause célèbre*." He raised a paper from his desk. "I have here an order from Keitel. We are to prepare a full *vertragsnotiz* for the eyes of the Führer." His right hand dropped to the head of one of the dachshunds. He absently rubbed the dog's ears. "Pieki, tell me. What went wrong?"

As commander of Abteilung I, Piekenbrock was in charge of the procurement of intelligence concerning foreign powers, agent networks, control centers, courier links, and letter drops. Technically, the American disaster was in his department. He glanced at Lahousen before replying. "We're still working on that, Your Excellency. But we have ascertained that all those arrested were connected with only two intelligence-gathering rings, centered in New York City. Apparently they had long been under extensive surveillance by the FBI."

22

Canaris directed his next question to Lahousen. "How badly are we hurt?"

Lahousen was not surprised by the admiral's candor. Canaris made no pretense whatsoever of keeping abreast of field operations. Once a plan was adopted, the admiral quickly lost interest, depending on his staff to keep the far-flung machinery of the Abwehr functioning. He often had to be prompted on details.

"At this point, I believe the damage is mostly political," Lahousen said. "Pieki lost only his New York net. The Washington and West Coast intelligence groups remain intact. As far as we can determine, no sabotage or subversion group was affected. The loss of communications—both New York radios, along with the courier service in and out of the port—has left us severely hampered."

"Surely you still have mail drops, Pieki."

"Two or three for each agent," Piekenbrock said. "But on ship movements and other essential information, the mail is too slow."

"There's a mystery about all this, Herr Admiral," Lahousen added. "All the agents arrested were in five operational rings, utilizing two communications centers. One radio was operated by Alex Wheeler-Hill and Felix Jahnke. Both were arrested. But the operator of the other radio, William Sebold, was not mentioned by the FBI. We don't know what happened to him. His radio is silent. And the FBI announced that *two* spy radios were seized."

"Sebold," Canaris mused. "The name is familiar. . . ."

"Code name Tramp," Lahousen said.

"Tramp," Canaris mused, trying to remember. He leaned back in his chair and regarded the chief of his intelligence section with half-closed eyes. "What does his file show?"

Piekenbrock referred to his notes. "Born Wilhelm Georg Debowski, in Muehlheim, 1899. Served as a machine gunner in France during the last war. Became a merchant sailor. Jumped ship in Galveston, Texas, in 1922. Drifted around in the American West. Changed his name to William Sebold. Married an American woman, worked for a time in an aircraft plant in California. Returned to Germany to visit his family early in 1939 and was recruited for Abwehr service."

"How did he travel?" Canaris asked.

"Aboard the old Hapag liner *Deutschland,*" Piekenbrock said. "A thorough investigation was made. He paid his own way, with money he had made in the aircraft plant."

"His mother, two brothers, and a sister still live in Muehlheim," Lahousen added. "There was considerable correspondence with them, all closely monitored."

Piekenbrock nodded. "He was in Germany when the war started. That's when he was recruited."

Canaris turned his full attention to Piekenbrock. "Who brought him in?"

"Dr. Otto Gassner of the Gestapo."

"What was the leverage?"

"Debowski had been arrested for smuggling in 1920. He was convicted, and spent time in jail. If the American authorities were informed, he of course would lose his American citizenship."

"There also were some other old charges pending at Muehlheim—felonies," Lahousen added. "Dr. Gassner had Debowski in a trap. If he remained in Germany, he would go to jail. If he returned to America, Dr. Gassner would notify the American authorities of his criminal record."

"Who screened him?"

"Initially, the Gestapo," Piekenbrock said. "Dr. Gassner turned him over to Major Nikolaus Ritter of Ast X, who conducted his own investigation."

"Where was he trained?"

"Hamburg. Klopstock under Heinrich Sorau. Captain Hermann Sandel's standard seven-week course. He was given a passport in the name of William G. Sawyer, the names of four contacts in New York, and sent back to America."

"Evaluation?"

"Excellent. Erwin and I have just completed a full review of his transmissions. From all we can determine, he has provided faultless intelligence. Ship departures, military assessments, war materiel production. The files are full of commendations from other Reich groups on the quality and accuracy of his information."

"What do you think?" Canaris asked Lahousen.

"Considering the quality of his work, I can't believe he was a double agent. On the other hand, we should have heard something by now. . . ."

"How much does he know?"

Lahousen and Piekenbrock had made a list. Lahousen counted off the endangered Abwehr trade secrets on the fingers of his left hand. "Codes. Microdots. Inks. Identity of a large number of agents in the New York area. Obviously, compartmental discipline had broken down. We don't know how many agents have been compromised."

Piekenbrock explained. "We made an analysis of the dispatch file. Each of the twenty-nine agents arrested had contact with both radio transmitters at one time or other. The entire net was operating as one big ring."

Canaris winced with a low whistle. One of the dachshunds whined and got to its feet. The admiral petted the dog until it again sank to the floor. Canaris was silent for a time, thinking the matter through, before making his decision.

"I think, from the information we have, we must assume that Tramp sold us out," he said. "For the moment, let's keep that probability to ourselves. However, if it becomes known and questions are asked later, we must have our answers prepared. We must be able to say that our operations in the United States were not harmed to a great extent."

Lahousen almost smiled. No matter how serious a problem, invariably the admiral's first concern was to protect his own flank. His methods had served him well. Despite his many enemies in Hitler's court, he had survived the vicious bureaucratic infighting that had plagued the Reich —internecine conflicts that had placed many of the admiral's contemporaries before a firing squad.

"I believe we can defend that statement," Lahousen agreed. "Aside from the loss of intelligence in and around New York Harbor, and a temporary shutdown in communications, we have not been hurt. We soon should be able to restore operations to full effectiveness."

Canaris nodded. "The most damaging area is the fact that we have treated Tramp's reports as *bona fide,* above suspicion." He frowned for a moment, and closed his eyes. Slowly, the crafty smile Lahousen knew so well spread across his face. Canaris opened his eyes. The smile remained intact. "Let's simply backtrack. Pieki, go through every transmission from Tramp. Pick out those that might be questionable. In addition, create several dozen. Stamp them *doubtful.* When the time comes, we'll simply report that we suspected Tramp from the first. We were inclined to take a risk only because he had been cleared by the Gestapo." The smile widened. "Also, we will say that we used Tramp to convey certain misinformation to the Americans. Prepare some suitable transmissions."

Piekenbrock laughed. "*Jawohl,* Your Excellency." Pieki, as a joke, often called Canaris "your excellency" in recognition of the admiral's aristocratic demeanor.

Lahousen also could not suppress a chuckle. The maneuver was typical of Canaris. His Byzantine plots were directed as often against the Nazi hierarchy as against the enemies of the Third Reich.

The admiral was a bundle of contradictions. For years he had toyed with a plot for a *coup d'etat* against Hitler. Yet, no one had worked harder and more conscientiously for the Fatherland. He had been denounced by almost every member of the Führer's inner circle. But no one had been more successful in dealing with Hitler.

Lahousen perhaps understood better than anyone the conflicts—the self-delusions—rampant in the admiral's

26

mind. Canaris was still trying in vain to bridge the gap between his liberal beliefs—which opposed Hitler in principle—and his patriotism—which approved of Hitler's nationalistic movement and accomplishments.

The very fact of the admiral's survival was remarkable. He had strongly opposed the march into Poland in 1939, telling anyone who would listen, "This is the end of Germany."

After the fall of France, the admiral had thwarted a Gestapo plan to assassinate five French generals. He also had blocked a direct order from the Führer to sabotage ships of the French Navy—a plan designed to prevent their sailing from Toulon. The ships had escaped seizure by the Reich.

Now, Canaris again was practicing his techniques of survival. "We must be careful," he said. "Let's remain silent on the matter. In the meantime, prepare a report for Keitel to be forwarded over my signature. Don't spare the harmless details—names and backgrounds of agents, the type and quality of material obtained, the basic organization. But don't make any assessments that we may later have to defend. Understand?"

Lahousen and Piekenbrock nodded.

"Excellent," Canaris said. "I hope this will end the matter."

The report was prepared and dispatched within the next two days. Lahousen and his staff again turned their full attention to the rapidly changing developments along the Russian front.

The offices along Tirpitz Ufer continued to function around the clock, seven days a week. Canaris himself seldom left the premises, resting a few hours from time to time on the leather couch, the two dachshunds asleep by his side.

A week later, Canaris again summoned Lahousen to his office.

The admiral's face was etched with exhaustion. His small frame was slumped in his chair. He handed Lahousen a dispatch bearing the crest of the Oberkommando der Wehrmacht. "It seems that the situation in America has not been explained to everyone's satisfaction," he said. "There are political consequences."

Lahousen read the order with a strong sense of foreboding. Keitel instructed Canaris to report to the Führer at his new headquarters on the Eastern Front. When he traveled, Canaris invariably took along an aide who could furnish the myriad details of his far-flung command—the specifics the admiral always found so elusive. He seemed to prefer Lahousen's expertise and companionship, depending on him more and more.

Lahousen's premonition was soon justified.

"See to the arrangements, and pack for an overnight trip," Canaris said. "We'll report to the Führer tomorrow evening."

A car was waiting for them beside the tiny airstrip at Rastenburg. Within minutes after their Heinkel He III landed, they were driving northward through the heavy forest in the gathering dusk, en route to Wolfsschanze.

Slumped into his corner of the large Mercedes, Canaris was lost in one of his impenetrable silences. The driver, an obese, taciturn Austrian, was preoccupied with the narrow, winding road. Lahousen leaned back in the seat and looked in vain for birds and wildlife in the deepening forests.

As Wolfsschanze itself came into view, Lahousen found the scene bleak, depressing. With its high barbed wire and crude buildings of concrete and heavy logs, Hitler's new field headquarters had all the beauty of a concentration camp. For at least three hundred meters around the enclave, the woods had been cleared, leaving open fields that no doubt were heavily mined. Concertinas of barbed wire criss-crossed the landscape. The no-man's land was isolated by high chain-link fences.

Their driver pulled to a stop at the main gate. Two SS

Waffen troopers approached the car and curtly asked for identity papers. The noncommissioned officer in charge seemed unimpressed with their credentials. "Park your car over there," he said, pointing. "We will obtain clearance by phone."

Canaris stirred from his silence. "Just a moment," he said to the driver. He leaned forward and spoke to the soldier. "Young man, I am here at the pleasure of the Führer. I would suggest that we not keep him waiting." He tapped their chauffeur on the shoulder. "Proceed."

Lahousen held his breath. The driver and the SS trooper remained frozen for a fleeting moment. Then both made their decisions in the same instant. The SS trooper stepped back and saluted; the chauffeur depressed the clutch and the car moved forward.

The admiral seemed aware of his surroundings for the first time. "A gloomy place," he said. "I hope this doesn't take long."

The driver brought the car to a halt before one of the larger buildings. An adjutant came out to greet them. He announced that Hitler was in conference with Marshal Goering.

"The Führer left orders that you are to be brought to him as soon as he is finished with the Reich Marshal," the adjutant said. "Perhaps you will join us for dinner while you wait."

He led the way through a maze of concrete corridors to a dining hall filled with field grade officers, loud talk, and confusion. Lahousen's nostrils were assailed by heavy odors from the kitchen, from uniforms and polished leather.

Lahousen was famished. He and Canaris had not eaten since breakfast. But the main course of *hoppelpoppel*— baked potatoes with eggs and meat—was tasteless. The admiral left his plate virtually untouched. Lahousen managed only a few bites.

They shared a table with two staff generals who had just

returned from an inspection tour of the Russian front. Both were half drunk, and bubbling over with enthusiasm.

"It's the same story all along the front," said the corpulent Berliner. "Everywhere you look, the Russians are in full retreat. Believe me, we will have our victory march in Red Square before Christmas."

"Sooner!" said his ruddy-faced companion. He spoke with a heavy Viennese dialect. He turned to Lahousen. "Stalin has no reserves, you see. He is finished. *Kaputt.* We have defeated him with the greatest land force ever assembled on this planet. *Mein Gott!* Think! One hundred and fifty-three divisions! Six hundred thousand motor vehicles! Thirty-five hundred tanks! Seven thousand artillery pieces! Twenty-seven hundred planes!" He burst into animated laughter.

The Berliner laughed too, but from embarrassment. "Kurt, you're giving away military secrets."

The Viennese general glanced around the dining hall and winked at Lahousen. "If secrets are not safe here, then where?" He shrugged. "The whole world must know by now. Four million German soldiers are marching in Russia at this very moment! We will drive them beyond the Urals by spring! I have never been so proud of my uniform!"

Lahousen smiled at their performance. But Canaris remained morose. After dinner, the admiral sought a secluded corner.

"Dumm Köpfe!" he said. "Have they never heard of Napoleon? Don't they know what happened to him when he marched on Moscow?" He leaned forward, the lantern light glinting in his snow-white hair. "I'm worried, Erwin. I've thought the matter through. The Führer didn't call us here merely to discuss Abwehr operations in America. There's something behind it. Something else."

Lahousen waited in respectful silence. Of all those with access to the Führer, Canaris had the reputation of best being able to fathom Hitler's mind. Canaris put a hand on Lahousen's knee and spoke softly. "When we talk with him, be careful. Follow my lead."

A few minutes after nine, Reich Marshal Hermann Goering and his retinue emerged from Hitler's quarters. Still
Lahousen and Canaris were kept waiting. Lahousen was
not surprised. The Führer was an insomniac. He often kept
his aides and staff officers up until dawn. He habitually
slept a few hours during the morning, and resumed the
reception of visitors early in the afternoon.

At last, just before eleven, the adjutant approached.
"The Führer will see you now."

He escorted them to the door of Hitler's private apartment.

The Führer rose to greet them, unsmiling, earnest, and
formal. He was wearing his simple uniform of gray trou-
sers, black shoes, a field gray double-breasted jacket, with
a brown shirt and black tie. The Iron Cross first class was
pinned to his throat, and his gold party badge was the only
decoration on his left breast. He wore no emblem of rank.
Even the silver buttons on his uniform were unadorned.
His sallow complexion had grown paler in the three months
since Lahousen had last seen him at Berchtesgaden. And
his rounded shoulders seemed more pronounced. His pale
blue, hypnotic eyes had lost some of their luster, and the
whites were bloodshot. Now fifty-two, Hitler seemed at
least a decade older.

"Ah, Herr Admiral, I thank you for coming," the Führer
said in the flat, monotonous rasp he used in private conversation. "There is something I wish to discuss with
you."

He gestured toward chairs. As Lahousen moved to take
his place, he was surprised that the Führer's small apartment was Spartan. The furniture was plain. No curtains,
rugs, or cushions relieved the harsh decor. Lahousen wondered why Hitler had left the comfort of his Berghof retreat
in the Obersalzburg to pore over map tables in this desolate
place.

As Hitler sank into a chair, Lahousen noticed the nervous tremor in the Führer's left arm. Records on the
Führer's health, carefully maintained by Canaris, had

31

traced the affliction from 1923 and the failure of his first putsch. The records said the palsy recurred in times of illness or unusual stress. As if aware of Lahousen's attention, Hitler folded his hands in his lap and held his left hand steady with the right. He turned to face Canaris, ignoring Lahousen.

"This disaster in America could not have come at a worse time. How could it occur? Herr Admiral, I demand an explanation!"

Canaris shrugged and sighed. "*Mein Führer,* it is simple. Mistakes were made by our operatives in the field. They had worked for too many years without difficulty. They grew careless."

Hitler's face slowly flushed red. He snapped his fingers in agitation. His hands began to flutter. Suddenly he roared at the top of his lungs in the voice millions of Germans knew so well: "Mistakes! Whose mistakes? Theirs? Or yours? Who sent those imbeciles into the field?"

Lahousen glanced at Canaris. The admiral was studying the floor, quiet but unperturbed. Hitler began pounding the arm of his chair, talking so fast that he stumbled over his own words. Lahousen had long heard of the Führer's legendary rages. Never before had he witnessed one.

"The Jew pig Roosevelt has used your carelessness to close our consulates! He is using your idiocy to inflame the American public against me! Against the Reich! This is a disaster! America must not come into the war! Not now! Not until the Reich stands supreme! A fortress Europe! Impregnable from all threat of blockade! The essential thing is to conquer! After all Europe is brought into the Reich, everything will be simply a matter of organization. Like the English, we shall rule our empire with a handful of men. . . ."

The Führer raged on as if he were addressing an audience of a hundred thousand in the Sportpalast. In a rambling tirade, he declared that soon the Reich would control the granary and oil production for all of Europe, that soon there would be sufficient slave labor for the immense factories now being designed and constructed by Herr Speer. It was familiar fare. Lahousen had heard it all before, under other circumstances.

It was an impressive performance. No one ever knew if these tantrums were genuine, or calculated role-playing. Lahousen suspected that Hitler was a consummate actor. No matter how heated his outbursts, Hitler never lost his self-control.

As the oration continued, Lahousen seized the opportunity to study the Führer. He wondered if the Abwehr medical files were complete. All sources agreed that the Führer suffered from a variety of physical disabilities. But as Lahousen watched Hitler in rage, he was struck by the unhealthy pallor of his skin now that he had lost the initial flush of anger. The Führer had the sickly whiteness of a man denied any glimpse of the sun. Moreover, he seemed totally exhausted, with swollen, puffed eyes, now frenetically glazed.

The eyes—metallic, frenzied—were by far the most arresting feature of his face. The irises were translucent, the pastel blueness sometimes pale green in certain light. They were so unnatural that Lahousen wondered if they had been seared by the temporary blindness the Führer had suffered when gassed at Ypres during the last days of the Great War.

The Führer's hair was a plastered, lifeless mouse-brown mop. The familiar forelock flopped as he swung his head in elaborate gestures. The toothbrush moustache now showed a few gray hairs. There also was a hint of gray at the temples, and more back of the ears. His voice seemed to have only two levels—the flat, almost inaudible monotone and the harsh, frayed shout of an exhausted orator.

As he continued his diatribe, he ceased pounding his chair to make his points and instead gripped the arm of the chair tightly. Lahousen sensed desperation in the way Hitler's hand clung to the wood. It was a small hand, with short fingers and square tips, the back completely white with no veins showing. It was the hand of a corpse.

The shouted oration continued more than ten minutes. Canaris remained immobile, head down, hands on knees. For a time, Lahousen thought Hitler had lost the thread of his rage. But at last, laboring for breath, the Führer returned to his subject.

"The drunkard Churchill is beaten! When he at last comprehends that he will get no help from Russia, he will come to us on his knees! We must conquer Russia! And now you have allowed these imbeciles to endanger Barbarossa! The cripple Roosevelt is doing all he can short of war to help Britain. And now he is sending war materiel to Russia! And you and your idiots have given him the excuse to close our consulates!"

Hitler collapsed, spent, his breath coming in short gasps. The tremor in his left arm was the only movement in the room for several long seconds. Then, as Canaris spoke, Lahousen understood why the canny admiral had endured the attack in silence, even when Hitler blamed the spy arrests, not the sinking of the *Robin Moor*, for the closing of the consulates. He had drawn Hitler's fire and set him up for the admiral's own broadside.

"Mein Führer," he said calmly, "I'm sure you recall the difficulties we have had in the past with our operations in the United States. You will remember that when I assumed command of the Abwehr, I attempted to reorganize completely our operations in America. At that time, the FBI had infiltrated every level of our espionage organization. I have taken every precaution. But we are still suffering the consequences. My failure is that I have been unable to overcome the chaos that existed in those days."

Hitler blinked at Canaris, speechless. Lahousen almost laughed aloud at the master stroke. With some caution, Canaris in effect had placed the full blame on the Nazi Party. When Canaris had taken over the Abwehr in 1935, the Party had been in charge of all intelligence, and almost every branch of the German government had been allowed to operate its own spy system in a massive hodge podge. Heydrich and his SS, the Air Ministry, the Nazi Party Bund movement, the Nazi Labor Front, even the travel agencies and shipping lines were into the game of spying on America. The field had been filled with amateurs. On assuming office, Canaris broke all connections with other groups. He formed his own professional spy rings, unknown to the Party amateurs.

Lahousen thrilled to the admiral's audacity.

Hitler was taken aback. He sputtered for a moment before speaking. "I'm told you are using Jews as *vertrauensmänner!* Trusted persons! Is this true?"

Canaris sighed. *"Mein Führer, vertrauensmann* is merely a term. In the world of spying, no one is trusted. Not truly. Our agents are guided by many motives. The best are inspired by their love for the Reich, their loyalty to their Führer. Others. . . ." He shook his head as if in sadness. "Valuable information can be bought from the Jews because of their greed. It is true. We make use of them. As you said, *Mein Führer,* it's unsavory. . . ."

"It must cease!" Hitler said. "That is an order!"

"Jawohl, Mein Führer," Canaris said.

Hitler drummed his fingers on the arm of his chair. His voice returned to its customary rasping monotone. "How badly are we compromised?"

Canaris lied easily. "We still have an elaborate network functioning. True, we have been hurt. Chiefly in communications. But we soon will repair the damage."

Hitler chewed for a moment on a fingernail. He carefully inspected the results and asked, "What have you learned about the *Normandie?"*

The abrupt change of subject was in keeping with a trait well known to Hitler's staff. Often one sentence spoken by the Führer had no connection to the next. Still, Lahousen was confused by the question, as was the admiral.

"I beg your pardon, *Mein Führer,"* Canaris said. "I do not understand."

Hitler's hands fluttered in irritation. "Why hasn't the

Normandie been returned to us? You were ordered to determine the situation!''

Lahousen had seen no such order. Direct commands from the Führer always were handled separately, and marked for special action. But with the flood of dispatches coming daily from the Eastern Front, a single communiqué could have been overlooked. Or, more likely, the Führer himself might be confused. He may have ordered some other agency to obtain the information.

But the admiral's memory seemed to jog. He glanced at Lahousen, silent appeal in his eyes.

Lahousen spoke on impulse. "The *Normandie* has been at Pier Eighty-eight in New York City since August of nineteen-thirty-nine, *Mein Führer,*" he said. He recalled specifics from some remote dispatch. "More than a thousand crew members were returned to Vichy France, through Montreal, early that September. A caretaker crew of one hundred and fifteen men remain on board, under the command of Captain Zanger. In May of nineteen-forty, after the French Armistice, she was taken into protective custody by the United States. A small contingent of Coast Guardsmen was placed on board, one man for each member of the French crew. . . .''

"I know all that!" Hitler shouted. "I asked you to determine why she has not been returned to us! What do they plan to do with her?''

"*Mein Führer,* there are no plans," Lahousen said, proving that he could match the admiral in audacity. "The United States is attempting to maintain diplomatic relationship with Vichy France. If she should seize and use the *Normandie,* or turn the ship over to Britain, Marshal Petain might well break off that diplomatic relationship. Then there is the matter of General De Gaulle, who is attempting to conduct his own war and has become a thorn in the side for Churchill. De Gaulle has organized his own intelligence network inside the occupied zone, in direct competition with Churchill's own. If the *Normandie* were put to use on behalf of Britain, De Gaulle's position would be enhanced."

"And there is no plan for the United States to use the *Normandie?*"

Lahousen spoke with conviction, knowing that what he said might well be true. "No, *Mein Führer.* As you no doubt know, the ship was designed to be converted quickly into an aircraft carrier, or into a troopship. That of course remains a possibility. But at the moment, there are no plans whatsoever."

Hitler shifted in his chair and pressed a hand to his abdomen. Lahousen wondered if the Führer's much-discussed, long-persistent flatulence and accompanying stomach pains also had returned.

"We must have the *Normandie,*" Hitler said to Canaris. "Admiral, this is an order! Get me the *Normandie!*"

Lahousen and Canaris exchanged glances. Canaris ventured the question. "How, *Mein Führer?* A commando force?"

"It shouldn't be difficult! Only one hundred and fifteen American sailors aboard her. The Frenchmen would be no problem. They're unarmed. A night attack, and she would be well out to sea before alarm could be raised. With her speed, no warship could catch her!"

The Führer was no seaman. He had never been off the Continent. Lahousen himself was no sailor, but even he could see immense shortcomings in Hitler's plan.

Canaris spoke softly. "What you say is true, *Mein Führer.* It's a daring idea. And it might be done. But there are some obstacles. For instance, a ship of that size requires several hundred men to get underway—the line-handlers, the engine rooms crews with knowledge of all the vast machinery, the lookouts who are the eyes and ears of the captain. Several hundred thousand gallons of fuel oil must be loaded. The massive canvas covers must be removed from the funnels. In that narrow space of the Hudson River, at least a half dozen tugboats would be needed

37

to prevent accidental grounding. Even then, there is the serious danger of collision in that busy harbor. . . .''

"You are telling me it can't be done?"

"No, *Mein Führer*. I am only pointing out the difficulties. Also, I wonder about the consequences. If the *Normandie* were stolen, right under the noses of the Americans, wouldn't that make them more predisposed toward war?"

Lahousen marveled at the admiral's technique. Canaris was not contradicting the Führer. He was merely feeding Hitler ideas and information, enticing him to change his mind.

Hitler thumped the arm of his chair with his fist. "The *Normandie* belongs to the Reich! It was specifically stated in the Armistice! All French ships in foreign ports were to return to their home ports. At once! The *Normandie* is ours, under all conventions of war!"

"The Americans will never return the *Normandie*," Canaris said quietly. "If they enter the war, they will need her."

Again Hitler became animated, his hands fluttering. "Exactly! Herr Admiral, we cannot allow that to happen! By Christmas, Russia will lie at our feet! Next spring, we will begin the complete subjugation of Britain. We will bring the drunkard Churchill to terms. I have conceived a plan!"

"Directive Number Sixteen will be renewed?" Canaris asked.

Lahousen tensed at the question. Directive Number Sixteen, code named Sea Lion, was the plan for the invasion of England. Since its conception, the Reich had lost air superiority over England. Britain also was making serious headway in the U-boat war. And the Führer had conveniently glossed over the fact that the French Armistice had decreed that all French ships would be disarmed and neutralized—a provision no one had taken seriously, especially the French Navy.

"No!" Hitler said. "After Russia is conquered, we will

turn south." He rose and crossed the room to a wall map. With a pointer, he traced each step of his grandiose plan. "We will push from Yugoslavia and Albania into Turkey, the Holy Lands—into Iran, Arabia. We will have the oil from the Caucasus, from the desert lands for our tanks and planes. We will seize the Suez Canal, and block the British empire from her raw materials. Only then will the entire Luftwaffe again be concentrated on England, and Britain brought to her knees."

Lahousen hoped his own face mirrored the admiral's calm as the Führer launched into another furious monologue.

"For this we will need ships! And the Reich has been robbed of all her shipping!"

His voice rising, he began a lengthy recital of the spoils of war won by the Reich, and lost through the ignorance, stupidity, and duplicity of the French. Two battleships, two cruisers, eight destroyers, submarines and two hundred smaller vessels of the French Navy had been seized in English ports. One battleship, four cruisers, and several smaller ships were seized by the British at Alexandria. A cruiser, an aircraft carrier, submarines, and smaller craft remained in port at Martinique, inaccessible to the Reich. And at Mers-el-Kebir, in the largest sea battle of the war, the British had opened fire without warning and destroyed the main portion of the French fleet.

"Remember the first Armistice!" the Führer shouted, returning to a familiar theme, oft repeated in his public speeches. "Germany was stripped of her entire commercial fleet! The *Vaterland!* The *Imperator!* The *Bismarck!* Monuments to genius! Models of design for everything that was to float on the seas for the next twenty years! And what happened! The *Vaterland* became the United States ship *Leviathan.* The *Imperator* became the British Cunard liner *Berengaria.* The Bismarck the British *Majestic.*"

The Führer's ability to absorb and retain specific information was well known. He frequently strutted this ability before visitors and members of his staff. But Lahousen was nonetheless impressed as Hitler demonstrated his extensive knowledge of the disposition of German shipping after defeat in the Great War. Ostensibly classed as a portion of war reparations, the forced sale of thirty large German ships had ended Germany's dominance of trans-Atlantic passenger service, and paved the way for the ascendancy of the British and American lines. Lahousen marveled as Hitler paced the room and went into minute detail.

"The *Kronprinzessin Cecilie* became the *Mount Vernon!* The *Kaiser Wilhelm II* the *Agamemnon!* The *Friedrich der Gross*, the *Huron!* The *Grosser Kurfurst* the *Aeolus!* The *Prinz Eitel Friedrich* the *De Kalb!* The *Kaiserin Auguste Victoria* the *Empress of Scotland!* The *Amerika* the *America.* . . ."

He raged for more than twenty minutes, reviewing the terms of the 1919 Versailles treaty at length, citing the ways in which it had been violated by the western governments. At last, he returned to the *Normandie*.

"And now, it is the same story. One hundred and eighty French maritime ships seized in foreign ports, the French Navy destroyed. All of those ships belonged to the Reich, the spoils of war!"

He crossed to a table, shuffled through maps and drawings, and returned with a large set of blueprints. He waved them in the air. "Here! Here is the *Normandie!* Eighty-three thousand tons. She can transport fifteen thousand troops across the Atlantic in four days. Men and equipment! An entire armored division! At more than thirty knots! She can outrun every submarine, all surface ships!"

Canaris cleared his throat. "*Mein Führer*, if it is your wish that we seize the ship, we will devise an elaborate plan. . . ."

Hitler paused, staring at the map. "No," he said softly. He was silent for a long moment. "We cannot give the cripple Roosevelt a cause to bring the United States into the war. Not now."

He resumed his earlier pacing the room, and spoke as if he were thinking aloud. "But if America *does* come into the war, England will be her stepping stone to invade the Continent. Roosevelt will be sending supplies, tanks, troops. Using England as the staging area. . . ."

He studied the map for a time. The Führer's obsession with maps was legendary. He began nodding, as if he had reached a decision.

"If America comes into the war, the *Normandie* will be of more danger to the Reich than a dozen battleships! We must not leave the *Normandie* in the hands of the Americans! She must be destroyed."

He turned to face Canaris. "Admiral, I order you! Sink the *Normandie!*"

"*Jawohl, Mein Führer,*" Canaris said. "It will be done."

Mollified, Hitler returned to his chair. For a time, he discoursed on the long-delayed invasion of Gibraltar, General Franco's probable reaction, and the possibilities of bringing Spain into the war, even at this late date. This had been a long project, involving Canaris from the beginning.

Toward midnight, an aide brought in a tray of white wine. Hitler's Alsatian dog Blondi shot through the open door and bounded into the Führer's lap. Hitler laughed and ruffled the dog's pelt. Then, for the amusement of his guests, he coached the dog through a number of tricks—begging, leaping over a riding crop, singing on command. As Canaris and Lahousen praised the dog's performance, the Führer beamed.

Lahousen noticed that Hitler scarcely touched his wine, yet retained his feverish animation.

Shortly after one in the morning, Hitler escorted Canaris and Lahousen to the door. He put an arm around Canaris. "You look tired, Herr Admiral. Why don't you speak with Dr. Morell? He has a tonic that works wonders!"

"Perhaps I shall, *Mein Führer,*" Canaris said.

The Führer had invited them to spend the night, but Canaris preferred to return to Berlin before dawn. A telephone call ascertained that English bombers had not penetrated that evening beyond Frankfurt-am-Main.

The same driver returned them to the airstrip.

Canaris did not speak of the visit until they were aloft in the Heinkel He III, safe from eavesdroppers.

"Your contributions concerning the *Normandie* were most timely. Where did you obtain your information?"

Lahousen regretted that the admiral could not see his smile in the darkness. "I made it up as I went along."

Canaris laughed. "Excellent. No doubt your assessment was as accurate as anything we could obtain from the field."

The admiral then sank into another morose silence. Several minutes later, he shifted in his seat and leaned close to Lahousen's ear. "What I'm about to tell you is in great confidence. I reveal my thoughts only in case something happens to me. I've seen more and more evidence of collusion between Heydrich and the Führer—some secret they are keeping even from the general staff. We know what the Einsatzgruppen are doing all along the Russian front. We also know their activities go far beyond relocation and slave labor. But Erwin, I'm beginning to suspect that the massacre of Jews, Gypsies, and misfits will soon be carried out on a scale beyond our wildest imagination. I fear that Hitler's obsession will turn us into monsters in the eyes of the world for all time to come. The more I learn, the more certain I am that Hitler must be deposed for the good of the Fatherland."

Lahousen did not answer. Canaris had been involved in various plots against Hitler for more than five years. But as the admiral's closest confidant, Lahousen also knew the admiral's greatest weakness: Canaris would never commit himself to a plan that would shed blood.

As long as he had known the admiral, Lahousen had not been able to penetrate this paradox: The director of the world's most effective clandestine agency was, in reality, among the most gentle of men.

Lahousen suspected that the admiral's assessment of the

national plan for Jews was correct. He also had read deeper meaning into the euphemisms growing more and more common in the *Sicherheitsdienst*—"sanitary measures," "special treatment," "emigration," "natural diminution," "change of residence." Rumors and reports persisted of impending Jewish extermination on a massive scale. The possibility was not so unbelievable, if one considered Hitler's speeches, or opened *Mein Kampf.*

"He is sick, you know. Mentally and physically," Canaris continued. "Hospital records attribute his blindness at Ypres, his frequent stomach pains to hysterical causes. The nervous tics, his constant suspicion, his mania for numbers and lists, his masochistic nature with women—all are of a whole. Dr. Morell is now giving him more than one hundred and twenty pills and injections a day. He can't last long under treatment by that quack. Morell is incapable even of reading the Führer's electrocardiogram. He recently sent an EKG to Dr. Karl Weber in Berlin. Morell gave his patient an assumed name, but of course the professor wasn't fooled. All the world knows Morell has only one patient. Weber concluded, and so informed Morell, that the electrocardiogram revealed a rapidly progressive coronary sclerosis. I don't know if Morell informed Hitler. In any event, the problem of Hitler may soon be solved."

They were approaching Berlin. Scattered fires could be seen from the bombings two nights before. Canaris turned to the window and resumed his brooding silence.

Lahousen waited until they were safely on the ground before he asked the question lingering in his mind.

"What shall I do about the Führer's order to destroy the *Normandie?*"

The admiral often conveniently overlooked direct orders if he happened to disagree with them, or if they could be circumvented. But once again, he surprised Lahousen.

"Why, we will obey it, of course. The Führer is right. The *Normandie* is a formidable weapon. We cannot allow her to be used against us."

Lahousen thought of the huge ship—more than three

hundred meters long, as large as a skyscraper, filled with hundreds of compartments. Its destruction would be a massive undertaking. And the Abwehr's penetration into America was at its lowest point.

"How large an operation? How many men?"

Canaris glanced behind him to make certain they were alone. "On a mission such as this, operatives tend to get in each other's way. And the more involved, the greater the risk. For the *Normandie,* we will need only one man." He smiled. "And as it so happens, I know exactly the man for the job."

The admiral remained silent for a moment, thinking. "Tomorrow, make me a list, complete with profiles, of our best agents left in America—those that remain beyond suspicion. We must select someone to help him."

2

Hudson River Pier 88, New York City

Late in the afternoon, with the sun low on the Jersey horizon, Captain Maurice Raynal left the *Normandie* via the gangplank, entered the Compagnie Generale Transatlantique terminal, walked through to the front door, and strolled up Twelfth Avenue to the center of the slip. There he smoked his pipe in the cool of the evening, as had become his habit in recent months, and stood gazing at the full grandeur of his majestic ship, reminiscing about all the good times, all the bad times they had been through together, and wondering what the future held for him, for her—and for France.

After almost two years at Pier 88, he had grown accustomed to the swish of tidewater lapping high against the pilings, the plaintive cries of the gulls circling overhead, the constant drum of traffic on the elevated West Side Highway just forward of the ship's bow. He had developed an intimate awareness of the incessant harbor dialogue of tugs, ferries, and excursion boats, the occasional chatter of cargo booms.

Raynal looked upon himself as a sailor who had left the

sea but failed to reach shore. He felt that the concept was apt: He, the *Normandie,* and France had all dwelled in limbo for two years, their lives drawn into an even tighter symbiotic relationship by cataclysmic world events.

France lay shattered into fragments that might never again be united. Raynal himself was a man without a country. The *Normandie*—all that was left of the France he had known—was more than just his home. She was his obsession.

She was so vulnerable, moored in the midst of a foreign city, virtually unguarded, slowly deteriorating despite all he could do.

She towered over him, her bow soaring higher than a six-story building, her massive anchors so large that an automobile could rest comfortably in their flukes. Farther aft, her superstructure rose another five stories, capped by three funnels so huge that each could serve as a tunnel for three locomotives traveling abreast. He recalled with amusement that American passengers invariably said with some wonder that the ship was longer than three football fields, laid end to end.

Despite her awesome size and weight, she was totally feminine. Raynal had always considered the use of the masculine gender for ships a perversity of the French language —one put to test by the *Normandie.* The French Academy after lengthy deliberation had ruled to make an exception in favor of the feminine article for the *Normandie,* taking refuge in the precedent of the German language deviation from the neuter gender in the case of the *Vaterland.*

Originally, the *Normandie* was to have been named the *Jeanne d'Arc*—not a wise choice, considering the propensity of French Line ships to burn at their moorings. Throughout her construction a national debate had raged over the selection of a proper name. Now, Raynal could not imagine her as other than the *Normandie.*

Her furnishings were so ornate that one critic had termed her "unrealistic, impractical, uneconomical, and magnifi-

46

cent." Certainly no one but royalty had ever lived amid as much luxury as her passengers. She was the ultimate in beauty, grace, and style.

He had loved her since the first time he had seen her, at St. Nazaire two months before her maiden voyage. He had known in one blinding instant that there was nothing he wanted more than to sail in her for the rest of his life. Although he had been offered a better-paying position with another line, he signed on as an assistant to Chief Engineer Jean Hazard on the *Normandie*.

Never for a moment had he regretted that decision.

She was simply the most magnificent ship ever built, different from any other afloat, an abrupt departure in design that would forever alter the thinking of those who followed the sea.

Her construction had been a national preoccupation. She was as much the living soul of France as the Louvre or the Palais de Versailles. She cost sixty million dollars in the depths of a world depression. The French government footed most of the bill. The *Normandie* was called, with some justification, the floating national debt of the French Republic.

Raynal never tired of looking at her.

He strolled a few more feet up the pier, carefully finding the spot that offered her best angle, chosen after many hours of experiment and contemplation. Viewed from that perspective, a few paces upriver from the center of the stringpiece, her sublime hull curved aft with Titian voluptuousness from her aristocratic bow.

Above the foredecks her bridge towered in haughty prominence, running completely athwartships, the largest and most impressive nautical command post afloat. Raynal had spent many hours there, in every kind of weather. He knew the ship and her capabilities intimately.

She was built for speed, elegance, and grace, and he had found delight in her myriad moods. At thirty knots and more, so gentle was her bow wake that she offered the illusion of skimming the ocean. She was wondrously efficient. When the *Queen Mary* was launched, the British ship needed thirty thousand additional horsepower to achieve the same speed.

There were those who said the *Normandie* was top-heavy. Raynal believed her high center of gravity only contributed to her perfection. She was *alive*. She did not lie dead in the water, a sodden, floating bathtub like so many liners, but responded to her exquisite balance with the alacrity of a destroyer. She might properly be called a tender ship—even delicate. But through 70 complete voyages, 141 crossings, Raynal had never known the *Normandie* to hang on the roll, even in the roughest seas. She did not fight or attempt to subdue the water. She was a sailor's delight—a ship that lived *with* the waves, one that reveled in the ever-changing temperament of the sea.

The Cunard side of the slip was now empty. The *Queen Mary* and the *Queen Elizabeth* were gone. Raynal had heard rumors that both were in the western Pacific. Seagulls now bobbed in the water near the empty pier, searching for scraps.

For twenty-two long months the *Normandie* had not moved from her moorings. Slowly, inexorably, she was succumbing to the ravages of inactivity. The scrape of her hawsers and fenders with the constant rise and fall of the tide had left discolored patches on her starboard side. Tenders and tugs had left their marks to port. The high, rakish funnels, now covered with canvas, were filmed with city grime. Along the white surface of the bridge, flaking of the paint was now visible from the pier.

The paint crew worked incessantly, but slowly lost ground. The boilers, turbines, and generators were gradually yielding to disuse. Her bottom rested in river silt. Raynal suspected that the massive propeller shafts were frozen in their bearings.

He sighed. With only 115 men, thorough upkeep was impossible. He and his skeleton crew had done their best.

All brightwork had been preserved in grease. Four tons of mothball crystals had been rubbed into the interminable lengths of famous blue carpeting. The companionways, all the walkways were covered with protective canvas. The furniture, the lacquered murals were shrouded. Bedding was stowed in the closets of each cabin, the doors open to allow air to circulate.

Yet an insidious mustiness prevailed throughout the ship.

Raynal had endured this slow deterioration with a painful sadness that grew from day to day.

But he had made his choice. Even now, he could not see how he could have done otherwise.

Upon the outbreak of war, he had watched with mingled emotions the departure of 1,230 of the *Normandie*'s crewmen. The temptation had been strong to return to France during the months of the "phony war." He had not shared the confidence of his fellow countrymen in the impregnability of the Maginot Line. He had been certain that France was approaching her darkest hour. Not yet thirty, and in excellent physical condition, he had thought seriously of accepting a long-standing offer of a reserve commission in the French Navy. But when word came that arrangements had been made for the trip home via Montreal, he simply could not bring himself to leave the *Normandie*. He had volunteered to stay with the caretaker crew.

With only 115 men aboard, the ship needed him more than ever. He could not abandon her.

Life on the idle *Normandie* had been eerie. Where more than 3,300 crewmen and passengers normally dined, played, and slept, there now was only a vast emptiness. So pervasive was the ghostly atmosphere that Raynal and his skeleton crew often found themselves speaking in hushed tones. Even after almost two years, they had not grown accustomed to the long, unrelieved silences of the forlorn ship.

With the reduction of the crew came greater responsibilities. From a middle-grade officer, Raynal had been elevated to second-in-command. He had just received his master's papers. Now, he was in effect both the executive officer and chief engineer.

Captain Zanger's duties were mostly political—dealing with the American authorities and the press, communicating with Transatlantique through embassies, and catering to the many Americans who felt it necessary to make a gesture toward their French allies with an occasional social invitation.

Most of the responsibility for the ship and crew fell on Raynal's shoulders.

Both men and ship rusted in port. Morale was low. Not even New York City—the best liberty town in the world —could divert sailors whose homeland lay under Nazi occupation. The worry over family and acquaintances back home was constant. Raynal had organized English lessons, cultural tours, literary discussions, and various competitive games. But as the months went by, attention waned. Now, most of the men performed their work like robots, sinking each night into wine-soaked lethargy.

During the first few months, security had been a major problem. Early, the ship had received several threats of bombs and sabotage. Most of the letters, phone calls, and reported plots had been treated seriously by agents of the FBI, who came aboard to talk with Captain Zanger and Raynal. The FBI agents had informed them that across America, and especially in New York, were small ethnic groups who no doubt would do harm to the *Normandie* if possible—Irish Republicans who assumed that the ship would be handed over to the British; Polish and Ukrainian factions who feared she might be returned to France and the Nazis; German sympathizers who believed she eventually would be put to use against Nazi Germany; American isolationists who saw her presence as an unnecessary involvement in the war; and even dissident Frenchmen, who did not wish her to be given to other French political groups, or to Nazi Germany.

Raynal had felt great concern. There were few uniformed guards around the pier.

Captain Zanger's initial plea to the Americans for protection brought only demurrals: The FBI could act only *after* a crime involving national security had been committed; the U.S. Navy did not have jurisdiction; the Coast Guard was a branch of the Treasury Department, with activities directed chiefly toward customs and coastwatch; the New York Police Department was cooperative, but explained that the city did not have sufficient men to guard the *Normandie*.

Advice had been plentiful, and bizarre. One FBI agent solemnly suggested that Raynal construct "some sort of sling" to scrape the hull below the waterline occasionally, to make certain no explosive devices had been attached.

As the months passed, threats dwindled. Security had not remained a constant problem, as he had expected. The ship's hull rose high above the pier. All portholes were kept closed and dogged. Only one gangway was rigged. Raynal ordered a stout door constructed at the head of the gangway, replete with a sliding-door peephole. Only crewmen —and the ship's company of Coast Guardsmen—were admitted aboard, except for the Coast Guard officer who came once each month to check the seal on the radio transmitter.

With the vast, empty expanses below decks, the possibility of fire was a constant worry. The *Normandie* had been called the most fireproof ship afloat. But her designer had no illusions. No vessel carrying fuel oil, boilers, wooden furnishings, and an extensive electrical system was invulnerable. As a safeguard, she was equipped with an elaborate fire-detection system. Thick metal bulkheads and doors were strategically situated to confine any fire to one-fourth of the ship. These 4 sections were subdivided into 36 subsections, and 126 elementary fire sections.

Raynal knew them all by heart.

The entire system was monitored by a central fire-control

station on B Deck, where a watch was maintained at all times. Members of the fire detail walked the ship around the clock, punching buttons at each station, lighting a series of red bulbs on a board in central fire-control. The progress of each member of the fire patrol could be followed from station to station. When a round was completed by a fire-watch, his lights were cleared and his new round began.

In addition, 224 fire alarm boxes throughout the ship were connected to central fire-control.

A fire brigade, rigorously trained by the Paris Fire Department, remained on duty at all times. Each man was drilled thoroughly on the locations of the 32 main fire cupboards and 211 general fire cupboards. Each cupboard was equipped with portable extinguishers, helmets, gas masks, special nozzles, extra lengths of hose, and tools. Each fireman was drilled until he instantly could locate any one of the 504 hose connections on board.

In addition, 74 fire plugs were within reach on Pier 88, providing city water pressure.

Raynal no longer spent much time worrying about security, or fire.

His major preoccupation now was with the future.

For twenty-two months Captain Zanger, Raynal, and their slender crew had fought their losing battle while France and half of Europe had fallen to Nazi Germany.

Now Raynal suspected that at last something was about to happen.

In May of 1940, 115 armed U.S. Coast Guard sailors had been moved aboard—one for each Frenchman—ostensibly to help protect the ship.

The New York press had reported that after the fall of France, American officials feared the *Normandie* might be sabotaged by her own crew.

Angrily, Captain Zanger had replied that if he wanted to sabotage the ship, he would only have to remove his crew and to turn her over to the inexperienced Coast Guard contingent.

Through discreet questioning of the Coast Guardsmen,

Raynal learned they had been ordered to observe the *Normandie* crew at work, and to learn all they could about handling the boilers, machinery, and other equipment.

Raynal felt certain that the United States at last was preparing to take some action concerning the *Normandie,* though what, it was hard to say.

He had spent much time thinking through the possibilities, and about what course of action he might take on each.

First, the United States Navy might deliver the *Normandie* into the hands of Vichy France. This seemed most unlikely. But it remained a possibility. For reasons Raynal could not fathom, the Americans were making every effort to court Petain and his Nazi-appeasers. Under the terms of the 1940 armistice, all French ships outside territorial waters were to be returned to France. Germany had voiced strong claim to the *Normandie.* If the *Normandie* were returned to France, she no doubt would be handed over to Nazi Germany.

Raynal had made an agonizing decision as to what he would do in that eventuality. He would destroy the *Normandie* himself before he would allow her to be turned over to the Nazis.

Second, the Americans might pledge postwar reparations, and give the ship to the British—the same British who had sunk the French fleet at Mers-el-Kebir, killing almost 1,300 Frenchmen.

Raynal would not allow the *Normandie* to be used to kill more Frenchmen. He would sink her himself.

Only one other possibility remained. The Americans might assume ownership of the *Normandie* and convert her into a troopship or aircraft carrier, stripping her furnishings, altering her configuration so completely that her beauty would be lost forever.

Raynal had not yet made his decision on what he would do in that eventuality. And he probably would be forced to make that decision soon.

He could not see how America could remain neutral

much longer. When war came, and the *Normandie* was seized by the Americans, he would have to take quick action. He and the *Normandie* had been through too much together for him to abandon her to an ignominious fate.

Four glorious years.

He remembered her maiden passage as if it were yesterday.

The passenger list had been fabulous—Colette and her poodles, Pierre Cartier, Mrs. Frank Jay Gould, the Maharajah of Karpurthala. The list could have served as a social register of the world. Thousands of bottles of the finest wines and champagne had been aboard for months, allowing ample time for them to settle in their seagoing *cave*. The Paris Opera's corps de ballet danced in celebration of her sailing. President Albert Lebrun came aboard to wish his wife *bon voyage*, and spent the night. Andre Dumas wrote a poem for the occasion. Cardinal Verdier came aboard to bless the ship—and to grant the nation a special dispensation from the sin of pride.

Problems arose. Some of the first-class cabins were without plumbing until the last moment. And once the ship got underway, tremendous vibrations from the four giant propellers made a few of the staterooms and cabins uninhabitable. There, trunks walked around the rooms. Conversation was impossible. Vladimir Yourkevitch, the ship's designer, was on board. He said he had expected the vibrations. He had been overruled on the shape of the propellers.

The liner arrived at Ambrose Lightship four days, eleven hours, and forty-two minutes after sailing. A blue ribbon thirty meters long was hoisted to the top of the after mast, proclaiming the *Normandie* to be the largest and fastest ship on earth.

With the Blue Riband of the Atlantic, France regained her national pride.

Raynal would never forget the first arrival of the *Normandie* at her New York pier. All the way upriver from

54

quarantine a swarm of fireboats arched great plumes of water around her. U.S. Army Air Corps planes flew low overhead in tight formation, banked, and returned again and again. Along Twelfth Avenue, thousands of New Yorkers waved and cheered. Twenty tugs provided escort—one with a huge, improbable Mickey Mouse balloon dancing aloft.

The *Normandie* was the first ship to dock at New York's superpiers, dug deep into the island at West Fiftieth Street —piers so new that the construction men were still at work. The West Side Highway had not yet been built, and from the *Normandie*'s bridge, the view of New York's skyline was magnificent. Twelve tugs were required to turn the *Normandie* into her slip. So untried were her capabilities that the first docking had taken more than an hour. On one attempt, a warping hawser parted, and disaster was narrowly averted as the *Normandie* almost rammed the adjoining Cunard docks.

That night, Madame Lebrun was entertained at the Waldorf by New York Mayor Fiorello La Guardia. On the following evening, she was hostess for a party on board, with the mayor as guest of honor.

Through the years, there had been many such grand nights.

And there were many hilarious stories. He had laughed often over the error once with an order of lobsters, when ''dozen'' was translated as ''gross.'' Twelve times the specified number arrived on board, filling the storage tanks, all the pots that could be found. Every meal on that cruise to Rio featured lobster. The ship's two hundred chefs exhausted their ingenuity to find one more way lobster could be served.

Such stories were legion. The *Normandie*, celebrated as the most aristocratic and stunning ship afloat, attracted gaiety, money, and elegance.

And now she had not moved from her berth in almost two years.

Raynal knocked out the ashes of his pipe, stowed it in a pocket, and studied the lines of the *Normandie* in the setting sun.

He had known many women. A few had filled him with unreasonable passions. But he had never loved a woman —or anything else on earth—as much as he loved the *Normandie*. She was perfection, his sole reason for existence.

He had vowed to defend her reputation with his life. In fact, for twenty-two months he had made that vow each night. And now, he once again pledged his life.

With a last, lingering look at the magnificent ship silhouetted against the deepening twilight, Raynal turned away and began his leisurely stroll uptown to dine alone.

3

Grid Square *CA*, North Atlantic

The U-boat lay low in the water, rolling gently to long, persistent groundswells, sixty-two statute miles east of Ambrose Lightship, her decks awash as she moved slowly westward on the dark surface of the sea, well protected by the blackness of the night. Two hours earlier, a brief summer squall had passed, leaving the sky heavily overcast. No trace of moon or stars remained.

On the open bridge, Oberleutnant Walther Von Beck trained his binoculars on the western horizon, where the lights of New York City were eerily reflected by the low cloud cover. To the north, a lesser glow hung over Long Island, the Hamptons.

Von Beck lowered his binoculars, sighed, and wondered what he should do.

He had been on station three days. And still there was no word on potential targets. The lack of communications was most unusual. He could not recall a similar period of silence at submarine headquarters since the war began.

He crossed the bridge and concentrated on the southern horizon, alert for shadows, pinpoints of light. During the last hour, three fishing boats and two well-lighted cargo ships had passed within five thousand meters, unaware of the U-boat. He knew that if a U.S. Navy destroyer should happen along, he might not be so lucky.

At his elbow, Navigator Jergensen muttered an obscenity and rubbed his tired eyes with the heels of his hands. "Cities shouldn't be lit like that in wartime," he said. "It's indecent. I'm half blinded."

Von Beck shifted his binoculars to cover Jergensen's sector. "We're not here as tourists," he said quietly.

Jergensen resumed his watch without answering. Von Beck turned to make certain the petty officer and two seamen were alert. Each was gazing intently into his assigned sector. Von Beck did not doubt for a moment the dedication of his crew. But the peaceful roll of the boat, the oedipal swish of water against the plates could lull even the most conscientious man into a moment of distraction.

That moment could be fatal to the boat.

Von Beck was now cruising well to the south and west of his assigned sector. With the lack of target reports, the temptation to approach the New York Harbor area had been irresistible. The risk could be defended. The region spawned the largest convoys. Ships from Houston, Galveston, New Orleans, Norfolk often clung close to shore until their convoys assembled along the northeast coast for the run past the Grand Banks, where U-boats often awaited in packs. He *had* to find a target soon. Fuel, supplies were running low, and half of his torpedoes remained unfired.

"Depth soundings!" he called down the tower.

"Two hundred thirty meters," a voice called up from the control room.

Von Beck's decision was made for him. He had ventured too close to land. The water might soon be too shallow to dive and maneuver if they were discovered. The Hudson Channel was deep, but erratic.

"Both engines full stop," he called down the hatch. The order was confirmed. Gradually, the sound of the bow wake, the wash of water across the decks eased.

58

As the boat slowed, Von Beck turned to study the western horizon with renewed intensity. At one point, the reflected lights now assumed a soft red tinge through his powerful binoculars. Calculating direction and distance, Von Beck suspected that he was seeing the glow from the concentration of neon around Times Square.

Unexpectedly, he was overwhelmed for a moment by a strong sense of loss.

He seldom allowed himself to think of that other life while on duty. But now, enticed by the aura of New York City, he had no difficulty in spanning the miles, the years, to the hot, humid streets of Manhattan on such nights, sweltering after similar summer rains. For a moment, he could imagine the yelling of the news vendors, the roar from the subway gratings, the honking of the taxis as they jockeyed for position, the bustle of the theater crowds as they made their way toward the better restaurants. . . .

"Ship, bearing zero three zero," Jergensen said softly at his elbow. "Range six thousand."

Von Beck shifted his binoculars. An almost imperceptible shadow moved against the horizon. He held his breath as he strained to see its shape.

Any dark ship was a probable target. Neutral ships now blazed like Christmas trees, with spotlights illuminating both the name on the hull and their ensign of registry flying at the stern.

Von Beck could not see even a hint of light on the darkened ship.

"An oiler," said the watchstander behind him.

The sailor had good eyes. Von Beck spoke down the hatch to the conning tower. "Come left to two seven zero. Both ahead half together."

The diesels responded. Vibration built in the deck plates as the submarine gathered speed. Von Beck grasped the bridge coaming for support as the boat heeled into the turn.

He had little doubt that the ship was a legitimate target. But his orders were clear. Another U-boat—the *U-203*—had encountered the U.S. Navy battleship *Texas* two weeks ago in the North Atlantic. The battleship was cruising in the war zone, obviously giving at least token support to convoys. The *U-203* had radioed submarine headquarters for permission to shoot. After several hours, the reply came in the form of a directive to all U-boats at sea:

BY ORDER OF THE FUHRER, ALL INCIDENTS WITH
UNITED STATES SHIPS MUST BE AVOIDED IN THE COMING
WEEKS. UNTIL FURTHER NOTICE, ATTACKS MAY NOT BE
MADE ON BATTLESHIPS, CRUISERS, AND AIRCRAFT
CARRIERS UNLESS DEFINITELY IDENTIFIED AS HOSTILE.
WARSHIPS STEAMING AT NIGHT WITHOUT LIGHTS ARE NOT
NECESSARILY HOSTILE.

Von Beck considered the mandate a waste of time, manpower, and fuel. He hoped the diplomatic advantages were worth the price.

"She's turning away," Jergensen said.

The shadow was now smaller, less distinct. Von Beck called below. "Sparks! Monitor radio traffic on the six-hundred-meter band. See if that ship is calling for help."

He altered course and increased speed. Slowly, the submarine closed the distance. Five minutes later, in another abrupt maneuver, the target began to move to the left.

"She's zigzagging," Von Beck said, satisfied. Clearly, the tanker was sailing under the registry of a nation at war. And no German or Italian surface ship would be in these waters. Her speed suggested she was under forced draft, perhaps rushing to join a convoy already at sea.

Von Beck called down the tower for a sound bearing on the target.

"Two nine zero," the word came back.

Von Beck cast the triangulation on his mental blackboard, made the calculations, and plotted his plan of pursuit. "Left to zero nine zero," he ordered. "Both ahead two thirds together."

If the tanker maintained her present zigzag course, she

would swing away for five minutes, then back again. With three thousand meters as the closest point during the tanker's zigzag, there was little danger the U-boat would be detected. Only a few feet of the superstructure rode above the surface—almost impossible to see on a dark night.

The boat began rolling, plunging to the combination of increased speed and the ground swells. Dawn was more than nine hours away. Von Beck and his crew faced a long night and an exhausting chase.

"I'm going below," he said to his navigator. "Call me if anything happens."

Fitting a pair of heavy, red-lensed goggles over his eyes to protect his night vision, he dropped through the hatch and down the ladder into the conning tower. He clapped the helmsman on the shoulder as he passed and clambered on down into the control room.

The boat's ventilators had now been open more than three hours, softening the all-too-familiar pungent smells of the boat. Despite three years of submarine warfare, he had never grown accustomed to the mingled, massive stench from the single toilet, the sweat of fifty men in cramped quarters, crude oil and bilge water, sausages and hams swinging from the overhead, and the acrid, ever-present fumes from the batteries.

The crew was quiet but animated. As Von Beck moved forward toward his tiny cabin, several of the men looked up at him and grinned, savoring the excitement. Every man on board knew the boat was only a few miles off the coast of America. Word already had spread that they had sighted, and were trailing, a potential target. The crew anticipated action. He hoped he would not disappoint them.

Stepping through the control room hatch, he paused to toss his binoculars onto his bunk, then walked on forward to the wardroom. Karl Mueller, first officer, sat at a mess table, working over the decoding machine and a pile of dispatches.

61

On forward, in the bow compartment, the torpedo crewmen were singing softly:

> No roses grow on a sailor's grave,
> No lilies on an ocean wave.
> The only tribute is the seagulls' sweeps,
> And the teardrops that a sweetheart weeps.

Mueller glanced up as Von Beck entered the compartment.

Von Beck sat opposite Mueller and adjusted the heavy red goggles more comfortably. "Find anything?" he asked.

"You were right, *Mein Kapitän*. Every convoy report for the last three days has been a sea sighting. Nothing has been received concerning convoys or ships leaving the American coast."

Von Beck found no satisfaction in the fact that his worst suspicion had been confirmed. Coastwatch operations in America apparently had been shut down.

He speculated for a moment on how seriously the situation might affect the success of the patrol—his first as a U-boat commander.

While off the coast of Newfoundland, the boat had monitored commercial broadcasts in America reporting the arrests of twenty-nine German spies. Almost simultaneously, messages from U-boat headquarters had dwindled. The two developments obviously were related. But to what extent? Almost every branch of the Third Reich had spies in America, each group working independently, unknown to the others. The Gestapo had its own spy apparatus, as did the SS. The Abwehr alone had more than a score of branches engaged in intelligence, sabotage, subversion, and counterespionage.

The spies captured in the United States could be of any group. Coastwatch operations might have been suspended temporarily as a simple precaution.

"Any problems in the boat?" he asked.

62

Mueller shrugged. "Nothing new. The chief says the toilet is fixed. I haven't the nerve to test it."

Despite his fatigue, Von Beck laughed. The intricate machinery of the toilet was designed to function at any depth down to twenty-five meters. But in practice it often malfunctioned at periscope depth, shooting offal and seawater back into the boat. Mueller once had said he himself would prefer a depth charge attack to a bout with diarrhea.

"What's new on the radio?"

"The Wehrmacht has captured Minsk. A pincer movement has trapped a huge Russian force between Minsk and Smolensk. Thousands of Russians are cut off. And we've taken Lwow!"

Von Beck tried to envision the sweep of the war. It was beyond comprehension. The speed of the German advance on the Eastern Front had been amazing. He wondered if the reports were exaggerated. "Minsk is halfway to Moscow," he said.

Mueller grinned. "Three-fifths of the way. I measured the distance on the map. Just think. My two brothers may be in the Kremlin before I get back to Brest."

If you get back to Brest, Von Beck thought.

"The Americans are upset," Mueller added. "Their Navy Secretary Knox made a speech, and said that the time has come for the United States Navy to clear the Atlantic. He said we are now sinking three ships for every one they build."

And at what cost to ourselves? Von Beck wondered. How long can we continue?

He rose from the table. The torpedo crewmen were now singing "Lili Marlene" in low, four-part harmony.

"I'm turning in," he said. "Call me thirty minutes before dawn—or if the tanker changes course."

He pulled the green curtain in his cabin and lay full length on the bunk, not bothering to remove his boots. He closed his eyes, forced himself to relax, and waited. But as on all the other nights, sleep would not come. Again, he endured the wide-awake nightmares that had plagued him through the last few months—Edvard Munch-like visions of explosions, crushed hulls, flooding compartments, drowning men. . . .

He no longer held any hope of outlasting the war. The odds had always been long. But with the incredible events of the last ten days, he now was certain his survival was no longer possible.

The first news of Barbarossa had come to the U-boat off Cape Race, Newfoundland, just after he had intercepted a convoy and sent two Belgian freighters to the bottom. The British escort corvettes had counterattacked, keeping the boat at a depth of 160 meters for more than eight hours. Eventually, the corvettes withdrew. Von Beck was unable to re-establish contact with the remainder of the convoy.

He had been cruising toward the southwest, searching for other targets, when Sparks picked up the nightly Armed Forces communiqué and its stunning announcement that the Reich had launched a lightning attack into Russia. Propaganda Minister Joseph Goebbels had proclaimed in person that the Wehrmacht was advancing along a 1,600-kilometer front from the Baltic to the Black Sea.

The crew of the U-boat could not have been shaken more thoroughly by a barrage of depth charges alongside the hull. Within moments, their own desperate war in the Atlantic had been relegated to secondary importance.

At last, they understood the long delay of the Führer in ordering the invasion of England. Goebbels explained that despite the existing Soviet-German nonaggression pact, Russia had shown by repeated provocations that she could not be trusted once Germany's back was turned.

Von Beck's crew had been excited, even exhilarated by the new turn of events. Von Beck could not share their enthusiasm.

He foresaw what lay beyond the invasion of Russia.

The war in the East would occupy the Führer's attention for many months, perhaps a year, even longer. The main forces of the Wehrmacht, the Luftwaffe would be committed to the Eastern Front.

All U-boats—including his own—would be sacrificed to a delaying action, continuing the blockade of England in the face of rapidly deteriorating odds.

He had seen growing evidence that the era of U-boat dominance in the Atlantic was rapidly drawing to a close. On his first war patrols as a junior officer two years ago, the boats had cruised along the English coasts unchallenged. Each combat cruise had ended in triumph, with at least five or six enemy ships sunk. But in recent months, long-ranged Catalina and Sunderland flying boats had pushed the defensive zone farther and farther from the British coasts, well beyond the Azores and Greenland, forcing the U-boat operations deeper into the waters of the western Atlantic.

The extended distances not only increased problems of fuel and supply, but also created a gantlet for the boats to run each time they moved to and from harbor.

Since early spring, fewer and fewer U-boats had returned from combat patrols. Random losses had always occurred among inexperienced crews. But for the first time, a number of veteran, even legendary crews were among the missing. The *U-99*, with Kapitän Kretschmer in command, and the *U-100*, under Kapitän Schepke, had been sunk. Von Beck had trained under both commanders. They had seemed indestructible. Kretschmer alone had sent more than three hundred thousand tons of enemy shipping to the bottom. Schepke had sunk more than a quarter of a million tons.

Since May, the number of U-boat losses had increased even more dramatically. Von Beck had heard persistent rumors that the British had a new secret weapon.

Day by day, the likelihood grew that America soon would enter the war. When that happened, the western Atlantic no longer would be a safe refuge for U-boats.

Von Beck could not shake his overwhelming sense of

fatalism. Although he forced himself to continue with his duties, he was filled with an omnipresent sadness. He was certain that for all practical purposes his life was over, that it would be only a matter of time before an enemy depth charge shattered the pressure hull, the sea would pour in, and his life would end.

Beyond these dark forebodings, beyond the anger, lay a consuming bitterness over the injustice.

He often tried to imagine what his life would have been like if the war had not intervened.

All through his childhood in America his family had assumed that he would follow in the footsteps of his father, eventually commanding an ocean liner for *Norddeutsher Lloyd.* An only child, he was kept home from public school to be trained toward that goal. He was educated by a private tutor, who drilled him in flawless American English against the time when he would deal daily with influential Americans as the captain of a great ocean liner.

His few attempts to make friends with his American peers during his boyhood had been unsuccessful. They considered him an oddity, a wind-up martinet. He had been unable to bend to the crass familiarity of American children. In time, he had retreated into a haughty, lonely silence.

His sense of identity had rested with his family, and with his future.

Standing on the *Norddeutsher Lloyd* piers in Hoboken, he had watched each arrival and departure of the *Bremen* and *Europa,* marveling that at one time his father had been captain of such beautiful ships. Twice each year, as a *Norddeutsher* director, his father sailed on inspection cruises. Often he took his family along, training Von Beck at sea for his future career. Von Beck came to know the ships, the crews intimately. Frequently, when his father lectured him on the finer points of shiphandling and navigation, or on the subtleties of gauging wind and current while docking, even the ranking officers of the ship would gather to listen.

Von Beck had grown into adolescence hoarding experience for his chosen career, and the responsibilities he some day would assume.

But that future never arrived.

In 1933, just after Von Beck's sixteenth birthday, *Norddeutsher Lloyd* transferred his father back to Germany.

The Von Beck family arrived in Berlin at the peak of excitement over the November Reichstag elections that swept Adolf Hitler into total power. Germany was in the grip of an exhilarating nationalism. Hitler had won ninety-two percent of the vote. His government was well on the way to relieving rampant unemployment, runaway inflation, economic depression. From the depths of despair, the whole country had been united into one large Germanic family, laughing, singing, working for the glory of the Third Reich.

Although his father laughed and called the Nazi government "an interesting social experiment," Von Beck thrilled to the mass demonstrations, the street marches, the stirring oratory.

He joined the Hitler Youth and was taught Strength through Joy, the inspiring camaraderie of shared work, and the Horst Wessel song. Soon, his quiet, lonely boyhood in America seemed no more than a dream.

At seventeen, he began with enthusiasm his compulsory term in the National Labor Service. The following year, he signed on as a naval cadet for training in the snow and mud of the Naval Academy at Flensburg.

He reported to the fleet on September 1, 1939, the same day the Wehrmacht marched into Poland and the war began.

Assigned to the Fifth U-boat Flotilla in Kiel, he made five combat patrols as a junior officer—months upon months of boredom, interspersed with a few brief intervals of absolute terror.

His superior officers were impressed with his thorough knowledge of the sea. On their recommendation, he was returned to Flensburg to be trained for higher command. After a single combat cruise as first officer, he had received his own boat.

The sobering responsibility of command, the deeper reality of the view through the periscope had brought overwhelming doubts. During the last few weeks, he had begun to question the war itself.

These things Von Beck kept from his crew, even from his fellow officers.

He recognized the increasing frequency of the daydreams—his persistent lament for what might have been—as a weakness. He had a job to do, one that demanded total concentration.

But more and more he thought back to that other world, to the clean lines of the great ships he had known, to the lingering sunsets at sea, to the exalted sense of pride and accomplishment from service aboard the liners.

His fondest memory was of the summer of 1936, just before his father died, and the last cruise his family had taken on the *Europa*. The highlight of the trip occurred in New York, where they were invited to a party aboard the *Normandie,* the largest and fastest liner afloat.

Captain Thoreux and Commissioner Villar had escorted Von Beck and his father on an extensive tour of the ship. Von Beck had marveled over the size of the liner, her tremendous power, her lavish appointments and superb styling.

On her massive bridge, awed by its sweeping expanse, Von Beck heard his father say softly, "Some day you will be captain of a ship such as this! You watch! Germany will build the *Normandie*'s successor. We will win back the Blue Riband and keep it, as we did in the days of the *Kaiser Wilhelm der Grosse,* the *Deutschland*, and the *Kronprinz Wilhelm*. And you will be her captain!"

On his return home to Bremerhaven, Von Beck had constructed a model of the *Normandie*, capturing every nuance of her graceful clipper bow and bulbous forefoot, the elegant flare outward along her upper decks. He doted on such innovations as the turtleback fo'c's'le. He memorized the statistics concerning her 170,000-horsepower turboelectric propulsion, the output of her 29 water-tube boilers. He learned many odd facts about her, such as the placement of the dog kennels in the dummy third funnel, added to her design only for esthetic reasons.

Von Beck and his father had spent many long, companionable hours with the model, blueprints, drawings, and diagrams, planning the perfect ship, carrying the advanced designs of the *Normandie* to even more lofty concepts.

In those days, he had been surrounded by beauty.

Now, he saw only ugliness—the stark, fetid efficiency of the U-boat, death, and destruction.

He could find no glory in killing from ambush, abandoning helpless sailors to drown, denying them even the human courtesy of a wireless message that might bring rescue.

It was a shitty war, devoid of all honor, gallantry, and hope.

He was thankful that his father had died before witnessing the collapse of values that had meant so much to him. And Von Beck's lingering grief over the death of his mother was eased by the thought that she had been spared the wearing anguish of the current wartime privations in Germany, the air raids, concern for her family.

Von Beck now had little family left. He and his sister, married to a shipyard owner in Bremerhaven, had never been close. They were separated by too many years. There were a few uncles, aunts, and cousins whom he barely remembered.

He knew it was fortunate that he had no strong emotional attachments, for he saw no way out of his situation. His only ambition was to return from his first combat command with a tonnage sufficient to earn the Knight's Cross—the third in three generations of Von Becks.

He had thought the matter through many times. He could see only one course open to him—to die with the knowledge that he had done all he could to uphold the family name.

Not until well into the early morning watch did Von Beck fall into a fitful, restless sleep.

The submarine continued to plow through the night, pursuing the unsuspecting tanker.

"Contact! Captain to the bridge!"

Even before he was fully awake, Von Beck swung his feet to the deck and reached for his bridge coat. He dashed through the control room and raced up the aluminum ladders into the pitch-dark night. Whipping off his infrared goggles, he crossed the bridge to Mueller, now officer of the watch.

"We're coming upon the convoy, *Mein Kapitän*," Mueller said.

The boat was pitching and rolling heavily. Von Beck hooked his coat harness into the steel eyelets of the bridge and trained his binoculars forward. A steady thirty-knot wind came out of the east, deepening the troughs. With each plunge of the bow, spray swept over the bridge, covering the watchstanders with brine. The distance to the tanker had lengthened.

"She increased speed a few minutes ago," Mueller said. "The convoy is hull-down on the horizon, to her port."

Von Beck searched the darkness. At first, he saw nothing but empty water. Then, as the submarine crested a wave, he caught a glimpse of specks along the rim of the sea. He checked the luminous dial of his watch. Forty minutes remained before dawn. Rough seas would make his approach more difficult, but the whitecaps would help hide the plume of the attack periscope.

He called down the hatch to the tower. "Both ahead full together!"

As the boat picked up speed, the plunging became even more violent. Solid seas reached the bridge. Von Beck clung to the bridge coaming to keep his footing under the weight of the water. Gradually, the tanker grew closer. Calculating speed and distance, Von Beck estimated that during the night they had traveled more than a hundred nautical miles. They were now well off the coast, and slightly north of the regular shipping lanes.

"Smoke cloud," called a watchstander behind him. "Oh five oh."

Von Beck shifted his binoculars. The first faint hint of dawn lay on the eastern horizon. A small dark smudge marred the surface of the sea. As the boat rode to the peak of a wave, he counted five ship superstructures.

He turned to Mueller and shouted into his ear against the wind, the waves. "Here's our plan. We'll follow the tanker right into the convoy. We'll stay on the surface until the last moment, then dive for submerged attack. I want you on the computer. We will make as many shots as possible."

He could hear excitement in Mueller's voice as he shouted his acknowledgment. *"Jawohl, Mein Kapitän!"*

Von Beck's plan was a compromise. The VII-C U-boat in practice was not a true submarine, but a motor torpedo craft that could dive, if necessary. On the surface, her twin diesels were capable of just over 17 knots, providing a range of 8,850 nautical miles. Submerged, using the electric motors, the boat had a top speed of 7.6 knots, and her batteries would be exhausted in two hours. The boat could remain submerged three days at much slower speed, maintaining only enough way to keep depth control with the hydroplanes.

Exercising caution, Von Beck maneuvered to within a thousand meters of the tanker's stern. He held that position as the leaden overcast began to lighten. Ahead, the ships of the convoy gradually assumed profiles. He could see another tanker, several freighters, and, off to port, two destroyer escorts.

He waited until he could see the pennant on the stern of the tanker.

She was Belgian.

"Dive alarm," he said.

The watchstanders hurriedly unhooked their harnesses and scuttled down through the hatch, their boots slamming into the deck plates below as they yelled "Alarm!" Von Beck heard the word passed through the boat, even before the alarm bell began to clang.

By the time he reached the control room, two machinists were dangling from the ballast tank levers, using their weight to open the valves more rapidly. Two other machinists were spinning wheels, opening flood valves. Above, Mueller closed the bridge hatch with a clang. One by one, all compartments reported to the chief of the boat.

After a moment, the chief turned to Von Beck.

"Ready to dive," he said.

"Take her to sixty meters," Von Beck said.

The hydroplane operators hit the buttons simultaneously with the palms of their hands. Von Beck could feel the boat taking on a sodden heaviness forward, losing buoyancy. All vibrations ceased. The stench of sweat, diesel oil, and bilge water returned in full force.

Even after hundreds of dives, Von Beck always was surprised by the sudden silence. Abruptly the hum of the ventilators, the roar of the diesels, the chatter from the radio shack were gone, replaced by the purr of the electric motors, the subdued gurgle of water in the buoyancy cells, and the soft hiss of compressed air clearing the tanks. It was now so quiet he could hear the drip of water into the bilge.

"Level at sixty meters," he said. "Maintain course zero nine zero."

The chief engineer was busy trimming the boat. Throughout each twenty-four hour period, the chief carefully monitored the weight of spent fuel, garbage discharged, salinity of the water. The accuracy of his calculations was tested with each dive.

"Forward tanks take on twenty," the chief said. "Release nine from aft."

Von Beck waited until the chief checked the results. A boat out of trim could mean disaster during a periscope attack.

"Boat balanced," the chief said.

"Periscope depth," Von Beck ordered.

He watched the depth gauge until the indicator rose to meet the red marker. Kneeling, he eased the periscope upward until it broke surface.

The tanker was still dead ahead. Slowly, Von Beck walked the periscope around a full circle.

"*Mein Gott,*" he breathed. He lowered the periscope.

They were surrounded by at least two dozen ships—tankers, freighters, a sprinkling of American destroyer escorts converted to British corvettes. The formation was staggered, ill-formed, almost motionless.

He apparently had blundered into a rendezvous. Ships were still assembling from every direction.

"The book," he said.

Jergensen knelt beside him with the silhouette recognition manual. Von Beck eased the periscope back to the surface. He made note of the tanker's superstructure, the distribution of the booms. He consulted the book briefly.

"The tanker is definitely Belgian," he said. "Fifteen thousand tons or so." He shifted the scope to the next target. "There is a large British freighter on our starboard beam. Make it eighteen thousand tons." He moved the view further to the right. "A Dutch tanker close off our starboard quarter. Fifteen thousand." He completed the sweep. "Two British corvettes on our stern, two more off to port, fifteen or twenty more targets sprinkled around like raisins in a pudding." He lowered the scope. "Ready tubes one to five. Prepare signal."

He would have preferred to launch a surface attack. But the corvettes were less than three minutes from effective gun range. He also wished he could maintain radio silence. But the admirals at headquarters had decreed that any U-boat sighting a convoy must radio its position before proceeding with an attack. He reduced the body of his message to three code letters—one signifying more than a dozen ships, another the speed, and the last conveying that he intended to attack. Even with the addition of his position and signature, the message could be sent in five seconds.

"Here's what we'll do," he called up the tower to Mueller at the controls of the attack computer. "A quick shot right up the ass of the tanker. Then we'll shoot the freighter on our starboard beam. Then the other tanker."

Mueller called down an acknowledgment.

Von Beck handed his message to Sparks. "As soon as the first torpedo is away, send this."

Again, he eased the scope to the surface. The tanker had moved slightly to the left, steering toward its place in the formation. He turned the scope to the right. The range to the freighter had narrowed—almost too much. The other tanker remained in the same relative position. Astern, the corvettes were approaching rapidly. Completing the circle, he brought the periscope back on the tanker.

"To the tower," he said, raising his voice. "Ready tube one. Target course eight knots, range five thousand five, torpedo four meters, bow left, angle ten, follow target." He heard the hum of the calculator as Mueller cranked in the information. The high-speed calculating machine would track the course, speed, and range of the target and communicate the data direct to the torpedo in the tube.

Von Beck gripped the handles of the periscope and held his breath until the lens cleared the surface again. "Stand by, tube one . . . tube one, shoot!"

The boat lurched as the torpedo left the forward tube. He heard the chief opening valves, frantically flooding ballast tanks to compensate for the sudden loss of a ton and a half of dead weight by the bow. Unless the chief acted quickly, the boat would broach. But Von Beck did not have time to worry. He shifted his full attention to the freighter.

"To the tower," he called. "Target course eight knots, torpedo six meters, bow left, angle twenty, spread three degrees, follow . . . stand by tubes two and three . . . tubes two and three, shoot!''

As he brought the periscope to bear on the third target, the first torpedo hit the tanker. So intent was Von Beck's concentration that he hardly heard the explosion. He continued feeding information to Mueller. An instant later, the concussion jarred the boat.

"Tubes four and five, shoot!''

The last two torpedoes were barely out of the tubes when numbers two and three hit, almost as one. The explosions from the near-by freighter rattled the submarine from stem to stern. For a half second, the lights went out.

The concussion from the more distant tanker was not nearly as pronounced.

Von Beck turned the periscope in a full circle for one last look. A column of black smoke three hundred meters high rose against the dawn, marking the spot where the first tanker had been blown out of the water. Not a sign of the ship remained on the surface. He could see only burning oil and gasoline. On the U-boat's starboard beam, the freighter was sinking. Even as he watched, her back broke and the two portions of the hull floated apart. The sounds of a breaking ship, something between the crack of a tree branch and the rip of heavy canvas, penetrated the hull of the submarine. The other tanker was burning furiously, the bow solid flames. Von Beck could see men jumping into the water. Then came a tremendous explosion, and Von Beck could no longer see the men.

Astern, the two corvettes were closing at flank speed. He saw the flash of gunfire from a five-inch turret.

"Flood!'' Von Beck ordered. "One hundred sixty. Hard left rudder. Starboard ahead full.''

He grabbed the overhead for support as the boat tilted. The corkscrew motion took them closer to two hundred meters before the hydroplanes brought the bow up. In the control room, the crew listened with apprehension as the hull creaked and popped under the pressure.

"Ahead very slow," Von Beck said. "All nonessential lights out. Silence in the boat."

Seated on the chart chest, he braced his sea boots against the bulkhead, his back against the sky periscope, and prepared for the pounding he knew was soon to come.

"Bearings!" he called to the sound man. "Keep them coming."

He stared at the deckplates as he listened to the monotonous drone of the sound man's voice, reconstructing in his vivid imagination what was happening on the surface.

The corvettes would be searching frantically, momentarily thrown off the scent by his erratic maneuver. Three pillars of flame would still be rising into the sky, with sailors swimming through burning oil, gasoline. The water would be filled with debris, the wounded, the dying, the corpses. . . .

In his peripheral vision, Von Beck saw his crewmen exchange glances, acknowledging to each other that yes, the Old Man again was in that dark, morose mood that always followed a kill.

He was twenty-four, and they called him the Old Man. Only the chief engineer was a few months older. Most of the men were eighteen, nineteen, twenty. He felt a generation removed from his entire crew.

"Bearings faint." The sound man spoke softly from the passageway forward of the control room. "Little movement."

Von Beck did not have to guess what was happening. The corvettes had stopped their engines to listen. Von Beck did not delude himself that they were picking up drowning men. They would not waste the time. His assessment was confirmed a moment later as the corvettes again got underway, dropping depth charges in their wake.

For the first twenty minutes, the explosions were safely astern. Von Beck's maneuver had taken the boat well into the wake of the corvettes. Gradually, the explosions grew fainter.

Mueller quietly descended from the tower. He stood by Von Beck, his head cocked toward the overhead. "Raking," he said. "I think they've lost us."

Mueller was wrong.

The corvettes soon returned with a vengeance. Once their sound gear locked onto the submarine, no maneuver Von Beck could concoct was adequate to break contact.

The attack lasted six and a half hours. Twice, explosions were so close and so violent that Von Beck held little hope his boat would survive. For a time, a leak in the after motor room threatened the E-motors. Eventually, the chief brought it under control.

Then, abruptly, the attack ended. The corvette screws receded.

Von Beck's desperate maneuvering had left the batteries low. He waited only twenty minutes before easing to periscope depth.

The corvettes were hull-down on the eastern horizon, hurrying to catch up with the convoy.

Von Beck called for damage reports. Every compartment had minor problems, but all the necessary repairs could be made underway.

He ordered the boat to the surface. As the diesels resumed their steady roar, restoring oxygen to the boat, charging the batteries, he set a course in pursuit of the corvettes.

At dawn the following morning, he again made contact with the convoy. He took up station well ahead, submerged, and sent his last two torpedoes into a large Dutch freighter. Again, the corvettes charged in and he was forced to dive.

The second depth-charge attack lasted more than twenty-six hours.

Not until two bodies, considerable debris, and a wide slick of fuel oil rose to the surface did the British corvettes break off the attack and jubilantly report the confirmed kill of a U-boat.

4

Kenmore Hall, New York City

The nights were the worst. During the days Rachael slept and lounged in bed, luxuriating in the clean sheets, the serenity. All the windows of her corner room were open for air, but the street sounds from below were distant, muffled. With the cross-ventilation, she did not mind the terrible heat. New York offered compensations.

Three times each day courteous young men wheeled sumptuous meals into her room. She devoured delicacies she had not tasted in years—fresh eggs, thick steaks, real coffee, crisp garden vegetables, chocolate mousse. She had almost forgotten that such pleasures existed. And she reveled in the precious comfort of a locked door.

Through the peaceful daylight hours, she regained a measure of self-confidence and restored faith in her elaborate, precarious plan.

But with the dark, her fears of failure returned. The consequences were too terrible to contemplate. Frantically, night after night, she pushed them from her mind.

She could not escape the feeling that she had been discovered, that they knew everything, that they were merely toying with her for their own purposes. She could end the mounting panic only by repeating to herself, over and over, what her father had told her, many times: "Rachael, you must learn the difference between your fantasies and the real world. You can't daydream your life away. Learn to deal with reality. If you can put your fantasies to work, you can move mountains!"

Soon her plan would prove that her father was right.

On the fifth morning, she awoke full of confidence, furious with herself. She had been ordered by the Abwehr to wait two or three days, remaining out of sight, before making contact with her control, in case she were followed. But she now had dawdled away too much time. Her control would be wondering what had happened to her.

She had endured too much during the last few months, putting her plan into operation.

She must not fail now!

Hurriedly, she began dressing.

She was uncertain what to wear. From what she had been able to see from her hotel window, jacket dresses with full padded shoulders seemed to be in style, with accessories of long gloves and portrait hats.

She had nothing so grand. No wonder the desk clerk had stared so disapprovingly the night she checked in.

As a matter of expediency, she chose the green silk peasant dress with the cloth-covered buttons, short gloves, and a wisp of a hat—the little-girl outfit that her father loved so much. It would have to do.

Besides, she did not want to leave the dress at the hotel, unguarded.

She took special care with her makeup. But the reality of the mirror almost destroyed her mood. She sat motionless for several minutes, analyzing all the things wrong with her appearance.

Her dark hair was gamin-cut at a time when fashion dictated that it should fall long and loose to her shoulders, maybe from a dramatic swirl about the face. Her brown eyes were much too big, their size accented by long, heavy lashes. Her lips were too full; she devoutly wished they were thinner, more conventional. Her hands were small, the fingers long and bony. The carefully polished nails only added to their length.

Her breasts were too small even for her thin build. She was much too child-like.

How could anyone take her seriously?

No wonder people stared at her.

Rachael sat for a time at the mirror, her eyes closed, concentrating on making her hands, her stomach, stop trembling.

Slowly, her confidence returned.

This *was* one of her good days.

She would make it so.

With one last look around the room, she forced herself to go back out into the world, to put her plan into action.

An elderly elevator man nodded a greeting. They rode to the ground floor in silence. When the cage opened, she crossed the lobby, her head high, taking care to walk properly, looking neither to the left nor right.

Outside the revolving glass doors, the streets were wet under a light rain. Surprised, she stopped beneath the hotel canopy in indecision.

A steady stream of traffic hurled by the hotel, horns blowing, motors roaring. She had always loved the sounds of New York, so energetic, so authoritative. By comparison, Paris traffic sounded like the bleating of sheep. But for the moment, she was overwhelmed.

The hotel doorman approached. "Taxi?"

She nodded. He signaled one to the curb and opened the door.

"Two hundred block of East Eighty-fifth," she told the driver.

He glanced at her in the rear-view mirror as he pulled away from the curb, and said something she did not understand.

"I'm sorry," she said. "I didn't hear you."

"The weddah," he said, turning slightly toward her. "I said, howja like this cool air?"

She had almost forgotten the gregarious, aggressive manner of Americans. "I'm sorry, but I've just arrived in town," she said.

He looked at her with renewed interest. "You're lucky, lady. We hadda heat wave. Seven days. People dying all over the place."

"That's terrible. I didn't know."

He smiled at her in the mirror. "That's why everybody's happy widda rain, see. Broke the heat wave." He dodged another taxi as it changed lanes. Sticking his head out the window, he shouted, "Creep!" and resumed talking as if nothing had happened. "Where you from, lady?"

Rachael decided she might as well take the plunge. She would try her story on this innocuous taxi driver. "France. I'm a French refugee."

He stared at her for a moment in the mirror. "Where the Krauts are? Paris?"

"A small town a little way out from Paris."

"You talk English real good," he said.

She raised her voice against the rush of wind, the noise. "Thank you. I lived here for a while, some years ago."

Abruptly, he again changed lanes, cutting off another taxi. The other driver honked and shouted something. Rachael's driver did not seem to notice. "What are the Krauts like?"

She was glad she had decided to talk. This was good practice. "We really didn't see very much of them in my small town," she said. "For the most part, they leave everything to the collaborationist police."

He kept glancing at her, then back to the street as he talked. "Pretty rough over there?"

"Very difficult for the Jews," she said. She watched for his reaction, wondering if he were Jewish. "Many are being relocated." He did not comment, so she went on. "The shortages are very bad for everyone."

"We're beginning to get that here," he said. "They're

talking about gasless Sundays. I ask you, what good'll that do? Everybody'll just fill up on Saturday. If you ask me, it's something the oil companies thought up so they can close gas stations on Sundays, see, cut down on overhead. We got plenty of oil! Pennsylvania, Texas, Oklahoma are fulla oil!'' He braked for a stop light, then, at the last possible moment, decided to run it. She gasped as the taxi almost brushed pedestrians in the crosswalk.

She glanced out at the street signs. They were now on Broadway, moving rapidly uptown. After several more blocks, she could see Times Square ahead. A huge crowd jammed the famous intersection. Rachael felt constriction around her heart. Crowds meant police, inspection of papers.

The driver was muttering under his breath. "My fault, lady," he said aloud. "I forgot about this. They got us blocked off. We gotta stop. The President's making a speech."

She did not understand. "The President is speaking? Here?"

"On radio. See, lady? That's a WNYC sound truck up there in front of Faddah Duffy's monument."

The amplified strains of "The Star Spangled Banner" penetrated the taxi. Around them, other cars and taxis were slowing. Her driver eased forward until they were in the midst of a sea of umbrellas. He stopped, switched off the ignition, and turned in his seat to roll down her window, despite the rain.

The national anthem ended. The crowd waited in silence. Then a voice filled the square. "Ladies and gentlemen, the President of the United States, Franklin Delano Roosevelt."

At first she had difficulty understanding the President. His words echoed off buildings and came back indistinct. She gathered that he was drawing parallels between the dangers during the American Revolution and the present threat from totalitarian governments. As she became accustomed to his unusual accent and style of delivery, she understood his words.

". . . we are engaged in a serious, in a mighty, in a unified action in the cause of the defense of the hemisphere and the freedom of the seas. We need not the unity alone, we need speed and efficiency and toil—an end to the backbiting, an end to the sabotage that runs far deeper than the blowing up of munition plants."

She felt a chill at the back of her neck. She clasped her hands to keep them from trembling. Her mouth was dry.

What munition plants had been blown up?

Were they searching for spies?

She sat for a time in a struggle to regain her composure. When she could concentrate again, the President was saying, "I tell the American people solemnly that the United States will never survive as a happy and fertile oasis of liberty surrounded by a cruel desert of dictatorship. It must be our deep conviction that we pledge as well as our work, our will and, if it be necessary, our very lives."

A hushed moment followed the speech. Then a murmur of approval and applause swept through the crowd.

"Ya gotta hand it to him," the taxi driver said. "He sure knows how to stir people up."

Around them, the crowd began to move. The street cleared. She heard pleasantries exchanged, laughter. The normalcy helped to relieve her fears. She had not heard such spontaneous gaiety in years.

When the taxi arrived at Eighty-fifth and Third Avenue, her driver leaned toward the mirror. "The two hunnert block is a long one. I can take you anywhere you wanna go."

She was prepared. She had been watching the numbers on the buildings. "Right there," she said. "Just beyond that parked car."

She gave him the fare and a generous tip. He touched the brim of his hat. "Good luck," he said. "And don't worry, lady. You're gonna do all right in this country."

She waited until he drove off, then walked back to the Little Casino Restaurant.

The door was locked. A handwritten sign in the window simply said, CLOSED. Stunned, she backed away.

It was then that she saw the swastikas painted on the glass. For a moment, she did not understand.

Then she did.

Fighting panic, she hurried back toward Third Avenue, ignoring the light rain.

From newspapers, she learned that twenty-nine German spies had been arrested.

All four of her Abwehr contacts were listed among them.

In the classes at Klopstock, she had been told that safety usually lay in making oneself as inconspicuous as possible. She was told never to run unless she had reason to believe she was suspected.

For the next three days, she remained in her room, uncertain what she should do.

How much did the Americans know? Were they onto her, watching her, waiting for her to make her next move?

She knew she had to think clearly. Too much was at stake. Canaris and the others had made it plain that she must perform as expected, and uphold her end of the bargain.

Thus far, she had seen no evidence that she was under surveillance. But the game of spying was far more complex than she had imagined. Perhaps she had missed something.

She made herself think back.

Lisbon was where the fear had started—the constant, paranoid fear that someone was watching her. She searched her memory for clues.

The city had been jammed with people desperate for the few scraps of paper that would take them from the hell of Europe to the heaven of Brazil, Argentina, Chile, Canada, the United States. She had waited for three weeks, visiting the American embassy almost daily. Each time, she had been questioned by the same dark-haired young man, rather handsome in a rugged way.

She remembered now that he had insisted on speaking French, claiming that he needed the practice. But his French was flawless. She was now certain that he insisted on the language to check her own lingual inflections.

He also had feigned unfamiliarity with her file. The pretense had been a trifle too elaborate. She recalled the way the conversation went on her first visit.

"Let's see, your full name is Annette-Marie. . . ."

"Annette-Marie Fourcade."

"And what is your reason for wishing to emigrate?"

Rachael had given the answer she had memorized and practiced even to the hesitations. "The . . . situation in Occupied France had become very difficult for me, and for my family. I could see no indication that conditions would improve. I thought that by returning to America, I would relieve the burden on them, and that I might be able to help them."

"I see. You have a large family?"

"Not immediate family. My parents are dead. An aunt and uncle are the closest. They are like my own parents. I also have several cousins, who are the same as brothers and sisters to me."

"And you have been to the United States before?"

"I lived there for a year on a student visa, while I taught piano and studied at Juilliard. I also made a concert tour of the United States, performing at colleges and universities, conducting master classes. I have many friends there. I'm sure I will have no problems."

As she had been warned, his questions were not in sequence. "How did you manage to leave France?" he asked abruptly, as if the thought had just occurred to him.

She was ready for him. In a way, the contest of wits had been exciting.

"It wasn't as difficult as I thought it might be," she said. "My uncle had friends who knew someone. I obtained the proper papers for passage into the Vichy zone, and made my way to the border of Spain. I bribed some officials, and was granted a pass-through visa to Lisbon."

"Alone?"

"My uncle insisted it would be safer."

He shuffled through her file. "Your uncle is your legal guardian?"

She recognized the question as a ploy to trap her. "Until I came of age."

"And what is his occupation?"

She paused, as she had been instructed. "He's an architect." Then she spoke hurriedly, as if to cover her hesitation. "That is a difficult question to answer, for he is also a recognized philosopher. He has written several books and is better known in that regard. But he earns his living as an architect, which is why I gave that answer."

For the first time, the young man had offered a trace of friendliness. "That's good. His recognition as an author will help greatly to establish your *bona fides*. What are some of his better-known books?"

She rattled off a half-dozen titles. He made careful notes. At the end of the interview, he smiled.

"As you probably know—but I'm required to explain it to you anyway—America has immigration quotas based on the country of origin. Those quotas were established in keeping with the ethnic heritages of American citizens. Fortunately, we've been granted some latitude in recent months to accommodate refugees, especially professional people and artists such as yourself. Even so, we have more than a hundred applications for each opening in the quota system. So I can't promise you anything, except that we will make every effort to process your case as rapidly as possible."

It was all play-acting on her part, and she had delivered her lines perfectly. But she still could not shake the feeling

86

that the Americans in the embassy had known all about her, and had allowed her to enter the United States for their own, mysterious purpose.

She had no grounds for her fear, except instinct.

But the feeling would not go away.

She remembered the knowing glances each time she entered the embassy, the quiet, persistent little man who hardly took his eyes off her all the way across the Atlantic.

The trip had been a nightmare—nothing at all like her magical, fairyland crossings on the *Normandie*, years ago.

This time she had spent twenty-two grueling hours on a huge, noisy Boeing 314 flying boat. And during the single refueling stop in Bermuda she had sat rigid with fear and anxiety through an unexplained twelve-hour delay. She had arrived in New York exhausted. Her clearance through Immigration and Customs seemed to take forever. And she remembered the strange attitude of the officials at La Guardia.

Did they know?

Now, sitting in a nest of well-explored newspapers, she tried to convince herself that they did not know—that she should remain in hiding for at least a week or more, then contact the Abwehr for instructions.

For the next four days she kept to her room, ordering all meals sent up. Then, shortly before noon on the fifth day, the persistent buzzing of the phone brought her seclusion to an abrupt end.

She lay motionless through six rings, staring at the ornately paneled ceiling, her heart racing, undecided whether to answer. She closed her eyes, clenched her fists, and fought off panic. She reminded herself that the call might be from the hotel desk. There could be some question about her room.

She gathered her composure, rolled to the edge of the bed, and answered in English, "Yes?"

The male voice was soft and polite. "Mademoiselle Fourcade?"

She hesitated, trying to place a suggestion of accent. "Speaking."

"I bring you greetings from Villeneuve-sur-Yonne."

The code phrase gave her a moment of sheer, heart-stopping terror. She gripped the phone with both hands.

Was it a trick?

Rachael remembered the warnings. The dangers had been stressed, over and over. Her head swimming, she spoke the oft-practiced line by rote: "Is this Uncle George?"

He did not respond for a moment. "Uncle George is . . . away just now. I have been asked to welcome you."

She had been told that sometimes she would have to think fast, and ad lib. But she could only repeat his words. "Uncle George is away? Away where?"

A tone of irritation came into his voice. "Look, I must talk with you. Meet me at three."

Before she could reply, he broke the connection.

Her hands trembling, she replaced the receiver.

Uncle George away?

What was the man trying to tell her?

The rain had ceased. The bench in Bryant Park remained slightly damp. Rachael had arrived a few minutes early and sat with the prescribed *New York Times* in her lap, folded at page eighteen. A few minutes later, a tall young man paused, glanced at the newspaper, and turned so she could see his own, carried in a coat pocket, also folded at page eighteen. He greeted her as a casual acquaintance.

"I'm Frank Pierce," he said, and smiled as he sat beside her.

She had practiced the meeting so many times in Hamburg that even with the sounds of the city around her, she found it difficult to believe that at last she was in America and it was for real. She wondered what her father would say if he knew how far the use of fantasy had taken her.

Pierce was a large man, well over six feet, and could be considered handsome. He had perfect white teeth, a firm jawline, and soft, curly blond hair. He was impeccably dressed in a double-breasted gray suit with the wide lapels that seemed to be the current style in New York. There was humor in his eyes. She could not detect any trace of German accent in his speech. She would have assumed that he was an American.

"We can't talk here, of course," he said, keeping his voice low. "But I assume you know that there have been difficulties."

Pedestrians were passing on the sidewalk only a few feet away. The benches nearby were crowded.

"What happened?" she asked.

He smiled again for the benefit of anyone who might be monitoring their conversation. He ignored her question. "Have a pleasant trip?"

What could she say? Rachael tried to imagine the answer that might be given by someone who had been everywhere, seen everything. She smiled back at him. "As pleasant as one could wish, I suppose, under the circumstances."

He lowered his voice. "We expected you sooner. Anything happen? You have any reason to suspect that they may be onto you?"

The role was becoming easier. "As far as I know, there's no problem."

"Thank God you didn't come earlier," he said. "The entire net has been broken. George, all the others were arrested."

She forced herself to remain perfectly motionless, and willed her face to show no emotion. "I know," she said. "I read about it in the newspapers."

A tall, thin man and a striking blond woman stopped at an adjoining bench, so close that they would have no trouble eavesdropping. They stood for a moment, discussing whether the bench was dry enough to use. As they sat down, Pierce glanced in their direction, then turned back to

Rachael. He spoke a bit louder. "Have you read William L. Shirer's new book, *Berlin Diary?*"

Rachael understood immediately—a play within a play for the benefit of the couple. "Not yet," she said.

"Absolutely fascinating. It's just been published, you know. Already more than a hundred thousand copies in print—the best-selling book in years. . . ."

He talked on, describing the book, telling anecdotes from it, performing for the benefit of the couple on the adjoining bench. After a few minutes, the couple ended their own brief, intermittent conversation and moved away.

Pierce leaned closer. "Look, we'll have to go someplace where we can talk," he said under his breath. She nodded agreement. The Bryant Park bench was the standard rendezvous, chosen to give anyone meeting her the opportunity to make sure she was not under surveillance. The procedure was routine, well covered in the Abwehr school on Klopstockstrasse in Hamburg. Now, they would go to a safe house.

Rachael did not feel right about the situation. But she could not think of a way to refuse.

They walked to the corner of Fifth Avenue, where Pierce hailed a taxi.

"Intersection of Madison and Eighty-fourth, please," he told the driver.

As the taxi moved into traffic, Pierce turned to look through the rear window. He was preoccupied for a time, watching to see if anyone were following them.

"Where are we going?" Rachael asked.

"To my apartment," Pierce said. Some of her concern must have shown in her face. "You'll be safe there," he added.

They rode up Madison Avenue in silence, the hot, humid air blowing through the cab. Rachael watched the display windows slide past, still full of merchandise despite the war. The sidewalks were crowded with pedestrians who moved along with an innocent normalcy she found difficult to believe. Only here and there did she see uniforms.

America was even less prepared for war than she had been led to believe.

"You're to work with me," Pierce said. "Duquesne left explicit orders. He told me to meet you, move you in here, put you to work immediately."

Rachael did not answer. Something was wrong. She felt boxed-in, overwhelmed. She did not know what to do. At the Abwehr school, she had been told that if she were separated from her control she should contact the Abwehr for instructions. No mention had been made about the possibility of a substitute control appearing on the scene.

Her instincts told her not to trust Pierce.

He was a strange man. He had a way of speaking in short, staccato bursts, pausing to flash his large white teeth in a wide, patronizing smile. He was pleasant, but there was a quality about him that was disturbing—a quality she could not define.

His apartment was on the eighth floor of a well-kept brownstone. The small living room faced uptown. The view through the windows was of tarred roofs and, a few blocks away, modestly taller buildings. The walls were unadorned except for three prints of various species of ducks in flight. From the faded, worn couch, she could see into a small bedroom. A tiny kitchenette was tucked into one end of the sitting room, separated only by thin paneling and a light louvered door.

Rachael sat quietly on the couch, assessing her chances of getting away from him. She needed time to think.

"Drink?" Pierce asked. "I have bourbon, gin, scotch, anything you want."

She accepted a glass of petit chablis. He brought it to her with great ceremony.

"To the Reich," he said, touching his glass to hers.

Aside from a token sip, Rachael left her wine untouched. Pierce quickly finished his and poured another.

"No one will ever suspect you're a spy," he said. "You look like someone's kid sister."

He leaned close and touched her shoulder in a way she did not like.

"You're not what I expected either," she said. "I would have taken you for an American."

He smiled. "I am. Born and reared in Milwaukee. But my father was a German soldier in the Great War. And I've been a member of the Bund more than three years."

Rachael kept her face expressionless. She had been given specific instructions to stay away from the Bund. Instructors at the Abwehr school had said the Bundists were closely watched by the FBI.

"You've never been to Germany?"

"No. But I've worked with Duquesne almost a year now. He has taught me everything he knows."

She understood. Pierce was the protégé, and Duquesne had been his hero.

Now, he wanted to become Duquesne.

Rachael tried to speak calmly, decisively. "I think I should contact the Abwehr and ask for instructions," she said. "That's what I was told to do."

Pierce frowned and shook his head. "That'd take forever."

"I'm sorry, but I specifically was ordered not to work with any other group," she said.

That was not exactly true. She had been warned about the necessity for tight compartmentalization, the dangers of working with amateurs.

"But with all the radios out, how will you contact Germany?" he asked.

"I have a method," she said.

"Not a mail drop, I hope. Duquesne is certain the English are opening all transatlantic mail in Bermuda. And they now share everything with the FBI."

Rachael remembered the long, unexplained delay of the Pan-American Clipper in Bermuda. She wondered if Pierce were right. The Clippers now carried the bulk of the mail across the Atlantic.

"I'm assembling a radio," Pierce said. "I almost have it ready. When it's completed, you can confirm what I'm saying."

His face was tinged with red from the wine. He moved closer and touched her cheek. "You're very beautiful. I understand now where you got your code name Princess. You have a regal way about you."

Again, Rachael did not answer. Their rendezvous had gone so smoothly. He had given her the right signals down to the finest details so that she could not possibly have suspected anything amiss. But as he talked, she at last realized what it was about him that bothered her most. Every professional she had met in the Abwehr had been of a certain temperament—cautious, quiet, reserved. They made a habit of fading into the furniture.

Pierce was too animated, too obvious.

He plainly was an amateur.

How could he have been left in charge?

The hazard was apparent, amply covered in the lectures at Klopstock. In time, the Americans would make Duquesne talk. There was a direct link to Pierce. And now to her.

"It'll be perfect," he said, stroking her arm. "You'll be my cover. Duquesne says that single people always attract attention. Married people go unnoticed. Your moving in here will solve problems for both of us."

He grinned.

Inwardly, she froze. The apartment was small and cramped. There was only one bed.

She tried a ploy to keep him talking. "I'm sorry, but I still don't understand. How did you escape arrest?"

He grimaced. "We had an FBI double-agent in charge of the Long Island radio. Code name Tramp. He blew the entire net. I never met him. He didn't know of my existence."

"Surely they're still investigating," she pointed out. "Maybe we should separate for a while. If we see no indication. . . ."

His face hardened. "We have our duty. Duquesne made that clear. Convoys are leaving every day, unreported. You know what's expected of us! The embargo against England must be total! We must get the coastwatch back into operation. I'll have the new radio ready within a week. Come! I'll show you!"

He rose and staggered drunkenly into the small bedroom. Reluctantly, she followed. There was space only for a chest of drawers, a small vanity, a double bed, and a long, plain table covered with radio parts and tools.

Pierce showed her the partially constructed radio, and explained that the Afu Apparat, the Telefunken suitcase radio ordinarily used by German agents, would not reach across the Atlantic. "It has only twenty watts. To reach Germany or even Mexico City for relay, we'll need at least a hundred, or better, two hundred."

She had received some training in radios. "What about American direction finders? Won't they locate you?"

"The Bund has bought a place out on the end of Long Island. Even with a directional antenna, it'd be difficult to find. They'd think the signals were coming from the sea."

Pierce aligned the loose radio parts on the table and explained the function of each. "Now I only need a strong rectifier tube, some crystals, and a good transformer. I can't just go out and buy them. The suppliers are suspicious of anyone hunting transmitter parts these days. But there's a member of the Bund who works in a radio manufacturing plant at Babylon, just south of Deer Park. He has promised to bring me the parts next week."

"Wonderful," she said with make-believe enthusiasm.

She glanced toward the door, thinking that if she could get away from him now, she could hide until she made contact through her letter drop. They would tell her how to handle this. "I'm sorry, but I'm tired," she said cautiously.

"I'll go back to my hotel and wait. I really feel that'd be best."

"I'll go with you to get your bags," he said. "We can move you in tonight."

Rachael involuntarily backed away from him, from the bed. "I can't do that," she said.

His eyes widened with understanding. He moved between her and the door. His voice took on a heavy tone of mockery. "Surely, mademoiselle, you have no qualms over a little charade of domesticity."

She remained silent, but she knew the expression on her face was eloquent enough.

He moved toward her, his grin intact. "Look, the Reich didn't train you and send you five thousand miles to play Pollyanna with me, sister. We're at war, and we all have our duty to do. I'm more than willing to do mine."

He reached for her. Eluding him, she backed into the long table, jarring it. Some of the radio parts fell to the floor.

She shook her head emphatically in mute appeal. All of her carefully rehearsed lines, her perfectly created character portrayal failed her. "I won't do it," she managed to say.

His laugh faded. "Listen, you Jew bitch," he said quietly. "Duquesne told me all about you. Don't try this high-hat act with me! You were sent here to do whatever I say!"

She backed the length of the table. She felt the bed behind her knees.

He grabbed her arm and twisted. The sudden pain made her cry out. He slapped her across the face with the back of his hand. "Shut up!" he said. "Shut up! If the police come we'll both hang! Remember that!"

She struggled silently, furiously. But he was too strong. He held her firmly against him, blocking her every effort to break free.

Their desperate, hushed battle continued for several minutes. Rachael felt faint. Her breath came in labored gasps.

With one arm, he held her tight, pinioned. His other hand began to roam. She could feel his erection against her stomach.

She sobbed in frustration and anger. But she knew she could not scream for help. What he had said was true: She could not risk the police.

Growing weaker, she stopped struggling.

He towered over her, grinning. "We're going to have a lot of fun, you and me," he said. "All we need is to break the ice, get to know each other." He shifted his grip. "Let's get this out of the way."

He seized the neck of her dress with his free hand and ripped downward. Buttons flew. She did not dare call attention to them by looking to see where they went. She felt his hands against her bare skin and tried to twist free. He covered her mouth with his own.

She bit hard and tasted blood.

"Bitch!" he yelled. He backed away, his left hand to his mouth. His right fist shot out and exploded against her face, spinning her around, slamming her across the table.

Head down, her senses reeling, she grasped the table for support. Her hand closed on a screwdriver. The shaft was long and sharp.

Rachael had been drilled in the use of such makeshift weapons.

She felt his hands at the back of her neck. Suddenly, he ripped the dress from her back, leaving her naked to the waist.

She turned, the handle of the screwdriver clutched firmly in her left fist, the shaft pointed toward him. Using the heel of her right hand as a ram, she drove the point of the screwdriver into his chest.

Her thrust met surprisingly little resistance. For a moment, she thought the point had been deflected by a rib.

Then the handle was torn out of her grasp.

Pierce staggered backward, clutching feebly at the handle of the screwdriver, his eyes wide in disbelief. His mouth worked desperately, but no sound emerged. He sat down heavily on the carpet. He tumbled over, his head striking the wall. Only a small stain spread across his shirtfront. The handle of the screwdriver made an effective plug for the wound.

Rachael stood over him, paralyzed. He looked up at her in astonishment, his mouth still trying to form words. Then, after an interminable minute, the mouth was still. Life left the staring eyes.

Numbly, Rachael backed away. She tripped and almost fell. Her dress and slip had fallen to her ankles. Stooping, still watching the empty eyes, she covered her nakedness with her ripped clothing.

She staggered to the bed and sat for several minutes, her head in her hands, and forced herself to regain control.

The Abwehr training center had projected many situations such as this. Invariably, the instructors had praised her imagination and resourcefulness.

She only had to think things through, as if this were one of those make-believe problems.

Gradually, she mapped out a plan of action.

First, she removed the chenille coverlet from the bed and spread it over the body, hiding the eyes. One by one, she found the buttons that had been torn from her dress. She counted them twice to make sure none was missing.

She could not find a needle and thread. She inspected the dress. Aside from a minor rip along the shoulder, the sturdy fabric itself had not torn. She hunted for something to anchor the buttons. On the table with the radio parts, she found some thin copper wire. With the help of a pair of needle-nosed pliers, she pushed the wire through the cloth and firmly re-attached the buttons.

In the tiny kitchen, under the sink, she found soap and a cloth. Retracing every move she had made in the apartment, she washed all surfaces clean of fingerprints.

Before leaving the apartment, she examined herself in the full-length mirror in the bedroom.

A dark bruise covered her left cheekbone. She masked it as well as she could with makeup. The dress would not bear close scrutiny—she could not hide the rip on one shoulder—but she thought she would be able to enter her hotel without its being noticed.

Rachael gathered her purse and stood in the middle of the room for two full minutes, making certain she had thought of everything.

Then she walked quietly out of the apartment, using her handkerchief to avoid leaving fingerprints.

Allowing the door to latch behind her, she moved past the elevator and down the stairs, pausing occasionally to listen.

At the ground floor, she cracked the door and peeked out.

The entrance was deserted.

Hurriedly, she walked out the front door and away from the building.

She did not look back.

5

Federal Building, Brooklyn

One by one they came, each in handcuffs, each escorted by four Special Agents of the FBI, a grim parade that paralyzed daily routine at the vast Federal Building in Brooklyn. The procedure was rigid, decreed in a lengthy memorandum from the Director. Two agents walked precisely six paces ahead of each spy to ascertain that no dangers lurked in darkened recesses, that no door or unexpected obstacle would distract the two agents who maintained firm grips on each prisoner's elbows.

Special Agent H. Shackelford Bonham stood motionless at the end of the corridor, a piece of federal statuary, and watched as quintet after quintet walked the length of the hall toward him, passing at exact ten-minute intervals. His job was to ensure that no threat, foreign or domestic, approached the spies and their escorts from the rear.

It was now two o'clock in the afternoon. Bonham was tired and bored. The hollow echoes in the vast corridor, the humid heat, the drowsy tempo of the building itself produced a stupefying, hypnotic effect. To his mild but anticipated disappointment, no Nazi Bundists or irate citizenry had enlivened his day. And the spies themselves were nothing to strike fear into the heart of anyone. Bonham had never seen such an assortment of misfits. Rumpled and scared, the dregs of international riffraff, they were far from impressive.

Across the wide hallway, Special Agent Paul Marcus was performing deep knee bends to restore circulation to his legs. Marcus was a small man, just over the Bureau minimum in height, with a thin face, big ears, and a sharp, prominent nose. His dark brown hair tended toward kinky curls. During their brief time in the New York office, Bonham and Marcus had been thrown together often enough to consider themselves working partners.

With a quick glance up and down the corridor, Marcus lit a forbidden cigarette, adroitly cupped it in his palm, and drifted over to Bonham. He raised a hand to cover his mouth as he spoke. It was a universal FBI habit, quickly acquired.

"I thought we swore to defend the United States against all enemies," Marcus said. "I don't understand this. Here we are, *guarding* our enemies."

"You haven't learned anything about enemies yet," Bonham said. "Wait till Bullethead catches you off your post."

Marcus remained unperturbed. "Shack, as long as I have you around, I've nothing to worry about. It's *your* ass he's after."

Bonham did not reply. Marcus was right. Frank Cato, the supervisor of the Security Squad in the New York office, never lost an opportunity to find fault with Bonham.

"How many more?" Marcus asked.

"One," Bonham said. "Bertram Zenzinger."

Three doors down, two secretaries peeked out, giggled at Bonham and Marcus, then scurried across the hall. The clatter of their high heels resounded up and down the long corridor, the echoes gradually blending into the new clamor of footsteps approaching on the stairs.

100

Marcus quickly snuffed his cigarette and moved back to his post.

Bertram Zenzinger and his escort appeared.

Arrested two months earlier for violation of the Alien Registration Act, Zenzinger now was to be charged with the higher crime of spying. He came toward Bonham with his head down, his thin body dwarfed by the two large Special Agents at his side. The trio passed Bonham without acknowledging his presence and disappeared into the courtroom, where Zenzinger was to be arraigned before United States Commissioner Martin C. Epstein.

As Bonham expected, the door did not remain closed. Frank Cato emerged, extracted his gold pocket watch, and studied it with great solemnity. He motioned to Bonham and Marcus. While they walked toward him, he ceremoniously lit one of his outsized cigars.

He was a huge man, taller than Bonham, wider, and solid. He weighed more than two hundred and twenty pounds. His head was bald, the skin wrinkled and metallic. The nickname Bullethead had not required much imagination. His black eyes were set well apart, and accented by heavy brows. A flat nose and thick lips gave him the aspect of a professional wrestler. He was an old hand in the Bureau, and had served with Melvin Purvis during the pursuit and arrests of Machine Gun Kelly, Pretty Boy Floyd, Baby Face Nelson, Frank and Ma Barker. His file bulged with commendations and letters of congratulations signed or initialed by FBI Director J. Edgar Hoover. One feat of heroism had merited not only a citation, but also a personal gift from the Director—a silver water pitcher and desk set. A first-year agent was now assigned the supplementary duty of keeping the pitcher eternally polished and supplied with ice.

Cato whipped the cigar out of his mouth and studied Bonham a moment before speaking. "A little change of plans," he said, his deep voice rumbling through the empty corridor. "You two'll handle backup on the transfer of

Zenzinger, Jahnke, and Stade. Shouldn't take long. You'll be free by four.''

Bonham nodded. The procedure was routine. The spies now had to be processed out of FBI Headquarters in Foley Square, and moved to the Federal House of Detention on West Street and the Women's House of Detention at Greenwich and Sixth avenues. He and Marcus would merely tail the transfer van to make certain no Bundists or lynch mob leaped out of a side street.

One more boring assignment.

Bonham's thoughts must have shown on his face. Cato's eyes narrowed behind a cloud of smoke. "Bonham, I've got my eye on you. No fuckups. Understand?''

Bonham did not answer.

Cato wheeled abruptly and lumbered down the hall.

Bonham watched him until he was out of sight. "Now why did he have to go and say that?'' he asked. "Just when I was beginning to develop a genuine affection for him.''

Marcus winced and shook his head. "Shack, why do you go out of your way to bait him? You're playing with dynamite.''

Bonham was genuinely puzzled. "What do you mean?''

"Well, shit. You stand there looking at him with that half grin on your face, staring him down with those baby blue eyes. Either that, or one of your great, glowering silences. You intimidate the hell out of him. Don't you know that? You look like you think you could mop up the floor with him without half trying.''

"What makes you think I couldn't?'' Bonham asked.

Marcus threw up his hands. "Shit! Why do I even *try* to talk to you?''

They walked down the stairs to the car. Marcus opened the trunk and lifted out the .45 caliber Thompson. He slid into the front seat, placed the gun between his knees, inserted the hundred-round drum, fed a round into the chamber, and double-checked the safety. Bonham drove across the parking lot to the transport van and turned off the ignition. They made themselves as comfortable as possible and prepared for a long wait.

After forty-five minutes, Marcus grew restless. He glanced at his wristwatch. "Bullethead said we'd be free at four."

"Free to start *our* work, he means."

"Shack, you're just not displaying the proper spirit," Marcus said. "A Special Agent does his work cheerfully and without complaint, no matter how much shit is dumped upon him."

Bonham grunted, conceding the point. A first-year Special Agent was expected to be a glutton for work. For five weeks he and Marcus had driven backup cars, manned radios on stakeouts, and served as lookout on black bag jobs during the roundup of the twenty-nine spies now in custody. In addition, they had spent at least eight or ten hours each day out on the bricks, conducting interviews and investigations for their own caseloads.

"Bullethead didn't brief us for this job," Marcus said. "What if a prisoner runs? Who are we supposed to shoot? The prisoner? Or the agent who let him loose?"

"I'm not authorized to make big decisions like that," Bonham said. "I'm just the driver."

Marcus sighed. "Shack, I'm beginning to understand Bullethead's attitude toward you."

Bonham saw movement at the door. "Heads up," he said. "Here they come."

The three prisoners emerged, escorted by a platoon of Special Agents. The spies were placed in the van and chained to heavy metal ringbolts in the floor. The door was closed, and the convoy formed for the trip back to Foley Square.

Bonham pulled into line, pondering what Marcus had said.

Was Cato really out to nail him?

Bonham had worked long and hard to become a Special Agent of the FBI. He could not allow one oversized, obnoxious blowhard to stop him now, even if Bullethead were part of an insidious clique within the Bureau.

The FBI was in the throes of the most rapid expansion in its history. A few short months before, the Bureau had consisted of less than 400 Special Agents scattered over forty-eight states, two territories, and a few assorted possessions. The authorized strength now called for 1,600 agents. With rapid recruitment, the Bureau was fast approaching that number.

This swift growth had allowed Bonham to realize his boyhood dream.

But it also had created problems.

The older agents, survivors of the gangster wars of the Twenties and Thirties, viewed the ballooning of the Bureau as a temporary condition, a necessary but lamentable product of the national emergency. They resented the mass hiring of new agents—and with considerable justification.

These older agents were the carefully selected members of an elite corps, sufficiently tough to battle the most hardened criminals in the streets, smart enough to prepare evidence that would prevail in court against the best defense attorneys organized crime could afford.

For years they had worked in an atmosphere of warm camaraderie. They took quiet pride in the knowledge that they were members of the best law enforcement agency on earth.

Now, by every action and gesture, they made plain that they perceived a sharp delineation between themselves and the flood of new, hastily trained recruits.

They were the Insiders.

Everyone who had come into the Bureau under the expansion program was an Outsider.

The Insiders protected their own. All major cases were assigned to the old hands.

The younger agents drew the shitwork.

Bonham still had eight months to go on his probational year. With completion of training at Quantico, he had been assigned to Philadelphia for his initial, three-month tour. There he had worked on the Applications Desk, ferreting out background information on applicants for government jobs. For his second tour, he had been sent to New York City, in keeping with J. Edgar Hoover's philosophy that an FBI agent should be familiar with every section of the country. He now was a member of the Security Squad, pounding the pavement to check on the character of defense plant workers, military men, government employees, anyone and everyone who might have access to sensitive information or material.

With the emergency growth of the defense industry and all branches of government, a tremendous workload had landed on the Bureau. Bonham did not mind. He was accustomed to hard work.

He could even tolerate boredom if some goal were in sight.

But day after day, by infinite vicious, subtle methods, the Insiders made it plain that nothing about Bonham qualified him for membership in their coveted circle—not his diploma from Abilene Christian College, not his law degree from the University of Texas, not his two years as an assistant district attorney in Cisco.

Only his high marks on the shooting range, his lean, rawhide strength in the combat courses had earned a grudging measure of respect.

For the most part, the consensus of the Insiders had been that H. Shackelford Bonham did not fit the mold.

He knew they were wrong.

He had spent most of his twenty-four years preparing himself to become a Special Agent of the FBI.

Most boys in Cisco, Texas, had been content to play cowboys-and-Indians until Shack came along. He had reorganized those boyhood games into the FBI and the gangsters.

Even then he had been an authority on the Bureau.

His father had served two terms as Eastland County sheriff, six terms as deputy, and varied periods as town marshal in Rising Star, Ranger, and Strawn. Before Bonham learned to read, he had doted on wanted posters and circulars. At eight, he could perform the FBI hip-pocket draw with his cap pistol. He could disarm any kid holding a knife or gun.

As he grew to adolescence in the depths of the Depression, the University of Texas School of Law had seemed as far away as the mountains of the moon. But Bonham had been determined.

Throughout his teens, he had picked cotton, branded cattle, chopped cedar, dug postholes, scooped wheat, roughnecked in the oil fields to earn his tuition to Abilene Christian College.

After graduation, he drove nitro trucks over the rocky terrain of West Texas to earn money for law school. Later, he worked with a Houston crew that specialized in capping runaway gushers and snuffing burning oil wells. It was dangerous work. He had acquired a reputation far beyond his years for tough, raw courage.

During his last two terms at the University of Texas School of Law, he served as an aide in the Texas Legislature to further his professional skills—and to polish some rough edges acquired in the oil fields.

Through all those years he had denied himself everything except work. While other students were drinking, dating, having fun, he had not indulged in one moment of relaxation.

He had accomplished the impossible. He had worked his way through college and law school in the worst economic depression the country had ever known.

After his admission to the bar, he spent two years in the district attorney's office at Cisco, gaining experience. He had tangled with—and defeated—some of the finest, craftiest legal minds Dallas, Fort Worth, and Houston had to offer.

Only then did he submit his application to the Bureau.

When his acceptance came a few months later, he thought his long battle was over.

Now he knew it was just beginning.

He was locked into the drudgery of security clearances. He spent his days visiting the former neighbors, teachers, employers, and acquaintances of each subject, asking dumb questions by rote. "Have you ever known him to make a statement disloyal to the United States?" "Has he ever expressed loyalty to any country other than the United States?" "Do you believe him to be of sound moral character?" "Do you know of anything that might tend to compromise him in being trusted with secret materials or information?"

The replies in turn were submitted to Washington by a formula so routine it was slow suffocation to Bonham.

His current job provided no opportunity for him to show initiative, ingenuity, or imagination. He saw nothing ahead but countless security checks—no member of the old guard ever would favor a new agent with a major case.

Bonham knew that unless he did something soon, his chosen career was at a dead end.

"You see the duty schedule?" Marcus asked.

Bonham shook his head.

"They nailed Walischewsky, Dold, and Clausing today."

Three more spies; only one remained on the apprehension list.

"Where?"

"Walischewsky and Dold when their ships arrived here at quarantine. Clausing in Brazil. They'll fly him back in a day or two. Walischewsky and Dold are scheduled to be arraigned tomorrow morning. Guess who drew corridor security."

Bonham groaned at the prospect of another weary, drab day. He glanced at his wristwatch. He had signed in at seven. After escorting the prisoners to Brooklyn, he had spent the morning and most of the afternoon in the corridor at the Federal Building. Through the remainder of the afternoon and the early evening he had walked the sweltering streets, conducting his security interviews. It was now past ten. And he still had more than two hours of work to do, completing his reports. "The more you give, the more they want," he said.

Marcus grinned. "You don't join the FBI. You enlist. Take the veil. Swear celibacy." He sighed. "At least you don't have to try to explain this place to a pregnant wife."

Bonham glanced around the office. Most of the old hands had signed out for the night. The first-year agents were still at their desks, laboring over reports, case files.

The competition was incredible. Every first-year man was determined to survive.

The old hands had a gravy train, with all the young eager-beavers doing the drudgery.

Bonham pulled out his typewriter and set to work. During the next two hours, he transferred his interview notes to FBI forms. He was thankful for his facility with words. Most of the agents—even some of the veterans—agonized over composition and spelling. All FBI reports were reviewed at several levels by supervisors alert for mangled words, grammatical errors, or awkward syntax. Great care was taken that no such lapse accidentally fell before the eyes of the Director. Discipline was rigid. A bobbled name or fact could constitute a "substantive error" that would place a letter of censure in the agent's personal file. The black mark would remain there throughout the agent's career.

A few minutes after midnight, Bonham at last completed a stack of reports. He gathered the material and cleaned off his desk. He picked up the forms and headed toward the in basket in Frank Cato's office. Each and every report had to be approved by Cato before being typed into a smooth draft by a stenographer.

Assuming that Cato had signed out hours earlier, Bonham pushed his way through the door without knocking.

The bald, bullet-shaped head of Frank Cato was still bent over the desk.

Cato looked up, scowling his irritation.

Bonham gestured with the material in his hand. "Excuse me. I thought you'd left. . . ."

"All right, all right." Cato reached for the stack. He flipped rapidly through the pages. In a moment, he found what he was hunting. Sliding out the thickest file, he slapped it on the desk in front of Bonham. "This report was due out of here yesterday." He glowered, waiting.

Bonham did not answer. He had spent two full days on the case, a special request from the War Department for a complete background on Lieutenant (j.g.) Hyman Roth.

Bonham had interviewed five neighbors, seven high school and college teachers, two rabbis, four college classmates, and three former employers. He felt confident he knew everything necessary about Lieutenant Hyman Roth. It was all in the report.

Cato pointed. "The War Department marked this case to be expedited. Or didn't you notice?"

Bonham spoke in measured words. "Sir, you're the one who assigned me all the supplemental duty during the last two weeks. You can't have it both ways, sir. Either I answer telephones, chauffeur people around, and stand all day in a courthouse hall, or I conduct my interviews. I can't be two places at once."

"Other first-year agents have managed to keep up with their work," Cato snapped.

"They haven't been handed shit details day after day," Bonham snapped back.

Cato's thick lips spread in a humorless smile. "You think you're overworked, Bonham? You should've been around during the early days. Hell, I once kept a stakeout forty-six hours straight on the Karpis case, without sleep, eating peanut butter and crackers and pissing in pop bottles. Now you're bitching about a few hours of supplemental duty. And they call you an FBI agent! Jesus H. Christ!"

Stung, Bonham lashed back. "I can outdo the best day you ever saw, Cato."

Bullethead's eyes narrowed. Purple veins slowly swelled along his temples. He rose to his feet and pointed at Bonham's chest with his cigar. His voice probably was heard out in the square. "You couldn't match my *worst* day, Bonham, not on your *best* day. You're not the first cracker smartass we've had in the Bureau. I've seen plenty of hotshots like you come and go. And you know something, Bonham? You're not going to make it. You young shitheads come into the Bureau, fart your way through a few weeks at Quantico, and you think you know it all. Well, you don't. After three or four years on the bricks, a few of you may begin to learn a little of what it's all about. But not you, Bonham. You haven't got it. You don't have enough brains to be a Grade Two file clerk around here, much less a Special Agent." He pointed to Bonham's stack of reports. "And I promise you if there's one single error, one fucking misspelled word here, it's your ass! Understand?"

Bonham did not move. He was riding high on the exhilaration of his fury. "I don't misspell words," he said. "I don't make errors."

Cato snorted. He came around the desk to bellow into Bonham's face. "You're goddamned right you don't! Not in my squad! Now you get your ass out of here. And when I give you a case to be expedited, you by God expedite it! Understand?"

Bonham delayed just long enough to show that he was not intimidated. Then he turned and walked back to his desk. Marcus looked up and gave an exaggerated, silent whistle. The door had been open. Marcus had heard everything.

Cato emerged from his office, slammed the door, and headed toward the front of the building to sign out. He did not bother to look in Bonham's direction.

Marcus waited until Cato was safely out of earshot. "Good God! What'd you do, Shack? Piss in his water jug?"

Bonham shrugged. "Ah, that cocksucker doesn't worry me."

Marcus looked at the ceiling and blew air up his nose. "You're crazier than he is. Come on! What was that all about?"

"We were merely exchanging confidences. We confirmed the fact that he doesn't like me any better than I like him."

Marcus studied Bonham with concern. "Want to go get a drink?"

At the moment, there was nothing Bonham wanted more. "I'm game," he said.

It would be a foolish luxury. In six hours they would be back in harness. And Marcus had a pregnant wife. Also, all first-year agents were cautious about drinking. FBI Director J. Edgar Hoover had decreed that agents should drink "with extreme moderation"—a phrase never specifically defined. A Special Agent in theory remained on duty twenty-four hours a day, seven days a week, always leaving word where he could be reached. The Director liked to tell Congress and the public that in case of an emergency, every man in the Bureau could be summoned within an hour.

And no agent could report for duty with liquor on his breath.

Marcus pushed himself out of his chair. "Listen, tonight I need a drink to *get* home."

In a secluded booth at a small bar two blocks away, they ordered boilermakers.

Bonham was still fuming. They drank for a few minutes without talking. But Bonham's rage kept building until he no longer could contain it.

"I just don't understand that son-of-a-bitch," he said. "He kept me on supplemental assignments, *knowing* I wouldn't be able to get that report in on time. Now he'll

111

probably fuck around with it two or three days, running it through the stenographer, just to give me a black mark. What's wrong with the fucking guy?''

Marcus shrugged. "Hell, you can't blame him, Shack. He's just like all the old hands. He's been a part of—helped to build—the best law enforcement organization in the world. He doesn't want to lose it to some green kids and a bunch of new procedures cooked up in the name of national defense. And of course you don't help matters any.''

"What do you mean?''

"Well, you're not . . . subservient enough. No, that's not the right word. Obeisant, maybe. Respectful. Good God, Shack! It wouldn't cost you anything to kow-tow a little around Bullethead. Not if you really give a shit about making the cut at the end of your probational year.''

"I've *got* to make it," Bonham said, surprised at the intensity of his own words.

Marcus gave him an appraising glance. "Then you owe it to yourself to play the game. Throttle yourself down. Quit trying to be the hottest FBI agent that ever came down the pike. Don't you see? That's why Bullethead's got it in for you. He's proud of the FBI. He's proud of his record in the Bureau. And you look at him like he's a pile of shit standing in the way of what you want to do. Why not try to work *with* him, Shack? Be content with routine! Be patient! Bullethead and his gang can't last forever. You'll be assigned some major cases, eventually.''

Bonham shook his head. "Suppose this national emergency ends tomorrow. Know what'll happen? They'll cut the Bureau back to where it was. Three out of every four agents will be dropped. That's why Bullethead and his gang keep us under their thumbs. When the ax falls, they can say hell, those guys have never done anything a file clerk couldn't handle. They've never even worked on one major case.''

Marcus disagreed. "No, you're wrong. I see their point, Shack. Let's face it. We don't know enough. If we're put on our own, outside these rote interviews, there's too much involved. We'd probably do something wrong and blow it. Those guys are the pros. They've been around long enough to have the necessary experience."

"Of course they're good," Bonham said. "That's why I wanted to join the FBI in the first place. But bullshit! Those clowns are beginning to believe their own press agentry. They're not saints! Just for instance, what's so great about catching this bunch of spies? To read the newspapers, you'd think the FBI performed miracles, and J. Edgar went in and rounded them up with his Thompson blazing. Hell, they had the whole thing dumped right in their laps. If Debowski or Sebold or Sawyer or whatever his name is hadn't gone straight to the American consul when the Abwehr put the squeeze on him, and turned double agent, would the FBI have landed all those spies? Hell no!"

Marcus frowned. "You're too rough on them, Shack. They did an excellent job of running Debowski. They landed the whole operation. They could easily have fucked it up."

"Sure. But what about other spies and saboteurs the Abwehr has out there, right now? Does the FBI know about them? And what about the replacements Germany will send during the next few months? Will Bullethead and his gang be able to nail them? Can they find, develop, and pursue a case without a Debowski on the inside, feeding information to them?"

Marcus scowled in irritation. "I suppose *you* could."

"Damned right," Bonham said. "I've been around police work all my life. A spy case is no different. You use the same procedures to go after them."

Marcus looked at Bonham, his eyes dark with growing irritation. "Shack, you're full of shit. There are hundreds, thousands of man-hours involved in something like that, all kinds of equipment, expertise, experience."

"Or one good man," Bonham said. "I'll bet you a hundred dollars that in six weeks I can go out and find a spy that nobody knows about."

Marcus started to speak, then changed his mind. He

shook his head. "No, I won't bet with you. First, I don't have the money. Second, I don't want to take advantage of your ignorance."

"Look," Bonham said. "There's nothing mysterious about it. Spies are bound to work within certain perimeters, just like any criminals. I'll study all the material in the Bureau's files, and analyze the methods of operations, techniques, and so forth, then go out and find them. Simple logic tells me there are others out there. And more coming in all the time."

Marcus now seemed more tired than annoyed. He rubbed his forehead. "Well, that's a problem for the Domestic Intelligence Desk. Right now, I've got about all I can handle. And if I hope to make it through tomorrow, I'd better get some sleep."

After Marcus had gone, Bonham ordered another boilermaker. He sat for a while and thought back over the conversation.

What he had said made sense. The Bureau files *could* be analyzed to ascertain the exact methods used by Abwehr spies. And no doubt there *were* other spies out there. And more *would* be arriving to replace those just arrested.

His complaints against the Bureau were valid. He probably would never handle a major case unless he found and developed his own.

Bonham ordered another boilermaker and thought about the plan beginning to form in his mind.

It was wild. And risky.

But it might work.

He slowly drank two more boilermakers and thought the plan through.

Later, on the way to his small room in a walk-up hotel on East Fortieth, he bought a *New York Times*. After undressing, he lay across his narrow bed and turned to page three and the pictures of twenty-nine of the spies now awaiting trial and sentence.

Lily Barbara Stein, twenty-seven, of 232 East Seventy-ninth Street, was listed as an artist's model. The newspaper quoted J. Edgar Hoover as saying she had moved in social circles, reporting on vital information she overheard. Else Weustenfeld, forty-two, of 312 West Eighty-first, was listed as a stenographer and notary public. Hoover called her "one of the paymasters in the ring." Joseph August Klein, thirty-seven, of 227 East One Hundred Twenty-sixth, was listed as a commercial photographer.

Headquarters of the ring had been the Little Casino Restaurant, 206 East Eighty-fifth. The proprietor, Richard Eichenlaub, was among those arrested.

Bonham examined the photographs with renewed interest. The spies all appeared to be such ordinary people. None would draw a second glance on the street. A porter. A stock clerk. A musician. A book salesman. A carpenter.

Bonham's plan was simple. But it might open the door to the Bureau's Inner Circle.

Major case files were retained in all Bureau offices. All Special Agents were expected to gain some familiarity with them.

Bonham would go much further.

In his off-duty hours, he would search for those new spies.

The odds against success were long. But the job might not be as impossible as it seemed.

Transatlantic traffic had slowed to a trickle. The big ocean liners were no longer in service. The *Queen Mary* and the *Queen Elizabeth* were somewhere in the Pacific hauling troops. The huge French liner *Normandie* had been tied up at her Hudson River pier for the last twenty-two months. Bonham had seen her many times. His work frequently took him to the piers.

Only an occasional passenger ship now risked the Atlantic to transport refugees. Practically all travelers arriving from Europe came on the Clippers, which were still flying from Lisbon to New York via the Bahamas.

Stealing time from his assignments, Bonham would examine the most recent passenger lists of every ship arriving in New York from Europe, every incoming flight of the Yankee and Dixie Clippers.

Most passengers would be above suspicion—government employees, diplomats, returning students, executives from well-known companies, volunteer ambulance drivers, nurses. . . .

But among them would be a few suspects that fitted within the perimeters he would establish by studying spy cases of the past.

Working day and night, he would investigate his suspects and trace them into their new lives.

Somewhere, he was bound to discover a link.

Such a thorough search would be difficult. But he was no stranger to hard work.

If Hitler sent more spies to America, he would find them.

He would show Bullethead and those other sons-of-bitches how to find, develop, and pursue a major case from scratch.

That night, Bonham slept little. Before dawn he was back at FBI headquarters in Foley Square, digging through the investigations summaries on sabotage and espionage.

The first file began with a bulging folder concerning threats made against the *Normandie*.

BOOK TWO

AUGUST-SEPTEMBER 1941

No French forebear prepared one for the Normandie; *neither the* France, Paris *nor* Ile *conveyed in their appearance any hint of their magnificent successor. She is a stunning departure from anything that has ever sailed the Atlantic.*

John Maxtone-Graham
The Only Way to Cross
(Macmillan, New York, 1971)

I have always extended to her more affection than I have to any other ship. I loved her for her gaiety, for her color, for the familiarity with all the world that was in her passenger list. She leaned to excesses in her decor, there was something of the fatal woman. . . . Like all aristocrats, she had abominable moods. I think she was more female than all other ships I have known. I think that's why I loved her so.

Ludwig Bemelmans
I Love You, I Love You, I Love You
(Viking Press, New York, 1942)

6

Bendler Strasse, Tirpitz Ufer, Berlin

In the soft glow from his desk lamp, Admiral Canaris seemed far older than Von Beck remembered. The rest of the office remained dark, despite heavy blackout curtains over the windows. The room smelled musty, lived-in, with the comfortable, lingering efficacy of tobacco, books, and dogs.

The admiral's blue eyes fixed on Von Beck. "What I want you to do is simple," he said with only the wisp of a smile. "You are to go to America and destroy the *Normandie*."

Von Beck's surprise was total. He sat facing the admiral, too stunned to speak. From his experiences, he was well acquainted with the disorientation common to the returning submariner. But this time he had been subjected to far more than he could assimilate.

The horrors of that last, long combat patrol still weighed heavily on his mind. On his arrival in Brest, he had been met by new orders and a herculean, marathon bout of bureaucracy complicated by the upcoming change of command. Within four almost sleepless days and nights, he had drafted and typed the official patrol log, completed a blizzard of forms on the final disposition of each torpedo, and evaluated the combat performance of each man aboard. He had presented a carefully prepared verbal report to the flotilla commander, and endured the lengthy conferences that followed. Accompanied by Todt Organization representatives, he had supervised the painstaking surveys of damage to the boat. The inevitable disagreements with repair personnel had erupted. Von Beck had been deluged by the red tape of work requisitions. Then came his mysterious new orders to report to Berlin for a special assignment. He had been given no time to speculate on them.

Admiral Donitz himself had driven down from his headquarters at the Chateau of Kernevel for the change-of-command ceremony. Standing on the gratings of his boat, Von Beck had received the Knight's Cross. Less than an hour later, he was on his way to Berlin.

The journey had contained its own traumatic shocks. The Armed Forces Radio had not hinted the extent of damage from the bombings. He had been appalled at what he saw of conditions. In every village, every town, whole sections had been razed by bombers. The people of Germany seemed poorly dressed, undernourished. Twice his trip was interrupted by air raids. In Frankfurt-am-Main, the railway yards were hit, and his train was delayed for twelve hours. He had arrived in Berlin tired, hungry, and bewildered.

And now this—a sabotage mission to America.

The admiral's smile remained intact as he watched Von Beck's reaction.

"I can't order you to take this assignment," he said. "Technically, I'm seeking a volunteer. But you're here because you're the perfect man for the job—maybe the only one. And I'm telling you this in all confidence: The order for the project came direct to me from the lips of the Führer. I can promise that if you succeed, your Knight's Cross will be weighted with clusters. Your place in the Reich will be assured."

120

Von Beck hesitated. Admiral Canaris had been one of his father's oldest and most trusted friends—an association that had dated back to their heroic service in the cruiser *Dresden* during the Great War. How could he convey to the admiral the doubts that now assailed him about the Reich? The anguish he felt over the deaths of so many fine young men in the boats? His strong sense of wrong over the abandonment of all conventions in submarine warfare? His suspicions, after viewing conditions in Germany, that the war might not be worth the price? His glimpse, in Frankfurt-am-Main, of a train with hundreds, perhaps thousands of Jews stuffed into the cars like cattle?

His thoughts would sound like treason.

He spoke cautiously. "I don't understand, Herr Admiral. Why me?"

Canaris regarded him with a glint in his eye that implied a shared secret. "When you were a boy, you built a large working model of the *Normandie*. Remember? Your father once showed it to me—quite a work of art, authentic to the last detail. Your father explained that you were being trained from boyhood to command such a ship. He said—with considerable pride—that you knew as much about ocean liners and sailing as he. And your father was generally regarded as the best in Germany."

Von Beck concentrated on keeping his face void of expression. He did not want the admiral to know how much those words affected him. His father had seldom given him praise. "That was a long time ago," he said.

"And now the boy has become the man—a submarine commander, expert in explosives, the sinking of ships. Don't you see? Probably no one else in the service of the *Vaterland* possesses that combination of knowledge, and certainly not to that degree."

Von Beck remained silent.

"Also, you have other unique qualifications for the job," Canaris added. "You speak American English, not the BBC English taught in German schools. You know American habits. You could enter America and blend into your surroundings. And your courage and resourcefulness are proven." He raised a folder from his desk. "I've read the report on your last patrol."

Von Beck did not answer. He did not consider his actions in bringing the submarine to the surface either courageous or resourceful.

The boat had lain at a depth of nearly two hundred meters for more than eighteen hours while the British raked relentlessly with depth charges. Each near-miss drove the boat deeper. Leaks erupted throughout, until, gradually, the submarine had lost buoyancy. Only the electric motors and hydroplanes kept it from plunging to the bottom. The frantic whine of the motors had brought more depth charges. A series of explosions close aboard had shaken the boat like a bone in the teeth of a hound. Two machinists, working on the E-motors, had been thrown off balance. They fell onto exposed wiring, and were electrocuted.

With his batteries near exhaustion, Von Beck had gambled everything on one last-ditch effort.

The bodies of the machinists were stuffed into torpedo tubes, along with various debris. Risking everything, he had ordered the outer torpedo doors opened. The odds had been long. The inner doors were not designed for that depth. If they had shattered, the boat would have been flooded within minutes. But Von Beck had no choice.

The inner doors held.

With a hiss of compressed air, the bodies and assorted debris were released through the tubes, and rose to the surface along with the ton of fuel oil bled from the forward tanks.

He ordered the electric motors silenced. The submarine slowly drifted toward the bottom.

It was a trick as old as submarine warfare. But it worked.

The corvettes had gone away, the sound of their screws gradually fading.

Again gambling, Von Beck had spent the last of his battery power in a speed run, using the hydroplanes to raise the boat to the surface despite the negative buoyancy.

The frantic maneuver succeeded. Once the vents cleared the surface and the powerful diesels were started, Von Beck was able to pump the boat.

He saw nothing of heroism or cleverness in his actions. Only desperation.

The destruction of the *Normandie* would be a different matter.

"You know ships," Canaris went on. "I needn't tell you what the *Normandie* in the service of Great Britain would mean—a monstrous amount of cargo delivered every eight days. Or, if America comes into the war, a full division of troops and their equipment each week. You are a submariner. You know better than I the odds against sinking her at sea."

Von Beck acknowledged the remoteness of such a chance with a nod. A U-boat on the surface could make only slightly more than seventeen knots—twice the speed of an ordinary convoy. But under forced draft, the *Normandie* could crank out twice the speed of a U-boat.

"If you volunteer for this assignment, you'll be given the names of various people in America who might be able to help you," Canaris went on. "They can supply the explosives, the necessary papers, safe houses, and so forth. But your dependence on them will be limited. For the most part, it would be a one-man operation. You will have absolute control."

Von Beck remembered the majestic size of the ship—more than three hundred meters in length. Eighty-three thousand tons of dead weight.

If he were to encounter her on the high seas, viewing her through the periscope, he would plan four torpedoes, with a spread of several degrees. And even four direct hits might not be enough to flood those cavernous spaces below her waterline.

He vaguely recalled that the *Normandie* had four zones of total watertight integrity. In wartime, the watertight doors would be closed even in harbor. At least two of those zones, and perhaps three, would have to be breached.

And there were other complications.

"Those Manhattan piers are shallow," he said. "She probably has no more than a meter or two under the keel, even at high tide. If she were sunk at her moorings, she could be refloated without much effort."

Canaris nodded. "That has been discussed. What about fire?"

Von Beck shook his head. He remembered the escorted tour he and his father had made of the ship. "She's as fireproof as any ship ever constructed," he said. "Her fire-fighting equipment is superb, perhaps the best afloat. The crew is well-trained. I would assume her firefighters were left aboard. Also, New York City firemen are authorized to respond to shipboard fires along the waterfront. The pier is loaded with fresh-water mains under city pressure. And the harbor itself has a number of fireboats capable of pumping a tremendous volume of water."

The admiral smiled. "See? Already you have told me more than all of my experts combined. As I knew from the first, Walther, you're the only man for this job. Will you take it?"

Von Beck hesitated. Clearly, he had been expected to volunteer. Canaris, everyone concerned would have presumed that no one would turn down a request direct from the Führer.

But he was in the grip of emotions he had not had time to assimilate.

He had just acquired that deeper appreciation of life accorded those who have returned from the grave.

Granted, the mission to America would hold its own dangers. Yet he knew his death was almost certain if he went back to sea in a U-boat. His transfer to the Abwehr no doubt would save his life.

But he knew himself. He would never shake his overwhelming sense of guilt if he left his boat and crew to their own fates.

And even submarine warfare seemed honorable, compared to spying and sabotage.

He thought it best to tell Canaris the truth.

"If the choice were mine, I would just as soon return to my boat," he said. "I have a responsibility. . . ."

The admiral nodded. "I understand perfectly. Any good commander feels a deep loyalty to his men. I'd think less of you if you felt otherwise. But Walther, let's be realistic for a moment. The decision really isn't yours to make, is it?"

Canaris was only pointing out the obvious. All doors had been closed behind him. He could not return to his boat. His crew, his entire command had been turned over to Mueller.

Von Beck paused, trying to put his objections into the proper words. "Herr Admiral, I mean no offense. But I prefer the life of combat."

Canaris smiled. "To the life of a spy?"

Von Beck did not trust himself to speak. He nodded.

"Walther, I've fought that battle every day since I came to the Abwehr. I can only tell you my conclusions: We must serve the *Vaterland* in the best way we can, wherever our talents lead us, no matter how objectionable the duty may be to us personally."

Canaris was silent for a moment. "I won't push you into making a decision. The idea of working with the Abwehr goes against the grain of any honorable man. But surely you recognize the necessity."

One of the dachshunds whined in his sleep. Canaris reached down and scratched his ears.

"In any event, you are here," he went on. "You possess knowledge we need. And you have already relinquished your command. So for the time being, why don't you take charge of our planning for the *Normandie* operation? Work out how it might be done. Get acquainted with Abwehr, the staff, what we are doing. If you decide not to volunteer, we at least will have a plan, which is something we don't have now. Is that agreeable?''

Von Beck felt that Canaris had just given him a way out. *"Jawohl, Herr Admiral,"* he said.

"Excellent,'' Canaris said. He rose from his desk. "Come! I'll introduce you to my assistant, Colonel Erwin Lahousen, commander of Abteilung Two. He's in charge of sabotage, subversion, and dark deeds. Erwin will find you a place to stay and some space where you can work. I'm sure you two will get along splendidly. You are much alike.''

As Canaris predicted, Von Beck was favorably impressed with the tall Austrian in charge of Abteilung II. Lahousen was every inch the aristocrat, from his ever-present monocle to his ramrod-straight bearing. But he possessed a ready, wry humor and an easy-going manner Von Beck found most engaging. He seemed genuinely interested in Von Beck's project and came by frequently to talk and to offer suggestions. Yet in no way did he make any attempt to establish himself as an overseer or supervisor.

As the days wore on, Von Beck learned that Lahousen was a descendant of French nobility who fled to the Polish Silesia during the religious wars of the seventeenth century. Lahousen spoke fluent French, Polish, Czech, and Hungarian, and could imbue his German with various authentic regional inflections.

From the first, Lahousen pledged his total cooperation. "If there's anything you want, just ask,'' he said. "If we don't have it, we'll steal it.''

Von Beck equipped his second-floor office with a complete set of blueprints of the *Normandie,* obtained from her builders in St. Nazaire. He also ordered navigation charts of New York Harbor, statistics on the capabilities of various explosives, and every handbook and pamphlet on sabotage and demolition published by the Abwehr.

Working long hours, he ordered the proper supplies and constructed a larger, even more detailed model of the *Normandie* than the one Canaris remembered. Again, the model was a labor of love.

Following the blueprints, he painstakingly re-created every line of the massive ship. For convenience, he made portions of the hull removable, to reveal the interior compartments.

The blueprints, the many hours of work on the model renewed his long-dormant passion for the ship. He was surprised at the wealth of detail he remembered. As he worked, the ship again came alive in his imagination.

Carefully, he made perfectly scaled replicas of the three gigantic funnels, each slanted by the designer at a delicate ten degrees, stairstepped slightly from forward aft to give the ship a rakish, streamlined air, as if underway. The masts also were tilted ten degrees, suggesting that they were bent by the speed of the ship. The dramatic flair of the hull along her upper decks complemented her soaring prow. He remembered how amused he had been over her wide, flat bottom. Afloat, the bulging hull was concealed, and provided her with a minimal entry through the water and a relatively small bow wake.

As the model took shape, he again marveled at her clean lines, the vast expanses of teak decks topside. Even her necessary deck machinery was concealed beneath a graceful turtleback.

As he worked, he remembered her opulent interior—the murals, the priceless furnishings and works of art.

He was certain he would never be able to destroy such a perfect ship.

But his calculations underscored the admiral's point: With her speed and tremendous tonnage, the *Normandie* would be a formidable weapon against the Reich. In the hands of the British—or of the Americans, if they came into the war—the *Normandie* would contribute immeasurably to the defeat of Germany.

When the two-meter model was completed, he constructed a water tank and put his calculations of her buoyancy, weight, and internal dimensions to the test.

He soon could foresee tremendous difficulties.

The *Normandie*'s design utilized her double bottoms for fuel and ballast tanks. A torpedo might penetrate the tanks, causing secondary explosions. But the force of a lighter charge—such as several sticks of dynamite—would be confined, cushioned. Toward the bow, all compartments below the waterline were small, except for the garages and baggage rooms on F and G Decks. Amidships, the boiler spaces and boiler uptakes were protected by the outboard fuel tanks. Under the rear funnel, directly below the Grand Salon and Smoking Room on the Promenade Deck, and the magnificent Dining Room on C Deck, were the turboalternators and the electric propulsion motors. They also were protected by baffled tanks. Further aft, below the waterline, were the four individual cold storage rooms for fish, pork, poultry and game, and beef.

The *Normandie* would be difficult to sink with explosives placed against her outer hull.

But Von Beck eventually determined that it could be done.

He carefully figured the volume of water—in various combinations—that would be necessary to send the ship to the bottom.

The results were surprising. He discovered shortcomings in the design of the *Normandie* he never had dreamed existed.

He wondered if the ship's original owners were aware of some serious flaws.

She was woefully topheavy. Doubting his own evidence, he rechecked his figures several times to be certain.

While the high center of gravity might be favorable under ordinary performance, tending to make a ship lively, the condition might become a tremendous hazard under adverse circumstances.

The *Normandie*'s flaw was not unique. Von Beck remembered his father's description of the old *Imperator* on her sea trials in 1913, so topheavy that she mysteriously listed to port, and then to starboard, with each turn or shift of the wind. She was taken back into the yards, and three meters were trimmed from her smokestacks. The extensive marble furnishings were removed from her upper decks, and cane furniture was substituted for the original mahogany. Even so, the *Imperator* had remained a perilously tender ship throughout her career, with an acknowledged tendency to hang on the roll.

Von Beck pondered his new discovery of the *Normandie*'s characteristics for several days. He became convinced that this Achilles heel might be the answer he was seeking.

Yet, the sheer size of the ship remained the principal obstacle. A single explosion to send her to the bottom in New York Harbor would necessarily be of monstrous proportion.

During three weeks of work, Von Beck projected twenty-two scenarios, ranging from one tremendous blast to a series of small shaped charges scattered throughout the ship.

At last, he reached the point where he could do no further planning. There were many unknown factors that could be considered only by someone at the site.

His work was completed. Still, he dallied, strangely reluctant to yield the *Normandie* project to anyone else, yet determined that he would not go to America as a saboteur.

For two more days he delayed his report, undecided how he would deal with Canaris.

He settled on a compromise. He had found that he liked the atmosphere of the Abwehr headquarters, the people on the admiral's staff. Lahousen had given him a general description of the Abwehr's worldwide operations. He was intrigued.

He was considering a proposal that he remain at Abwehr headquarters to direct the *Normandie* operation in America. He could argue that the saboteur would need a wide base of advice and support, available only from a well-equipped facility in Berlin.

His speculation was interrupted one evening by Lahousen, who seemed troubled. "Something has come up that concerns your project. The chief is waiting to discuss it with us."

As they entered the admiral's office, Piekenbrock was seated on the leather couch. Canaris was at his desk, his dachshunds lounging at his feet. Both the admiral and Pieki were unusually solemn. As Von Beck and Lahousen took their places, Canaris finished reading a report and tossed it aside. He spoke to Von Beck without preamble.

"Walther, we've been handed a problem. Perhaps you can help us decide what to do. Erwin, why don't you fill him in? Then we'll discuss it."

Lahousen was polishing his monocle. He carefully replaced it in his eye. "I'll have to give you some background," he said. "Immediately after the arrests of the spy rings in America, the admiral and I were summoned to the headquarters of the Führer on the Russian front. There he gave us verbal orders concerning the *Normandie*. A few weeks later we again were summoned, and given a directive to place high priority on the re-establishment of an effective intelligence network in America. We have acted on both matters."

He paused and glanced at the admiral. Canaris gave him the barest hint of a nod. Lahousen went on. "Today we received a visit from a Leutnant Werner Kappe, who came to us straight from the Führer, bearing sufficient papers to support all he told us. Kappe is German-American, a journalist by profession. He once worked as a reporter on a New York German-language newspaper, and made himself conspicuous as a member of a Nazi Bund in the United States. Kappe gave us a list of ten men, all former residents

130

of America, who would be able to pass as Americans. All are now serving the Reich, most in uniform. Kappe, a party member, has sold the Führer on a plan for himself and his men to return to the United States as saboteurs."

Von Beck nodded his understanding. As former residents of America with known pro-German sympathies, all the men no doubt had extensive dossiers in the files of either the FBI, Naval Intelligence, or other organizations.

Admiral Canaris was watching Von Beck's reaction. "The problem is, of course, that we must put your *Normandie* project into operation as soon as possible," he said. "We can't ignore Kappe. The entire party structure is behind him." He leaned forward in his chair and checked the positions of his hounds before moving his feet to a more comfortable position. "Disaster is inevitable. None of those men has been investigated—we know absolutely nothing about them. Any one of them may be a double agent. They have no training, no skills, It's sheer idiocy!"

"This man Kappe was most arrogant and overbearing," Lahousen said. "He came to us with his own complete plan —he has even made arrangements for transportation. Two submarines have been placed at his disposal by order of the Führer. His plan is to concentrate on sabotage at aluminum plants and electrical power stations."

Canaris shook his head. "I feel sorry for the deluded men involved."

Lahousen agreed. "They probably will be caught within a week. The arrests of ten more spies in America will set off a witch hunt. That's going to bring heightened security along the docks, aboard ships, in factories. Suspicions and rumors will be flying. And all that is certain to hamper the *Normandie* project."

"We have two choices," the admiral said. "We can either subvert the Führer's plan in some way, or we can cooperate fully, maintaining as much control as possible, and delay Kappe long enough for the *Normandie* mission to succeed."

131

"Either choice holds hazards," Lahousen added. "If we ignore a direct order of the Führer, someone on his staff certainly would remind him of that fact. If we cooperate, blame for the failure of the mission will be placed on the Abwehr."

"And it *will* fail," the admiral said.

Von Beck hoped his expression did not reveal the turmoil raging in his mind. First, he was shocked that anyone would dare hint that an order from the Führer might be circumvented. He'd had no suspicion that dissatisfaction with the Reich existed at this level, that there was anyone in Germany who might share his own views. He waited until he could keep his voice devoid of emotion.

"How long could Kappe be delayed?"

Canaris glanced at Lahousen.

"Two or three months, maximum," Lahousen said. "We can subject Kappe and his men to as much innocuous training as possible—codes, explosives, communications, all the triviality we can devise, yet teaching them nothing that will compromise our secrets with the Americans. If we delay longer, our tactics would be obvious."

"We might find other methods," Canaris said. "Kappe's men are scattered. Perhaps we will encounter exasperating delays in locating them, processing their orders." He turned to Von Beck. "How much time do you need?"

"My research is completed," Von Beck told him. "The *Normandie* project is ready to be put into operation."

The admiral's gaze fixed on Von Beck. "Except that we don't have a trained man ready to go," he said.

Von Beck did not answer. The silence lengthened.

Canaris picked up a letter opener and tapped the knuckles of his left hand with the blade. "Walther, I can't ask you to volunteer," he said. "But you see the problem. We don't have time to train a man in the skills and knowledge you possess."

Von Beck hesitated, uncertain how best to phrase his feelings. "I've always thought of myself as a military man," he said. "I just can't see me doing this work."

Piekenbrock laughed. "Welcome to the club."

Canaris frowned. "Walther, the three of us understand what is in your mind. We've fought that battle. Indeed, we fight it every day. But please consider this: You were brought here for a specific mission, on the direct orders of the Führer. You are now deeply involved. If you do *not* volunteer to complete that mission, a question mark will remain in your service record for all time to come."

Von Beck wished he had more time to think. He did not answer.

"Walther, you can look upon this operation as just another way to accomplish our purpose," Canaris said gently. "If the *Normandie* were at sea, flying the British ensign, and you had her lined up in your periscope, you wouldn't hesitate to shoot. Your tonnage of enemy shipping would be increased by eighty-three thousand tons, and your Knight's Cross would be weighted with clusters. The fact that she lies in New York Harbor and that you would plant the explosives by hand does not alter the result, except that fewer people would die."

Von Beck was aware of the admiral's reputation for cleverness. But he also knew that what Canaris was telling him was true.

If he did not accept this assignment in America, the fact would dog him throughout his career.

He would never hold another command.

The Knight's Cross he had just won would forever be tarnished.

Canaris was merely pointing out the obvious: He had no choice.

He could only accept the inevitable gracefully.

Von Beck smiled in defeat. "You are correct, Herr Admiral," he said. "I will put my personal considerations aside. I volunteer for the assignment."

"Excellent, excellent," Canaris said, rising to shake hands. "I'm so pleased." The admiral waited while Von Beck received congratulations from Lahousen and Piekenbrock. "Then we are of accord," he said. "We will delay

Kappe and his men as long as possible, giving Walther time to do the job." He turned to Von Beck. "You will leave as quickly as feasible. Erwin will work out the details with you. Come back to see me before you go."

Von Beck and Lahousen spent the following day in hurried preparation for Von Beck's departure. A Luftwaffe plane would be leaving for Greece shortly after midnight. Arrangements were made for Von Beck to be aboard. From Greece, he would fly to Lisbon, where he was booked under an assumed identity for passage to Rio. He would travel to Argentina, where he would receive a new passport. He then would make his way to Mexico and the U.S. border. At Juarez, he would cross on a lazy Sunday afternoon with the usual crowd of American tourists. Lahousen explained that papers were seldom checked. Aside from a friendly question—"Where were you born?"—Americans of suitable appearance were never bothered, and wandered in droves back and forth from their hotels on the American side to the nightclubs, bars, and whorehouses on the Mexican side.

From El Paso, Von Beck would take a train for New York, under his new identity as Walter Beck, diesel engineer. A complete biography had been drafted for his American background. His wealth of documents claimed that he had been born in New Jersey, educated in public schools, and held a master's degree from Massachusetts Institute of Technology.

"We are according this mission the highest secrecy," Lahousen said. "No records containing your name will exist within the Abwehr apparatus. You will have the code name Sailor. Only the admiral, Pieki, myself, and one or two others will know of your true identity. We hope we don't hear from you until the job is done. But in case of emergency, you can communicate through a drop in Milan. Any message, or reference to you by anyone, will be brought to our immediate attention."

Von Beck was fitted with two Brooks Brothers business

suits and other authentic American clothing. He also was given a list of contacts, along with the code of introduction for each person. After memorizing it, he destroyed the list.

"The mission itself is in your hands," Lahousen said. "If I were in your shoes, I'd depend on those other people as little as possible. I'd stay away from areas where European dissidents hang out—like the Yorkville section in New York City. German sympathizers, various ethnic and political groups probably have been infiltrated by the FBI."

Two hours before his flight, Von Beck went up to the admiral's office. The door was open. He entered without knocking.

Canaris was dozing in his chair, his hounds curled on the carpet. Von Beck stopped in indecision.

The admiral's eyes opened. "Yes?"

Again, the room was illuminated only by a desk lamp. In the shadows, Canaris seemed smaller, more wizened. "Excuse me, Herr Admiral. I didn't intend to wake you. But my plane leaves in two hours, and. . . ."

Canaris stirred. "Of course, Walther. Come in, come in." He rose from his chair and moved a stack of papers that blocked his view. "Sit down, sit down. Maybe we can rescue a few minutes from this terrible war. Brandy?"

"If you please, Herr Admiral."

Canaris poured two snifters, handed one to Von Beck, and raised the other in toast. "To the *Vaterland*."

Considering the time and place, the omission of the Führer and the Reich seemed pointed. Von Beck had noticed a dearth of "Heil Hitler" exchanges in daily life at Abwehr headquarters. The admiral's sharp, analytical eyes locked on him for a moment.

Von Beck touched his glass to the admiral's. "To the *Vaterland*," he repeated.

The reply seemed to answer an unasked question. The admiral's speech became less guarded.

"I'd hoped that while you were here, we could have long talks, learn what is in each other's minds." Canaris said.

"But there's no time for anything these days, not even between old friends. Yet, when you take away old friends, what is left?"

The admiral seemed greatly fatigued. He slouched deep in his chair, his small frame almost lost in his clothing. The lines in his face had deepened.

"My father always valued his friendship with you most highly," Von Beck said.

Canaris nodded. "Your father was a splendid example of the kind of man that once was the backbone of Germany. Industrious. Loyal. Honorable." He sighed and made a helpless gesture with his snifter. "And look how I'm repaying his friendship—by sending his only son on a mission such as this!"

Von Beck did not know how to respond, so he remained silent. The admiral obviously was near exhaustion. His speech was low, halting. He continued as if he were talking to himself.

"Sabotage, the gathering of intelligence is necessary, I suppose. Unfortunate, but necessary. I'm glad I have Erwin to run Abteilung Two. I've always felt that sabotage is something less than honorable. Whatever else happens, please be assured that your feelings toward this mission are understood, and appreciated."

Von Beck took a deep breath. Never before had he confessed his full thoughts about the war to fellow officers—or to anyone. But he now felt compelled to do so.

"Perhaps it's as honorable as U-boat warfare," he said.

Canaris glanced at him in surprise. Again, the admiral's analytical gaze locked on him. "I've never thought of it that way," he said. "Perhaps I've been away from the sea too long. Tell me, is that a universal feeling? Is the ruthlessness of U-boat warfare a matter of morale among the boats?"

Von Beck paused, uncertain how far to go. "No, Herr Admiral. If the men feel that way, they keep it to themselves, as I've done. Or perhaps the things I have seen through the periscope have altered my thinking. You shoot

136

from ambush on an unsuspecting enemy. You see him roasted alive. If he survives you leave him floating in the cold sea, without any probability of rescue.''

Canaris stared at his brandy for a long moment. "I suppose your father and I were fortunate that we served at sea in a more honorable time.''

Von Beck answered obliquely. "I would have preferred a billet on the *Bismarck,* despite the odds against her.''

Canaris wearily massaged the bridge of his nose. "This is a terrible, terrible war,'' he said. "Horrendous things are being done. . . .''

He stopped, leaving the specifics unspoken. Von Beck remembered the *Judenzug* at Frankfurt-am-Main and the stench from the cattlecars filled with human cargo. The trainmaster had told Von Beck that such trains had become common.

The admiral fell silent, lost in his own thoughts. When he spoke, his voice was so low that Von Beck barely heard.

"That madman is destroying Germany. He must be stopped.''

The treasonous words lingered in the air. Von Beck felt a chill along the short hairs of his neck. He had not suspected that anyone at command level held that thought—not in all Germany.

"We can only try to salvage what honor we can from the disaster,'' Canaris went on. "We must continue to work for the good of the *Vaterland.*''

Von Beck finished his brandy and rose from his chair. "I'll do my best, Herr Admiral.''

Canaris came from behind his desk to walk him to the door. "I'm confident you will. And I promise you this. I'll see to it that full recognition comes to you for your services. I'm proud to have known your father. And I am proud to have known you.''

The finality of the past tense was disturbing. Canaris seemed aware that he had been more revealing than he had intended. But he did not retreat.

"Put your trust in no one, Walther,'' he said. "For me,

it's too late. I'm in too deep. But you take care to survive. And if I have helped you to escape this disaster that is Nazi Germany, then at least I've done something worthwhile."

He gripped Von Beck's hand.

Before Von Beck could reply, Canaris turned and walked back toward his desk, his head down, his small, stooped frame bent as if he carried the weight of the whole world on his shoulders.

Von Beck returned to his room to await his summons to the limousine and the start of his long journey.

7

St. Luke's Place, Greenwich Village, New York City

Drifting from one dingy hotel to another, carefully covering her tracks, Rachael hunted two weeks before she found the basement apartment. It was perfect, reminding her of the dollhouse her parents had given her on her fifth birthday. Located on a quiet street not far from Washington Square, it contained a small bedroom, a larger living room, a luxurious bath, and a tiny kitchenette.

Outside, lavish trees sheltered the smooth, unbroken sidewalk. The building itself was of red brick, with ornate leaded-glass and sculptured-cement appointments in the Italianate style. Each building in the block was served by matching marble steps graced with charming flourishes of wrought-iron railings.

Inside, the furnishings were undistinguished, but serviceable. From her front window, Rachael could look through the gauze curtains at the shin-level of passing pedestrians, and she could see without being seen. The view amused her. The apartment was ideal for a spy.

The Frank Pierce incident now seemed no more than a bad dream. With deliberate patience, she severed every link to him. She destroyed all documents, everything that existed of the Annette-Marie Fourcade identity.

She leased the apartment in her own name.

"I'm a French refugee," she told the landlady, a Mrs. Anne Adler. "My parents were too ill to come with me. But they insisted that I make my way to freedom."

Short, rotund, and gushing, Mrs. Adler literally opened her arms to Rachael. "How awful! Is there anything I can do?"

"You've already done enough, letting me have this wonderful place," Rachael told her.

"Do you have enough money?" Mrs. Adler asked. "How will you live?"

"Oh, money's no problem," Rachael told her. "My father has excellent contacts in this country. I'm an artist and illustrator. Fortunately, my work is in demand."

As Rachael suspected from that first meeting, Mrs. Adler was nosy, and a gossip. The following day she heard herself referred to as "the little French refugee in the basement apartment."

Mrs. Adler made certain that she quickly became acquainted with other residents in the house. On the first Saturday afternoon, despite Rachael's protests, Mrs. Adler took her on a whirlwind tour of the upper floors, introducing her to a ballet dancer and an actress who shared an apartment on the top floor; two male musicians on the second floor; a librarian and her unemployed boyfriend, also on the second floor; and a male poet who lived alone in a single room on the third floor.

Mrs. Adler imposed herself into each introduction, talking incessantly, not allowing Rachael opportunity for even the most cursory polite remarks. Mrs. Adler's tenants seemed accustomed to her idiosyncrasies. Rachael received several knowing smiles. Apparently the tour of introduction was a ritual with each new arrival in the apartments.

On the second landing, Mrs. Adler paused and gestured

toward the front apartment. "And we have a young actor who will be famous some day—James Brighton. Remember, I told you! Already he's playing second lead in *Watch on the Rhine*. You simply must meet him. But he has a matinee today."

Pleading a prior appointment, Rachael managed to escape tea in Mrs. Adler's apartment. The landlady's overpowering personality was wearing. She had a way of standing too close, leaning forward, using her hands to emphasize her words. Rachael found her stocky build, mannish haircut, and familiar manner offensive in ways she could not define. Instinctively she tried to back away from further involvement, sensing that Mrs. Adler might become a major problem.

The deposits and lease for the apartment took most of her available cash. With the arrest of the spy rings so recent, she remained wary of picking up the money that the Abwehr had deposited for her at Chase Manhattan. Reluctantly, she went to a dealer on Forty-seventh Street and sold one of her diamonds. She regretted the necessity, but saw nothing else she could do.

She ordered an unlisted phone, and pulled a board loose in the bathroom closet, making a cache for her secret ink.

Although she had been warned by the Abwehr not to do so, she wrote her parents the good news that she was safely in America and "at work," explaining no further.

Rachael could not lie to her parents. She felt to some degree estranged from them. Yet in other ways she had never felt closer. She remembered that after she received the dollhouse on her fifth birthday, she had played elaborate games, entering a far more complex, ethereal world, from which her parents were necessarily excluded. Her refuge of make-believe was beyond their care-bound comprehension.

Her new life was something like that.

She had to travel through this new experience alone.

As soon as she was certain the address on St. Luke's

Place would be permanent, she established contact with the Abwehr through a Milan drop.

The first reply was cryptic but specific, ordering her to monitor and report all ship traffic, and to forward whatever information she could obtain on U.S. war materiel production and military preparedness.

She set to work with a vengeance, quickly establishing a routine she felt would not attract suspicion. She left her apartment promptly at eight-thirty each morning, carrying art materials and a sketchbook. By a circuitous route, she made her way to the Battery and the Staten Island ferry. Although new signs warned against the use of cameras, no one seemed to find harm in an artist sketching views of the docks. In time, she grew so confident she bought small, delicate opera glasses to ascertain the names of the more distant ships.

On arrival of the ferry at St. George each day, she boarded a bus for the first of several trips about the island, checking ship traffic not only in Raritan Bay, but also along the Jersey shore. Usually several warships were riding at anchor off St. George Terminal.

Returning to her apartment late in the afternoon, she assimilated all her information on ship movements.

She then wrote her reports in the way she had been taught at Klopstock, using secret ink buried between the lines of long, rambling letters of nonsense family chatter. The Klopstock instructors had praised her neat penmanship, her carefully crafted letters.

Recognizing the necessity of speed on the details of ship traffic, she rushed each letter directly to the main post office on Eighth Avenue to catch each outgoing Clipper.

On the way back home, she stopped by news kiosks and purchased the daily newspapers. She spent her nights reading through each, gleaning pertinent information for her longer letters.

Rachael entered into her game with total concentration. Nothing escaped her notice. She reported fully on the new

7 P.M. curfew placed on service stations along the Eastern Seaboard to ease the gasoline shortage. She analyzed the many complaints about the curfew, the expressions of public acceptance that appeared in the letters-to-the-editor columns. She followed closely the debate in Congress over extension of the draft, and the heated controversy over Senator Wheeler's charge that the movie industry was glamorizing warfare in an effort to get America into the war. Strikes for higher wages plagued war-production efforts at East Coast shipyards, the munitions plants in St. Louis, and aircraft factories in New Jersey and upper New York State. When silk was banned for civilian use, Rachael made certain that the Abwehr knew that Macy's added thirty-five extra salesgirls at the hosiery counter to handle the rush, and Gimbel's added nineteen.

She also reported the speculative stories rampant in the newspapers—the dire warnings of inflation, a proposal to build an oil pipeline from Texas to New York, a scheme to construct a highway to Alaska, a plan to shift university curricula from pure science to the applied sciences of metallurgy, munitions chemistry, and industrial X-rays.

The newspapers contained an unbelievable wealth of detail. Each Saturday, many pages were devoted to the activities at military camps all across the United States—their weaponry, type of training, their authorized and actual strength.

A half million men were engaged in Army maneuvers in the swamps of Louisiana. Rachael provided the Abwehr with a complete examination of the tactics involved, as gleaned by military editors on the staffs of the daily newspapers.

The financial pages were even more specific. Reynolds Metal Company proudly announced the sale of two million pounds of aluminum to Russia. Packard Motor Company used full-paged advertisements to reveal the start of production on nine thousand Rolls-Royce aircraft engines for Britain. The Berwick Plant in New Jersey conducted an ornate ceremony, complete with pictures, to celebrate completion of the thousandth thirteen-ton tank for the Army. Speed, armor, weaponry, and performance of the tank were published in full.

She even included information she doubted—such as the description of an Army project to use trained falcons, equipped with special knives, to rip up the parachutes of invaders.

The work kept her hours filled. She completed her assignments competently, swiftly, working far into each night.

Only the few brief moments she had to herself were difficult, when dark thoughts came and she sometimes doubted the wisdom of her grand plan.

Certainly her father would never comprehend what she was trying to do, just as he had never understood about her music.

From her earliest memory, music had been her life, and no one else had recognized that fact—not her mother, her older sister, her brother, and especially not her father.

"Rachael, music is fine for diversion," he had said, over and over. "But don't you see? It's just not practical."

Her sister Lillian was studying to become a medical doctor, her brother Theodor a research chemist. Her father praised them as examples she should follow.

"Rachael, you *must* think of the future," he had said. "Acquire a reliable profession!"

He lamented her less-than-brilliant grades in the sciences, while ignoring the praises her teachers heaped upon her for musical prowess, for her feats in literary composition.

This conflict smoldered until her mid-adolescence, when she received a music scholarship to the university. It was the realization of her every dream: She would be studying with the world-famous Max Schoenberg.

Her father insisted that she decline the honor.

Rachael rebelled.

At the time she was confused. She did not understand that the issue was not so much music as a way of life, that she was the only artist in a family of practical, science-oriented Austrian Jews. All of her cousins and uncles were professors, doctors, or lawyers. They were incapable of understanding her impractical ambitions, just as she was incapable of understanding their logical approach to life.

The heated argument with her father raged for weeks. Only reluctantly, after Rachael lost weight and spent most of her time crying, did he give his permission for her to accept the scholarship.

He stressed that he was doing so only because of her poor grades in other subjects, because she had failed as a student.

His voiced disappointment had been devastating. For a time she had wavered, torn between her love of music and her need for her father's approval.

He had never relented in his view that she had made the wrong choice.

Instinctively, she had known she was right.

When she entered the university, she became friends with several students like herself—artistic students deemed misfits by their families. Only then did she understand.

Enrapt in the excitement and glamour of the university, she had been able to endure the pain of her estrangement from her father.

In her second year, she was asked to serve as roommate and translator for an older scholarship winner from France, Annette-Marie Fourcade. Despite two years' difference in their ages, they soon became close friends.

Annette-Marie was a child prodigy coming into full fruition of her talents. Rachael's own musical education had been stunted by the indifference of her family. For a time, she was quite content to walk in the French girl's shadow.

Annette-Marie had difficulty with language. Her German was minimal, and she found the *Wienerisch* dialect of Vienna confusing. Rachael was fluent in French and English, and she was a natural mimic. Her imitations of the *Hochdeutsche* of Prussia or of the rote phrases of American tourists asking directions, sent her friends into gales of laughter.

Annette-Marie's father indulged her. When Annette-Marie was invited to America for a concert tour, her family's only reservation was that Rachael must be allowed to accompany her.

They had traveled first-class on the *Normandie,* surrounded by unbelievable magnificence and luxury—a fairy tale come true. Every venture from their stateroom was an experience dazzling to such young passengers. Each night they made the ritual descent of the grand staircase into the Main Dining Room and its splendor. Longer than the Hall of Mirrors at Versailles, towering thirty-five feet to the coffered gilt ceiling, the room was breathtaking.

They sunbathed on their private terrace outside their stateroom, and visited the Winter Garden with its lush greenery, exotic birds, and marble waterfalls. Each time they left an elevator, one steward held the cage open while another leaped ahead to open doors for them. Some passengers found such an abundance of attention wearing. Rachael and Annette-Marie reveled in it.

Their New York debut had been a complete success, with Annette-Marie in excellent form. Rachael performed with her on the double piano, offering Tchaikovsky's First Piano Concerto. They played the *Ritual Fire Dance* for an encore. Rachael won her own paragraphs in the reviews.

The trip to colleges and universities around America had been hectic, but fun. The dark news from home seemed far away, of no significance.

Rachael returned to Vienna in March of 1938—just in time for the *Anschluss.*

The insanity of Germany had invaded Austria. The Nazis had won the country without firing a shot.

Rachael was on the subway to *Karlsplatz,* en route to the

university, when she was swept into the streets by a hysterical crowd of Nazis. The shouting, crazed mob moved past the Ring, the Opera, to the German Tourist Bureau, long used as Nazi Party headquarters. Rachael had trembled in fear as the crowd chanted *"Sieg Heil!"* and *"Ein Volk, ein Reich, ein Führer!"*

When she at last found a policeman and moved toward him for protection, she saw that he was watching the demonstration with approval.

It was the end of the Austria she had known.

Overnight, Nazi flags appeared all over Vienna. Within a week, Austria was thoroughly Nazi.

Some Jews fled. A few committed suicide.

Rachael's father refused to budge.

"Our family has lived in Austria more than two hundred years," he said. "There are two hundred thousand Jews in Austria. What can they do? Kill us all?"

He was dismissed from the university faculty and put to work sweeping the streets. When he protested, he was made to clean the latrines at the SS barracks.

Her sister Lillian was turned away from her classes at the medical school. Her brother Theodor was threatened with a beating if he returned to the research laboratory where he had worked for four years.

With only a minimum of income, the family subsisted on savings, and waited.

When Crystal Night came in November, Rachael's father was caught by a Nazi mob, beaten, and dragged through the streets.

Afterward, he was jailed.

Rachael went to the authorities and pleaded for his release. As she talked with an unsympathetic police captain, a rotund man in a business suit listened intently from a corner of the room. After several minutes, he approached her and asked several questions. He seemed especially interested in her proficiency with languages.

A few days later, she herself was arrested and taken to

the police station. The rotund man escorted her into a small room.

"There is a possibility that I can help you, and your family," he said. "If you will work with us, your family will be accorded preferential treatment."

"What kind of work?" she asked.

He studied her a moment before answering. "The Reich has special use for persons of your talents," he said. "You are fluent in languages. You've traveled in America. You can pass as a refugee. No one will suspect you."

Rachael was desperate. Her father remained in jail. She herself had been given a glimpse of a cell. Her mother was ill with worry.

"What do I have to do?" she asked.

"Almost nothing," the man said. "Just write to us, from time to time, to keep us informed of conditions in America."

Rachael's initial impulse was to refuse. But she had second thoughts.

If she could get to America, perhaps she could make arrangements for her entire family to flee Austria—maybe even to America.

The fat man had been persuasive. He promised that if she cooperated, no harm would come to her family.

She had accepted on one condition. "My father must never know."

The fat man laughed. "I was counting on that," he said.

He left the room, and within minutes her father was freed.

Rachael told her parents that the universities in America had offered to sponsor her emigration as a refugee. The fat man provided a letter that convinced her father.

"I don't know what will happen to Austria, or to us," her father said. "But I do know that this is a heaven-sent opportunity. Go to your friends in America! Tell them what is happening over here!"

Rachael had some money of her own—an inheritance

from her grandparents. But before she left, her father took her into the basement and gave her ten diamonds from the secret hoard behind a loose brick.

"These will help you to get started in America," he said. "They are small, but of good quality."

She sewed them onto the silk peasant dress as cloth-covered buttons. She kept the dress all through the Abwehr training in Germany, and wore it on the flight across the Atlantic.

The diamonds made her plan even more logical.

While she cooperated with the Nazis, she would work to get her family out of Austria.

She held fast to a dream of her father arriving on the Clipper, hugging her, and telling her what a wonderful thing she had done, and how proud he was of her.

But that scene was growing more remote every day.

Instead of improving, political conditions had grown steadily worse. She had phoned the World Jewish Council —anonymously at first—seeking information. She was referred to a smaller group, the Jewish Agency, and a young man named Hillel Goldman. She was told he had been successful in bringing many Jewish refugees out of Europe. Reassured by his promise of secrecy, she visited him one afternoon at a small synagogue in Queens, explained her concern for her family, and asked if he would help her bring them to America.

Goldman was small, dark, and earnest. His face was gaunt, and he spoke with a nervous intensity. His eyes were bright and intelligent. Rachael found his analytical stare disturbing.

He was not encouraging. "We are bringing out only a few now, from time to time, mostly from Poland and Czechoslovakia. German and Austrian nationals are much more difficult to help, almost impossible. But I'll see if anything can be done."

Rachael filled out a form, listing the names of her parents, her brother and sister, the address of the family home, and the date of her last communication with them. Hesitantly, she included her own address and phone number, remembering that Goldman had promised complete secrecy.

He walked her to the door. "Don't get your hopes too high," he warned. "At this point, it would take a miracle to get your family out of Europe. But on the other hand, don't lose faith. It could happen. We are in a continual process of assembling information, learning more and more about conditions over there. Check with me in a few weeks."

Rachael left the synagogue convinced that for once in her life she must accept reality.

Apparently her only chance was to cooperate with the Nazis, in the hope that they would uphold their end of the bargain and give her family special protection.

And despite her constant worry and concern, she felt a certain satisfaction.

For the first time, her father—and her entire practical-minded family—were dependent upon her for their very lives.

Rachael was pulled more and more into the social life of the apartment building, even though she resisted at every turn. The tenants were terribly gregarious. They constantly trooped in and out of each other's rooms. An evening seldom passed that someone did not knock on Rachael's door to invite her into another apartment for a party or to join a group walking over to drink wine in some cafe. She did not know how best to deal with the situation. She knew she should keep her distance, that danger lay in any close relationship. But she instinctively sensed that aloofness might lead to suspicion, and even more danger.

Worse, she found herself enticed by the promise of fun and companionship. The poet on the third floor, David Reed, was especially attentive. He seemed to contrive ways to encounter her in the hall or along the sidewalk in front of the building. He was tall, pleasant, and had a very nice smile. She liked his quick wit, his boyish charm. She enjoyed talking with him. Repeatedly he invited her to a movie or party, and she was tempted. She responded to his advances with warmth and friendliness. On several occasions when the whole house was included in a party, she let it be assumed that she was David's "date." But she declined to go out with him. She knew that once her barriers were lowered, she would never be able to re-establish the proper distance.

She told him that her work load filled her evenings, that after her ordeal, she badly needed quiet and solitude. He was patiently persistent, and turned his constant presence into a standing invitation.

Even more difficult to handle was the problem of the actor, James Brighton. With his dark hair, firm jawline, and graceful movements, he was remarkably handsome. He possessed the deep, rich baritone of the polished actor, practicing faultless diction and modulation. In his own way, he was even more persistent.

He laughed when Rachael repeated Mrs. Adler's remark that he was playing second male lead.

"Chief spear carrier would be more descriptive. But it *is* a speaking role. And I would have paid *them* to work with Paul Lukas. I'm learning so much, just studying him night after night, the tricks he uses to bring freshness to every performance."

He asked her to attend *Watch on the Rhine* as his guest.

"I would be interested in your impressions," he said. "In many ways, I think the play may be one of Miss Hellman's best efforts. Certainly, it's timely. But we have had so little real-life experience in such things. I would like to know what you think."

Against her better judgment, Rachael agreed. Although the story of a German and his wife, harassed in Washington by Nazi agents, bore little relationship to her own past, the

151

accuracy of the aura conveyed was devastating. Rachael emerged from the theater emotionally shattered.

Brighton perceived her mood. He took her to a small, secluded cafe in the Village. There they sat talking for a long time, mostly about the play.

She had been impressed with his performance. He had played one of the Nazi agents. His demeanor onstage had been so altered that at first she had not recognized him.

In the context of discussing the play, he probed gently into her own feelings about the Nazis. Mellowed by the wine, disarmed by the first pleasurable conversation in months, Rachael almost launched into a description of Crystal Night. She caught herself at the last possible moment.

The slip would have been ruinous, and irreversible, revealing that she was not French, but Austrian. Her masquerade would have been beyond explanation.

The close call left her weak and sobered. Pretending sudden nausea, she asked Brighton to take her home. In the days following, she assiduously avoided him. She knew that she must never allow herself to be trapped into another such relaxed conversation, where the slightest mistake could betray her.

But it was the poet David Reed who demonstrated the full extent of the dangers posed by her surroundings.

One afternoon she arrived home to find a group assembled on the front steps, painting cardboard signs that read:

YOU'RE NOT OUR HERO,
EX-COLONEL LINDBERGH!
HEROES FIGHT FOR FREEDOM!

WRITE THE PRESIDENT
TO CLEAR THE ATLANTIC
AND STOP HITLER NOW!

WE'RE NOT HITLER YOUTH!
WE'RE AMERICAN YOUTH
WHO BELIEVE IN FREEDOM!

"The Nazi Bundists are marching on Staten Island to-morrow," David explained. "We're going over to picket them. The newsreels, radio, and newspapermen will be there. You ought to come with us."

He introduced her to members of the group, who called themselves American Youth for Freedom.

Rachael politely declined. "As a refugee who has been given political asylum, I shouldn't be demonstrating."

David seemed puzzled. "We have several refugees in our group."

Rachael was confused and frightened. "But my family is still over there," she said, turning away.

He followed her into the hall. "Rachael, I'm sorry. I certainly didn't intend to upset you. I just thought that with your situation, and knowing that you're politically aware, you might like to participate."

His choice of words alerted her. "Knowing that I'm what?" she asked.

He spread his hands in a helpless gesture. "That you read every newspaper, every day. I see them sometimes in the trash. You mark all the political stories, sometimes underlining them. I don't know of anyone who reads as much of the news."

Thoroughly alarmed, Rachael accepted his apologies and hurried on down to her apartment.

How could she have been so dumb? The disposal problem of daily newspapers had never been mentioned at the Abwehr Klopstock school, but she should have foreseen the hazard. If David Reed had noticed, then no doubt so had everyone in the house—especially the nosy Mrs. Adler.

Rachael spent a sleepless night, worrying about the speculation she may have caused. But she concluded that to alter her habits would attract even more attention. She continued to read all the daily newspapers, and to put them in the trash behind the building.

But she stopped marking and underlining the information she selected to send to Nazi Germany.

Rachael was well into the third week of her new life before she noticed the men.

She had left the apartment, taken the subway to Forty-second Street, and wandered erratically around Times Square for an hour, reading the theater marquees, checking her back trail as she had been trained to do.

She saw nothing unusual.

Adhering to her daily routine, she then took the subway to the Battery and boarded the Staten Island ferry.

She was on the upper deck, sketching ships at anchorage off St. George, when she saw the first man.

He was standing at the opposite end of the ferry, munching on an apple, gazing into the middle distance as if totally bored with his surroundings. He was of ordinary height, with short-cropped, rust-colored hair and bushy eyebrows. He was well-dressed in a gray business suit, and carried a small, dark briefcase. As the ferry docked on Staten Island, he moved on ahead of her and was soon lost in the crowd.

The fears of her first days in New York returned with a rush.

She was certain she had seen the man before.

Leaving the ferry, she boarded the bus for the ride down Richmond Terrace to Western Avenue and Howland Hook. Taking a seat toward the rear, she carefully monitored the other passengers. She did not see the man with rust-colored hair again.

But she saw two other men who seemed familiar.

One boarded the bus as the other stepped off—a technique of surveillance she had been taught at Klopstock.

Heart pounding, she remained on the bus while she decided what to do.

If she broke her routine, she might throw them into a

154

panic. They would have to readjust their coverage. They might become obvious, and her suspicions would be confirmed.

But her fixed schedule had been her cover. As a daily schoolgirl-commuter, she tended to blend into the woodwork. If she broke that schedule, she would attract attention.

Fighting her every instinct, she remained on the bus and continued her tour of the island.

On the bus that went along Hyland Boulevard to Raritan Bay, she decided her fears were groundless.

Everything around her seemed ordinary.

She stepped off at Craig Avenue and walked over to catch the Rapid Transit train back to the St. George Ferry Terminal.

As she boarded, she saw the rust-haired man again.

This time he wore a light blue sports shirt. Instead of a briefcase, he carried a newspaper. And in place of a snap-brim hat, he wore a dark blue cap.

But it was the same man.

He settled into a seat opposite and a few rows behind her. She felt his eyes on her all the way back to the ferry. He boarded the boat ahead of her, and walked to the far end of the upper level.

He seemed completely oblivious of her. But as she watched, he seemed *too* disinterested in his surroundings. His every movement was a bit too casual.

When the ferry arrived at the Battery, he again moved ahead of her to wait for the big doors to swing open. And again, he disappeared into the crowd.

Rachael took the subway north to Columbus Circle and walked into Central Park. From a bench, she watched her back trail for half an hour. She did not see the man again, or any face that seemed familiar.

In time, she convinced herself that she had been mistaken. She remembered her earlier fears, when she often awoke at night in a cold sweat, certain that the American authorities knew all about her and were merely toying with her.

She remembered that one of the Abwehr instructors had said that paranoia was a spy's stock-in-trade. "When you cease to be frightened and suspicious of everyone around you—that's the time to start worrying," he warned.

Walking southward toward a newsstand, she bought the evening papers and scanned the front page headlines.

Her fear faded as she became excited over a news story she did not find.

Hailing a taxi, she hurried back to her apartment. There she went through the newspapers carefully, to make sure she was not mistaken.

Several days ago, a brief item had announced that President Roosevelt was leaving on the presidential yacht for several days of fishing. A separate story had mentioned the concern among members of the press corps that no provision had been made for them to cover the trip.

Two days later a reporter had written that Washington was buzzing with rumors speculating that Roosevelt and his yacht were en route to a secret meeting with British Prime Minister Winston Churchill. White House spokesmen had denied the rumors, insisting that the presidential staff was in radio contact with the presidential yacht.

Then, for the last four days, there had not been a single mention of President Roosevelt's location—not in any newspaper.

No doubt if such a conference were in progress, the Abwehr would know about it.

But Rachael also knew that if she were to report the possibility, and it proved correct, her status at Abwehr would be elevated considerably, ensuring further protection for her family.

And if by chance the Abwehr did *not* know about the conference, she would be moved into the front ranks of operatives in America.

She had been instructed to use the cable system only for

emergencies, or for major reports when time was of the essence.

Rachael felt that the current situation met those requirements.

Carefully, she drafted a brief message: "Unable to locate Uncle Ben. Not at home. Further news expected."

Uncle Ben was her code for Roosevelt. Abwehr would quickly interpret the meaning of the message.

She sent the cable from the Western Union station on Broadway just below Times Square, and returned to her apartment with the sense of a job well done.

She read the daily papers, making notes. After checking the lock on the front door, she started her daily letter to the Lisbon drop.

When the phone rang, she was completely absorbed in her work. The sound was so unusual that for a moment she did not recognize it. In all the time she had lived in the apartment, the phone had rung only twice. Both instances had been wrong numbers.

Hesitantly, she picked up the receiver.

"Mademoiselle Rachael Moser?"

The voice was low, friendly, richly masculine.

"Yes?"

"This is Walter Beck, mademoiselle. I bring you greetings from Villeneuve-sur-Yonne."

8

Foley Square, New York City

Each night, Bonham worked late in the file room. He usually returned well before dawn the following morning. Gradually, he accumulated a list of 126 known or suspected Abwehr spies investigated by the Bureau during the last six years. But when he attempted to codify them, his theory collapsed. A common denominator seemed impossible to find. The subjects ranged from the highly educated to the practically illiterate, from industrialists and government officials to itinerant sailors and adventurers. Not until Bonham placed the spies into ethnic categories did he emerge with his first discovery—one he was ill-equipped to handle.

That night, he took the problem to Paul Marcus.

They were seated in their favorite bar, drinking the boilermakers that had become routine after each long, exhausting day.

Bonham waited until they had finished their second round before he broached the topic.

"Paul, you're Jewish, aren't you?"

Marcus glanced at him uneasily. "You looking for proof or something?"

Bonham ignored the question. "Paul, I've found something strange. Did you know that a fair percentage of the spies the Abwehr sends into this country are Jewish? Several of that last bunch were Jewish. Were you aware of that?"

Marcus remained guarded. He accorded the question a single, abrupt nod. "I've wondered about it."

"Well, what's going on?"

"What do you mean?"

"Jews helping the Germans! Come on, Paul! Why? I need to know more! I'm so goddamned ignorant about Europe. About this Jew business over there. Honest to God, if I ever met a Jew in West Texas, I never knew it."

Marcus looked at Bonham for a moment before answering. "Don't expect much help from me. I'm third generation."

"Just tell me this. How many of that last bunch *were* Jews?"

Marcus checked to see if he were serious, then shrugged. "Shit, I don't know. You can't go by names. Three or four, probably. Maybe more." He did not seem to want to talk about it.

Bonham persisted. "But why would they do it? The money?"

Again, Marcus shrugged. "From what I saw in the reports, there wasn't much money involved."

"Why, then? Any theories?"

Marcus glanced around to make certain they were not overheard. He leaned forward on the table and spoke quietly. "Shack, nobody knows for sure what's going on over there. And nobody seems to give a damn. You hear rumors in the Jewish community that people are being shipped off to labor camps. Relocation, they call it. The Jews that remain can't attend theaters, concerts, use the parks. Jewish doctors and lawyers are barred from practicing their professions. All that kind of shit. Jewish families can't even have a telephone."

"You mean they take up spying just to have a job?"

Marcus frowned in irritation. "Hell, no! It goes beyond that. Look at it this way. Suppose the Krauts take over, make you register your family and property, and surrender your means of livelihood. You have a big family. You don't know how you'll keep from starving. Your neighbors are being shipped off to the labor camps. Then, suppose some Kraut officer comes around and says, if you'll cooperate, do a little job for us, we'll see that nothing happens to your family."

"You think that's what happened to these people?"

Marcus shook his head. "Hell, I don't know. From what I could see, that last spy ring was a mixed bag. Brown Shirts. Screwballs. A few Nazi patriots. Anti-Communists. Mostly garden variety scum. Out of the bunch, there are maybe a half dozen who might have been coerced into spying."

"You studied German in college, didn't you?"

Marcus raised an eyebrow in surprise. "Who told you that?"

"It's in your service jacket."

Marcus scowled. "You nosy son-of-a-bitch."

"Well? didn't you?"

"I took German because it's close to Yiddish, which I've heard all my life. For me, it was simply the easiest way to get a language requisite out of the way."

"But you learned German, didn't you?"

Marcus snorted. "The only thing I learned was that with all their terrific marching music, and their vigorous language, it's easy to see why the Germans get to feeling like they've got to go out and whip somebody's ass every twenty-five years or so."

"Paul," Bonham pleaded, "don't you know anybody that could help me with this German-and-Jew business? I just don't understand it. But I do know that the small percentage of Jewish refugees among German spies has been the *only* consistent thing about them. If I could learn more about it, I could set my perimeters."

Marcus sighed. "Shack, did anybody ever tell you you're stark, raving crazy? If they even get a hint down in Washington of what you're doing, you won't even finish your probational year. And you *will* get caught. It's inevitable! You're a bull in a china closet. I used to think it would be a virtue for someone to be totally devoid of ethnic bias. But after knowing you, I'm not so certain. Shack, don't you understand? This is a delicate, sensitive thing with these people. It's not cowboys and Indians."

"I know," Bonham said. "That's why I've got to get to the bottom of this Jew business. I need to talk to someone who can listen to the background information on the Jewish refugees coming into this country and say, yes, that sounds right, or no, that sounds fishy."

Marcus sighed. "All right. Bring your stories to me. If I don't know the answer, I can check it out in the Jewish community. I'll be your rabbi."

Bonham gave him a blank look. Marcus explained.

"In this context, a rabbi is like a Dutch uncle."

The next afternoon, Bonham began assembling his list of suspects, and the background on each. For the first time, he allowed his personal project to interfere with his routine duties. The act was indefensible. He was leaving his assigned cases to pursue a whim. If he were discovered, he no doubt would be dismissed summarily from the Bureau. He was violating a cardinal rule. Spies were the concern of other desks. His meddling conceivably could jeopardize an investigation in progress.

Moreover, it was the first time he had purposefully misrepresented himself. As he obtained the necessary information from the Immigration and Naturalization Service, Pan-American Airlines, shipping lines, or police, he flashed his credentials, leaving the implication that his inquiries concerned an active case.

He had found that despite their code names in the Abwehr files, spies usually traveled under their own names, or

161

under the name of someone recently deceased. He did not waste his time seeking clues to false identities.

Gradually, he compiled a list of 176 suspects. The requisites he established were simple: a Jewish refugee from a German or occupied country, traveling alone. Sandwiching his investigations into his regular case load, he obtained minimal background on each.

Working night after night over boilermakers, he and Marcus managed to cut this initial list to thirty-one prime suspects.

During his off-duty hours, through persistent legwork, Bonham cleared six of the thirty-one. For eight straight nights he tailed a middle-aged violinist who left his apartment each evening for mysterious and erratic jaunts about the city. Not until the ninth evening did Bonham learn that the musician was searching for a long-lost brother.

A professor of medieval literature, an aircraft mechanic, a baker, an encyclopedia salesman, an accountant—one by one, Bonham traced each into a new life in America.

Still, he was only beginning to grasp the scope of what he was trying to do. Again, he took his problem to Marcus.

"We've got to cut the list further," he said. "Let's pick out the most likely suspects."

They went painstakingly through the files, narrowing the field to three prime suspects.

Janusz Szewczyk was a Warsaw tailor who claimed to have escaped Nazi persecution by fleeing over the mountains into Yugoslavia and eventually to Greece where, aided by a longtime friend, he was able to make his way to America.

Marcus gave Szewczyk's story an elaborate shrug. "Different. That's all I can say. Why go east to get west?"

Herman Kornfeld was an Austrian professor of philosophy who said he fled into Italy shortly after the German Anschluss. Masquerading as a sailor, he reached Brazil, where he jumped ship. When he earned enough money, he came to the United States.

"I think he stole his plot from Homer," Marcus said. "It's too elaborate. Liars tend to overexplain."

Annette-Marie Fourcade claimed to be a French pianist who once had made a concert tour of America. After the Nazi invasion, she had made her way alone to the Spanish border, where she bribed officials and was able to reach Portugal. After a wait of several weeks for her entry papers, she came to the United States on the Clipper.

"All by herself?" Marcus said. "Who is she? Joan of Arc? It's my impression that the Resistance sends refugees across the border in small groups—a few at a time—in unpatrolled areas. You don't just walk up to a border guard, hand him some money, and say, 'Let me through.' "

"Her story was cleared by the U.S. Embassy in Lisbon," Bonham pointed out.

Again, Marcus shrugged. "Maybe it's all true. But maybe you should find out. It can't hurt."

Bonham spent the next few nights shadowing Janusz Szewczyk. For an immigrant who had been in America only a few weeks, Szewczyk had many friends—a fact that struck Bonham as highly suspicious. But through discreet inquiries, he soon learned that Szewczyk had been featured speaker at meetings of fraternal groups in Polish-American neighborhoods, where he was warmly received. For many Polish-Americans living in New York, Szewczyk provided the first complete description of conditions in Warsaw and the Ghetto.

Bonham crossed Szewczyk from his list.

Herman Kornfeld was more difficult to locate. He had moved from the address listed in the files of the Immigration and Naturalization Service.

"He's ill," a friend explained to Bonham. "Nothing permanent—total fatigue from the terrible experiences he has suffered. We've sent him to my brother's farm in Iowa, where he can rest. In the fall, if he's able, he'll join me on the faculty at NYCC."

163

Bonham did not cross the name from his list. But at the moment, there was nothing more he could do. He would wait.

Annette-Marie Fourcade had checked out of her club-hotel on East Twenty-third. She had left no forwarding address. The man on the night desk did not remember her.

The next day, Bonham phoned the Immigration and Naturalization Service. Annette-Marie Fourcade had not reported a change of address. Bonham was preparing to leave FBI headquarters and return to the hotel to question the manager, when he was called into Bullethead's office.

Bullethead shoved an envelope across his desk. He did not seem pleased.

"Bonham, you've been summoned as a supplemental witness in the spy trials opening Monday. Get your ass over to the U.S. attorney's office this afternoon and find out exactly what they'll be wanting from you. Fortunately, I doubt that the conviction of thirty-three German spies will rest on your testimony. But just the same, we want no fuckups. Understand?"

Bonham nodded.

"Then get your ass over there," Bullethead said.

Bonham learned that the prosecution simply wanted his testimony to the effect that, while assisting in the arrest, he had indeed observed incriminating evidence in the possession of two of the defendants. Furthermore, on instructions from the arresting officers, he had duly logged the incriminating evidence, which he would identify for the edification of the court.

An assistant prosecutor explained that a jury of nine men and three women had been selected Wednesday in only three hours and twenty-five minutes. Both the prosecution and defense attorneys were taken by surprise. Jury selection had been expected to consume the remainder of the week. In a rare moment of agreement, both prosecuting and defense attorneys had requested an extended recess.

164

The judge had postponed the opening of testimony until Monday.

"Be here at nine sharp," the assistant prosecutor said. "You are free until then."

Bohmam glanced at his watch.

He still had time left in the day to pursue his own spies.

Kenmore Hall was a resident hotel featuring separate floors for women, and offering such diversions as table tennis, Ping-Pong, Chinese checkers, a gymnasium, and a steam room. Bonham asked for Manager Anthony Stark, and was directed to a small office behind the registration desk.

A thin, light-haired young man was on the telephone as Bonham entered. The man listened for a moment, grunted a few times for someone's benefit, then hung up.

"Yes?" he said.

Bonham flashed his credentials. Stark's eyes widened. He made no comment.

"Miss Annette-Marie Fourcade was a guest in your hotel a short time back," Bonham said. "I'm attempting to locate her."

An almost imperceptible flicker of expression on Stark's face told Bonham that the name had meaning. But Stark remained guarded. "Is she in trouble?"

"Do you have reason to think she may be?"

It was a shitty question, but it sometimes brought results.

Stark spread his hands. "I don't know anything at all about her. But then we don't have the FBI come around every day."

Bonham nodded. "May I see her registration card?"

Stark glanced at a file cabinet. "If it's necessary. . . ."

"It's necessary."

Stark searched for more than five minutes. Bonham waited. At last, Stark produced the card.

"Here it is. She checked out on the tenth of July."

Bonham studied the card. The signature at the bottom suggested a person of introverted nature. The loops were tight, the lettering small, wispy. The handwriting was extremely feminine.

"She checked out after only ten days," Bonham noted. "And she prepaid a month's rent?"

Stark bit his lower lip. "Well, you see, she didn't actually check out. So we had to hold her room. . . ."

Bonham understood. This creep had pocketed the extra cash. Bonham sat on Stark's desk and leaned over him. "Look, I don't give a shit about the money. I only want to know about the woman. You *do* remember her, don't you?"

Stark relaxed perceptibly. "Of course. I remember her well."

"Then tell me. Everything you remember."

Stark frowned with the effort. "She was . . . well, unusual looking. At first, you thought she was a little girl. But on second glance, you saw she was a mature woman. A beautiful woman. Very small, different. Stayed in her room, day and night. Ordered all her meals sent up. I thought maybe she was sick, see. We have some weird things happen here—things you wouldn't believe. So I asked around among the staff. They said she seemed all right, that she just seemed to want to stay in her room."

"She go out at all?"

"Just twice, that I know of. Once, about a week after she checked in, she was out no more'n an hour or so." He frowned, remembering. "That was July fourth. I know because I had the radio on, waiting for the President's speech. She went out through the lobby, and the doorman signaled a cab for her. The President's speech started a few minutes later."

Bonham nodded. The taxi was something he could check.

"Then she was out for a while on that last day. She got a telephone call. . . ."

"Who from?"

"I don't know. They didn't say."

"Did they ask for her by name, or for the room?"

Stark hesitated. "By name, I think. It was a male. They talked for a while. Then, in an hour or so, she went out."

"How long did the phone conversation last?"

Stark considered his answer. "Two minutes. Maybe less. Certainly not much more."

"Have any idea what the call was about?"

"Of course not." Stark's tone was indignant. "Any employee who listens in on a guest's phone line is fired on the spot."

Bonham waited.

"About three or four hours later, she came back," Stark said. "I remember I had closed the office and was ready to leave. She came through the lobby and went straight to her room. She seemed scared."

"What gave you that impression?"

Stark shrugged. "Well, she was mussed-up, like she had been running or something. And her dress was ripped."

"Ripped?"

"Here, at the shoulder. Her hair needed combing. And she had a frozen look on her face, like she was holding herself in, to keep from crying."

"You didn't talk to her?"

Stark shook his head. "It happened so fast. She was by me and into the elevator before I could say a word." He shrugged again. "And that night, she left."

"Anyone see her leave?"

"The night clerk. He noticed she was carrying a shopping bag. He thought she was just going out. But she didn't come back."

"She left her clothes in her room?"

Stark nodded. "A few things. I figure she left the suitcase so she wouldn't have to check out."

That made sense. Apparently she waited around the clock at the hotel for days—for something, probably for the phone call. She went out once, probably in an effort to contact someone. Then, when the call came at last, she went out to meet someone. Something happened. She came back scared. She panicked, made a clean break, fleeing from someone—or from whatever happened.

"You still got the suitcase?"

Stark hesitated. "It's in the storage room. But there are laws, you know. We're supposed to hold it. . . ."

"Look," Bonham said, "I can get a court order. But there's no need to go through all that legal shit unless we have to."

"Well, I guess it wouldn't do any harm. . . ."

"Right now, I just want to see if there's anything there to help me find her. If there *is* something, I'll get a court order. Okay?"

"Okay," Stark said.

Stark fished a ring of keys from the middle drawer of his desk. He led Bonham into the dark basement. Unlatching a wire cage, he hunted through storage bins until he found the suitcase. He placed it on a small table at the center of the room, beneath a naked bulb.

"It's unlocked," he said. "There were no keys. . . . And we didn't know what might be in it. . . ."

Bonham nodded. He was in no position to make a case out of Stark's illegal search.

Opening the suitcase, Bonham began stacking the material on the table. Two dresses, size six. Three slips. Two brassieres. Four pairs of panties.

The clothing conveyed an uncanny sense of intimacy. As he worked, Bonham began to envision the woman as Stark had described her—small frame, short dark hair, large brown eyes.

He had never thought of himself as psychic. But as he searched through the suitcase, he began to sense more than he could explain. He had the strong premonition that he was on the right track.

He dug deeper.

Beneath two scarves, a woolen sweater, and a light

jacket he found another dress—a green-striped silk with a full, flared skirt. It had no labels. As he pulled it from the suitcase, he discovered that all of the buttons on the front had been removed, torn from the cloth.

"That was the dress she was wearing when she went out that last day," Stark offered. "I remember it because . . . well, she looked terrific in it."

Bonham examined the dress carefully. The fabric was torn along one shoulder. He could find no bloodstains.

The dress posed a puzzle, If it had been ripped from her, either through violence or accident, the buttons most likely would not have been torn loose all the way to the hem.

"Was it buttoned when she came through the lobby?"

"I don't know," Stark said. "It happened so quick. And I was looking at her face. But her dress wasn't gaping open. I'd have noticed that."

Bonham examined the front of the dress with care. At the site of one missing button he found a piece of thin copper wire, just over an inch long. He explored further. He found no more wire, but holes had been punched in the fabric—holes larger than those made by an ordinary needle. Bonham surmised that wire had been used to replace the top five buttons.

He was mystified. Why had she decided to scrap the dress? Was it because she might have been seen wearing it —somewhere that might connect her to something incriminating?

And why had she removed the buttons?

He palmed the bit of copper wire as he put the dress aside.

At the bottom of the suitcase he found a few small boxes and tubes. He opened and smelled each. All contained cosmetics. In the corner, sitting upright, was a small, unlabeled bottle. Bonham held it up to the light. Only a few grains of substance remained. Uncapping the bottle, he cautiously tested the aroma. The smell was strongly medicinal.

"Nothing here," Bonham said.

He repacked the suitcase. Catching Stark's eye averted, he slipped the small bottle and the piece of copper wire into his coat pocket. He waited until Stark had relocked the storage cage, then gave the hotel manager his card.

"I don't think she'll come back," he said. "But if she should, please call this number." He lowered his voice to a confidential tone. "And don't talk about this to anyone but me. This is a very sensitive case."

During the weekend, the nation took one more step toward the inevitable. War headlines dominated every street kiosk, every radio newscast.

En route to Iceland with the mail, the U.S. Navy destroyer *Greer* was fired upon by an unidentified submarine. The *Greer* dodged the torpedoes and retaliated with depth charges. The submarine was driven off. President Roosevelt promptly ordered the Atlantic Fleet "to eliminate" the offending U-boat. He said that in the future such action would be taken against any submarine or surface ship that attacked an American ship on the American side of the Atlantic. In a subsequent and unprecedented order, he commanded all American warships to "shoot first" if Axis raiders entered American defense zones.

The German government said the American destroyer *Greer* had initiated the incident, and that Roosevelt's order was simple provocation for war.

American isolationists vociferously agreed with the Nazis.

The American flyer-hero Charles A. Lindbergh told reporters that the British, Jewish groups, and Roosevelt were in a conspiracy, pressuring the country toward armed conflict.

Democrats, interventionists, and militant patriots came to Roosevelt's defense. The issue grew heated in radio debates, and in the nation's newspapers. The Texas Legislature adopted a resolution informing Lindbergh that if he were planning a trip to Texas, he would not be welcome.

In this stormy atmosphere, U.S. Attorney Henry M. Kennedy electrified the U.S. District Court in Brooklyn—and the world—with his opening remarks to the jury as the spy trials got underway.

Kennedy said the prosecution would prove that Nazi Germany had stolen such U.S. defense secrets as the design for the coveted Norden bombsight—a device so hush-hush that it had not been shared even with the British until late in 1940.

Kennedy said other secrets sought by the Abwehr included automatic range finders, methods of bacteriological warfare, electric-eye anti-aircraft shells, gun-turret designs for the Sunderland flying boat, and textiles for Army uniforms that would neutralize mustard gas.

Moreover, said Prosecutor Kennedy, for the last sixteen months the Federal Bureau of Investigation had been in constant communication with the Nazi secret service in Hamburg by means of a short wave radio station on Long Island. He said this radio, utilizing the call letters CQDXVW-2 and broadcasting on wavelengths from 14,300 to 14,400 kilocycles, was operated by FBI Special Agents J. C. Ellsworth and M. H. Price, aided by a German double-agent, William G. Sebold, known to the Abwehr under the code name Tramp.

While Bonham was kept in the limbo of waiting rooms, Sebold's testimony consumed most of the week.

Artfully led by questions from the prosecutors, Sebold provided lengthy detail on the type of information Germany wanted—the number of Allison motors manufactured at the GM works, specifics on the aircraft carrier *Saratoga*'s delivery of planes to Halifax, the number of Curtis P-40s, Lockheed P-38s, and Bell P-39s being produced each month, production statistics on the Fairchild aviation plant at Jamaica, Queens, the Grumman plant at Bethpage, Long Island, the Republic aircraft factory at Farmingdale, Long Island. Sebold said the Germans especially were interested in American shipyards, their arrangements, the numbers of slips and docks.

He said much specific information was requested over a long period of time.

For instance, he said that two weeks before the fall of France, he first was ordered to keep close observation on the transatlantic liner *Normandie*. He said the order was repeated every few weeks.

Each day Bonham was kept waiting until noon. When it became clear that Sebold would be on the stand the remainder of the day, Bonham was released for the afternoon.

The trial was a terrible waste of time. His assigned work continued to pile up on his desk. And his free-lance investigation of Annette-Marie Fourcade remained at a standstill.

Bonham felt stymied. She no doubt had assumed a new identity, moved to a different section of town. She would not return anyplace where she was known as Annette-Marie Fourcade. The trail seemed to be at a dead end.

But as he paced restlessly in the halls, waiting to testify, he had plenty of time to think. And the more he reconstructed what he knew about her, the more certain he became that something significant had happened the day she disappeared—something that had thrown her into blind panic.

Friday noon, he was told by one of Prosecutor Kennedy's assistants that the government felt it had an airtight case. His testimony would not be needed.

Inspired by the high drama of the spy trials, and driven by the almost certain knowledge that he at last was on the right track, Bonham turned his full attention to the problem of tracking Annette-Marie Fourcade. He all but abandoned his assigned work. He consistently had closed more cases than the other first-year agents. He felt he could risk coasting for a few days.

First, he took the small brown bottle he had found in Annette-Marie Fourcade's suitcase to a commercial chemical laboratory and ordered a complete analysis. Although he flashed his credentials in the hope of quicker service, he explained that he was working on a special case and would pay cash.

The frail, stooped, gray-haired chemist in charge promised to give it his personal service. "Some of the tests will take several hours," he said. "Check back with me the day after tomorrow."

Bonham then took a taxi out to La Guardia Airfield. In the publicity office at Pan-American, he gave the manager a peek at his credentials. He was rewarded by the manager's full attention.

"I'm interested in the pictures of arriving passengers that appear in the newspapers," Bonham explained. "Who takes those photographs?"

"Depends," the manager said. "The larger newspapers usually send out their own photographers. But we also take pictures, just in case. The smaller newspapers and magazines frequently use ours."

"Do you photograph *every* incoming passenger?"

The manager hedged. "Not always. Just those who may be newsworthy. But of course, people who fly the Clipper are the type who make the news."

"Would a concert pianist—a young woman—be considered newsworthy?"

"Probably. If you're looking for a specific person, you might talk with Walt Fallowfield, our photographer. He's waiting for the Dixie Clipper now. It should be coming in any minute. If you'd care to wait. . . ."

"I'll wait," Bonham said.

He strolled out into the warm sun and stood on the concrete apron, watching the knot of people at the ramp by the East River. After a few minutes, he heard a shout. Someone pointed. All turned to look.

The Boeing 314 flying boat had appeared to the south, a dark speck against the pale blue sky. The speck grew until the flying boat took form, lumbering along noisily several hundred feet in the air. It made a pattern to the east of the airport, then banked and settled slowly onto the surface of

173

the East River, its hull sending up twin spouts of water. The boat taxied to the dock. A crew made it fast. Bonham walked out to watch the passengers disembark.

Framed in the doorway, each set of passengers paused and smiled for a photographer. Bonham moved closer.

The camera was held by a short, red-haired, freckle-faced youth with a perpetual grin. He manipulated a large Speed Graphic, flash gun, and photographic plates with impressive skill. Of the thirty-eight passengers on board, he took pictures of thirty.

Bonham waited until Fallowfield finished, then walked over as he gathered his exposed plates.

"Need some help?"

"No thanks," Fallowfield said without looking up. "I can manage."

Bonham introduced himself and showed his credentials. "I talked with your manager. He said you might be able to help me."

He explained what he needed.

Fallowfield seemed puzzled. He glanced around to make certain they were not overheard. "Listen, I send a print of *every* picture I make to you. If I made it, you've already got it."

For a moment, Bonham did not understand.

Then he did. He groaned inwardly. He should have realized that all incoming passengers were monitored.

He started talking, inventing as he went along.

"Your photographs go direct to the Domestic Intelligence Division in Washington," he explained. "We in the New York office seldom see them. I need just this single picture. I thought it'd probably be easier to get it from you here than to go through the red tape of requesting it out of Washington."

Fallowfield hesitated. "It might take a while to find the negative," he said. "That far back. . . ."

"No problem," Bonham lied. "I've got plenty of time."

He waited in a small office while Fallowfield searched. In a few minutes the photographer returned triumphant with a packet of negatives. He disappeared into the darkroom. When he emerged, he was holding three eight-by-ten glossy prints.

"This the one?" he asked.

Bonham stared at the photograph. Although he often had attempted to visualize Annette-Marie Fourcade, and felt he had a clear image of her in his mind, he was unprepared for the emotional impact of the picture. Poised on the steps of the Clipper, she seemed on first glance childlike, frightened, vulnerable. But there was something about her dark eyes that conveyed a strong sense of resolution. Almost in defiance of her delicate features and petite size, she seemed determined, tenacious.

"That's the one," he said. "How much do I owe you?"

"I'll just put this on my next bill," Fallowfield said.

Bonham kept his eyes on the photographs to hide his hesitation. If he insisted on paying for the prints, he would plant an element of suspicion. Fallowfield might mention the extra pictures, the visit of a Special Agent from the New York office.

But if he allowed the bill to be sent to Washington, chances were good that it would slip through unnoticed.

"That'd be fine," he said.

He spent the remainder of the afternoon spreading the word among cab companies that he had ten dollars for any driver who remembered picking up a young woman at Kenmore Hall just before noon on July fourth.

Then, armed with the photograph, he began a tour of musicians' unions and booking agents.

None remembered the young pianist.

On the fourth day of his search, in a sixth-floor studio near Columbia University, he found a music teacher who thought she remembered the name.

The large, efficient woman was teaching a class of six students, demonstrating technique at the keyboard. She frowned for a long moment at the photograph while Bonham and her class waited.

"You're talking about three or four years ago, right?"

175

she said. "A classical pianist, strong on Chopin, Liszt. Played the small college circuit."

"That may be the woman," Bonham said. "Do you recognize the photograph?"

The teacher shook her head. "I never saw her. I just remember the name. I could be wrong. She may have been on a church-concert circuit. Or maybe civic music. Why don't you check with Juilliard? They might know."

The tip led him to the offices of Mrs. Samuel Yunich, a middle-aged woman with a pleasant, open face and a ready smile. Her response was immediate. "Annette-Marie? Of course, I remember her very well. Why do you ask?"

Bonham explored cautiously. "I understand she may be back in this country."

Mrs. Yunich seemed totally without guile. A frown crossed her face. "So I understand. Someone called my attention to a mention in the *Times* of her arrival on the Clipper."

"Have you seen her?"

The frown deepened. "No, I haven't."

"Do you think that's unusual?"

"Frankly, yes. We weren't close friends, but we did have dinner together several times while she was here before. I felt certain she would call."

Bonham held out the photograph. "Is this Miss Fourcade?"

Mrs. Yunich glanced at the glossy print, then back to Bonham. "There's some mistake. That's not Annette-Marie."

Bonham managed to retain his professional poise. "Do you recognize the person?"

She nodded. "That's the little Austrian girl, Annette-Marie's assistant and traveling companion. I don't remember her name." She thought for a moment. "It was Rachael. Rachael something or other. I'm sure I have it in my desk. I probably could find it, if you wish."

"Please," Bonham said. "It's most important."

She pushed her way through the thick, soundproofed door and strode down the hall, leaving the heavy scent of jasmine in her wake. Bonham followed her past a long line of music-room doors and the muffled sounds of violins, pianos, woodwinds, and horns. She entered a dark, cluttered office, and Bonham waited patiently while she searched through the bottom drawers of her desk, pulling out folders, notebooks, scratchpads. At last, beneath a stack of sheet music, she found an address book and grunted in relief.

She flipped rapidly through the pages, then pointed with a long, crimson fingernail. "Here it is. Rachael *Moser*." She rattled off an address in Vienna.

Bonham wrote down the information. "What do you know about her?"

"Only what Annette-Marie told me. Annette-Marie considered her competent, talented, a budding pianist of first rank. I only saw her two or three times, you understand, and never really got to know her. She seemed . . . reserved. Much more so than Annette-Marie, who was rather outgoing."

"Did you correspond with Annette-Marie?"

"Just an occasional exchange of holiday cards, a note now and then." She paused. "The last letter I sent her—a little more than a year ago—came back stamped 'address unknown.' "

Bonham returned to the commercial chemical laboratories. The stooped, elderly chemist greeted him with a smile.

"You must have an interesting case, young man. Do you have any idea what you brought me?"

Bonham shook his head.

"It's a preparation called Pyramidon. Do you know its use?"

Again, Bonham shook his head.

The old chemist laughed. "Lucky you came to me. Not many young people would know about Pyramidon. It's a prescription drug, used in Europe, mostly by dentists, as a pain-killer. But it has interesting properties. If you dissolve the tablets in water and use the solution as an ink, it becomes invisible as it dries. Then, it can be restored to visibility with a reagent, much in the way a photograph is put through a developer.''

"Secret ink?'' Bonham asked.

"Exactly. The reagent is a simple solution of one percent ferrous-chloride, twenty-five percent ordinary table salt in water. You just dip a cotton swab in the developer, and gently rub the letter until the writing reappears.''

He handed the bottle back to Bonham. "It was a device commonly used by German spies during the Great War,'' he said. "I had no idea they still used it.''

Everything fell into place. That evening, the phone on Bonham's desk rang.

"You the FBI man who put the note on our bulletin board about the woman at Kenmore Hall?''

"Yes,'' Bonham said.

"I'm the guy that picked her up,'' the voice said. "It was just before noon, July fourth. I remember because we had to stop in Times Square for the President's speech.''

Bonham held back his elation. He wanted to be certain. He placed the photograph on his desk and looked at it. "Describe her.''

"Sure,'' the voice said. "Good-looking young lady. Very small. Black hair cut kinda short, where it just covered her ears. Big, dark eyes—really pretty.''

The description fit. "What was she wearing?''

The line was silent for a moment. "A green dress, I think. Some kinda stripes to it. High neck. Buttons down the front. Skirt was fuller than most you see these days.''

That cinched it. "How did she act?''

"She didn't talk much. But friendly. Hadda foreign accent of some kind. Said she was French, from a little town just outside Paris.''

178

"Okay. One more thing. Do you recall where you took her?"

"She didn't give me an address. Just the two hunnert block of East Eighty-fifth. I let her out about a third of the way down the block."

Bonham remembered instantly: The restaurant used as headquarters by the captured spy rings was located in that block.

He took the man's address and phone number, promising to send the ten dollars. He hung up the phone with a deep sense of satisfaction.

He had his spy.

And he had her photograph.

She was somewhere in New York, practicing her trade.

All he now had to do was find her.

BOOK THREE

NOVEMBER-DECEMBER 1941

We cannot lose the war! Now we have a partner who has not been defeated in three thousand years!

Adolf Hitler
December 7, 1941

9

Bryant Park, New York City

Rachael arrived at the rendezvous fifteen minutes early,
thankful that she had chosen her pale yellow, backless sun-
dress. The sky was clear and the day stifling with no
breeze. Heat rose in shimmering waves from the pavement,
and the streets were jammed with the usual noon-hour
traffic. She stepped out of the pedestrian stream on Sixth
Avenue and pretended to fish in her purse. From under the
rim of her portrait hat she carefully monitored the pas-
sersby to make certain she was not under surveillance.
After a full minute, she was satisfied. Abruptly, she turned
and entered the park.

The benches were crowded with office workers seeking
brief respite from the unseasonable heat of the buildings.
Many had brought their lunch. Rachael walked through to
the northeast corner near the library and stood, hoping that
someone would soon relinquish his seat.

The voice over the phone had sounded quiet, confident,
and authoritative—nothing at all like Frank Pierce. But she
had no way of knowing if the man who called himself Walter Beck was truly from the Abwehr, or merely another

Bundist. She had delayed the meeting as long as she dared, anticipating that she would receive some kind of a directive. But none had arrived.

She still did not know what she would do if he were another American Bundist, with questions about Frank Pierce.

Nervously, she again glanced at her watch. Seven minutes until one. A few benches away, several office workers rose, carried their brown paper bags and napkins to a trash container, and walked toward the street. But the Abwehr-designated benches near the corner remained full. Rachael waited, alert for any indication that anyone there was leaving.

At three minutes until one, three young women left their bench and hurried toward Sixth Avenue. Rachael quickly claimed the bench, ignoring a middle-aged couple moving toward it.

Carefully, Rachael placed the folded newspaper across her lap, gazed into the middle distance, and waited.

The man who called himself Walter Beck arrived almost on the stroke of the hour, carrying his folded newspaper in his left hand. He stopped in front of her and stood so long gazing at her that she grew concerned that something might be wrong.

"Miss Moser?"

She looked up, as if startled. "Yes?"

He did not smile. "I'm Walter Beck. I believe we have mutual friends. Do you mind if I sit down?"

"Not at all," she said.

He was a tall man, broad of shoulder, with large, strong hands and the saddest eyes Rachael had ever seen. He was dressed in a dark gray business suit that highlighted the blue of his eyes. His face bore the deep tan of an outdoorsman. In his bearing Rachael recognized the unmistakable stamp of aristocracy.

He glanced at the other benches, gauging the distance to other ears, and spoke softly.

184

"My name is Walther Von Beck. Please call me Walter. Our mutual friends have sent me here on a special assignment. They gave me your name, thinking you might be able to help me."

Rachael felt a wave of relief. If he had just arrived from Europe, he probably would not know about Frank Pierce. And she took comfort in his serious, direct demeanor.

"I'll do whatever I can to help," she said.

He paused and again checked the distance to the nearest benches. "The main thing I need at the moment is a safe place to stay. Some kind of cover. I'm now at the Taft, just above Times Square. I feel conspicuous. Our mutual friends had the feeling that all hotels might be under surveillance these days. I understand you have an apartment in Greenwich Village. If you could manage to take me in for a short while, I would try to be no bother."

Rachael hesitated. She could not risk appearing uncooperative. If he saw the flat, surely he would think it too small for his purposes. She did not want to take him there. His presence would complicate her already difficult situation in the apartment house. But she could find no other solution.

"I've only two tiny rooms and a bath," she said. "But if you don't mind a couch. . . ."

"That'll be fine," he said. He paused, and spoke in a sad, measured, off-hand manner. "You see, I have a great deal of work to do, and very little time. Why don't we pick up my bags and go there so we can talk?"

From the moment Von Beck rose from the bench, Rachael knew her period of seclusion had ended. Quietly, effortlessly, but with complete authority, Von Beck immediately took charge, firmly escorting her with a soft word, a gentle touch toward a taxi stand.

Rachael stayed in the taxi while Von Beck retrieved his bags at the Taft.

On the way to the Village, Von Beck watched the sidewalks, apparently lost in his own thoughts. When they arrived, he paid the driver and lingered for a moment at the curb, studying the street before following her into the apartment.

He stood in the middle of the floor, his height and size making the room seem even smaller. "Very nice," he said. He pointed to the corner behind the door. "If it isn't too much of an imposition, I can string a wire, and drape off a small nook. You'll hardly know I'm around. I promise you it won't be for long."

Rachael fought to keep her face devoid of expression as she thought frantically, seeking some way out.

She could not make her refusal obvious. Her lack of cooperation would be reported to the Abwehr, and her family would suffer. The duty of an Abwehr agent to provide other agents with safety and cover had been made plain at Klopstock. But she had never dreamed it would be so difficult. She now thought of her apartment as private, a part of herself. She could not imagine sharing it with a German Nazi.

"There is a problem," she said cautiously. "This is a townhouse, converted into small apartments. I have established myself as an artist . . . a single person. Your presence might create suspicions."

Von Beck nodded solemnly. "Let's sit down and discuss it," he said. "We may find a solution."

Rachael did not wish to appear inhospitable. "Coffee?" she asked. "Or wine, perhaps?"

"Coffee, please," he said.

While Rachael busied herself in the kitchenette, Von Beck sank into a meditative silence. But when she returned with the serving tray, he resumed the conversation as if there had been no interruption.

"Tell me about the other people in the house," he said. "Describe each—everything you can remember."

Rachael began with Mrs. Adler, and worked her way upward through the building. Reluctantly, she told him of Jim Brighton and David Reed, their attentions to her and the steps she had taken to discourage them. As she talked,

Von Beck gave her his complete attention, listening somberly without comment. She was fascinated with his eyes, the way the upper lids curved downward at the outer corners, in an expression so calm, yet sad. They were eyes imbued with world-weariness. He had none of the arrogance she had learned to expect of a German Nazi. She felt that he was competent, autocratic, perhaps even ruthless. But she was thrown off stride by his casual gentility.

He waited until she worked her way up to a description of the two dancers in the back apartment on the top floor. He gave her the ghost of a smile.

"And you've been here less than six weeks? You're very observant." He frowned in thought and toyed with his coffee cup. "Perhaps we can approach the problem logically. First, we both will be going in and out of the apartment often, at all hours. We will need a cover story to make this seem natural. Second, two persons of opposite sex, living together, will attract curiosity. I think we can use this to our advantage. Third, we may have to use the apartment as a safe house occasionally, for meetings with various people. We must plant a cover story in advance, so this will not seem suspicious. Can you think of any other necessities?"

Rachael desperately wanted to offer some obstacle. But she could think of none. "No," she said.

He slowly sipped his coffee. Rachael was impressed with the deliberate way he approached the problem. She would not have been so practical.

"If I remember correctly, Greenwich Village has always taken considerable pride in defying social conventions," Von Beck said. As he smiled, his whole countenance changed in the most intriguing way, his eyes conveying a twinkle of amusement, his face losing its habitual solemnity. He had a nice smile. Rachael felt that at some time in the past, Von Beck had smiled often.

"I shouldn't be making premature judgments," he went on. "But from what you've told me, some of the relationships in this house seem anything but conventional—homosexuals and lesbians. I think we can give them a cover story that will divert their attention, even enlist their aid."

Rachael was appalled at her own naiveté. She had remained unaware of—had not even given a thought to—the personal situations of others in the house. But she instantly realized that Von Beck's assessment probably was correct.

"You have established yourself as an artist. Do the other people in the house visit you?"

Rachael shook her head. "I've implied that I need seclusion for my work."

"Good. Have you visited in the other apartments often?"

"Just for occasional parties. I've tried to preserve my privacy. So I've taken care not to intrude on them."

Von Beck hesitated, as if making certain he was taking the right course. "Let's give them this story: I'm a nautical design engineer, the scion of an established New England family. We leave the implication—just a hint—that I'm involved in secret government projects. During the last few weeks, we have worked together. You've done artist-concepts of my designs. We have fallen in love. But my blue-nosed family is scandalized because you are Jewish. I've been forbidden to see you again. My father has even gone so far as to hire private detectives. Does this sound too melodramatic?"

Rachael shook her head. She was enchanted to be outdone in the area of make-believe, but she felt threatened by the way Von Beck was taking complete control of her life.

"We'll tell it little by little, a few facts at a time," he went on. "First, to Mrs. Adler, to explain my presence. Then perhaps you can query one or two of the other tenants, asking if they've seen private detectives lurking around, and confide part of the story. That should do it. I'm certain the drama will be all over the house within a week. Attention will be focused on the story—not on the realities."

188

Reluctantly, Rachael nodded agreement. A few tidbits to Mrs. Adler would be sufficient.

"The situation will explain my presence. Our work will explain our erratic schedule, an occasional visitor. And the other people in the house will become our eyes and ears, to alert us if we are under surveillance."

Despite her aversion to her part in it, Rachael thought the plan wondrously clever. She took some comfort in Von Beck's expertise and confidence. But she felt suffocated by the sudden invasion of her privacy. She still could not imagine sharing the apartment with him.

Von Beck seemed to read her thoughts. He glanced at the corner behind the door. "I'll go out and buy some drapery this afternoon. I promise you, you'll hardly know I'm here. I'll not intrude on your life. We will have to give the appearance in public that we are lovers. But the charade will end at the door."

Intermingled with Rachael's immediate, overwhelming relief at the promise was the disturbing knowledge that she had been put in her place. She was aware that the Nazis considered sexual intercourse with a Jewish woman among the most serious of crimes.

Von Beck had just reminded her that she was a Jew, he a dedicated Nazi, and the fact that they were living under one roof would not make it otherwise.

At first, Von Beck's plan worked perfectly. Rachael confided her "situation" to Mrs. Adler with carefully feigned reluctance and timidity. Mrs. Adler was enthralled. She soon proved that in her short, stocky frame beat the heart of a true romantic. Not only was the cover story spread throughout the building, but Mrs. Adler also invited Von Beck and Rachael into her apartment for dinner. Von Beck was utterly charming, and soon had Mrs. Adler blushing and giggling like a schoolgirl. He fended her questions concerning his work with disarming evasions, and was so attentive to Rachael that she occasionally had difficulty in remembering that it was only make-believe.

As the days went by, Rachael and Von Beck fell into a rigid, constrained routine. In his curtained portion of the living room he used only a chair and small table. He spent most of his time there, poring over figures and drawings. He slept on the couch, leaving her the privacy of the bedroom and bath. In the mornings, he made coffee, then used the bath while she fixed breakfast.

His constant presence was wearing. She no longer felt that her lovely apartment was her own. He often was morose, moody, and uncommunicative. Her only relief came when he went out, or during the few hours she spent away from the house each day. More and more she found excuses to dawdle, dreading and delaying the return to her own apartment.

Although he had said he would need her in his work, he gave no further hint about his project. She only knew that each day he left for several hours, and spent most of each night working at his figures and slide rule. Rachael continued her own routine, visiting the waterfronts, sketching various ships, searching through the newspapers, and preparing her long letters to the Abwehr.

He left her little time to herself. In the evenings they usually went out for dinner at some quiet restaurant in the Village, returning to the apartment for a few more hours of work.

Rachael anticipated that Von Beck's presence would alter her relationship with others in the apartment house, but she had not dreamed that the change would be so extensive and drastic.

Within a week, she noticed that David Reed was avoiding her. Where once he always seemed to be coming in or going out each time she entered the hall, he now simply was not in evidence. Once, when she accidentally encountered him on the street, he saw her first, crossed to the opposite curb, and pointedly looked the other way.

Rachael understood the reasons behind his jealousy. He had made his interest in her obvious to everyone in the house. Now, without warning, she had moved a lover into her apartment. Clearly David thought she had taken him for a fool.

She worried over the course his jealousy might take, if he should have second thoughts about those marked newspapers, or if he should disbelieve the story Von Beck had concocted.

Mrs. Adler's curiosity was insatiable. Von Beck was adept at parrying her questions, so she centered her efforts on Rachael, wanting to know the details about his family, the exact status of their Romeo-and-Juliet romance.

Rachael was by nature too honest to lie spontaneously, not devious enough to invent with facility. After she blushed and stammered her way through several of Mrs. Adler's quizzical assaults, Rachael tried to avoid her, even though she knew that by doing so, she was raising doubts in Mrs. Adler's mind.

In fact, she now wondered how widely Von Beck's story was believed. The two dancers in the back apartment on the top floor had once been friendly, always stopping to chat. Now they smiled but remained wary.

Jim Brighton put it into words, perhaps unwittingly. "Well, you're not the naive little waif we thought," he said. "Only here a few weeks, and already you've got your life organized better than most of us. We'll have to take a second look at you."

That was what Rachael feared was happening, throughout the whole building. She saw the re-examination in their eyes.

One more mistake—such as the marked newspapers—and someone might arrive at the right answers.

She told Von Beck about the changed attitudes toward her, and suggested that they move to a new apartment. He listened to her reasoning, but quickly rejected the idea.

"You're imagining things," he said. "What you've explained is to be expected. It's natural that your relationships would be different. We can't move. Without a radio, your address is our only link in case the Abwehr needs to contact us in a hurry. A new address would take weeks to establish, and we don't have the time. Just do your job. Don't worry about it.''

Sometimes he was curt to the point of rudeness. One night she broached the subject of the Jews in Germany, and asked if he knew what was happening to them. The question seemed to make him angry.

"How would I know?" he snapped. "I'm not a Jew."

He went to his corner and did not speak to her again all evening.

Many such incidents occurred between them. She learned that Jews, U-boats, and the Klopstock school were delicate subjects, apt to trigger his black moods. She avoided those topics, even when she obtained some bit of information she felt she should tell him.

There were other worries Rachael did not share.

On a Monday afternoon in the third week of November, she again visited Hillel Goldman of the Jewish Agency at the small synagogue in Queens. He remembered her, and did not bother to pull her file. He took her into a dimly lit room. There were no windows. The air in the room was hot, humid, and musty. They sat at a small table. An elderly woman came in to pour coffee, then left them alone.

Goldman sat facing Rachael. She noticed that he now had dark circles under his eyes. He gestured toward a stack of papers on the end of the table.

"The situation over there has become more and more confused," he said. "We've received isolated, unconfirmed reports of wholesale massacres of Jews in Poland, Czechoslovakia, and in the Ukraine. Thousands upon thousands have now been relocated. There are rumors of death camps. Communication is poor. We really don't know what's happening.''

"What about Austria?" Rachael asked.

"Apparently the Austrian Jews are now going through the experiences of the German Jews during most of the last decade. Confiscation of property, loss of all professional rights, relocation. I haven't been able to learn anything concerning your family. However, we may be able to arrange something. . . ."

He wiped the perspiration from his forehead with a white handkerchief, and carefully folded it before continuing.

"Before I tell you what might be done, perhaps I should explain the situation. Understand, Jewish leaders throughout the world, government officials in Washington are divided on what is happening to Jews in Europe, or what can be done about it. Too many people—including Jews—remember the exaggeration of atrocities during the Great War. There were stories about German soldiers tossing Belgian babies in the air and catching them on the points of bayonets, and so forth. After the war, those stories were disproven. Now, even when we receive eye-witness reports that several hundred Jews have been murdered somewhere in Poland, there is widespread skepticism, not only in Washington, but also in the World Jewish Council. Some Jewish leaders believe that the German relocation program for the use of Jews in war work may be the salvation of the Jews in Europe, that Hitler will protect them because he needs them. At the other end of the spectrum, very much in the minority, are those who believe that the relocation program is the first step in the mass murder of European Jews."

"What do you believe?" Rachael asked.

Goldman did not answer for a moment. "I've read *Mein Kampf.* I'm convinced that if it is within Hitler's power to murder the Jews—and apparently it is—then he will do so."

Rachael remembered the insanity of the mob around Karlsplatz during the Anschluss. She remembered the terror of Crystal Night. The possibility of mass murder did not seem remote under such circumstances.

"Negotiations are now in progress to bring out several German Jews, perhaps in the next month or two," Goldman went on. "It is a trade—some people we want, in exchange for German spies and criminals held by several countries. The negotiations are very expensive, and the German government is demanding bonus money. The American government won't contribute. We can't use Jewish Council funds. Many of the directors are opposed, on principle, and we can't risk dissension by showing favoritism to special groups. If someone—some individual—is willing to pay the German price, and to help finance the negotiations, it might be possible to add two or three names to the list."

Rachael hardly dared to breathe. "How much money?"

"I don't know," Goldman said. "Probably in the neighborhood of ten to twenty thousand dollars for each person."

Rachael felt a rush of relief. Her diamonds were worth much more.

"I'll pay it," she said.

Goldman held up a hand. "Remember, I can't promise results. We may never know the details. The odds are long. Do you still want to try?"

Rachael did not hesitate. "Yes," she said.

"Then I will make preliminary arrangements," Goldman said. "I'll call you, perhaps within the next few weeks. It probably would be best to put up a sum of money, say five thousand dollars each for your parents, brother, and sister, with the understanding that more money is available if we have some indication of success. Would that be satisfactory?"

Rachael left ecstatic. Despite Goldman's warning of caution, she felt that her plan to rescue her family might be working.

She would have to sell two or three more diamonds from her safety deposit box. Only a few hundred dollars remained in her checking account—all that was left from the sale of one of the smaller diamonds. After leasing the apartment, she had spent money too lavishly on furnishings and decoration. She also had overspent in replacing the clothing she had abandoned at Kenmore Hall.

She still had qualms about claiming the money the Abwehr had placed on deposit at Chase Manhattan under her Annette-Marie Fourcade identity. She strongly suspected that the FBI might have the account under surveillance.

Although she trusted Goldman implicitly, she knew she should attach some stringent demands when the time came to put up the money. She was inexperienced in such matters and wanted to ask Von Beck's advice. But his formidable reserve discouraged any talk of personal problems.

Rachael decided to sell two or three more diamonds, make the arrangements with Goldman, and say nothing about it.

Von Beck felt disoriented on the streets of New York. After so many years in the military, the absence of uniforms was bewildering. For several days he roamed Manhattan, reveling in the atmosphere of a nation at peace. He had forgotten that people could live concerned only with their work, their families, their small pleasures. He had grown so accustomed to faces eroded by fear and fatigue that American countenances now seemed as unblemished as those of newborn babes. The few uniformed servicemen he saw on the streets appeared a decade younger than the nineteen- and twenty-year-olds in his U-boat crew.

The aura of political innocence in America was amazing. The whole country seemed awash in total naiveté.

Von Beck remembered a random remark once made by his father, that Americans for some reason lacked the tragic sense of life that was deeply ingrained in every European. Americans had remained relatively untouched by the Great War. And now they had no concept of the horror looming on their horizons.

195

Von Beck was convinced that after the incidents involving the American destroyers *Greer, Kearny,* and *Reuben James,* war was inevitable between Germany and the United States. The *Greer* had dodged torpedoes, but the *Kearny* had been hit, and 11 Americans killed. The *Reuben James* and crew of 115 had gone down 600 miles west of Ireland. The final provocation might come any day. And Americans seemed blind to the situation in the Far East. Announcements that Roosevelt had imposed severe embargos on Japan were relegated to the inside pages of the newspapers. No one seemed to realize that Japan desperately needed the oil, aviation gasoline, and scrap metals to feed her far-flung war machine.

Von Beck was certain war would come to America soon.

And little time remained for him to complete his mission.

He desperately sought a solution to the problem. Twice each day he walked down Twelfth Avenue, past the *Normandie.* To avoid attracting attention, he never slowed his pace, glancing but briefly at the ship. He carefully timed his visits, to give the impression that he passed the ship as part of a daily schedule.

As he suspected, the *Normandie* was virtually impregnable. Each day as he walked along the stringpiece under her soaring bow, he could see that only one gangplank was rigged from the French Line terminal. Apparently, access to the ship was rigidly controlled. The sides of the ship were too high, too exposed for grapnels. Occasionally he glimpsed a Coast Guardsman walking her decks, carrying a rifle.

After all his planning, all the calculations, he still was undecided on the best course of action.

If he could get aboard, several options were available. At least one boiler would be in operation, vulnerable to sabotage and, with luck, an explosion that would flood the engine spaces. He could set off a series of explosions in her wing tanks that would open up her sides. Or, on some dark night, he could open and damage her seacocks in a pattern designed to capsize her.

But since he could find no way to get aboard, his attack would have to be made from outside the hull.

For this, he would need to recruit help, a step he was reluctant to take.

He did not know yet if Rachael Moser was capable of doing the work or—more important—if he could trust her.

She was vastly different from what he had expected.

When Lahousen had discussed the Abwehr personnel available to him in America, Von Beck had been intrigued with the lengthy, elaborate reports written under the code name Princess. After Lahousen explained that she was a Jewish woman, working in exchange for the Abwehr's protection of her family, Von Beck had pictured Rachael Moser as a businesslike, hefty, perhaps even mannish opportunist he could deal with on a pragmatic level. Not until he was preparing to depart and Lahousen showed him her file picture, did Von Beck learn that his initial impression was wrong, and that her code name Princess was not sarcastic humor.

"Actually, she's quite good-looking," Lahousen said. "And one of the most efficient agents we have had in New York. It's a pity we don't have a radio in operation. Some of her best information arrives too late."

She was still restrained and distant with him. But he now had been with her long enough to know that she was an unusual woman. She was extremely intelligent, completely feminine, yet childlike and vulnerable in so many ways. She kept much of herself hidden behind that elfin face and those large, innocent eyes. Her body and manner implied immaturity, but he had learned that her personality was strong and compact.

He sensed from the first that she was frightened by his unannounced arrival. He admired her for the way she masked that fear behind an artful bravado.

Yet, he was reluctant to bring her into the project.

Her motivations were too tenuous. She had made a Faustian pact with the Devil to protect her family. In her eyes, he was one of the Devil's minions. The slightest shift of

197

events might end her cooperation with the Abwehr. He simply could not depend on her in a crisis situation. If the Abwehr lost its leverage, she would betray him.

And he could not forget the fact that she was a Jew.

Since boyhood, he had been conditioned never to trust a Jew.

The training had begun in the Hitler Youth. He remembered the documentary film, *Jud Suss*, that had depicted Jews as depraved, the carriers of loathsome diseases, the disseminators of a defective genetic strain that would turn all mankind into subhumans unless checked. He remembered the stereotyped Jew that appeared everywhere in posters and cartoons by artists such as Philipp Rupprecht, demonstrating the typical features of Jews as crooked short legs, large flat feet, dangling hairy arms, a hunchback stance, a coarse-featured face, large hanging ears, and distended lips. Later, there were other documentary films, such as *Der Ewige Jude,* which traced the scourge of mankind. Under the constant barrage of such propaganda, the later confiscation of Jewish department stores such as Wertheim's on Alexanderplatz in Berlin by the government seemed a fitting and natural first step to the seizure of all Jewish property.

Lost in the excitement of the Hitler Youth, the naval academy, and later the U-boats, Von Beck had never thought much about the so-called Jewish problem. It was an abstraction. The Jews he had known did not seem much different from other Germans. He had assumed that they were the exceptions—the few Jews who were not "subhumans."

His brief glimpse of the *Judenzug* in the railroad yards at Frankfurt-am-Main continued to haunt him. He remembered that momentary view of thousands of Jews crammed into the freight cars like sheep headed for the slaughterhouse. He had heard of the *Arbeitseinsatz*—the "mobilization of labor"—involving the Jews. But he wondered what prospective employer hoping to achieve maximum production would treat his employees in such a manner.

The *Judenzug* in Frankfurt-am-Main had not been created for propaganda purposes—nor for optimum use of labor.

Neither was Rachael an abstraction. After his few weeks with her, he had learned that she was honest, warmhearted, even lovable. With her delicate build and exquisitely planed features, she was the antithesis of the Jews depicted in the Hitler Youth documentaries.

His every instinct told him that under ordinary circumstances he could trust her.

But he could not trust his own feelings. He was attracted to her both physically and intellectually. He was repulsed —and fascinated—by her Jewishness.

Yet, he had to remember that the Abwehr had sent him to America with instructions to trust her. In a sense he would be defying orders if he failed to put her talents to use.

Time was growing short. The two submarine loads of Nazi Party amateur spies might arrive and be captured any day now, launching the FBI on a witch hunt. He could not delay his project much longer.

Eventually, he decided that he had no alternative. He would have to trust Rachael, simply because he could not complete his mission without her.

But he also resolved that he would exercise the utmost caution, and tell her only as much as she needed to know.

He waited until they were settled in for the night. Rachael had completed her dissection of the newspapers and was laboring over one of her lengthy letters. For an hour or more, he had been refiguring the weight of the *Normandie*'s turboalternators.

He put his slide rule aside with an exaggerated sigh of exhaustion. Rachael looked up from her letter.

"My preliminary work is completed," he said, unconsciously assuming his tone of command. "After you finish that letter, I think you can forget about your normal duties for a few days—perhaps a few weeks. I am authorized to ask you to perform certain important work for me."

Rachael's expression did not change. The hand holding

the pen tightened, and her eyes seemed wider. But she said nothing.

"If you wish, you may check my credentials with the Abwehr," he said. "Perhaps a note at the bottom of your letter. Of course you are not to use my name, only my code designation of Sailor."

"I already have," she said.

He tried not to show his surprise. "And what did they say?"

Rachael gave great attention to recapping her fountain pen. She did not look at him. "I was told that I am to consider any order from you as coming from Admiral Canaris himself."

He rose, crossed to the table, and sat down facing her. "This is an important project," he said. "Your role will be essential. If you have any doubts . . . if at any time you feel you cannot do the job . . . I want you to tell me. Do you understand?"

She met his gaze. He thought he saw her lips tremble, but she regained control before he could be certain. "What is it you want me to do?" she asked.

He pointed to the apartment house overhead. "The most important portion has begun—our cover. A lone man prowling around the waterfront attracts attention. If he is seen several times, he draws suspicion. But two lovers can dawdle, spend an afternoon on the docks without anyone giving them a second thought. During the next few days, we'll pose as lovers strolling around the waterfront, while I make certain observations."

He paused, wondering how much he should reveal.

"Afterward, I'll need to make contact with an individual or two. You'll help me find those people."

Her eyes did not waver. "Walther, what is it we are about to do? Can you tell me?"

He hesitated. Perhaps the fact that she had called him by his first name caused him to lower his guard.

"Sometime during the next two or three weeks, you and

I are going to sink the *Normandie*." He paused, but her expression had not changed. "There will be only the two of us," he added. "But I have now determined how it can be done."

10

Aboard the *Normandie*, Pier 88, New York City

For two hours, Maurice Raynal and Captain Zanger explored the depths of the *Normandie,* and still their tour was only half completed. At last they reached the propeller mounts, as deep in the stern as one could go without removing the keel plates.

Raynal placed a hand on the cantilevered supports for the huge drive shafts, the gigantic screws. "The bearings may be frozen, for all we know," he said. "I've never heard of propeller shafts remaining immobile for two years. I don't know what to expect."

Ventilation had been cut off in the after part of the ship. The space was hot and humid. Captain Zanger removed his hat and wiped his forehead. "How much of a job would it be to test them?"

Raynal had given it much thought. "We would need outside help, divers to disconnect the screws, perhaps a fireboat to wash away river silt. Twenty of our men could do it in a week or ten days."

Captain Zanger winced. "Already we are short for the fire detail and simple maintenance. Could we assign men?"

Raynal gave the only possible answer. "Other tasks would suffer."

Captain Zanger considered the problem for a moment. "Let's forget it then, for the time being," he said. "But we will make note of the situation in our report."

They switched off the lights, left the machinery spaces, and moved on forward by flashlight, into the vast compartments devoted to linen storage. The musty smell of unrelieved dampness grew stronger. Zanger found the switches and flooded the spaces with light.

Raynal stood for a moment, making additional notes for the full report requested by Transatlantique on the condition of the ship.

What else could he say, other than the fact that the *Normandie* was slowly rotting? The entire ship was ventilated on the premise that she would be spending at least half of her time at sea, with air flowing through every one of the hundreds of compartments throughout the ship. Now, dankness persisted even in the well-ventilated engine rooms and crew's living spaces. In the many sections of the ship where the air ducts were shut off, mold, rust, and rot were making headway.

They entered the huge cavern where fish had been kept in isolated refrigeration. The room was now empty, but even after two full years the smell lingered. On forward were the individual cold storage rooms for pork, poultry and game, and beef.

"The refrigeration system should be overhauled before it is returned to use," Raynal told Zanger. "There will be a tendency for the compressor valves to stick after such long inaction. The Freon should be checked."

"Make note of it," Zanger said.

They climbed up through the deserted Engineers' Mess and quarters for the engine room crew on E Deck, to the food preparation area on D Deck. There they spent more than an hour examining the bakery, the icing room, butchers' shop, fish preparation room, the massive larder, cold

203

room for fruit, cutlery storeroom, glass storeroom, and the scullery with its famous electric range, eighteen meters long, where seventy-six master chefs and a hundred assistants once prepared more than four thousand individual, gourmet-quality meals each day.

Raynal had seen the entire area teeming with unbelievable activity. He now found the oppressive, hollow silence deeply disturbing.

They moved on forward, past the first-class passengers' gymnasium, to the twenty-five-meter swimming pool, where they found the enameled sandstone and ornate mosaic wall friezes in a good state of preservation.

Their footsteps echoing, they walked on through to the stairways, where they climbed up six flights to the Boat Deck and, at last, fresh air. The early December sun was surprisingly warm on Raynal's face, the sounds of traffic along Twelfth Avenue and the elevated West Side Highway reassuring after the spooky silences below decks.

Zanger strolled to the Forward Promenade, just below the ship's bridge, well away from earshot of the crewmen busy painting lifeboats, the Coast Guardsman walking his post on the fo'c's'le. He then turned to face Raynal.

"Well, Maurice, what are your recommendations?"

Raynal glanced up to where paint was peeling from the forward stack. He thought of the lacquered gold flaking on the bas-reliefs in the Smoking Room, all the rusting, inactive machinery.

"She badly needs a long period in drydock," he said. "Complete restoration, bowsprit to stern. That is my recommendation."

"I agree," Zanger said. "Write your report. Explain your reasoning. I'll sign it. The company will spend much time deliberating upon it. And nothing will be done. This whole thing is an exercise in futility."

"Then why do it?" Raynal asked.

Zanger looked away. "What else can we do? They've put us in charge of the ship. We'd be derelict in our duty if we didn't inform them of the situation, offer our recommendations as to what is required. But what can *they* do? If she is returned to France, she will be made into a garbage scow to haul the Nazis, or bombed by the British. How can we expect them to spend one or two million American dollars to repair her, idle in a foreign port? She is a millstone around their necks—a thousand dollars a day for pier space, another two or three thousand dollars a day for maintenance expenses, and subsistence and pay for the crew. She has not returned a single franc to the company in two years. Nor can they expect a single franc from her for years to come." Zanger shook his head sadly.

Raynal asked the question that was constantly on his mind. "What do you think will happen to her?"

"If America doesn't enter the war, she'll continue to deteriorate. How long will it take the British and the Russians to drive the Nazis from Europe? Five years? Ten? What will the *Normandie* look like in only two more years? In five years? Ten?" Zanger turned his face away. "I must tell you, Maurice. I see no hope for our ship."

"What if America does come into the war?" Raynal asked. "Has anything been said to you about the possibilities?"

"Only in the form of rumors and opinions," Zanger said. "There's considerable concern that the American Navy urgently needs more large aircraft carriers, fast transports. I've heard the mention of immediate conversion of the *Normandie* to one or the other. A controversy seems to exist as to which they need most."

Raynal watched the painters complete one lifeboat and shift their dropcloths to the next. He once had seen blueprints for rapid conversion of the *Normandie* into an aircraft carrier. The revamping would be extensive, and drastic. Less time and work would be required to remodel her into a fast transport, but ultimately the results would be just as damaging. The *Normandie* was built on the metric system. The Americans would have no facilities to service and repair her machinery and equipment. It would have to be replaced.

"I'd hate to see that," he said.

Zanger nodded. "It is a terrible thing to contemplate." He looked up at the forward stack, the sky. His voice trembled with emotion. "But what other hope is there for her to survive?"

He turned abruptly and walked rapidly aft. Just before he disappeared behind the freshly painted lifeboat, he reached into his jacket pocket and pulled out a white handkerchief.

Raynal lingered for a while at the rail of the promenade. Facing forward, he watched the constant stream of traffic on the West Side Highway. He dreaded the return to his cabin and the report still to be written.

Captain Zanger had provided him with a new thought. Never before had he considered the possibility that the only salvation of the *Normandie* might lie in her confiscation by the Americans. He had been so concerned with her gradual decay during the past two years that he had not looked forward to the probable results of far longer idleness.

Zanger was right. After five years of continued inactivity, the *Normandie* would require renovation so extensive that the costs might be prohibitive. After ten years, she would be beyond restoration as a first-class passenger ship.

Conversion to an aircraft carrier or transport would bring the long-needed repairs. A return to sea would send oil circulating through her machinery again, remove the tarnish from the coils of her turboalternators. A crew of a thousand experienced men again would keep her in top condition.

The price would be great. Some changes in her design would be irreversible.

Any hope of eventual return to her original grandeur would depend on the amount of care put into her conversion.

Raynal lit his pipe and stood at the rail, watching the

gulls sweep low along the water as they searched for offal pushed into the slip by the tide. A group of workmen hurried by on Twelfth Avenue, headed in the direction of the taverns on Eleventh. Three Coast Guardsmen left the ship and walked toward Times Square. Two lovers stood on the stringpiece, their arms around each other, gazing up at the ship.

Something about the man was familiar. Raynal removed the pipe from his mouth and stared, certain he had seen the man several times, walking along the near side of the avenue, covertly but intently studying the *Normandie*.

Raynal lingered at the rail and watched the couple, curious about the fact that the man obviously was giving more of his attention to the ship than to the lovely woman at his side.

Moving with controlled casualness, Raynal walked up the ladder to the bridge. Inside, he uncovered the powerful ship's binoculars, adjusted the lenses for short range, then trained them on the couple.

The woman was remarkably pretty. But Raynal scarcely noticed.

He was intently studying the man, carefully noting his every feature before going below to phone the information to the FBI.

11

Pier 88, New York City

Von Beck stood with his arms about Rachael, monitoring movement on the *Normandie*. A single Coast Guardsman walked the fo'c's'le, his rifle slung at his right shoulder. Farther aft, a ship's officer leaned against the forward promenade railing. He was looking in Von Beck's direction. Behind the officer, crewmen were painting a lifeboat. The only other visible activity was at a cargo door on the port side aft, where a lighter was delivering supplies. From so close to the bow, Von Beck could not see into the opening in the ship's side.

"Let's walk over to the Cunard pier," he said. "I want to study her from that angle."

Rachael did not answer, but responded to his light touch. He was uncomfortably distracted by her nearness, the feel of her movement inside his arm, the faint hint of her perfume.

The day was amazingly warm for early December. The newspapers had termed the late Indian summer a phenomenon. Misled by the false spring, trees were budding in Central Park.

They reached the head of the Cunard pier, where the *Queen Mary* had moored in normal times. "This is far enough," he said.

Across the narrow strip of empty water, the *Normandie* towered over them, her canvas-draped funnels and masts soaring to the sky. From this perspective, they could see the full length of her, from the outward curve of the bow to the third-class passenger promenade deck on the fantail, more than three hundred meters away. At the cargo hatch, the lighter was using a small boom to swing a load of supplies through the opening. Inside the ship, three men maneuvered the load to a soft landing on cargo mats. Von Beck was curious about the procedure. He assumed that all work inside the ship was being done by the ship's crew, and that no men from the supply vessel were allowed on board.

He had to be certain.

"Let's stand here for a few minutes, as if we're talking," he said.

With Rachael at his side he did not feel so conspicuous. Nothing seemed more natural than two lovers spending an afternoon poking around the waterfront. Earlier, when he had made brief visits to the piers alone, he had felt that the guards on the docks, the seamen on the decks of the *Normandie* had watched his every move.

Now, no one seemed to be giving them a second glance.

"Oh, look!" Rachael said in dismay. "The Winter Garden is gone."

Von Beck grunted an acknowledgment. The glass-enclosed greenhouse under the bridge would have demanded far more attention than could be provided by a skeleton crew. He wondered what other functions of the ship had been closed down.

He recalled the routine for a ship undergoing extensive repairs in drydock. Even then, with the ship surrendered to the care of the contractors, a full quarter of the ship's crew remained aboard. He could not imagine life aboard a ship as large as the *Normandie* with only a few more than a hundred crewmen to assume all responsibilities. If he were in command, he would shut down all boilers except for the bare minimum needed for lights, ventilators, and pressure in the ship's water mains. He would severely limit access to the ship, and maintain extremely tight security, allowing no one on board not well known to every member of the crew. He would limit shore liberty each evening to a third of the crew, with at least a third on watch at all times. His chief concern would be the cavernous spaces below decks, where fire or mischief might get a good headway before discovery. To prevent this, he would establish elaborate fire patrols throughout the ship, covering every companion-way, each compartment, at least hourly.

The French Line was known for a high degree of competence among its commanding officers. Von Beck could assume that all this had been done. And that assumption severely limited his own options.

He was resigned now to the probability that he would have to use a chain of explosives below the waterline, in the hope of capsizing her at the pier. The odds were long against success for such a plan. He would explore every possibility before committing himself.

As he monitored the work aboard the supply lighter, Von Beck saw movement in his peripheral vision. The officer on the promenade deck had moved up to the bridge. He was now inside the glass-enclosed wheel house, and was peering through the giant, pedestal-mounted binoculars. He seemed to be watching them.

"Say something," Von Beck said to Rachael. "Just talk. It doesn't matter what you say."

She grasped the situation instantly. Turning to face him, she began random chatter while he continued to watch the lighter operation. He was careful never to look directly at the officer on the bridge. But by glancing occasionally in that direction, he could see that the officer was still gazing intently through the binoculars. Although Von Beck was preoccupied with the loading procedure and the danger posed by the nosy officer, the meaning of Rachael's words came through to him.

"When I first came to America with my friend, our room was up there on the Promenade Deck, starboard side, just in front of the entrance hall," she said. "On the return trip, we asked for the same room, and managed to get it. We had special permission from the captain to go into the theater to practice on the piano, any time the theater wasn't in use. And I'll never forget. From the theater stage, it seems as if you can see all the way through the ship—past the Upper Entrance Hall, the Vestibule, the Grand Salon, the Smoking Room, and up the Grand Staircase to the Grill Room on the Boat Deck."

Von Beck also remembered the much-celebrated vista— more than half the length of the ship. No other vessel afloat could boast such immense open interiors.

He allowed Rachael to continue her description while he watched the loading, the officer. Although she had told him of her crossings on the *Normandie,* he had not mentioned that he also had been aboard the ship, that he had studied the ship extensively. He had told her nothing of his background.

"The Dining Room is beyond belief," she went on. "Never in my whole life have I seen anything so elegant, all crystal and hammered glass. The ceiling of the Dining Room is three decks high. It's one of the biggest, and certainly the most magnificent, rooms I've ever seen. But I think my favorite is the Grand Salon, with its murals, etched in glass. They reach almost to the ceiling."

Von Beck remembered. The murals depicted the history of navigation.

"From there, if the huge doors are open, you can see into the Smoking Room and its murals of lacquered gold bas-relief. They're Egyptian hunting scenes, for some reason I've never understood. The furnishings are morocco leather, and the carpets a lovely shade of blue. . . ."

The lighter had completed its off-loading. As it moved away from the ship, the big cargo door was winched shut.

It fitted so tightly that its outline could no longer be discerned from the pierhead.

As Von Beck had suspected, no crewman from the lighter had been permitted aboard the ship.

"The cuisine is absolutely the best in the world," Rachael went on. "I don't know how they do it, with that huge dining room, so many people. . . ."

Von Beck casually glanced to his left, far enough to see that the ship's officer had vanished from the bridge. His sudden disappearance was strangely disturbing. Von Beck interrupted Rachael by encircling her waist with his arm.

"Let's walk away, slowly," he said. "We've been here too long. I think that man was suspicious."

They crossed Twelfth Avenue under the overhead highway, walking like two casual tourists with an afternoon to kill. They strolled all the way back to Times Square without speaking.

Rachael seemed to be under a pall of memories, cast by her own long monologue.

Von Beck remained engrossed in his elaborate plan to sink the *Normandie*.

Some aspects were in his favor. In general, security along the docks was far more lax than he had anticipated. The chief danger lay in some careless mistake, an exceptionally observant sentry or crewman.

He probably would be able to work underwater, along the pier, undetected. A series of shaped charges attached to the outer hull would blast holes large enough for a number of compartments to be flooded almost instantly. If these compartments were carefully selected, the *Normandie* might be made to capsize at her pier before her crew could counterflood.

The high center of gravity he had discovered back in Berlin might be her fatal weakness.

They dined that evening in a quiet French restaurant on East Fifty-second Street. Von Beck remembered the place fondly. His father had taken him there many times. But the decor had changed, and he recognized none of the staff. Not trusting his limited French to hide his Germanic inflections, he ordered in English.

Rachael remained quiet and withdrawn. Von Beck made jokes and talked of other things, for their table was totally lacking in privacy.

But as soon as they returned to the apartment, he tried to learn what was weighing so heavily on her mind.

"Everything," she said. "The war, the way things are."

"Anything specific?" he prodded gently. "If it has to do with the operation, I must know. We both have to be totally committed."

She looked at him for a moment before replying. "There are other ships," she said hesitantly. "Why does it have to be the *Normandie?*"

Von Beck remembered that he more or less had asked the same question. He felt that Rachael deserved an answer.

"The *Normandie* belongs to the Reich, under any interpretation of international law," he explained. "The Americans have refused to give her up. The high command believes she eventually will be turned over to the British, to be used against us. We can't permit that to happen."

Her next words came in a burst of self-righteous anger. "I just don't understand how anything so beautiful could be so important in war."

He gave her the logic he had been feeding himself.

"Rachael, the *Normandie* will be destroyed as a thing of beauty, no matter what we do. When she's converted to war use—and that's inevitable—she'll be stripped. You wouldn't recognize her. All the hammered glass and crystal in the Dining Room, all the carpets, the furnishings, the murals, the artwork, everything will be removed. They'll hollow her out to the bulkheads. They'll install tiers of bunks. She'll become a floating dormitory. If they convert her to an aircraft carrier, there'll be even more damage. She'll never be the same again.''

"That's an atrocity!'' she said.

Again, he could not allow her to know how totally he agreed. But he gave away more than he intended.

"War itself is the atrocity,'' he said. "We are only pawns. In time, you get used to it.''

Little by little, Von Beck developed more confidence in Rachael. She was an effective cover. She lacked the guile one would expect in a spy. Her deceptively childish appearance, her unflagging directness raised her above suspicion.

After dinner one evening, as they dawdled over coffee, he carefully explained exactly what he wanted her to do.

"The Irish Republicans have promised the Reich that they will furnish the explosives for missions such as this in America. We must make contact with them, set up meetings, make all necessary arrangements. I think you'd arouse far less suspicion than I in making the initial contact.''

She listened without comment.

He hesitated, wondering how much to tell her. "I'm concerned that the Irish may want to participate in the job itself. We've heard that they have their own plan to destroy the *Normandie,* to prevent her being turned over to the British. If necessary, we may even hint that we will work with them. But our orders from Canaris are specific. We're not to bring them into it. They're too volatile, too emotional. We must keep them out of the actual operation.''

She nodded her understanding. "When will I go?'' she asked.

"Tomorrow. We'll have to move fast. Conditions could change any day now.''

He gave her four names, along with the last addresses known to Abwehr. He watched her as she wrote them down. She spent several minutes memorizing them, then burned the list.

The way she rigidly followed Abwehr procedure like an obedient schoolgirl never ceased to amuse him.

That night he heard her moving about in her room. Once he thought he heard her crying. The next morning, distraught and sleepless, she emerged to face him.

"I don't think I can do it," she said. "I can't be responsible for the destruction of that ship."

His surprise was total. He was thoroughly shaken, but he could not allow her to see that.

He stood staring at her while he decided what tack to take. His silence pushed her into an explanation.

"It was bad enough before," she said. "I didn't fool myself about the coastal watch reports. I knew they probably cost people their lives. But that is a part of war. If I didn't do the work, someone else would." She shook her head. "I can't fool myself about this. It's just you and I, and that ship! We alone would be responsible. I can't shift the blame to anyone else."

He was furious with himself for involving her in the project. He had suspected from the first that she was a much more complex person than she appeared on the surface. And now she knew too much about the plan. He could not simply walk away from her.

She sank into a chair by the breakfast table and lowered her head into her hands. She seemed pathetically small and defenseless. But he knew what he had to do.

He reached down, seized her wrists, and forced her to look up at him. "Don't talk that way," he said. "Don't even think that way. Think of yourself. Think of me! Think of what I would have to do—to you—if you jeopardized our mission." He shook her in rhythm to his words, knowing he was hurting her. "Please, please don't make me do it."

She sat staring up at him. Blood drained from her face. The moment of silence lengthened.

"You would do that?" she whispered.

He met her gaze, hoping he was managing to convey some of the anguish he felt.

"I would *have* to do it," he said.

In an instant she again became the frightened child he had encountered on that first day. He felt her arms tremble.

He released her wrists and sat down facing her. "Rachael, get this through your head and don't forget it. We're locked into this together. And you must understand one thing: What we ourselves feel has nothing to do with it."

She was looking at him, her eyes wide with a new understanding. "Pawns," she said, remembering what he had said earlier. To his surprise, she gave him a rueful smile. "You're right, of course. I really have no choice. I'll go and make the arrangements. I'll do what you expect of me."

Without answering, he rose from the table and turned his back. He pretended to work with the coffee pot until he again had his emotions under control. She watched as he poured the coffee. He placed a cup in front of her. He then made toast and brought it to the table.

"It's just that the *Normandie* means so much to me," Rachael said. "All the memories of the good times I had aboard her, the people so happy—dancing, dining, playing games. They lived as if they never knew a single care. Somehow, I feel we will be destroying all that."

He reached to take her hand. "Listen to me, Rachael," he said. "That way of life has disappeared from the face of the earth, perhaps forever. Nothing we do will bring it back."

Rachael left the apartment shattered to the core of her being, overwhelmed by the variety of conflicting emotions sweeping through her. She was frightened, shocked, and hurt. But most of all she was angry at herself for her naiveté. Always, she wanted to see the good in people. For

216

some reason she did not understand, she forever remained blind to their worst side.

Von Beck had made a fool of her. She cringed to think that she had been on the verge of confiding in him about her nest egg of unmounted diamonds, her plan to rescue her family—and to ask his advice on the best way to proceed.

Von Beck had just reminded her of something she had chosen to ignore. He was the enemy.

She had allowed herself to be misled by his manners, his gentle, understanding ways. He had seemed so sensitive to her fear when he arrived, and made every effort to put her at ease. She had been beguiled by his aristocratic bearing and quiet dignity, his considerate gestures. She had even begun to find comfort in his presence in the apartment.

He had lived up to his promises. He had never intruded on her privacy, spending most of his time in his curtained-off corner, calculating with a slide rule, filling page after page with figures.

He had always been exceptionally polite and thoughtful. He had observed that she had a weakness for little cones of Hershey's chocolate wrapped in tinfoil. Once, returning to the apartment, he brought her a bag of the candy, handing it to her in silence, with only a wisp of a smile.

And he had a soft, wry humor she found appealing. Yet, he was reticent. She knew absolutely nothing about his background, other than what she could derive from his speech and bearing. He spoke the *Hochdeutsche* of educated Germans. His English was unmistakably American, but devoid of regional inflections. His French was fluent; only an occasional guttural consonant hinted his native language.

She had known he had a dark side. But in her ignorance, she had imbued his silent moods with romance and mystery.

During the last few weeks, the curtain in his corner had been drawn less and less. Repeatedly, she had seen him

217

break off with his calculations, sigh, and stare at the wall, lost in some private anguish he would not share.

She often spent idle moments wondering about him, doting on the way he held his pipe when absorbed in thought, the firm, full curve of his mouth when he sought some elusive answer to his mathematical computations, the way the shade of blue in his eyes altered in certain light.

More and more, she had found herself excited by his nearness, his clean, strong, quiet, confident maleness. She had known she was falling in love with him. And, imbecile that she was, she had believed that he had shared her feelings.

Now, in so many words, he had just told her that if she did not obey him to the letter, he would have no qualms about killing her for the glory of Nazi Germany.

How could she have been such a fool?

Rachael soon found that the addresses from the Abwehr files were outdated. Moreover, the Irish Republicans were an elusive, nomadic bunch. She spent three days searching in Yorkville before she managed to contact William O'Neill, leader of the group, through an intermediary.

O'Neill was cautious. Two more exchanges of *bona fides* through third parties were required before O'Neill would agree to a meeting. He insisted on a casual encounter at Grand Central Station, in the corner near the passageway to the Biltmore Hotel.

Von Beck and Rachael arrived a few minutes early. They stood facing the concourse, watching the commuters scurrying to catch trains. Von Beck held a folded edition of the *Times*. A tall, husky blond man passed them twice before returning a third time, his own newspaper showing, folded to the code page.

He walked close so he would not have to raise his voice over the noise of the station. "I'm O'Neill," he said to Von Beck. "You have some business with me?"

Von Beck measured him a moment before answering. "I hope we can do business," he said. "I'm Walter Beck."

They did not shake hands. Both were completely preoccupied with their battle of wits. Rachael was ignored.

"What can I do for you?" O'Neill asked.

He was even taller than Von Beck, with pale blue eyes and thinning blond hair combed straight back. His complexion was ruddy, his skin rough and flaked. His suit was light gray, rumpled, and ill-fitting. The pattern of his green tie was marred by what looked like a small catsup stain. He faced Von Beck with hands on hips, his feet widespread.

Von Beck spoke softly. "I need explosives. Plastique C-Four."

O'Neill's eyebrows raised in amusement. "Well now! How much you need?"

Von Beck did not hesitate. "At least six boxes."

O'Neill laughed. "You're dreaming. I haven't seen more than a half dozen blocks of C-4 since I've been in America."

The discussion was interrupted by two middle-aged couples heading for the hotel, a redcap wheeling their luggage on a handcart. O'Neill waited until they were out of earshot.

"And what would you be wanting with so much explosive? Six cases would bring down this station."

"That's my business," Von Beck said.

They stared at each other for a long moment.

"Let's understand one thing," O'Neill said. "You have come to me, asking me to commit a criminal act. The authorities would welcome that information. In other words, I'm in control of this situation. Do you understand me?"

Von Beck watched the concourse while he considered the matter. At last, he turned back to O'Neill.

"It will be used to sink the *Normandie*," he said.

O'Neill laughed—a braying hoot. He glanced at Rachael to include her in the joke. "My boys have been trying to do that for some time now."

"So we've heard," Von Beck said. "And the *Normandie* is still afloat. That's why I was sent over here. The job must be done. It can't be botched."

"My boys don't botch jobs," O'Neill said evenly.

"Listen to me," Von Beck said. "I was sent personally by the Führer to sink the *Normandie*. I will have your cooperation."

O'Neill stared at Von Beck, his mouth slightly open. Rachael was certain her own reaction was no less obvious. Von Beck had made no mention of direct orders from Hitler.

Von Beck's flat, detached manner left no doubt he was telling the truth. He continued in the same indifferent tone. "Surely I needn't point out that if you give us your cooperation on this, the Führer later will give special consideration to your own cause."

O'Neill recovered. He gave Von Beck a slight shrug. "I can't promise anything."

"I'll be expecting results in a few days," Von Beck said. "Rachael will contact you."

Von Beck remained silent and glum for hours after the meeting. He returned to his corner of the room and stared at his figures. He did not reveal his thoughts until late in the evening.

"It's too late—too much risk—to find another source of supply," he said. "I wish we didn't have to depend on O'Neill. I don't trust him. But I see no alternative. We'll proceed on the assumption that he will deliver. If he doesn't, we'll try to establish another contact."

On each of the next four days, Rachael accompanied Von Beck to the docks during the noon hour. They strolled close to the Cunard and French Line piers while Von Beck studied the pilings, the lay of the ship.

During the mornings and afternoons, they bought and assembled the gear Von Beck would need—a diving suit from a salvage yard, hooks, ropes, diving weights, suction cups, flexible rubber hose, a hand-driven portable air pump.

Under an assumed name, Von Beck leased warehouse space on the top floor of a building on Eleventh Avenue, only two blocks from the superpiers. He explained to the rental agents that he needed a place to store antique furniture. He paid cash for a six-month lease, and no questions were asked.

By the end of the week, they had completed the purchases, and stored them in the warehouse.

On Saturday, O'Neill sent word that he could deliver the C-4 the following Monday. Von Beck considered the price outrageous, but he gave Rachael the money and sent her to close the deal.

That night, Von Beck took her to dinner at the French restaurant. Throughout the evening he was so pleasant that she sometimes had difficulty remembering that only a few days before, he had threatened to kill her.

On Sunday, they slept until almost noon. After a late breakfast, Rachael worked on a coded letter while Von Beck drew a painstaking diagram of the *Normandie,* pinpointing the exact location where he would attach a charge of C-4, and the relationship of each charge to the adjoining piles along the pier. He became so engrossed that he did not go out for the Sunday papers until midafternoon. When he returned, his face was ashen. He sank into his chair and stared at the diagrams.

Rachael thought he was ill. She felt a rush of concern. "What's wrong?" she asked.

"The man at the newsstand had a radio," he said. "I heard it with my own ears." He looked up at her. His voice was drained of emotion. "The Japanese have bombed Pearl Harbor," he said. "America is in the war."

Rachael knew that Von Beck's thoughts were of the *Normandie,* of his plans that probably would have to be revised.

But for her, the news had another, far more personal meaning.

The bombs at Pearl Harbor had destroyed the last chance she had of bringing her family to America.

She would have to contact Hillel Goldman immediately and make new arrangements. Her only hope now lay in getting her family into some neutral country.

Until then, she would have to give Von Beck and the Nazis her full cooperation.

12

Foley Square, New York City

By early evening, FBI headquarters at the Federal Building in Foley Square had settled into a model of efficient, highly organized bedlam. Within minutes of the news from Pearl Harbor, machinery had been set in motion to summon all Special Agents, stenographers, file clerks, switchboard operators, and building guards. Downstairs, security was now tight. The entire building was off-limits to the public. No one, not even the federal judges, were admitted without proper identification.

The long-rumored, long-secret war plans were put into effect. More than a hundred Special Agents received previously prepared orders dispatching them throughout the city to arrest all known and suspected Japanese sympathizers.

Bonham and Marcus drew telephone duty, recording and evaluating the hundreds of frantic tips pouring in from alarmed, concerned, and suspicious citizens.

Bonham had not stopped for a late lunch after receiving his summons. He now was hungry, and there seemed to be no relief in sight. The telephone switchboard remained a

223

solid array of tiny red lights. There was no way to know how many more callers were attempting to get through.

The nut ratio was high. But even as he logged the calls, Bonham groaned inwardly at the number that expressed potentially valid suspicions and would merit further investigation.

A real estate broker reported that the owners of Japanese restaurants had not been renewing their licenses during the last few months. He suggested that perhaps they had known of the impending attack. Bonham recorded the details and promised that the information would be given proper attention. An elderly woman phoned from her Park Avenue apartment to whisper that her houseboy was Japanese. She had caught him several times speaking in a foreign language over the phone. She said he was a barbarian, and ate his fish raw. She was now alone in the apartment with him, and scared to death. Bonham wrote down her address and promised that an agent would be out within a few hours to take her resident Jap into custody.

From Newark, an hysterical woman sobbed out her story. Her husband had been dragged off a train and taken to jail by a group of men who claimed to be with the Newark Police Department. Bonham checked, then phoned the woman back to report that Newark police had indeed been ordered to board all trains and interstate buses and to take into custody all persons of Japanese descent. The woman explained that her husband was not Japanese. Bonham again phoned the Newark Police Department to inform them that one of the suspicious Orientals they now had in custody might possibly be Chinese and, he reminded them, an ally in the war against Japan.

As Bonham worked, bulletins fresh off the teletype were laid on his desk to keep him informed. In this way he learned that Mayor La Guardia had heard the news about Pearl Harbor in his home at 1274 Fifth Avenue and immediately summoned commissioners into an emergency meeting at City Hall, where a blizzard of edicts had just been released. The mayor had announced over the radio that all Japanese nationals were to remain in their homes pending determination of their status by federal authorities. He ordered the Nippon Club at 161 West Ninety-third Street, as well as all other places where Japanese congregated, closed and padlocked by police. He said diners in Japanese restaurants could finish their meals, then the establishments were to be closed until further notice. He also ordered armed guards posted at all waterfront facilities, power plants, public utility sites, armories, bridges, tunnels, water supply sources, shipyards, aviation fields, piers, and defense plants.

Police Commissioner Valentine issued instructions that all officers on duty were to inform every U.S. serviceman that he was to return immediately to his ship, post, or station, that all military leaves and passes were canceled. Within minutes, further bulletins informed Bonham that Grand Central, Penn Station, all subway and bus terminals were jammed by military personnel. He also was advised that Greater New York service station employees had voluntarily ended their week-old strike, and had resumed work to assist military men in returning to their posts.

Now, in these early evening hours, the flow of Japanese suspects began arriving at headquarters—a mere trickle at first, then a flood. The Japanese, with reactions varying from stark fear to vocal amusement, were taken, one by one, into the bullpens for thorough interrogation. Stenographers recorded all questions and answers in shorthand.

After interrogation, each suspect's statement was compared with existing material in the FBI files. All information was then assembled and accompanied the suspect to Ellis Island.

Flanked at the telephone desk by other first-year men, Bonham could hardly hear the incoming calls above the din around him.

Most of the tips probably would be ignored. Bonham alone recorded the specific locations of more than a hundred suspicious radio aerials sighted by alert citizens. But occasionally, the calls were disturbing. One man phoned to report that he was of Japanese descent, and had practiced law in the courts of New York State for twenty-two years. He asked, in a calm, reasonable voice, for Mayor La Guardia's legal premise for suspending the constitutional guarantees of American citizens. Bonham pointed out that La Guardia was not only mayor of New York City, but also national director of Civilian Defense, and that he was operating within the guidelines established with the full support of Congress and the President. Bonham further pointed out that the President was scheduled to go before Congress the following day to request a formal declaration of war and, no doubt, extraordinary wartime emergency powers.

The Japanese suspect did not argue. "My father always said that every man has a tendency to become what he hates," he said. "I confess I didn't know what my father meant, until now."

At 9 P.M., Bonham, Marcus, and six other first-year men were relieved from telephone duty. Bullethead had prepared a stack of assignments for them.

"Read this directive," he said, handing out copies to be passed around. "And follow it to the fucking letter. Get going."

Bonham hurried through the lengthy directive, digesting its main points. The text was couched in the usual governmental gibberish.

Marcus struggled to make sense of the convoluted prose. "I thought wars were simple," he whispered to Bonham. "This one's already getting too complicated for me."

The assignment sheet decreed that Bonham and Marcus would constitute a team. They were to rendezvous at Sixth Avenue and Fifty-ninth Street with a detective from the New York City Police Department, and proceed to arrest various designated individuals known to be of Japanese descent, and suspected of Japanese sympathies.

The crowd jamming into Times Square had stalled crosstown traffic. Bonham and Marcus sat at Sixth Avenue and Forty-second waiting for a harried policeman to clear the intersection.

"I thought of every way it might come," Marcus said. "But I never thought it'd be like this."

Bonham watched the stream of demonstrators shouting and yelling as they crossed the street in front of them. Many were waving American flags. The din of car horns penetrated their government Ford.

Bonham had not yet had time to think about the meaning of the war. "One thing for sure," he said. "Nothing will ever be the same again."

He saw a chance to slip through the cross-traffic against the light. Nudging the car forward, he held his badge out the window and eased through the pedestrians. Someone thumped a rear fender and yelled an obscenity. The policeman spotted the government plates, stopped traffic, and waved them on.

A few minutes later, they found Detective McMullan waiting in a police car at Fifty-ninth Street. Bald and rotund, with a loud, raspy voice, McMullan introduced himself, shook hands, and climbed into the back seat of the car.

"I'd 'bout given up on you guys," he said. "I've been waiting a fucking half hour."

He was smoking a big cigar that smelled as if he had found it in a dog kennel. Marcus rolled his eyes at Bonham, and pointedly lowered his window.

"I know this town like the back of my hand," the detective said. "Where you guys wanna go?"

The first subject on their list was a Japanese physician, residing on East Sixty-eighth. The doctor's wife answered the door, bowed, and stepped back to allow them to enter. The foyer and living room were decorated with Oriental screens, lacquered wood, and painted vases.

After a moment, the doctor came into the room and greeted them without a trace of accent. He was of short stature, with a stocky build and close-cropped, iron-gray hair.

"Gentlemen, I've been expecting you," he said. "I heard the speech by our illustrious mayor. And since I'm a founding member of the Nippon Club, I assumed I would be one of the first arrested. What's the procedure?"

Marcus glanced at Bonham, then answered. "You may bring a small suitcase. It's recommended you include only traveling essentials."

The doctor nodded. "This is absolutely ridiculous, you know. I've practiced medicine in New York City for fifteen years. I'm a graduate of New York University, class of twenty-two. Surely you can check that. I haven't been back to Japan since my mother died in nineteen-seventeen."

"We have our orders, sir," Marcus said.

"Of course," the doctor said. He nodded to his wife. She disappeared into a bedroom.

The doctor glanced after her, then spoke quietly. "How long will I be gone?"

Marcus seemed at a loss for words.

"We don't know, sir," Bonham said. "We're just here to take you into custody."

Detective McMullan had been standing in the middle of the room, stinking up the apartment. He now moved toward the bedroom door, keeping the Japanese woman in sight. The doctor walked to a hall closet for his suit coat and overcoat.

The doctor's wife returned a few minutes later with a small, smooth-leather suitcase. While Marcus frisked the doctor, Bonham placed the suitcase on the back of a chair, opened it, and glanced briefly through its contents. The doctor was taking two extra white shirts, one pair of pajamas, socks, and underwear. Bonham lifted out a travel case and checked its contents. He returned it and closed the suitcase. He remembered that a safety razor was permitted.

"Let's go," he said.

The doctor kissed his wife good-bye. Her hands trembled as she reached to touch his cheek, but her face remained impassive.

They drove the doctor to the station house, where Detective McMullan booked him as "a prisoner of the federal authorities." The doctor then was placed in the holding tank.

During the next four hours, Bonham, Marcus, and McMullan made five more arrests—a silk importer, the president of a Japanese bank, a broker, an insurance man, and a merchant who specialized in fine lace.

Bonham and Marcus then said good-bye to McMullan and requisitioned a van. They hauled their catch to Foley Square, marching their prisoners past the cordon of security guards downstairs.

By the time they arrived in the FBI offices, the procedure had settled into a fine-tuned routine. A team of interrogators took each subject into a small room and put him through the paces—his place of birth, date of entry into this country, close associates of Japanese ancestry, the names of his relatives still residing in Japan, and a battery of questions designed to determine his true loyalty.

The interrogations lasted the better part of an hour. Bonham and Marcus waited.

When the subjects returned, they again were loaded into the van. Bonham and Marcus drove them down to the Barge Office in the Battery. Bonham was startled to see the building surrounded by Coast Guardsmen in leggings, carrying rifles with fixed bayonets. The Japanese were marched onto a waiting ferry. At Ellis Island, Bonham and Marcus signed them over to the Immigration and Naturalization Service.

Dawn was breaking as they rode the ferry back to the

Battery, the sun lighting the tops of Manhattan's sky-scrapers.

Marcus sprawled on a ferry bench. "I don't understand it," he said. "We've processed these people through the city jail, FBI, Coast Guard, and Immigration. Why?"

"Elementary law," Bonham pointed out. "Broadens the base of responsibility. With everybody in charge, nobody's in charge."

They rode for a time, watching the phenomenal view as the sunlight spread to encompass the whole of Manhattan Island. Marcus looked at Bonham.

"Shack, I don't know whether you realize it or not, but this is your golden opportunity. With all this confusion, you can blow the whistle on your spy and let things take their course. You'll be off the hook."

Bonham shook his head. "They can bring in half the country, and I don't give a damn," he said. "But that one's *my* spy—if I can find her."

The roundup continued through Monday. After a few hours of sleep, Bonham and Marcus joined another city detective for the procedure that quickly became routine—apprehending subjects, booking them into station houses, taking them to Foley Square for interrogation, then transporting them to Ellis Island.

On that second day of the war, as President Roosevelt went before Congress to request a formal declaration, the FBI net was enlarged to include suspected German and Italian sympathizers.

That afternoon, the President revealed that the toll of dead at Pearl Harbor might exceed 1,500.

On Monday night, hostile aircraft were reported over blacked-out San Francisco. The planes were tracked over the bay before they turned southward, then headed back out to sea. The theory was voiced that when San Francisco radio stations went off the air at the time of the warning, the pilots became confused and could not find their targets.

New York's first air raid warning came at 1:30 P.M. Tuesday. More than a million children were released from their schools and told to go home.

The all-clear came seventeen minutes later.

A second warning was sounded at 2:02 after a wave of several hundred enemy planes was reported approaching New York from the Atlantic. Families were evacuated from Mitchel Field. Air raid wardens and police made a futile effort to evacuate Times Square, where a large crowd remained glued to the lighted bulletins.

In the skyscrapers, where warnings were posted that everyone was to avoid windows during air raids, office workers could be seen peering at the sky, watching for enemy planes. A wave of selling swept Wall Street and continued until the all-clear thirty-nine minutes later. Work in the shipyards was halted for four hours.

Most New Yorkers emerged from the experience more bewildered than alarmed. A battle of recriminations erupted between the Army and the Civil Defense over the validity of the reports. Visiting Britons were horrified that with enemy planes believed to be approaching, schoolchildren had been sent out into the streets. Mayor La Guardia said the practice would be stopped.

Bonham and Marcus continued their work through the air raid warnings, bringing in another twelve aliens to add to the totals reported by the New York office—205 Japanese, 105 Germans, and 54 Italians.

On the Pacific Coast, the military searched for the aircraft carrier that had launched the Monday night raid on San Francisco.

Tuesday night, enemy planes were reported over Los Angeles.

New York's third air raid warning came Wednesday morning as thousands of office workers poured out of the subways and buses and onto the streets. After the earlier false warning, the public calm now bordered on indifference. With an occasional glance at the sky, commuters scurried on to work, accepting the air raid alert as one more

231

irritation to life in the city. The all-clear did not come until 9:01, when the approaching planes were identified as an unscheduled U.S. Navy patrol.

An argument erupted among officials over the potential danger. Some military spokesmen argued that the width of the Atlantic would protect New York City from air raids.

William L. Shirer, deemed the outstanding authority on the war by virtue of his best-selling *Berlin Diary*, pointed out that the German Heinkel III bomber was perfectly capable of crossing the Atlantic to bomb New York.

Shirer said he fully expected several nuisance air raids on New York City, each consisting of about 150 planes. His opinion was widely quoted in the newspapers and on radio.

On Wednesday, windows of the Museum of Modern Art and many major stores were taped. All large buildings in the city issued directives to tenants on what to do in case of an air raid.

Working through the confusion, Bonham and Marcus brought in 16 more aliens as the count in Foley Square rose to 256 Japanese, 139 Germans, and 66 Italians.

That night, the Japanese cherry trees in Washington's Tidal Basin were attacked and severely damaged by patriotic Americans. San Francisco endured another sleepless night of air raid warnings. Los Angeles was blacked out for three hours while an unidentified plane circled over the city.

In the Pacific, Wake and Midway islands were still holding out against superior attacking forces.

On Thursday, Mayor La Guardia flew to the West Coast to direct Civilian Defense efforts. San Francisco had begun extensive sandbagging. A plan for evacuation of the city was reported ready, if needed.

In Los Angeles, more than a hundred persons were injured and one man was killed during a blackout.

New York City announced contingent evacuation plans.

On Ellis Island, several aliens were released after convincing authorities that they were loyal Americans. Others were transferred to Camp Upton, Long Island.

All telephone and cable links overseas were closed.

And, in the early hours of Friday morning, Bonham at last found time to resume his search for Rachael Moser.

Turning back through the major crimes blotter for Greater New York, Bonham found that only two murders, three armed robberies, and a rape had been reported on the afternoon of July tenth.

The armed robberies appeared routine—a jewelry store and two pawn shops. The rape case involved a youth who had dated his victim for several months, and who apparently was carried away by passions of the moment.

One of the murders arose out of a family squabble. The husband made a habit of beating his wife senseless. For once, he fatally misjudged his depth of anger.

The other murder seemed much more interesting.

That evening, Bonham visited the precinct involved and asked for the homicide detective who had handled the case.

"You want Gabrielli," the desk sergeant said. "Up the stairs, second door on the left. Next to the can."

Bonham thanked the sergeant and climbed the well-worn marble steps to the second floor. In the crowded squadroom, the plainclothesman pointed out to him as Gabrielli was on the phone. Bonham used the brief wait to study him.

A large man with dark, deep-set brown eyes and thick black hair combed straight back, Gabrielli had a no-nonsense manner about him. He was giving someone hell over a delayed report from the medical examiner. His huge beefy hand almost covered the receiver cupped to his ear. At last, with a choice bit of profanity, he hung up the phone.

Bonham approached his desk and flashed his credentials.

233

Gabrielli did not bother to stand or to shake hands. He merely pointed Bonham to a chair.

"I want to talk to you about the Frank Pierce murder," Bonham explained.

Gabrielli shook his head in disgust. "I sent you fucking people everything I know."

Bonham winced inwardly. He should have checked the files in Foley Square. "The case conceivably could be connected to something I'm working on," he said. "I'm just here to see if there's anything that was too insignificant to put in the report."

"Nothing," Gabrielli snapped.

Bonham sighed. "I guess what I really want to do is to get your impressions—the type of material you ordinarily don't put into a report."

Gabrielli regarded him warily. "What do you mean?"

"Well, what's your theory of what might have happened?"

Gabrielli thought it over. "One thing, right off the top of my head. It wasn't premeditated. To me, a screwdriver stuck through somebody's heart shows that whoever did it just picked up whatever was handy at the moment."

"Any idea on the motive?"

"Only a guess. Want to hear it?"

"That's what I'm here for."

"With all that radio gear lying around, it had to be the British."

"Who?"

"The fucking British. They're killing people all over town, you know."

"I didn't know," Bonham admitted.

Gabrielli gave him a look. "Shit yes! We had a case last week. Guy found with his neck broke in the basement of his apartment house. It seems he was a sailor selling information on ship movements to some people from the German embassy in Washington. Fucking British *told* us they did it. They knew the government wouldn't let us do a fucking thing about it. Good riddance, everybody said. So forget it. Then they killed a guy right in Times Square. Hit-and-run with a fucking taxi—some Nazi bigwig. Nothing was ever done about it."

"I don't know if my case ties in," Bonham said. "What do buttons ripped off a dress mean to you?"

"You mean *all* the buttons ripped off?"

Bonham nodded.

"The dress come from overseas?"

"I think so."

"Then I think diamonds."

"What?"

"Diamonds. Women cover the diamonds with matching cloth and sew them on as buttons. They used to stick the diamonds in their pussy. Now that's the first place the customs men look."

Bonham left the precinct exhilarated, even though he had little solid information.

Everything fitted into place. The cloth-covered diamond theory was the only thing that made sense.

Early the next morning, he began a systematic search through the diamond district, showing Rachael Moser's photograph to every dealer in diamonds and rare gems.

The hunt lasted for three days.

At the twenty-sixth shop on his list, a gray-haired, prune-faced dealer named Schwartz examined the photograph with more than passing interest.

"Sure! I remember her. Very young woman. Brought in a small but rather elegant stone. Good color, high refraction. What about it?"

"How many times has she been in?"

"Only that once."

"How long ago?"

The dealer thought for a moment. "Four, five weeks ago. Maybe longer. I can examine the records, if you'd like."

"I'd appreciate it," Bonham said. He lowered his voice to a confidential tone. "This is a very important case."

The dealer found the records, but they were of no help. No address was listed.

Bonham left with the dealer's promise to call him if the woman visited him again and, if possible, to delay her until Bonham could get there.

For a time Bonham considered ordering several dozen copies of the photograph and distributing them throughout the diamond district. But after reflection, he abandoned the idea. He reasoned that eventually she would return to the dealer who bought one diamond without complications, rather than risk another dealer.

That night, Bonham told Marcus about the new lead and asked him for assistance in catching the possible incoming phone call.

Marcus groaned. "Goddamn it, Shack, you've already made me into an accessory before the fact. When they tack your ass to the wall, they're not going to give me any medals."

"All you've got to do is take the call if I'm not there, and get the word to me," Bonham explained. "Every day, I'll give you a schedule of where I'll be, from minute to minute. No one will ever know."

Marcus remained reluctant. But he eventually agreed.

With his trap set, Bonham plunged into his assigned work.

The roundup of enemy aliens was virtually completed. Bonham concentrated on clearing the backlog of security investigations on his desk. He resumed his long hours on the job, skipping meals, going for days with a bare minimum of sleep.

Slowly, he gained ground.

Somehow, the work grew easier. Bonham was gradually acquiring the FBI *patois*—an obscure jargon that conveyed meaning far better than extensive detail or explanation. For instance, the simple phrase "neat and clean in his personal habits and generally considered a loyal American" implied that the subject seemed all right to the agent who conducted the interview. The phrase that "this investigation has failed to disclose that the subject is engaged in any activities inimical to the welfare of the United States" simply meant "this thing doesn't seem worth fooling with any further." Bonham learned that the Director doted on such phrases as "the subject maintains a well-kept, orderly house," suggesting that the subject was a typical, patriotic American.

With the rapid changeover from defense contracts to full war production, the workload of Bullethead's security section mushroomed. More new men were coming aboard each week. Soon Bonham and Marcus found themselves regarded as relative veterans. Bullethead was kept so busy with the new men that he no longer had time to harass Bonham. Gradually, as the section grew, Bonham and Marcus began to feel a measure of security.

On a cold, nippy afternoon in late December, Bonham had just conducted his sixth interview of the day. He returned to Foley Square to write his reports. Marcus met him at the door to the squad room.

"Where the fuck you been? I've been calling all over! Schwartz the jeweler left a message. Twenty minutes ago! The girl is there, selling a diamond!"

Bonham didn't say a word.

He slammed his folders into Marcus's chest, turned, and ran out the door, unaware that he almost knocked Bullethead sprawling.

"That's her," Schwartz said. "The one in the brown coat with the fur collar."

Bonham looked through the grill separating Schwartz's office from the public area. Rachael Moser was seated at a small, velvet-covered table, deep in conversation with the lean, elderly man facing her. The man adjusted a telescoping desk light, pulled down his green eyeshade, and squinted through a jeweler's glass at a stone he held with jeweler's tongs.

"She brought in two small diamonds," Schwartz said in Bonham's ear. "I delayed her by saying that if she would wait for our appraiser, we probably could give her a better price. Actually, they're of excellent quality. Good color. High refraction. I've seen very few of that type in recent years."

Bonham paid little attention to Schwartz, or to the transaction taking place less than fifteen feet away. His full concentration was on Rachael Moser.

She was much smaller than he had imagined. Yet she revealed considerable presence and authority as she countered something the elderly man had said.

As she glanced toward the office, Bonham was momentarily disoriented. He had become so familiar with her features that in the flesh she somehow seemed larger than life. She had apparently reached an agreement with the appraiser, for she smiled, nodded, gathered her coat closer, and reached for her purse.

"She gave us an address in the Village," Schwartz said, handing Bonham a slip of paper. He looked at it, then stuffed it into his pocket. The address might be false. He could not gamble on it.

"You can let her go now, anytime you're ready," he said. "I'll follow her out."

He waited in Schwartz's office while the sale was completed. Schwartz filled out the check himself. She tucked it into her purse, thanked both Schwartz and the appraiser, then turned and walked out the front door.

Bonham gave her a fifteen-second head start, then followed, signaling his thanks to Schwartz as he strode through the outer office.

She was on the staircase, almost to the ground floor. Bonham fell in behind her, walking casually, never letting her out of his sight.

They emerged on Forty-seventh Street, between Fifth and Sixth avenues. Without hesitation, Rachael turned toward Fifth. Bonham closed the distance, fascinated by her walk. She took very short steps, her body unnaturally erect and poised, as if balancing a book on her head. He remembered that the manager in Kenmore Hall had mentioned her unusual way of walking.

At the intersection, Rachael headed toward the taxi stand. As she stepped into the front cab, Bonham walked on past and entered the second, flashing his credentials to the driver.

"Just keep that taxi in sight," he said. "I think it's going to St. Luke's Place, But I want to be sure."

Traffic was thin. They made most of the green lights, moving rapidly downtown. When Rachael's cab angled off to the right at Washington Square, her destination became more certain. As her taxi turned onto St. Luke's Place from Seventh Avenue South, Bonham reached forward and tapped his driver on the shoulder.

"You can pull up at the corner," he said. "I'll take it on foot from here."

As he walked around the corner, Rachael was paying her driver. She left the taxi, walked up the steps and into the building.

Bonham walked on across the street, into the small park facing the row of apartment houses, wishing to hell he had a dog. He knew he could not loiter long without attracting attention, but he urgently needed to find some way of setting up surveillance.

The buildings were well protected by trees along the sidewalk. The fronts were uniformly recessed from the street. He would not be able to see the steps to Rachael's apartment house from any other along the street.

He walked on westward to the end of the block and the intersection with Hudson. He stood for a moment at the curb, figuring angles.

Even if he could find a place across Hudson, the line of sight was wrong and the distance too great.

He crossed the street and walked back eastward along the row of apartments toward Seventh Avenue South. He paused to light a cigarette, and examined the front of the red-brick buildings, trying to fathom their interior layouts. He resisted the temptation to walk up one of the marble and wrought-iron steps to examine the mailboxes.

He was approaching Rachael's apartment, uncertain of its exact location, when she emerged, accompanied by a tall, solidly built blond man. The man had his right arm around her, guiding her down the steps.

Surprised, Bonham almost broke stride, but quickly recovered. He slowed, edging toward the curb so they would be down the steps and onto the sidewalk before he reached them.

The maneuver worked. At the foot of the steps, they turned left, toward Seventh Avenue South.

But the man glanced back over his shoulder at Bonham. For a fleeting instant, their eyes met.

He had the look of an outdoorsman—a rancher, oil worker, seaman—with weathered skin, rugged features, and a self-confident stride. His blue eyes were heavily lidded, with a droop at the outside corners that gave him the doleful expression of an old sheep hound. He showed no fear or alarm, only mild curiosity.

Bonham tried to keep his own face expressionless.

The man turned away, and the moment passed.

Shaken, Bonham let them go on ahead. By the time he reached the corner, they were stepping into a taxi.

He did not follow.

Lingering at the curb, he looked back, fixing in his memory the exact location of Rachael's apartment house. He then studied the buildings across Seventh Avenue South.

St. Luke's Place angled into Leroy Street at a triangular block enclosed by Bedford, Carmine, and Seventh. Some of the windows along Seventh Avenue South had possibilities.

He found two apartments for lease. The first offered only a view of the treetops down St. Luke's Place. But the second, a small one-bedroom flat, was better situated. From one corner of the living room, standing against the wall, he could see not only the steps, but the doorway of Rachael's apartment house.

"I'll take it," he told the landlord.

He posted the necessary deposits and signed the lease, instantly elevating his standard of living tenfold. He was unconcerned about the added expense; his spartan way of life had helped him to accumulate a modest bank account.

He spent the remainder of the afternoon moving into the apartment and arranging for utilities and a telephone.

Just before dark, he went into the bedroom and examined the small dresser.

It was of the type that had a large central mirror, flanked by two narrow, hinged mirrors. Bonham shoved it into the living room, against the corner, next to the windows.

He then arranged an overstuffed chair, facing the large mirror. By properly positioning the wings, he had a bank-shot view of the steps and doorway to Rachael's apartment.

Satisfied, he settled down to wait.

Now that he knew where they were holed up, a wealth of possibilities lay before him. They would not be able to make many moves without his knowledge. And when he was ready, he would smoke them out, applying pressure, spooking them into a fatal mistake.

13

Aboard the *Normandie*, Pier 88, New York City

"I think we've found it," Raynal said.

He carefully unlatched the separator ring, aligned the inner and outer races, and extracted a steel ball from the bearing. A quarter of the ball was worn flat.

Raynal laughed and handed the ball to his assistant, Pierre. "A five-year-old mystery solved," he said.

Disassembled parts of the turboalternator lay scattered around the compartment. Raynal dug deeper into the race and removed three more steel balls. All were worn lopsided.

The turboalternator had been emitting a troublesome clicking noise for years—enough to worry about, not serious enough to demand drastic action. But when Raynal ordered the turboalternator put on line two days earlier, the bearing showed signs of overheating. Raynal had decided to make immediate repairs. Engrossed in their work, he and Pierre had continued on through the noon hour. Now, a few minutes after one, Raynal felt a gnawing hunger.

He put a forefinger into the race, trying to determine if

the grooves were scored. He felt a definite roughness and muttered an obscenity. The whole housing would have to be replaced.

Behind him, the wall telephone rang. Designed to be heard over the running machinery, the sound was ear-splitting in the quiet compartment. Pierre moved to answer it.

"For you, Maurice," he said.

Raynal wiped the grease from his hands and took the phone.

Captain Zanger's voice was low and intense. "Maurice? Would you please come up to the Main Entrance Hall immediately? Don't say anything to the crew."

Raynal was instantly alerted by the emotion in Zanger's tone. "What's wrong?" he asked.

"Just come up, please," Zanger said. "I'll explain."

Raynal finished cleaning his hands, rolled down his shirt sleeves, and put on his coat and hat. "Go ahead and disassemble the bearing," he told Pierre. "I'll be back in a few minutes and we'll go to lunch."

He walked forward to the main elevators and punched the button for the Promenade Deck. When the doors opened at the Main Entrance Hall, Captain Zanger was waiting, surrounded by a phalanx of U.S. Coast Guard officers.

"Maurice, this is Captain John S. Baylis, commandant of the New York Coast Guard district. He is taking possession of the *Normandie* in the name of the United States government."

Baylis was tall and resplendent in a dark blue uniform. The visor of his hat was decorated with gold. Stunned, Raynal did not know whether to salute or shake hands. He did neither.

"We are to assemble the men here," Captain Zanger went on. "They will be escorted to their quarters to gather their gear. No one is to be allowed to return to the lower spaces."

Captain Zanger seemed close to tears. He put a hand on

Raynal's shoulder. "Maurice, help me keep the men under control. We don't want any incidents."

After two years of waiting, the shock of the actual seizure of the ship was almost anticlimactic. But the manner of the boarding party seemed ominous.

Raynal looked at Baylis. "Captain, what is the exact status of the crew?"

The Coast Guard captain's answer seemed well-rehearsed. "That's still to be determined," he said. "Officers and crew will be escorted to Ellis Island, where you will be handed over to the U.S. Immigration and Naturalization Serivce. There, disposition will be made on an individual basis."

"And the ship?" Raynal asked. "What's to happen to her?"

"I'm not at liberty to say," Baylis said. "Nor, may I add, is it germane at the moment. Under terms of the seizure, your company and government will be paid restitution. Please assemble your men. We are on a close schedule."

Raynal gave the order, and word was piped throughout the ship that all Transatlantique employees and crewmen were to assemble in the Main Entrance Hall.

Raynal's mind remained numb. He wandered like a sleepwalker among the men as they came up from below. Most were confused, puzzled, and apprehensive. Raynal could think of no words to put them at ease.

Captain Zanger made the announcement of what everyone now knew: The *Normandie* had been seized by the American government. The men were told to gather their gear and reassemble in the Main Entrance Hall.

The crew went below, accompanied by a squad of Coast Guardsmen. Raynal followed. He spent only a few minutes in his room, packing a single suitcase.

When he returned to the Main Entrance Hall, an argument was in progress. Several FBI agents had arrived at the gangplank. They claimed they also had orders to take the crew of the *Normandie* into custody.

244

"My instructions are to turn the crew over to the Immigration and Naturalization Service," Captain Baylis said. "There was no mention of the FBI."

He refused to allow the FBI agents to come on board. Both the Coast Guard and FBI groups dispatched aides to phone Washington and request clarification of their orders.

For the next two hours, Raynal and the crew waited for the matter to be resolved. And with each passing minute, his frustrations grew. He kept thinking of the disassembled turboalternator. At the moment, the uncompleted job seemed to symbolize the plight of the whole ship.

Most of the French crewmen drifted forward into the theater and were venting their anxieties in nervous, boisterous chatter. The Coast Guard officers strolled aft into the Grand Salon, where they stood in small groups.

At last, Raynal could stand the inaction no longer. Marshaling as much military bearing as he could manage, he approached Captain Baylis, who stood in the salon with Captain Zanger. They were surrounded by a large contingent of Coast Guard officers.

Raynal gave Captain Baylis a salute.

"Captain, with all due respect, I am signatory officer for the condition of this ship. I don't question your nation's right to seize her, under the provisions of international law. But, sir, I do protest the method in which it is being done! You have a hundred and fifteen men aboard this ship. I have had the opportunity to work with them during the last eighteen months. Only a handful are qualified to stand the most elementary underway watch. This is an intricate, delicate, complex ship. My men and I know her. As I understand the international situation, we are your allies. I'm sure the crew of the *Normandie* would welcome the opportunity to volunteer their expertise to your cause."

Captain Zanger was looking at the deck, his long, sad face enclosed in silence.

Captain Baylis seemed irritated by Raynal's offer. "Thank you, Captain Raynal. Your suggestion will be taken under advisement. . . ."

For a moment, Raynal's emotions overrode his better judgment. "Without us, you will never get this ship underway," he said.

A flash of anger crossed Captain Baylis's face. "I assure you, Captain Raynal, we have plenty of men in the Navy and Coast Guard capable of taking a ship to sea."

"I'm talking about her conversion, sir," Raynal explained. "What do they plan to do with her?"

Captain Zanger interrupted. "Maurice, please. What the United States plans to do with the ship is beyond our purview."

Raynal spread his hands in appeal. "Gentlemen, there should not be one item of discord among us. We all know ships, the sea. We know what has to be done. Why the secrecy? We all know that plans exist to turn this ship into an aircraft carrier. And I'm telling you that it can't be done. The superstructure is not strong enough. She is too top-heavy. If you'll allow me, I can explain this to your technicians, and save everyone much grief. Any attempt to convert the *Normandie* into an aircraft carrier will destroy her."

Zanger remained silent. Captain Baylis spoke direct to Raynal. "This is neither the time nor place for such speculation," he said. "Any plans that exist for the ship are highly confidential."

Raynal knew he had overstepped. But he could not find it in himself to retreat. "Captain, it's so confidential that any man on board or on the docks can tell you the basic plan. The boiler room intakes would be diverted to a new superstructure to be erected on an island along the starboard side. The Sun Decks and Boat Decks would be stripped away, the Promenade Deck reinforced and extended some distance aft. The Main Dining Room, this hall, the Chapel would be cleared to serve as a hangar deck. It would destroy her!"

"Captain! There's no need to go into all this!" Captain Baylis said.

Raynal ignored him. "She conceivably *could* be turned into a fast transport. But there are certain idiosyncrasies to the ship that cannot be ignored. . . ."

Captain Baylis stared down at his shoes a moment before answering. Then he surprised Raynal with a sympathetic smile. "Captain, I remember how it feels to leave a ship. And I'm sure the qualms are greater in your case—and with justification. But the fact is, I'm aboard to take custody of the ship for the United States Government, and more specifically, the Department of the Navy. I'm only a caretaker. In a few days, I'll be handing her over to someone else. So I'm really not in a position to help you."

"I should talk to someone," Raynal insisted, hearing the note of desperation in his own voice. "There are so many things you should know about the ship. She grounds each day at low tide. The bottom of this slip is not level. Unless the ship is given proper ballast, she takes on a list to port. . . ."

"Knowledgeable shiphandlers will be aboard," Baylis said.

"She is encased in mud," Raynal went on. "She'll have to be scraped. The boilers are in good shape, but it's been two years. . . ." He shook his head in frustration. "There are so many things. There are twenty-nine cats aboard. Who is going to feed them? The fire alarm system is very complex. I've not been able to instruct your young men satisfactorily, because of the language problem. The propeller shafts haven't turned in two years. The main bearings should be taken down. . . ."

Captain Baylis held up a hand. "Captain, I see your point. But there's really nothing I can do. However, I'll put a recommendation in my report, urging strongly that your experience be put to use, if at all possible."

Raynal suddenly felt defeated. His frustration-driven energy was spent. He gave Baylis a salute. "Thank you, Captain," he said. "I can't ask for any more than that."

A young ensign approached from the lounge, saluted,

and handed Captain Baylis a sheet of yellow paper. Baylis glanced at it, then reread it more slowly. He turned to his aides.

"Our position has been clarified," he said. "We are to take control of the ship. The FBI is to take the crew into custody. However, the Coast Guard is responsible for the transportation of the crew to Ellis Island."

Captain Baylis walked to the center of the hall and raised his voice. "The formalities of seizing the ship have been completed. Members of the ship's crew will report to Mr. Foxworth of the FBI at the gangplank."

The Special Agents of the FBI were admitted as far as the head of the gangplank. The Special Agent in Charge, introduced as P. E. Foxworth, spoke to Captain Zanger. "Are your men prepared to leave the ship, Captain?"

"We have been expecting to do so for two years," Zanger said.

"Very well. If you'll call your men together. . . ."

Captain Zanger turned to Raynal. "Maurice, summon the men."

"One moment, sir," Raynal said. He turned to Foxworth. "You used the terminology that we are being 'taken into custody.' I would like to know, on what charge are we being arrested?"

Foxworth waved a sheaf of papers. He seemed embarrassed. "It's only a formality. But since you ask, the technical charge states that you have overstayed the maximum on your visitor's permit."

The members of the crew who understood English laughed. They quickly interpreted for the others, and the laughter became general.

Raynal brought them to order. "Attention to roll call," he said.

Raynal fought to keep his emotions under control. He was certain that the remnants of the crew of the *Normandie* had gathered for the last time—115 Frenchmen who had served her through four years of Atlantic service. They had made 141 crossings together, carrying 133,170 passengers. Almost every man aboard was a plank owner, having served from her maiden voyage.

The members of the crew had other things in common. To a man, they were opposed to the Vichy regime. And they did not want to return to Occupied France.

Raynal faced his men. One by one, he called out their names. An FBI agent stood by Raynal's side, making a checkmark as each man stepped forward.

A brief silence followed the roll call. Then Raynal spoke to his men in French.

"Whatever else we do with our lives, we may be content that we have had our moment of greatness," he said. "We have sailed the most magnificent ship ever built, and we have served her well. We have just given her two more years out of our lives, in an effort to protect her from harm. Let us hope that our sacrifice has not been in vain. Let us pray that we have preserved her for a mission, a mighty contribution that will help to drive the Nazi invaders from French soil! *Vive la France!*"

The reply came back in a roar: *"Vive la France!"*

And from the rear, a husky baritone began the "Marseillaise." By the second note, 115 men were singing the anthem, filling the hall with sound.

Raynal turned and led his men toward the gangplank, blinded by tears he did not wish the Americans to see.

Light, swirling snow gave the twinkling skyscrapers of New York the soft vagueness of a Cezanne painting. The short winter day was ending on Ellis Island. Raynal watched the distant harbor, where tugs were moving a freighter out into the stream. The strident voice of his interrogator brought him abruptly back from the view out the window, to the matter at hand.

"Have you ever been a member of, or ever participated in the activities of, the Communist Party?"

"No," Raynal said.

"The Nazi Party?"

Raynal sighed. "I am opposed to totalitarianism in any form."

"Answer the question, please."

"No. I have never been associated with the Nazi Party."

Raynal was tired and irritable. He had endured three long sessions of grilling within the last two days. The questions were repetitive. He recognized the technique. The authorities thought that by asking the same question many different ways, they eventually might receive a different answer.

"Have you ever advocated the violent overthrow of any government?" asked his questioner, a Mr. Carlson.

"Yes, I have."

Carlson looked up in surprise, his eyebrows raised.

"For the last six years, I've been advocating the violent overthrow of Nazi Germany," Raynal said.

Carlson grunted. He shuffled his papers around nervously. "Some of our questions have become a bit dated. Good answer." He reviewed his notes, leafing through the pages slowly. At last, he leaned back in his chair and looked at Raynal. "That about wraps it up."

He paused, and ceremoniously placed his pencil on his desk. "This is off the record, Captain. We're talking informally. You say you don't wish to return to Vichy France. You say you have reservations about joining any faction of the Free French. Tell me, Captain, what *would* you like to do?"

Raynal did not hesitate. "Remain in America. Help the war effort, in any way I can."

"If you are paroled, granted residency in America, how will you support yourself?"

Raynal shrugged. "I'm an educated man. I know ships, navigation, turbines, high-pressure boilers. I could teach French, if nothing else. Or dig ditches."

Carlson studied him for a long moment. "As you may know, German and Italian merchant crews in your circumstances are being interned for the duration. French citizens pose an unusual problem. While we feel we're allied with the French people, generally, we must recognize that the Vichy regime is repressive, increasingly collaborationist. Therefore, we must make our decisions on the individual merits of each case. I hope this in part explains the necessity for the lengthy questioning."

"I understand," Raynal said. "I take no offense."

"Ordinarily, the normal disposition of your case would be to go forward with deportation proceedings. Obviously, these are not normal times. We must decide with justice, compassion."

He paused, uncapped a pen, and wrote several words on Raynal's papers.

"This decision will be subject to review. But my recommendation is that you be granted parole, and residency, for the duration of the war."

Raynal thanked him.

Carlson reached for a yellow slip on his desk. "There's just one more thing," he said. "The FBI has placed a hold on you. An agent is waiting in Room Five-B now to interview you."

Raynal felt a moment of acute apprehension. "What do they want?" he asked.

"I have no idea," Carlson said. "I've only been advised that it has nothing to do with your Immigration and Naturalization status."

When Raynal found Room 5-B, the door was standing open. The FBI agent was seated behind a bare wooden desk in the middle of the sparse, drab room. He stood as Raynal entered.

"I'm Special Agent Lester J. Halbouty," he said. "I would like to ask you a few questions."

He gestured toward the only other chair in the room. He was small, rotund, and graying, with black, piercing eyes. A single folder lay on the desk. He waited until Raynal had settled into the cane-bottomed, ladder-backed chair.

"It has been called to our attention that you once made a report to the FBI concerning suspicious persons loitering about the *Normandie*."

His tone gave the statement the aura of an accusation.

"Yes," Raynal said.

"What did you think they were up to?"

Raynal had difficulty with the colloquialism. "I beg your pardon?"

Halbouty tried again. "What made you think they were acting suspiciously?"

Raynal explained. "I had seen the man several times before, studying the ship. On that day, he was obviously attempting to look into a cargo door open on the port side. Through the ship's binoculars, I could see his eyes. They were very alert, analytical." He shrugged. "I acted more on what I sensed than what I saw."

"Have you seen the man since that time?"

Raynal shook his head.

"You also described the woman with him," Halbouty said. He handed Raynal a photograph. "Is this the one?"

The woman was stepping through the doorway of an airplane. There was no mistaking the small build, large eyes, and gamin face.

"That's she," Raynal said. "I'm certain."

Halbouty retrieved the photograph. "Would you recognize the man if you saw him again?"

"Of course," Raynal said.

Halbouty slid the photograph back into the folder. "Thank you. You've been most helpful. I wonder if I could have your permanent address."

"I don't know where I'll be—what I'll be doing," Raynal said.

Halbouty's hesitation was brief. He handed Raynal a card. "When you do know, would you please call me? We may be needing to ask you to identify this man."

Raynal promised that he would do so.

He then returned to his tiny room at the end of the hall.

252

Darkness was complete, and through his window the swirling snow turned the lights of the city into a veritable fairyland. Irresistibly, Raynal was drawn toward the spectacle.

He stood for more than an hour, picking out landmarks, trying to ascertain the exact direction of the *Normandie*.

No matter what her fate, he was determined that he would be a part of it. He had served in her long enough, devoted to her a measure of his life significantly sufficient to know he could not abandon her now. His burden of responsibility toward her was heavier than ever.

Toward midnight, he undressed and crawled into bed, wondering if anyone had remembered to feed the cats.

Three nights later, Raynal returned to his room at the Seamen's Church Institute in the Battery, dejected and despondent.

That morning, he had said good-bye to the last of his crewmen, now on their way to England to join the Free French.

Through the remainder of the day he had gone from office to office, making application for a position—any position—on the *Normandie*. He had received no encouragement.

No one seemed to know who was in charge of the ship. Some said she had been transferred from the Coast Guard to the Maritime Service. Others said the Army had taken her over as a troop transport. Rumors along the docks persisted that the Navy was moving swiftly to convert her into an aircraft carrier.

Raynal had walked up Twelfth Avenue several times, passing the *Normandie*.

Negro soldiers now guarded her with bayonets. Pedestrians were not allowed onto the pier or stringpiece. Raynal had stood for a while on the opposite side of the avenue, gazing at her from a distance.

He had bought a bottle of California wine and smuggled

it into his room. He sat for a while, listening to his radio, sipping the wine, worrying about what would happen to the *Normandie*, France, himself.

The American radio stations were devoid of significant news. And after two years of trying, he still could not fathom the intricacies of Jack Benny, Fred Allen, Charley McCarthy, and the other purveyors of American humor. He grew bored with the chatter and switched it off.

For a while, he dozed.

Just before midnight, he was awakened by a knock on his door. He opened it. A tall, robust U.S. Navy officer stood in the hall, hat in hand. "Maurice Raynal?"

Raynal nodded, and invited the man into his room.

The officer sank into a chair. "Thank God I've found you. I'm Lieutenant Commander Victor Weldon, Materiel Office, Third Naval District. I've been put in charge of the conversion of the *Normandie*. Three thousand shipyard workers are reporting aboard her tomorrow, ready to go. And it's a total mess. Can you believe it? We don't even have a set of blueprints! Everything's in metric. We can't even read some of the signs on the switchboxes. And they want her ready for sea in six weeks! We have tons upon tons of furnishings and precious art to strip and store, and we are told to do it with minimum damage. An impossible job!" He leaned forward. "Captain Raynal, would you consider helping us out?"

Again, Raynal could only nod at the heaven-sent opportunity.

Weldon laughed with relief. "Good! When'll you be able to report for work?"

Raynal reached for his bag. "I'm ready now," he said.

14

Twelfth Avenue, New York City

Light snow had been falling since early morning. The arrival of much colder temperatures in midafternoon brought larger flakes and a new intensity. Snow was now accumulating on the sidewalks, and the streets were filled with slush, gradually turning to ice.

Carefully stepping over the crisp, muddy drifts in the street, Von Beck crossed Twelfth Avenue. With his head buried in a heavy peacoat and turned-down watch cap, he tried to appear oblivious of his surroundings, hoping that anyone who noticed would assume him to be a dock worker, returning from a pier somewhere up in the Fifties.

Overhead, the sparse traffic on the West Side Highway had slowed to a crawl. Von Beck walked southward, his head lowered, watching for patches of slick ice. Not until he was even with the Cunard Terminal did he cast a disinterested glance in the direction of the piers.

Despite the cold, the black soldiers were still stationed in front of the *Normandie*. A sentry box stood just inside the sawhorse barriers, where a uniformed guard checked the papers and identity badges of everyone going onto the pier.

All this Von Beck saw in his peripheral vision. He was concentrating on the ship itself.

Already the *Normandie* appeared greatly altered. Welders were at work sealing her portholes. Painters were changing her to battleship gray. Cranes, motors, winches filled the decks.

The conversion was progressing much more rapidly than Von Beck had expected. He had not dreamed the project would be given such high priority.

Von Beck risked only one glance, then he turned away. He recrossed Twelfth Avenue, and walked east on Forty-eighth.

Pearl Harbor had brought vast changes to the waterfront. Almost overnight the docks had gone from unbelievably lax security to armed suspicion. The daily newspapers reflected a national tension that bordered on panic. Preoccupation with loyalty and citizenship was intense.

In the weeks since Pearl Harbor, Von Beck had remained close to the apartment. He was certain that the momentary excitement would ease as the Americans became accustomed to war. But until then, he could not risk attracting attention. His forged draft registration card, his Social Security number and university degrees would bear only cursory inspection.

America's entry into the war had given his mission far more importance. But the increased security had wrecked his original plan. He had to devise another—and soon. At the present pace, the work on the *Normandie* would not take long to complete.

Clearly, she was not being restructured as an aircraft carrier—an extensive overhaul job that would take months. He could only assume she was being refitted as a fast transport—a simple alteration that could be done within a few weeks.

But he could be certain of nothing. With Rachael as cover, he had visited several waterfront bars during the last two weeks, listening for talk about the *Normandie*. He had overheard only brief, jocular exchanges alluding to chaotic conditions aboard the ship. He had not placed much credence in the loose talk. Shipyards were always permeated with noise and confusion. Simple workers often did not understand the comprehensive planning that brought unity out of chaos.

His brief glimpse of the *Normandie* had convinced him that someone knew exactly what was being done with the ship.

She was being rushed into shape for a purpose.

The efficiency of American industry continued to amaze him. Just the day before, Rachael had learned that a new, sixteen-floor headquarters building at the New York Navy Yard in Brooklyn had been completed in only forty-eight working days. He had seen other examples of American construction and production speed that were truly astonishing.

If such attention were devoted to the *Normandie,* she could be converted and ready for sea in a matter of weeks.

He had to find some way to get himself—and his six cases of plastique explosive—aboard the *Normandie* before she sailed.

Walking cautiously on the thickening ice, he trudged on toward Times Square, devising his new plan.

The knock at the door was quiet but insistent. Cleaning up in the kitchenette, Rachael froze, plate in hand. In his corner, Von Beck raised an eyebrow. Rachael shook her head, signaling that she had no idea who it could be. The knock came again.

Von Beck rose soundlessly. He slid the curtain closed, hiding his notes on the *Normandie,* then walked quietly into the bedroom and closed the door. Rachael put the plate in the sink, wiped her hands, and crossed to the entry. She gave the apartment one last glance to make sure that all seemed normal, then unlatched the door.

A tall, thin young man stood at the foot of the stairwell, his hat in one hand, a briefcase in the other. His tone was apologetic.

"Miss Moser? I'm Special Agent H. Shackelford Bonham of the FBI. I wonder if I might ask you a few questions."

He held out a leather folder of credentials.

Rachael hardly noticed. She felt faint. The young man's face was blurred. Her mind was blank. She was saved by her deeply ingrained habit of courtesy. She reacted automatically.

"Of course. Won't you come in?"

She stepped back from the door and Bonham entered. For a moment Rachael did not know what to do or say. She was saved only by her instinctive politeness. "Won't you be seated, Mr. Bonham? Would you like some tea? Coffee?"

"Coffee would be fine," Bonham said, moving to the couch.

Fortunately a fresh pot was on the stove. Rachael poured, then served each cup with both hands to keep from showing her nervousness.

Bonham waited until she was settled into the armchair facing him. His face was lean and weathered, with prominent cheekbones. Rachael was chilled by the coldness of his pale blue eyes. She wished Von Beck were in the room.

Bonham slowly sipped his coffee, obviously in no hurry.

Rachael could not stand the tension any longer. "What did you wish to see me about, Mr. Bonham?"

With visible reluctance, Bonham opened his briefcase and took out some papers. "Miss Moser, are you acquainted with David Reed?"

"Yes, I am," Rachael said, wondering. She had not seen David in days. "Is he in trouble?"

Bonham regarded her with a bold stare. "Do you have some reason to suspect he might be?"

Flustered, Rachael felt blood rise to her face. "No, of course not," she said, angry at him for setting the trap, even angrier at herself for having fallen into it. "I consider David a good friend. Naturally, I'm concerned."

Bonham gave a single nod of acknowledgment. He was silent a moment. He seemed to be delaying his questions to make her nervous. With an effort, she forced herself to relax.

"If you're good friends, then I suppose you know that he has enlisted in the Marine Corps," Bonham said.

Clearly he was trying to provoke her. An Abwehr school warning popped into her head: *During interrogations, never explain beyond the question.*

"No, I didn't know," she said.

In another exasperating pause, Bonham seemed to give her answer much thought. "There's a problem in connection with his enlistment. Perhaps you could help us. We've had reports that he was involved in some political activity. Do you know anything about that?"

Another Abwehr rule came to mind: *Always tell the truth, whenever possible.* She assumed that Bonham knew the answer to his question, or he would not have come to see her.

"I know only that he once asked me to go with a group picketing a Nazi Bund march somewhere. On Staten Island, I believe."

"Did you go?"

"No."

"Any reason?"

Rachael hesitated. Bonham probably had questioned other people in the house, and expected certain answers from her. "I explained to him that as a refugee seeking asylum in this country, I didn't feel I should participate in its internal politics."

"What was the name of the organization?"

Rachael honestly did not remember. "I can't recall," she said.

Bonham referred to his notes. "Student Defenders of Democracy? Student League for Democracy? Union for Democratic Action? Vanguard of Democracy? Democracy's Volunteers? Cardozo Group? The Mazzini Society? American Youth for Freedom. . . ?"

"That was it," Rachael said. "American Youth for Freedom." She was struck by the incongruity of the questions. "I don't understand. Isn't that a patriotic group?"

Bonham nodded. "Ostensibly. But you see, so many of those organizations were infiltrated by Communists."

Rachael spoke before she thought. "But what difference does that make? As long as they're anti-Nazi?"

Bonham glanced at the bedroom door before answering. "In these times, a person's loyalties are most important," he said slowly. "Not necessarily loyalties to a country, but to an ideal. Wouldn't you agree, Miss Moser?"

Rachael felt a chill up her spine as she realized he was conveying meanings beyond his words.

"Yes," she said.

"And timing," Bonham went on, as if speaking his thoughts aloud. "Timing often determines the penalties for misplaced loyalties." He paused, and looked at the curtained-off corner of the room. "For instance, the peacetime spies who were arrested last summer received relatively short prison terms—eighteen years or so. Now, the only way they would escape execution today would be to give themselves up voluntarily."

Rachael did not answer. She was stunned into silence.

"Of course, David Reed's activities apparently were not serious, but we had to make certain." He rose, and held out a card. He smiled down at her. Again, he seemed to be imbuing his words with weighted meaning. "If you should have any second thoughts, Miss Moser, please call me."

Numbly, Rachael took the card and walked him to the door.

Bonham paused in the entrance.

"Remember, Miss Moser," he said. "Any information whatsoever, call me. Please!"

260

"He knows," Rachael said. "There's no doubt in my mind. Everything he said was full of innuendo."

Von Beck had heard the entire conversation. He was disturbed, confused. The FBI man's visit did not make sense. "That isn't the way the FBI would handle it," he insisted.

Rachael sank onto the couch. "I think we should abandon the project. Maybe they don't have enough to arrest us. But I'm sure they're watching us."

He moved to stand over her. "Rachael, if they had any suspicions at all, they would take us into custody for extensive interrogation. You're imagining things."

She shook her head. "No. You should have seen his face. He all but offered to help me if I would turn myself in. He looked at the bedroom door as he said it. He *knew* you were in there."

Von Beck turned away. He walked to his corner and sat down. He tried to put his own feelings aside. The situation demanded cold logic.

The FBI agent's phrases had struck him as unusual. For a simple security check, the questions had been rambling, disorganized. And he wondered why the FBI would be investigating possible Communists, when they surely were swamped with the work of arresting enemy aliens and clearing thousands of workers for war production.

And his logic kept taking him back to a simple fact: If the FBI suspected him, platoons of agents would be assigned to the case for around-the-clock surveillance. They would not send a lone agent to make oblique remarks.

"If we go ahead with what we're doing, we'll be caught," Rachael said. "I think we should abandon the mission."

Von Beck spoke with an intensity he hoped would penetrate her fear. "Rachael, we're so close to success. We can't quit!"

She did not answer. After a few minutes, she went into the bedroom and closed the door.

There the matter stood for the next few days. Von Beck worked on his new plan, gathering materials, further information concerning the security along the piers.

Rachael had described Bonham. Although Von Beck kept a close watch, he saw no signs that they were under surveillance.

But he continued to worry about Rachael. He now had known her long enough to realize that she was an unstable person, given to brief, intense passions.

She might go to the authorities.

He had to consider that possibility.

The silence of the unresolved situation lay heavy between them.

On a Friday evening in early January, snow began to fall. By Saturday morning, the drifts were deep in St. Luke's Place, the trees weighted with their burden. Rachael remained in bed until midmorning. When she at last came into the living room, her mood was gloomy. She went to the front window and stood for a long time, watching the snowfall. Von Beck was deeply engrossed in his figures.

Rachael suddenly turned from the window. "I can't do it," she said. "I don't care what you do to me. I simply can't do it."

He had anticipated her reaction. But he was undecided what to do about it. He had commanded men through many difficult and terrifying situations. Now he found himself helpless before the insubordination of an obstinate woman.

"Think of your family," he said quietly.

She looked at him. Her eyes filled with tears. "Don't you think I haven't? For two years I've thought of nothing else. I don't even know if my family is still alive! I've written. I've asked my control in Lisbon. If the Abwehr wants me to keep my end of the bargain, why don't they keep theirs? Why can't they keep me informed about my family? Don't they owe me that?"

Von Beck remained silent. He had always suspected that whatever protection Admiral Canaris could offer her family

262

would be limited. He had avoided revealing to Rachael his glimpse of the *Judenzug* in Frankfurt-am-Main. He would not be surprised to learn that her family was already dead.

Rachael had washed her hair earlier in the evening and it remained damp and clinging about her face. She hugged her breasts in a habit he now found familiar, and disturbing.

"Listen to me," he said. "If you refuse a direct order from the Führer, no one can save you, or your family. Not me. Not Canaris. Not anyone."

She whirled on him and spoke with surprising anger. "I certainly wouldn't expect anything else! I saw my father dragged through the streets by men like you! I just don't understand. How can you spend your life destroying and killing?"

Von Beck did not answer for a moment. He was thinking of the many sailors he had left to drown, of Rachael's supplying Germany with information on ship departures, condemning men to death in order to save her own family.

"We all do what we have to do," he said.

"Spoken like a true Nazi!" Rachael said. "Can't you think for yourself? Do you always have to follow orders?"

"In this instance, we both had better follow orders," he said.

"I'm not a machine like you," Rachael said. "I have feelings!"

"And you think I don't?" Von Beck asked quietly.

"No," Rachael said. "If you did, you couldn't bring yourself to destroy that magnificent ship. How can you do that? It's like killing a person—someone you know and love."

Von Beck changed his tack.

"Rachael, come down to the docks with me. Look at what they've already done to her. You'll realize she'll never again be the ship you and I have known and loved."

Even as he spoke, he realized he had revealed something of himself. She looked at him with no effort to hide her curiosity.

"You? You know and love the *Normandie?*"

He laughed, strangely embarrassed. "Why do you think they picked me for this job? Of course I know the *Normandie,* every rivet, every beam in her. I've been fascinated by her—doted on her—from the day she was launched."

She was frowning at him, as if trying to understand. "If you feel that way about her, how can you destroy her? What are they holding over you?"

Von Beck moved to stand over her. "Rachael, I'm a German officer. My country is at war, and my family has served Germany for centuries. The *Normandie* will be used to transport soldiers to my country, to kill, rape, plunder. With that thought in mind, I can destroy her, no matter what I feel. Americans have no corner on patriotism."

Rachael sat down at the kitchenette table. "And I'm Austrian," she said. "My family has lived in Austria more than two centuries. Now they're held hostage in their own homeland. Why? When they have never had anything in their hearts but love."

She lowered her head into her hands and sobbed as if her heart would break. "Why do we have to live in such times?"

Moved by her anguish, Von Beck crossed the room and put his hand on her shoulder.

The effect was electric. Rachael looked up at him, her eyes filled with tears.

Von Beck's concern for her was intermingled with all he had witnessed through two years of war—sailors plunging into blazing oil, ships and men disappearing into awesome palls of towering black smoke, the corpses lying in the streets of Frankfurt, Berlin, Munich.

Much of what he was feeling must have been mirrored in his face.

With a strangled cry of despair Rachael came out of the chair and into his arms. He tried to hold her, to comfort her, but she showered him with kisses he could not resist.

He was defenseless against his own hunger. Consumed

264

by emotions that had lain dormant too long, he carried her to the bed where they made love with an intensity that seemed to know no limits.

They were perfectly attuned, altering their pace in a marathon dance, moving from gentleness to the wonders of deliberate exploration, to the fury of desperation. Von Beck had never dreamed that such unbridled passion could be so tender. Again and again they renewed the delicious savagery, reaching higher and higher plateaus.

At last, fulfilled, they lay in peaceful silence, contented.

Snow continued to pile against the window the whole night through, enhancing the illusion that they were alone, secluded and protected from the city, from the war.

Hesitantly at first, wary of breaking the spell, they began to talk.

Snowbound through the long weekend, they lay in bed, confiding thoughts, feelings, and memories long guarded from each other, from the world.

She told him about the happiest day of her life—her fifth birthday, when her father took the family on a picnic into the Obersalzburg. She told of her persistent, troubled sense of estrangement from her practical, science-minded family, of her early passions for dance, music. She talked of her life-long frustration over her weakness—the subjugation of her own personality to serve others.

He told her of his own childhood, how he had been reared to revere honor, tradition, and class responsibilities, and how he still believed in those qualities, yet found no place for them in the modern world. He described his early ambitions, his extensive training for a life at sea. Hoping she might to some degree understand, he told her of the excitement of Nazi Germany in the mid-Thirties, the universal sense of a destiny fulfilled. He told her of his long war patrols, the terrors of the depth-charge attacks, his growing disenchantment.

He described his last patrol, when he had given up the boat as lost, and the one-in-a-million gamble that had brought them back to the surface, closer to death than to life.

As he talked, she clung to him, sharing, reliving the experience with him.

He had never felt so close, so totally involved, with anyone in his life.

But the snow against the window melted. The weekend ended.

With the dawn on Monday, Von Beck prepared to leave to make arrangements to go aboard the *Normandie* so he could put his new plan into action.

Rachael begged him not to go.

"I love you," she said quietly. "But I know that what you are doing is wrong."

Von Beck did not answer. He had to force himself to accept the fact that despite all that had happened to them during the weekend, nothing had changed.

He knew he had to accept the fact that she might yet betray him.

What was love between two people, when all the world was at war?

15

Yorkville, New York City

The German-language movie posters were gone from the Garden and Casino theaters on Eighty-sixth Street, replaced by simple, hand-lettered signs in English announcing that the houses were closed, soon to be reopened under a new entertainment policy. Along Eighty-sixth, the main street of Yorkville, little knots of troubled housewives stood talking in the windy cold, their expressions pinched and worried. At the corner newsstands, groups of men gathered to read and discuss the headlines of each edition as it arrived.

Wherever he went in Yorkville, Lieutenant (j.g.) Hyman Roth and his uniform drew long, hard stares.

He now considered his assignment futile. How could anyone track down a rumor? Especially in Yorkville, wearing a U.S. Navy uniform?

During the last two days, he had visited twenty bars, at least fifteen restaurants, and several churches. The results were the same: Everyone agreed that Yorkville contained only loyal Americans.

But the admiral and most of his staff had a different view.

"We should've cleaned the place out during the last war," the admiral had said. "The bastards up there were actually celebrating German victories. Feelings ran high about it. But nothing was ever done. This time, it's going to be different."

The admiral had made it plain he expected a detailed report.

And now, after two days of search, Roth had nothing.

The wind had grown sharper, colder. The heavy Navy overcoat was warm, but his cheeks, ears, and nose were numb.

On impulse, seeking a few minutes of warmth, he turned into yet another neighborhood bar.

The place was almost deserted. Crossing the bare wood floor, Roth ceremoniously unwrapped his scarf, removed his gloves, and placed them in his upturned hat while he surveyed the bar. Four men were seated at a back booth, talking in low tones. The bartender was perched on a stool, wiping a row of whiskey glasses. Roth walked over to him, placed his hat on the polished wood, and unbuttoned his coat.

The bartender was short, bald, and in his middle forties. He regarded Roth with the friendliest smile Roth had seen in Yorkville. "What'll it be, Lieutenant?"

"Beer," Roth said. "Draught."

As the bartender set the beer on the bar, he gave Roth's uniform unguarded study. "You off a visiting ship?"

Roth hesitated, uncertain how to answer. The bartender slapped his forehead.

"Shit, I forgot," he said. "It's a military secret, right?" He laughed. "This fucking war's gonna take some getting used to." He resettled himself on the stool, his forearms on the bar, and leaned toward Roth. "Reason I ask, I'm an old Navy salt, see. I was in tin cans during the last war. Machinist mate. Two hitches. I was up for chief. I shoulda stayed in."

Roth sipped his beer. "They're hunting experienced men," he said.

The bartender grinned. "You think I could get my old rate back, Lieutenant? At forty-six?"

Roth thought of the long lines at 90 Church Street every day for the last three weeks, including Sundays. "A lot of old hands are reupping," he said.

Again the bartender laughed. "Hell, I guess I ain't so old, at that. You see in the paper the other day about that old guy, ninety-two, trying to enlist in the Marines?"

Roth nodded.

"And I read about a woman up in Connecticut, ninety-seven, working as a plane spotter for Civilian Defense. Said she was a nurse in the Civil War! Can you imagine that?" He shook his head in amazement. "We'll probably be hearing a lot of strange things before this one's over."

Roth saw his opening. "We've been hearing some unusual things," he said. "We're told it's common talk in Yorkville that the *Normandie* will never sail. You ever hear anything like that?"

The bartender glanced at the back booth, then looked at Roth. He grinned ruefully. "Lieutenant, what kind of business will I have if it gets around among my customers that I'm talking to Navy Intelligence?"

Roth gave the bartender a long, blank stare. "You say you're a former Navy man. Where are your loyalties? Don't you know we're in one hell of a tough war? What about your old shipmates?"

Again, the bartender glanced at the back booth before answering. He spoke in a lowered voice. "Lieutenant, I know it's hard for an outsider to understand. Most of the people in Yorkville are all right. But a lot of them were *born* over there. You see that story in the papers the other day? A woman from down the street here committed suicide. Her son was home on leave from the American Army. She got to brooding over her son fighting against Germany. It was just more than she could take. A lot of people here

269

are like that. They've got divided loyalties. But when the chips are down, they're Americans."

"We've had reports that remarks about the *Normandie* were made right here in this bar," Roth lied.

The bartender considered his answer carefully. "Lieutenant, I've heard people say the *Normandie* may never sail. But I'm sure they didn't mean anything by it."

"Heard it from whom?"

The bartender shrugged. "Hell, Lieutenant, they were just talking. Like last summer, after Joe DiMaggio got hits through thirty, maybe forty straight games. People would come in here and say he couldn't keep it up, that he was bound to have a hitless game soon. And look what happened. DiMaggio got hits through fifty-six straight games."

"I don't see the parallel," Roth said.

"The ship's just something to talk about, see? That doesn't mean they're gonna *do* anything about it."

"Who are 'they'?" Roth asked.

The bartender hesitated. "Welders, pipefitters, joiners —some of the people working on her. We get quite a few of them in here, especially during the weekends."

"What do they think might happen to her?"

The bartender spread his hands, palms up. "Shit, they're just talking, see? They don't know anything's going to happen to her. They just say things are so screwed up aboard her they can't see how she'll ever be in shape to leave. The way they describe that conversion job, it sounds like the Three Stooges hanging paper."

"Mismanagement? Is that what they're talking about?"

"In a way. It's a hurry-up job, right? No secret about that. You can read about it in the fucking newspapers. They're getting her ready for sea. No trained crew. All kinds of shortcuts. Talk is that they're taking big risks every day."

"What kinds of risks?"

"Oh, shit, go see for yourself, Lieutenant. From what I've heard, they've had several fires, a blizzard of contra-

270

dictory orders, everything you can imagine. From what they say, the ship's in terrible shape. Any sailor knows what two or three months in a yard can do to a ship. Right? The *Normandie* has been tied up two fucking years! Even with an experienced crew, it'd be a hell of a job to get her ready for sea. How they gonna do it with a green crew?''

"You've got a point," Roth said. "But I imagine they've thought of that.''

"I wouldn't be so fucking sure, Lieutenant. If I was you, I'd find out.''

Roth put on his scarf, hat, and gloves. "I will," he said. "Thanks for talking to me.''

The bartender picked up the empty glass and plunged it into the sink.

"Who's been talking to you?''

Two Negro soldiers were on patrol in front of the French Transatlantique terminal as Hyman Roth arrived by taxi. Bundled in heavy overcoats against the swirling snow, with rifles shouldered, the soldiers were marching their posts just inside a sawhorse-and-rope barrier bordering Twelfth Avenue.

A week before Christmas, three thousand Negro soldiers had been moved into New York City for permanent guard duty. Quartered at the 13th Regiment Armory at Sumner and Jefferson in Brooklyn, the 369th Coast Artillery Armory at One Hundred Forty-third Street and Fifth Avenue, and the 165th Infantry Armory at Twenty-sixth and Lexington, the regiment patrolled all bridges, tunnels, piers, and other points deemed vulnerable to saboteurs. Despite the new blackout on troop movements, Mayor La Guardia received special dispensation from Washington to announce their arrival. The mayor had argued that the sudden appearance of three thousand armed soldiers in the streets might cause even New Yorkers to panic.

The two soldiers glanced curiously at Roth, but did not

challenge him. He stepped over the barrier and walked toward the pier, awed by the monstrous size of the ship looming over him.

A uniformed civilian guard at the head of the pier gave Roth's papers a brief glance. "Who you want to see, Lieutenant?"

The guard was stamping his feet, clearly eager to return to the warmth of his hut.

"I'm just here on an inspection tour," Roth said. "If it's all right, I'll just look around."

The guard nodded and stepped back into his hut. Roth walked on past, onto the narrow pier.

With some incredulity, he realized that anyone wearing the uniform of a Navy officer could have gained entry.

The guard had not even glanced at his special credentials from Admiral Andrews, obtained with considerable effort.

The walls of the terminal building, three stories high, rose to Roth's left. On the right, the sides of the *Normandie* rose even higher. The outward flare of the hull created the unsettling optical illusion that the vast bulk was about to topple over onto the pier. The narrow canyon was bridged by four gangways, rigged on the second and third levels of the terminal.

Roth was reminded of a college friend who once took his poodle along on a trip to California, anticipating with glee the impact the giant sequoias might have on the dog. But to his friend's disappointment, the poodle paid no attention. The trees were so big that the dog could not conceive of them as trees.

Walking alongside the *Normandie*, Roth understood the dog's lack of perspective. Viewed from such close quarters, the *Normandie* was a solid cliff of metal plates.

A shower of sparks fell near him. Roth looked up. On scaffolding high overhead, welders were cutting away the huge gold-leaf letters, each more than six feet high, that spelled the *Normandie*'s name across the bow. Farther aft, painters were covering the French Line's traditional black, white, and yellow decor with wartime gray. As he watched, another cascade of sparks drifted down from the welders' torches, mingling with the falling snow.

A deafening cacophony assaulted Roth's ears, drowning the sounds of traffic on the West Side Highway behind him. Along the pier, twenty-eight motor-driven generators roared, serving the arc welders at work on narrow scaffolding as they sealed portholes with metal plates. Further aft, motor-driven winches whined continuously, delivering equipment to the workers, lowering material stripped from the ship. Three hundred yards away, near the stern, debris rained down on the pier, tossed from somewhere near the fantail.

Stepping around the occasional wooden toolsheds along the pier, Roth saw a workman drawing liquid into a five-gallon can from a fifty-gallon drum. He walked closer, to confirm what he suspected.

"Is that gasoline?"

The worker looked up, saw Roth's uniform, and decided to be civil. "Sure thing, mate."

"Is it a common practice to keep gasoline on the pier?"

"Ain't my idea," the man said. "It's what I was told to do." He pointed toward a generator. "We need it for the motors."

Roth walked on. He found four more drums of gasoline. Near the stern of the ship, debris continued to fall into a growing pile on the dock. Roth walked as close as he dared.

The material varied from scraps of metal to polished veneer. Much of it was plain plywood.

He walked back, entered the terminal, climbed to the second level, and crossed the gangway into the ship.

The first space he encountered was so vast he found it difficult to believe he was inside a ship. The ceiling was at least twenty-five feet high, and the hall was filled with so many workers the scene resembled the filming of a Hollywood biblical epic. At least fifty men were rolling up huge sections of blue carpeting. Others were on scaffolds, re-

273

moving veneer from the walls. A few carried furniture, lumber, or heavy tools. Some just seemed to be passing through.

A large diagram posted near a bank of elevators informed Roth that he was in the Main Entrance Hall. After studying the diagram for several minutes, he walked aft, down a flight of stairs, and into the gigantic First-Class Dining Room.

The entire three-hundred-foot length of the room was in an uproar. High on pipe-metal scaffolding, workmen were removing the mirrored glass that covered the walls. Even higher, up against the thirty-foot ceiling, others were stripping away lavish wooden panels. Shouts of warning were almost continuous as material dropped from above. Husky movers were carrying off the ornate furniture, dodging around the workers removing the carpet.

Roth watched the bedlam for a few minutes, then retreated. He returned to the bank of elevators, restudied the posted diagram, and went up to the Promenade Deck.

As he stepped off the elevator, Roth once again found himself in a sumptuous entrance hall. Although the ceiling was not as high—a mere twenty feet—the spaciousness was even more pronounced. To his left, up a flight of six steps, was the entrance to a large theater. To his right, he could see open spaces all the way aft, up a great staircase to daylight, almost two hundred yards away. In the sweeping vista were more than four hundred workers.

Roth began picking his way aft, dodging around the various projects, making mental notes for his report.

In what he determined was the Grand Salon, much of the furniture had been removed. The murals, etched in glass, were being taken down and packed in boxes. For some reason, most of the carpet remained in place. At least twenty men were involved in the removal of the huge doors into the Smoking Room, where carpenters on scaffolding were peeling away the gold bas-relief hunting scenes.

Roth examined the walls closely. Beneath the massive

panels was plain plywood, coated with some kind of lacquer.

Walking up the grand staircase, Roth entered the Grill Room. He went to the windows and looked down on the Tourist-Class Promenade, where welders were installing a three-inch gun, their torches showering the area with sparks. On further aft, another massive pile of debris almost covered the Third-Class Open Promenade. Roth estimated that the pile was fifty feet square, and at least twelve feet high.

Returning to the Promenade Deck, he moved to the starboard side and examined some of the staterooms. The doors were open. Inside, the furniture was still in place, the bedding stuffed into the closets. Inside several rooms, he found stubs of cigarettes ground into the carpets.

Roth had seen enough.

He returned to the main elevators and began a search for the Chief Naval Inspector.

His name was Harold Malone, he was a full lieutenant, and he bristled the moment he caught the drift of Roth's assignment.

"Look here, it's not your place to be running around the ship, interfering with the contractors," Malone said. "I'll thank you to get off this ship, Lieutenant. If there's any question, I'll be glad to take it up with your commanding officer."

Malone was tall, big-boned, and swarthy. Well into his forties, he looked like an old China hand. Roth suddenly found his mouth dry, his tongue thick. He disliked arguments, and as a lieutenant, junior grade, he had a one-bar disadvantage.

"Lieutenant, I'm on direct assignment from Admiral Andrews to track down rumors about this ship," he said. "I can't file a report to the admiral unless I consider the possibility that those rumors may be true."

Malone looked at him for a long moment. A rivet gun started up somewhere aft of the inspector's office. The sounds were deafening.

"What rumors?" Malone asked.

"They're saying in Yorkville that the *Normandie* will never leave her pier."

Malone hooted. "That's not rumor. That's opinion—and one held by some people in high places. You don't have to go to Yorkville to hear that. You probably could hear the same thing all over Washington, or from anybody working on this ship."

Roth managed to hide his surprise. "Then why isn't something being done about the hazards?"

Malone re-established his one-bar edge. "Be specific."

"The pier, for a start. Right this minute, debris is piled to the second level of the terminal. Also on the pier are two hundred and fifty gallons of gasoline. Sparks shower down constantly from the welding torches. It's a miracle you haven't had a fire."

"We've had a dozen," Malone snapped. "The miracle is that we haven't had a big one."

Roth was confused. "I don't understand. If you know about these risks, why do you take them?"

Malone pointed to the work schedules on the bulkhead behind him. "As you may or may not know, Lieutenant, we're supposed to have this ship ready for sea by February fourteenth. There's no way to do that without taking short-cuts."

"Like gasoline and debris on the pier?"

"Congratulations, Lieutenant. You've got the picture. We have to keep the generators running. If that means keeping fuel on the pier, then we'll take the calculated risk. And you can tell the admiral that I've filed a complaint every day for the last two weeks about that debris on the pier. You can also remind him that technically, we're not in command. The ship has been turned over to the Robins Dry Dock and Repair Company. All we can do is complain."

"I've found cigarette butts ground out in the carpets of the staterooms," Roth said.

"The prime contractor has promised that any man caught smoking on board is fired on the spot. I have no doubt many aren't caught."

"What about the welders? The sparks? Don't we have any control of them at all?"

"Under the contract, all welders are supposed to use asbestos shields when making sparks. They're told to burn metal only in the presence of a fire watch, with hoses laid. But sometimes the safety standards we would like to maintain simply aren't practical."

"Who's responsible for the fire watch?"

"We have two. The Coast Guard maintains a patrol. The contractor also maintains a fire watch on all three shifts. So far, they've been amazingly effective. The ship is still afloat."

Roth was writing the report in his head. He wanted to leave no questions unanswered. "What about the confusion? People are stumbling over each other all over the ship."

Malone sighed. "Lieutenant, there are thirty subcontractors on this job, and two thousand, four hundred and twenty-five men, working three shifts. Each subcontractor has his own jobs to perform elsewhere, and devises his own schedules. Most contractors shuffle men from other work they're doing for the Navy, in the shipyards in Brooklyn, over in Jersey, or maybe even from Norfolk and Newport News. If you can figure a way to dovetail everything, we'd be happy to hear about it."

"What about security? Has everyone—like those people in Yorkville—been cleared?"

Again Malone gave a laugh that was more a bark. "Shit, Lieutenant, we can't even get a *list* of the people working on this ship. You can make this plain: There's been no security check. All we know is what the contractor tells us." He picked up a sheaf of papers. "According to Robins, we have about twelve hundred American-born citizens, three hundred fifty-some-odd naturalized citizens, about a hundred who claim citizenship from birth but who can't prove it, and a dozen or more enemy aliens who have received first papers. And those figures change from day to day, even from hour to hour."

"What about the FBI? Aren't they working on it?"

"Shit! By the time we got a third of those men cleared, the *Normandie* would either be at sea or on the bottom. And security? It's a joke. All you need to get aboard this ship is a union badge or a pass. You can find one on the floor of most any of the saloons around here. Or you can buy your own for a fifty-dollar union initiation fee."

Roth was shaken. What he had just heard bore little correlation to what he had been taught in Reserve Officers Training. "Surely, something should be done," he said.

"You haven't heard the half of it," Malone said. "The confusion on board this ship is nothing to the fuckup in Washington. Follow this if you can: On the eighth of December, the Coast Guard was transferred from the Treasury Department to the Navy Department. Four days later, still acting on Treasury orders, the Coast Guard took over the *Normandie*. To straighten out that screwup, the ship four days later was signed over to the U.S. Maritime Commission. Three weeks after that, the Maritime Commission signed her over to the Navy. The initial idea was to make her into an aircraft carrier. We had no blueprints of the *Normandie*, much less a conversion plan. So a survey was made, and drawings were done. Then some asshole decided that the ship wasn't sturdy enough, that it would take too long, or some goddamn something. So they decided to make her into a boxed cargo transport. More designs were done—and scrapped when new orders came for a hurry-up conversion to a troop transport. Now, the big argument is over who will operate her—the Navy or the Military Transport Service. For a few days, we had some high-ranking Army brass aboard with their own conversion plans, throwing their weight around. At the moment, she's back in the jurisdiction of the Navy, except that technically this pier has been designated an extension of Todd Shipyards, parent company of Robins Dry Dock and Repair, which, if I understand it right, has full responsibility for the ship, except that a convenient clause in the contract limits their liability to three hundred thousand dollars.''

"On a sixty-million-dollar ship?''

"Perhaps because she *is* a sixty-million-dollar ship,'' Malone pointed out.

"Why don't they extend the yard period?''

"Lieutenant, you'll have to ask Washington. Apparently they have a mission for her. In fact, the sailing date has been advanced, twice, and other safety measures eliminated. A week or two back, someone discovered that she's tremendously topheavy. Her own captain warned us about that. So we drafted plans to peel about fifteen hundred tons of dead weight off the Promenade and Boat Decks. Those plans were canceled in the interest of time. When we stressed the danger of her capsizing in heavy seas, the simple answer from those armchair admirals in Washington was that we could keep the bottom tanks ballasted as long as the ship is at sea.''

Roth considered all he had learned—the hazards, the confusion, the lack of security. "Have you mentioned all this in your reports?''

Malone shook his head slowly. "Certainly not.''

"Why?''

Malone gave him a cool stare. "Lieutenant, how long have you been in the Navy?''

Roth remained silent. His fresh uniform, his bright new shoulder boards spoke for him.

"I'll bet I've wrung more salt water out of my socks than you've seen in your whole lifetime,'' Malone said. "And there's one thing I've learned. You might bear it in mind. Sometimes your superior officers don't *want* a full report.''

"They're going to hear it from me,'' Roth said.

Malone sank into his chair. He peeled off his hat, tossed

it onto his desk, and ran his fingers through thinning hair. "You may prove me wrong, Lieutenant," he said. "I hope you do. But I have the definite feeling that Washington knows all about the conditions on the *Normandie*. I further hold strong suspicions that for reasons of their own, the people in Washington *want* these conditions to exist—have planned for these conditions to exist. Why? I don't know."

He looked up at Roth. "Go ahead. File your report. Maybe it'll do some good." He hesitated, lowered his voice, and spoke in a tone deadly serious. "On the other hand, Lieutenant, I won't be at all surprised if you disappear off the face of the earth."

Flanagan's Bar was widely proclaimed in Lower Manhattan as the last surviving outpost of the free lunch. But for those who worked in the Federal Building at 90 Church Street, the bar's proximity was its greatest asset. In essence, Flanagan's had become an annex of the Office of Naval Intelligence, privy to administrative gossip, rumors, and carefully crafted nonofficial exchanges. When Hyman Roth's immediate superior, Lieutenant Commander Richard Barthelmess, sent word for Roth to meet him in Flanagan's, Roth suspected the reason.

Barthelmess was not the only well-known movie actor in Naval Intelligence, nor was he by any means the only member of the staff whose name and face were instantly recognizable by the public. Gertrude Lawrence's husband, Richard Aldrich, was a full lieutenant. Nat Benchley was a lieutenant, junior grade. Famous visitors were common. Lieutenant Commander Jack Dempsey and Commander Walter Winchell often dropped by, as did Madeleine Carroll, Gertrude Lawrence, Vivian Della Chiesa, and Conrad Thebaldt. Moreover, the staff was filled with well-known reporters and sportswriters from New York daily newspapers.

But Barthelmess maintained his own calm, handsome

aloofness, as befitting a former matinee idol. Roth and Barthelmess had worked together almost two months, but Roth had yet to lose his sense of awe in the actor's presence.

Barthelmess met Roth at the door and ushered him to the bar, where they gathered drinks and complimentary food.

They carried their plates to a back table, where Barthelmess kept Roth diverted with small talk until they had finished eating. He then glanced around to make certain they were not being overheard, and got down to the matter at hand.

"Your report concerning the *Normandie* is on my desk," he said. "I can send it up, if you want. But I thought you might like to reconsider."

"Why?" Roth asked, knowing.

"Roth, I can't exaggerate the kinds of hell that report will bring down on us. At the moment, I see three courses of action open to you. First, we could forget about the report."

Roth shook his head. "The investigation was instigated by Admiral Andrews," he said. "I know it was a low-level, low-priority assignment. No one expected anything to come out of it. But that report contains exactly what I found."

Barthelmess gave him his famous wry smile. "I doubted you would back off. I just thought I should mention it for the record. Second, you could rewrite the report, softpedaling the material."

Again Roth shook his head. "There's no way to minimize conditions aboard that ship."

"All right. That's exactly what I anticipated you'd say. But I still doubt you know how much of a furor that report will cause. No lieutenant junior grade should have to bear such pressure. Did you put *all* the material you have into the report?"

Roth thought about it for a moment, and nodded.

"Then there's only one thing for you to do," Barthelmess said. "Go back to the *Normandie*. Pile up even *more* material. Get the specifics. When the brass descends on you—and they will—you can use your new material as ammunition to go on the attack. You can let them know right off that you only put *half* of what you know in the report. Understood?''

"Yes, sir," Roth said.

"All right. I'll shove the report into the mill. You'll have about three days before the fireworks go off. You'd better spend those three days aboard the *Normandie*. I don't know at this point whether you'll come out of this with another stripe, or be busted to seaman second. But good luck, Roth. You're going to need it.''

16

Eighth Avenue at Fiftieth Street, New York City

Beyond Eighth the sidewalk traffic thinned. Bonham dropped back, keeping Von Beck in sight. He was now certain that Von Beck was headed for the warehouse with the material he had just purchased in a sporting goods store.

During the last three weeks Bonham had become an expert in surveillance, a master of disguise. He now carried a nondescript canvas bag containing his briefcase, a coat of a different color, two hats, and a variety of moustaches and beards. Within ten seconds, Bonham could alter his appearance sufficiently to fool all but the most astute observer. The canvas bag could disappear into the briefcase, his knit cap could be replaced by a snap-brim, and a tie and coat could turn him from a laborer into the model of a young executive.

In keeping with his expertise, he had become increasingly daring. The night before he had actually sat next to Von Beck and Rachael in a waterfront saloon, his eyes fixed on the floor in the sullen, unseeing stare of a drunk while they nursed their drinks and eavesdropped on the conversations around them.

He had followed them almost every day for three weeks, piling mystery on mystery.

His visit to Rachael's apartment had not produced the results he expected, but he did see a few aftereffects. Both Rachael and her friend were more wary, nervous. They might yet make that fatal error.

Rachael had made twelve trips into the cafes and taverns of Yorkville, where she met briefly with five different men. Abandoning her each time, Bonham had tailed the men, and managed to make three. All were carried on the FBI Subversives List as known members of the Irish Republican Army. Once she had gone to a synagogue in Queens. He had been unable to discover her contact there.

He had followed Rachael and her companion to marine supply stores, downtown restaurants, to the Eleventh Avenue warehouse, and to the waterfront piers.

Nothing they did made much sense.

Bonham had heard Rachael call her companion Walther. In a Yorkville tavern, the Irishman named O'Neill had referred to him as Von Beck. The residents of the apartment house knew him as Walter Beck. Bonham had put all combinations of the names through the FBI files, and through the Immigration and Naturalization Service records.

He had drawn a blank. After all his work, he had no solid evidence.

He was certain of only one thing: The case was far more important than he had even dreamed.

In some way, it involved the *Normandie*. From the way they paused and looked at the ship on their walking tours of the docks, no doubt remained in his mind.

He was certain that Rachael and Von Beck were close to the execution of some major act of sabotage.

And he had nothing but an intriguing string of circumstantial evidence. He had no facts to connect her with the murder of Frank Pierce—nothing but his own suspicions. He had no idea of the subject of her conversations with the men from the IRA. He had not seen Rachael or Von Beck commit a single illegal act.

If he were to submit a report containing only what he knew and suspected, he would be laughed out of the Bureau.

Ahead, Von Beck turned left toward the warehouse. Bonham quickened his pace. By the time he reached the corner, Von Beck was entering the building.

Bonham drifted on across the street. In a recessed doorway, he reversed his windbreaker, turning it from red to blue. He replaced his knit wool cap with a floppy hat. Removing his glasses and moustache, he donned a thick, scraggly beard. Satisfied, he staggered out to the curb. Wine bottle in hand, he sat down to wait for Von Beck to emerge.

And while he watched the doorway to the warehouse, an idea he had been entertaining for the last week grew into a full-blown obsession.

Through the ruse of making a delivery to Von Beck, he had entered the building and learned the exact location of the space Von Beck had leased.

He now had to determine exactly what was in the warehouse.

It might hold the one concrete, solid piece of evidence that would put all his other material into perspective.

The warehouse was five stories high. A laundry covered most of the first floor. At the rear, an inset from the street housed a truck dock. Inside, a freight elevator serviced the top four floors. Each level contained four individual storage spaces, accessed by a wide central hallway off the elevator. At night, the heavy freight doors were closed and locked, as was the front entrance to the stairwell. Power to the elevator was killed. Von Beck's space on the top floor was protected not only by a sturdy deadbolt, but also by a heavy hasp and padlock.

After reconnoitering the building several times in daylight, Bonham could find no way to make his entry from the ground floor.

But from an aerial map of New York City on file at FBI headquarters, he had determined that the four compartments on the upper level were each serviced by a small skylight.

Shortly after midnight on a morning in late January, Bonham slipped into the recess behind the building and stood for a long time in the darkness, watching, waiting, shivering from the cold.

A freezing wind had struck just after midnight. The sky was overcast, and the temperature had dropped into the upper twenties.

Bonham waited patiently until the foot patrolman passed the intersection on his regular rounds. He counted off four more minutes, to give the policeman time to reach Twelfth Avenue and the noisy West Side Highway. He then quickly crossed to the rear of the building. With a small boat grapnel, he pulled down the balanced fire escape. The pulleys were rusty and squealed in protest. Bonham climbed the steps until the counterbalance took over, then eased the fire escape section back into position.

He remained motionless on the landing for a full minute to see whether the noise had attracted attention. Then, slowly and cautiously, he climbed upward.

At the fifth-floor landing he paused. A small, rusty iron ladder went straight up to the roof. Bonham doubted that anyone had tested it in years. It felt frail and inadequate.

As he put his full weight on it, the ladder rattled against its supports. Hardly breathing, Bonham inched up the ladder to the roof.

Using his penlight cautiously, he walked softly across the graveled tar roofing to examine the skylight over Von Beck's warehouse space. Much to his disappointment, the framework was solid, designed for providing light, not ventilation. The heavy glass was reinforced with imbedded chickenwire.

With one last glance around to make certain he was not

being observed, he assembled his tools. From around his waist he unwrapped the hoisting pulleys, rigged with fifty feet of manila rope. From his tool kit, he assembled the suction cup with its swivel and large diamond-tipped glasscutter. Bearing down gently, he rotated the brace-and-bit arrangement until he had a neat, pieplate-sized circle cut through the glass. Gently, he lifted it out with the suction cup.

With a screwdriver, he reached inside and removed the brackets that held the glass to the frame. As the panel came free, he lifted it out and placed it on the roof. He reinserted the plate-sized plug, taped it thoroughly on one side, and filled the cut with model-airplane glue.

He then turned his full attention to the loft.

Peering down from the ceiling, Bonham judged the room to be roughly twenty feet square. His large flashlight revealed a stack of wooden crates in one corner. Various cartons were arranged along the opposite walls. The floor directly beneath the skylight was bare.

Bonham attached his hoist to the skylight base. Easing his body through the opening, he hunted around with his right foot until he found the loop in the rope. Slowly, he lowered himself the sixteen feet to the floor.

He stood motionless for a full minute, listening, making sure no one else was in the building. He heard nothing except the wind whipping over the open skylight.

He switched on his flashlight and started exploring.

The stack of plain wooden crates offered no clue to their contents. With his screwdriver, he pried open the top of one box. Inside were two smaller wooden boxes, each clearly labeled:

DANGER
Composition C-4
Trimethylene trinitramine

Cautiously, Bonham inserted his screwdriver and opened the smaller box. Inside, the two-and-a-half-pound demolition blocks of plastique were packed sixteen to a bag, two bags to a box, all arranged in neat rows. Bonham copied down the markings on both the box and the demolition blocks.

Using the wooden handle of the screwdriver, he forced the nails back into their holes and gently tapped the lids securely closed.

Item by item, he inventoried the equipment at the far side of the room—a box of number-six blasting caps, four fifty-foot rolls of Primacord, a suit of the type used by commercial divers, a box of plumber's friend suction cups, a portable air pump, and several lengths of flexible rubber hose.

Bonham made one last survey of the room to confirm that he had missed nothing.

Placing his foot in the loop, he hurriedly lifted himself back to the roof.

He reattached the inner brackets. With a pair of pliers, he bent the outer frame and slipped the glass panel back into place.

The skylight probably would leak. But no glaring signs of entry would be evident from below.

He reattached his gear to his body and retraced his route to the street. He walked away from the building, satisfied with the night's work.

He now knew exactly what Von Beck intended to do.

The outbreak of war probably had stymied Von Beck's timetable, forced him to seek an alternate plan. But whenever and however Von Beck moved, Bonham intended to be there.

Now he could catch Von Beck red-handed.

"How do you know it wasn't *your* Nazi, Shack?" Marcus demanded. "What if it *was* sabotage? What if they trace it to your man, and they learn that you knew about him? Goddamn it, you've got to tell them what you know!"

Bonham shook his head doggedly. "It wasn't my guy," he said.

They were seated in their favorite bar, enjoying their late-night ritual after a long day. Bonham was tired and chilled to the bone. He pulled his overcoat closer about him and shivered. New Yorkers now were calling it the coldest winter since 1936. Outside, the temperature had fallen to four degrees. The newspapers had said that no relief was in sight.

The night before, three thousand bags of copra had caught fire at Pier 83. Two buildings at Forty-third Street and the North River were destroyed. Almost simultaneously, another major fire had broken out in a six-story loft building on Thirteenth Street, between Fifth and Sixth avenues. Eight firemen had been injured, not counting Mayor La Guardia. Not content with his dual roles as director of the national Civilian Defense and mayor of America's largest city, La Guardia also had responded as a fireman. He was undergoing treatment for frostbite.

The FBI, Naval Intelligence, and Marcus suspected sabotage.

"How can you be so certain?" Marcus asked.

Bonham had grown increasingly reticent with Marcus. Repeatedly, Marcus had voiced his concern over his status as an accomplice.

He felt he now had to keep Marcus quiet only a few more days.

"I'm certain, because I know exactly where my man was when the fires started," he said. "I know where he stores his explosives, exactly what he plans to do with them."

Marcus stared at him. "Explosives? What the fuck *is* he going to do?"

Bonham looked away. "All in good time," he said.

Marcus turned in the seat to face him. "Shack, how the fuck will you *ever* explain all this? All the tailing, interrogations of citizens, everything! Even if this woman is Mata Hari, and you hand her over to them on a silver platter, they'll send you right to the can along with her. How are you going to handle all this?''

Again, Bonham shook his head. "You already know more than you want to know.''

Bonham had made his point. For a while, they talked of other things—Bullethead's latest decrees, the mounting workload, interoffice gossip, the rash of brown-nosers in the latest crop of new men.

As usual, Marcus left after two drinks.

Then, as usual, Bonham lingered for another.

He was exhausted. The night before, while the two major fires were in progress, he had tailed Von Beck into York-ville. There, in a tavern where German was spoken freely, Von Beck had met once again with O'Neill the Irishman.

Despite his efforts, Bonham had been unable to get close enough to hear the conversation. He had sat at the bar and tried to read lips. He knew only that the word *Normandie* had been used, at least twice.

Afterward, he had tailed Von Beck back to his apartment on St. Luke's Place, then gone to his room for a few hours of sleep.

He had spent a full day at work. Then, while ostensibly out conducting interviews, he followed Von Beck and the woman to a waterfront bar. He had watched them from a distance while they sat for almost two hours, drinking little, talking only once, when a brief argument seemed to flare.

The tail was made even easier now that he knew Von Beck's nature. Some men simply functioned better at night. Bonham was of this ilk. Others awakened before dawn, spent their energies mostly in the mornings, and coasted through the afternoons and early evenings.

Von Beck was of this type.

Bonham had learned to anticipate Von Beck's morning movement, his early retirement at night.

Bonham had adjusted his own work to accommodate Von Beck's habits. Most of the time, he now remained one step ahead of Von Beck. And he no longer had to spend so much time at his mirror arrangement in the window, waiting for Von Beck to appear.

He was certain that Von Beck's next morning activities would be a followup to whatever he had worked out with the Irishman.

The thought sent Bonham into motion. He rose from his booth and searched in his pocket for money to pay the check.

It was then that he saw the two men on the opposite side of the room, watching him.

Bonham stood, pretending to count change, while he looked them over, careful to keep his eyes focused slightly to their left.

One was a big man, well over six feet. Broad-shouldered. Perhaps 225 pounds. Thick black hair, combed straight back. Bushy eyebrows and a wide, square face. The dark eyes were slightly protruding.

The other was slimmer, more the wiry type, with curly rust-colored hair closely cropped. Both were dressed in neat, conservative suits, with overcoats. At the same moment, they grew suspicious of Bonham's ploy and quickly looked away.

A dead giveaway.

The two men smelled of cop. But Bonham could not decide what kind. They were a trifle too well-dressed for the city variety. And he had never seen the two men around Foley Square.

He left a tip, paid the check, and pushed his way out the front door. After the partial warmth of the bar, the cold wind hit his face with a sobering chill.

Bonham turned left, hurried a third of the way down the block, then stepped abruptly into a recessed doorway.

He did not have long to wait. The two men emerged, walked to the curb, and seemed to stand for a minute in indecision. As if on impulse, the slim one hailed a passing taxi.

Bonham waited until the cab door closed, then rushed

out into the street. The next taxi was not far behind. Bonham stepped in its path, waving his badge.

"I just want to know where that cab goes," Bonham told the driver. "Don't get too close."

The taxi cut over to Sixth Avenue and turned uptown. Bonham's driver followed, lingering about a block behind, slipping and sliding over the ice to stop at some intersections, spinning the wheels to slip through others. The windswept streets were practically deserted.

The driver kept chattering away, griping about the plans for a new municipal airport out in the Idlewild meadows. "I ask you, what the fuck do we want with an airport way out there?" he demanded. "We gotta fucking airport that's as big as we'll ever need."

Bonham made sounds of agreement. He leaned forward to keep the other taxi in sight, despite the heavy fog inside the windshield.

"That old man is within his rights," the driver said. "If that land was mine, they sure as fuck wouldn't take it."

Bonham grunted assent. He vaguely knew what the driver was talking about. An eighty-year-old eccentric was blocking condemnation proceedings. The newspapers called him "the hermit of Thurston Island."

"Who the fuck's gonna pay two bucks or more for a taxi ride way out there?" the driver asked. "Rockefeller?"

Ahead, the other taxi turned right at Fifty-ninth Street. Bonham grabbed the driver's shoulder. "Slow down," he ordered, pointing. "Stop over there, just short of the intersection."

He left the cab and hurried to the corner.

The other taxi had stopped. As Bonham watched, the two men stepped out and started across Fifty-ninth Street toward Central Park.

Bonham returned to his cab and paid the driver. Not bothering to wait for change, he sprinted across the rockhard slush, keeping his attention focused on the two men.

They disappeared into the trees, heading toward the pond.

292

The park was well-lighted, the reflections glistening from the snow trapped in the trees, the drifts piled alongside the walks. Bonham stopped and stood for a long moment, listening. He heard only the muffled sounds of the city, the faint stir of wind in the treetops.

Unbuttoning his overcoat and jacket despite the cold, Bonham walked down the path toward the pond.

Abruptly the two men emerged from the shadow of a tree, not ten feet away. Startled, Bonham put his weight on his right foot, stepped sharply left, and flung the flaps of his coats aside as he went for his gun.

"Pull that gun and you're a dead man!"

The voice boomed from behind Bonham. He froze, his gun clear of its holster but still hidden by his coats.

The man with the rust-colored hair took a step forward, smiled, and pointed. "Drop your pistol in the snow, Bonham. Hurry up! No tricks! Let's get this over with before we all freeze our asses off."

Bonham knew he had been hopelessly mousetrapped. He had no choice. He tossed his .38 into the snow.

The big man picked it up, opened the cylinder, and dumped the cartridges into his hand. He turned and drew back an arm to throw the ammunition into the snow-covered pond, then reconsidered. He dropped the cartridges into his overcoat pocket, nodded to the man or men behind Bonham, and started pulling off his gloves.

Bonham instantly understood what was about to happen. But the realization came too late. A brawny forearm encircled his neck, pulling him off balance. He was held helpless in an iron-firm headlock. He tried to kick. The arm tightened.

"Just relax, Bonham, and it'll go easier," said the man with the rust-colored hair.

The beating was done dispassionately, and with highly professional skill. No skin was broken, but Bonham knew he would piss blood for a week. His chest was alive with pain, yet he did not hear the snap of a single rib. The muscles of his stomach were pounded methodically into agonizing jelly. His kidneys were battered until paralytic twinges radiated into his shoulder blades.

When it was over, he lay crumpled in the snow. The man with the rust-colored hair knelt beside him. With a vise-like grip on Bonham's left ear, he lifted his head clear of the ground. With the other hand, he slapped Bonham's face to get his attention.

"You couldn't leave it alone, could you?" he said. "This is just a friendly warning, Bonham. Take it. Lay off. Mind your own business. In a few days, it'll all be over."

He dropped Bonham's head back into the snow. Rising to his feet, he gestured to his men, and they walked away.

Bonham fought against the pain and nausea. Every movement was agony. But he knew he had to get out of the park or he would freeze.

Holding his breath against the stabbing pain, he rolled over, and managed to rise to his knees and elbows. He pressed a handful of snow to his face. Slowly, he staggered to his feet.

His empty pistol had been returned to its holster. He fumbled with the latch until it was secure.

As he stumbled out of the park, he thought back over the incident.

In a few days it'll all be over, the man had said.

That could only mean one thing. Whatever Von Beck was planning was about to happen.

Whoever the men were, they only wanted Bonham out of the way for a few days, and they thought an expert beating would suffice.

Bonham hugged his battered stomach as he made his way back to Fifty-ninth Street.

Whoever they were, the bastards were wrong. They would have to give him more than a few aches to take him out of the running. He would be back on Von Beck's tail at dawn, if it hare-lipped the governor.

17

Ninety-second Street, New York City

Seated in O'Neill's apartment, Von Beck had been explaining his plan for more than an hour. He had brought his diagrams. Painstakingly, he described how a half dozen well-placed charges could destroy the *Normandie*'s watertight integrity, sinking her within minutes.

O'Neill listened impatiently. At last, he pushed Von Beck's drawings back across the table.

"There's no need to go through all that," he said. "The whole ship's a tinder box. All we have to do is put a torch to her. She'll go up like a Roman candle."

Von Beck wished he had been able to establish other contacts, other sources of supplies and assistance. O'Neill lacked discipline, logic, dedication. And he knew nothing about ships. But Von Beck knew of no other way to get aboard the ship. O'Neill held the key.

"If the *Normandie* burns at her pier, the Americans will simply scuttle her, extinguish the fire, and repair the damage within weeks," Von Beck explained. "We will have accomplished nothing."

"Fire has destroyed other French Line ships," O'Neill

argued. "The *Georges Phillipar,* the *Atlantique,* the *Lafayette,* the *Paris.* They burned, and never sailed again."

"Only because they capsized," Von Beck explained. "The land-based firefighters poured too much water into them. The Americans surely would know better." He rolled up his diagrams. "All you have to do is help me get aboard her. I'll put her on the bottom of the ocean."

O'Neill sipped his beer for a moment before answering. "Too risky," he said. "And we might miss our only chance. If your plan failed, we'd never get another crack at her." He rubbed his knees nervously. "My boys have been waiting for two years to put the torch to her. I don't think I could stop them now if I tried."

Von Beck shifted to a different approach. "O'Neill, who do you think will win this war?"

Surprised, O'Neill hesitated. "I don't know," he said. "From what I read, things don't seem to be going well on the Russian front."

"A winter stalemate," Von Beck said. "You can bet the Wehrmacht is preparing a spring offensive. England is whipped, a plum waiting to be picked. Five ships have been sunk off the East Coast of the United States during the last week—three on the approaches to New York Harbor. Japanese submarines are harassing the West Coast. Japan's participation in the war will turn the tide. Everyone said Germany couldn't survive a war on two fronts. But tell me this, can the Americans fight a two-ocean war?"

O'Neill nodded. "I've said it myself. Germany may win yet."

"And when she does, what'll be your country's position? Who will become regents for the Reich in England?"

O'Neill could not see the connection. "What does that have to do with the *Normandie?*"

Von Beck leaned forward and put a hand on O'Neill's knee. "Remember this! The Führer himself sent me to America to destroy the *Normandie.* I was selected because I'm experienced with ships, explosives. I was trained spe-

296

cifically for this one job. What I'm saying, O'Neill, is that the Führer didn't send me to America to toss a match into a pile of lumber."

He paused, giving O'Neill time to absorb his words.

"My report of the mission will go direct to the Führer," he continued. "If you help me, you'll be remembered."

O'Neill was silent for a moment. "What do you want me to do?" he asked.

"First, get me aboard the *Normandie*. Second, once I'm on board, I must be able to slip away for several hours at a time, without arousing suspicion. Can you do this?"

Slowly, O'Neill nodded. "All the unions are hiring." He paused while he considered the problem. "The pipefitters would be best. The man who runs the shape-up is sympathetic to Germany. If we paid him a hundred dollars or so, he would pick you for the *Normandie,* look the other way when you disappeared. He can assign you to loading and off-loading supplies for the job. You will be able to get the plastique aboard yourself. The major difficulty will be to get you through the hiring process—filling out forms, answering questions. I can coach you on what to say."

Von Beck reached into his coat pocket for a small notebook. He uncapped a pen. "The sooner the better," he said.

Two days later, after O'Neill completed arrangements, Von Beck filled out the forms and made application for union membership. The procedure was much simpler than he had anticipated. Following O'Neill's instructions, he gave his birthplace as a small town in Nebraska. When asked, he said he had been unable to obtain a birth certificate, as the county courthouse had been destroyed in a fire. He gave his address as general delivery, explaining that he had just arrived in town and had not located a permanent place to stay. No one seemed to consider his answers exceptional; the whole nation seemed to be on the move, relocating for wartime jobs.

Von Beck left the union hall with the most profound

sense of accomplishment he had experienced since his arrival in America.

He not only had his credentials to go aboard the *Normandie,* but as a pipefitter handling supplies for his crew, he also had the means of moving his explosives into the hold of the ship.

For a time Rachael considered suicide. The letter lay on the end table by her bed, an everpresent accusation.

It contained the pathetic ramblings of an old woman, half out of her mind. Rachael read it once and knew it by heart:

> Your father passed away a few weeks after you left. He was frantic with worry. We had heard nothing from you. I only regret your father was not alive to know the joy your letter brought us last week.
>
> Your brother has been relocated to a forced labor camp, somewhere in Prussia. We have not heard from him direct, but have heard from someone who knew someone who saw him there. Your sister went on the last conscription. I have not heard from her either. They tell me now they are taking the older people. I expect to be summoned soon. . . .

Rachael was consumed by total despair. She fell into lassitude. By day, during the hours Von Beck worked on the docks, she wandered aimlessly about the apartment, agonizing, weeping, hardly aware of her surroundings. With darkness she retreated into bed, spending long hours in a strange, listless stupor. She felt incredibly weary, her limbs so heavy every movement required tremendous effort. She could not eat. She lost weight. Her comatose intervals in bed grew longer and longer.

Von Beck read the letter, offered a few words of condolence, then retreated into his impenetrable shell, his great, brooding silences. He often studied her with a troubled expression, but said nothing. Only at night when he held her, comforted her with his closeness, did she regain some measure of the intimacy they had shared on that magic, snowbound weekend.

But even that brought further anguish. She hated herself for the contentment she found in his arms. She knew what he was, what he represented. She castigated herself for acquiescing to his will, for continuing as an accomplice on his project. Several times each day she took out the card the FBI agent had left and looked at it, wishing she had the strength and courage to do what her conscience dictated. But she remained passive, constantly fatigued without reason, brooding away hours at a time. She seemed unable to organize herself to do anything.

As the days passed, she made the decision to quit the Abwehr more by default than by conscious effort. January ended, February began, and she simply could not force herself to leave the apartment. Her stationery, her invisible ink remained hidden away, unused. The longer she procrastinated, the more she grieved over her family, and the more she thought of suicide.

Von Beck made special dishes and tried to tempt her into eating. Sometimes, to please him, she would take a few bites. But most of the time she was nauseated by the mere thought of food.

On a night in early February, Von Beck put aside the broth he had been trying to feed her. He sat on the edge of the bed and reached for her hand.

"We've got to talk."

She waited while he searched for words.

"Rachael, I have to go away. . . ."

Alarmed, confused, she struggled to raise her head, to make sense of the words. "Go? Where?"

He evaded her questions. "I don't want to go. I have no choice. You know that. But I'm concerned for you . . . that you'll be all right."

She had not dreamed that she might have to face the future alone. The prospect was overwhelming. She could not speak.

"I'm aware of what you've been going through," Von

Beck said. "It's something you've had to resolve for yourself. I couldn't help you. But you can't go on like this."

She did not answer. She felt completely drained of emotion. For weeks, he had been the only thing that made life worth living.

"I have about five thousand American dollars left," he said. "You can use it to get away. You must put distance between you and the Abwehr."

He paused, as if considering how much to tell her. "You see, there are too many Abwehr people on the East Coast. Dedicated, overly patriotic people. Someone might find you. It would be best if you could move inland. With the war, jobs will be easier to find. You have talent. Perhaps you could teach music."

She tried again. "Where are you going?"

He looked at her a moment before answering. "The *Normandie* is scheduled to sail Saturday. I'll be aboard."

She had assumed from the beginning that he would simply plant the explosives, timed to explode at sea, and that they would flee.

"Why?" she asked. "Why do you have to be aboard?"

"There's no other way to be certain. I must plant the charges, light the fuses." He squeezed her hand. "There's nothing new about this. It's what I was sent to America to do."

Only now did she understand. "You're *planning* to be killed!"

He gave her a faint smile. "Not planning. There may be time to get off before she goes down. I'll have a raft. We won't be a great distance out. I should be able to make it."

She was desperate for hope. "Shall I wait for you here?"

"If you wish. But if I don't come within a week or ten days, you'd best leave."

For a few minutes, she was content with that. Then, unexpectedly, she was overwhelmed by uncontrollable anger.

"How can you sacrifice your life—my life—to this stu-

300

pid war? My family is gone! And now you. How can you do it to yourself, to me? Where is the sense in it?"

He sat calmly through her outburst. He rose and paced the floor for a moment before returning to the bed.

"Rachael, don't try to make me deny who I am. We can't make these judgments for each other. I should be telling you not to quit the Abwehr, that it's dangerous, likely to get you killed. But I can't. The choice is yours to make, according to your nature. I feel that for you—with your temperament and beliefs—to continue to work for the Reich is wrong. But I can only offer understanding, not advice or help."

"Why is it wrong for me? And not for you?"

He did not answer for a long moment. He turned out the lamp, and spoke in the darkness.

"If I were to turn my back on Germany now, I would be making a statement that all the killing I've done in combat was wrong. I'm not prepared to do that. It would be too much to bear. I'm a third-generation naval officer. I wear the highest military decorations of the Reich. How can I turn my back on what I am? You can't ask it of me. I can't ask it of myself."

Rachael had never felt so desolate. It was the worst night of her life. She was consumed by agonizing grief, weeping for her family, for him, for herself. She now faced facts she had long denied: Her friend Annette-Marie Fourcade was dead. Otherwise, the Germans would not have selected her identity for Rachael's use. She spent most of the night in recriminations. At last, exhausted, she fell into a troubled sleep.

When she awoke, just before dawn, Von Beck was beside her, still asleep. As she memorized the lines of his strong, peaceful face and took comfort in his deep, labored breathing, she was filled with a new resolve.

She would not stand by idly and allow him to sail to his death.

Somehow, she would find a way to stop him.

BOOK FOUR

FEBRUARY 1942

The Normandie *was one of the proudest gestures the Third French Republic ever made. She was built in strength, in luxury and in loveliness. . . . Yesterday the smoke of her burning floated over this city. . . . Now we have smelled what offended the nostrils of the people of Rotterdam, of London, of Coventry, of Warsaw, of Belgrade, and what now floats over Singapore. Says the smoke of the* Normandie: *This is our war. The fumes can sting us to action. We can see in them the shapes of a greater burning in which an evil system shall go down. Let us close ranks.*

New York Times
February 10, 1942

18

Pier 88, New York City

Braced against an icy wind sweeping across the Hudson, Maurice Raynal waited patiently for his line to move. Around him, the workers were quiet, subdued by the cold. The glare of the floodlamps, the darkness were grim reminders of an hour of sleep lost as clocks were adjusted to the first day of Eastern Standard Wartime.

The morning papers had reported that much colder temperatures could be expected by early afternoon.

The bow of the *Normandie* loomed overhead. From somewhere deep inside her came the burst of a rivet gun, the screech of a cargo boom under heavy strain. The steady roar of the motors for the electric welding torches echoed over the waterfront.

Raynal moved past the civilian guards, who gave only the briefest glance at the badge of each worker. Raynal had seen at least thirty different kinds of badges on board. He wondered how the guards managed to recognize all. On the other side of the makeshift gate, other guards were checking the lunch boxes of the departing night shift. Raynal never ceased to be amazed at the naiveté of the Americans.

The lunch boxes were not examined as the men went aboard, only when they left the ship, to prevent theft. Incendiary devices, even small bombs could be carried onto the *Normandie* at any time.

In some quixotic gesture, the Americans had renamed her the *Lafayette,* either in ignorance of, or ignoring the fact that another Transatlantique ship had borne the name. But as yet the rechristening had not taken effect; both workers and the newspapers still referred to her as the *Normandie*.

Raynal crossed the gangway with mixed emotions. He felt fortunate that he had managed to remain with the *Normandie* a while longer with his new job. He had helped to minimize the irreversible effects of her conversion. But he could not ignore the pain of seeing what they had done to her.

She would never be the same. Throughout the past six weeks, in his capacity as consulting expert, he had witnessed her transformation from the most beautiful ship afloat to a monstrous, oversized transport.

He could voice no valid complaint. His recommendations had been followed, often to the letter. But such an intricate work of art as the *Normandie* could not be disassembled with any hope of complete restoration.

More than 2,400 van loads of material had been removed, dismantled, catalogued and carted to warehouses in the greater New York area. Working twelve to fourteen hours a day, Raynal had examined and logged each item.

Some of the problems had seemed insurmountable. The hammered glass panels in the Main Dining Room alone weighed forty-five tons. The great twenty-foot high bronze doors to the room had to be removed and transported safely. The huge Lalique glass chandeliers had to be lowered and packed. Wrought iron, bronze, lacquer, plaster, tile, parchment, leather, molded decorative glass paneling —each work of art contained its own hazards.

The job had been done with amazing dispatch, without

interrupting other work as the ship was readied for sea. Her boilers had been cleaned and tested. River silt had been washed from beneath her with high-pressure hoses. Three-inch naval guns had been installed. The first contingent of Navy men had just reported aboard.

Raynal was exhausted, depressed, and fearful of the future.

On Saturday, the *Normandie* would leave harbor for the first time in two years with—the ultimate folly—a green crew.

He had protested. Officially he was not even supposed to know of the plans for sailing. But everyone aboard knew she was scheduled to depart for Boston, final fittings, and a brief round of sea trials.

First, Raynal had gone to Commander Weldon, officer-in-charge of the conversion, and volunteered his services as a consultant in ship handling.

Weldon had replied that although his offer would be appreciated, it probably would not be accepted. Weldon had added that he would speak to the ship's new captain about it.

Raynal also had written to the commandant of the Third Naval District, Secretary of the Navy Frank Knox, and, just for good measure, President Roosevelt.

As yet, he had heard nothing.

After picking up his material in the inspector's office, he took a starboard elevator to the Promenade Deck and walked aft toward the Smoking Room.

As he moved through the Grand Salon, more than fifty men were milling about in the extraordinary confusion that reigned during each change of shift.

As was his custom, Raynal stopped for a moment and assessed the permanent damages. The room had been his favorite on the entire ship.

Most of the blue hand-knitted Aubusson carpet had been removed. The carpeting had been a masterpiece of workmanship—eight million stitches, knotted by ten craftsmen, who had spent three months on the job. No doubt it would never be restored to its former magnificence. Some of the remnants lay about the floor. As he watched, workmen with their filthy shoes carelessly walked on the rolls on their way across the room. The parquet dance floor at the center of the room also was being removed. The wood was scattered in a disorderly fashion. Linoleum had been laid over a small portion of the room.

The rapid change from carpet and parquet to linoleum was hampered by burlap bags piled almost to the ceiling in the after portion of the salon.

Varnished plywood had replaced the ornate etched-glass murals, leaving the walls bare, ugly. Four steel stanchions that once supported the ornate indirect lighting rose naked from the floor. From the dirt, disorder, and the rude noises of the workmen, no one would believe that this room once had been the scene of elegance and culture equal to any the world had to offer.

Moving on aft, Raynal entered the Smoking Room. Considerable furniture from the first class cabins had been stored there overnight. Raynal walked through the rows of chairs, examining their condition. He was bent over a chair, checking its stenciled number, when he heard his name.

"When will you have this material off the ship?" Commander Weldon asked.

Raynal threaded his way through the chairs toward Weldon. "Two, maybe three days yet, Commander," he said.

Weldon frowned. "Could you possibly make it two, Mr. Raynal? We've yet to complete the work in here. We can't take up the rest of the carpet until this material is out of the way."

Raynal pointed to the huge stacks of burlap bags in the Grand Salon. "Those bags are taking up a lot of space. Couldn't they be moved? That would give us room to process the furniture."

Weldon shook his head. "Those are kapok life preservers, waiting to be stenciled before they are distributed throughout the ship. There's nowhere else to put them. We'll just have to work around them. If we could get rid of the furniture, it'd be a blessing."

"I'll do my best," Raynal promised. He hesitated. "Commander, have you had time to mention my offer to the new captain?"

Weldon nodded. "His answer was exactly what I expected. No provision exists for a civilian to serve aboard a Navy ship, especially in wartime. It's impossible."

"I understand the problem, Commander," Raynal said. "But surely this is a special case. The *Normandie* simply can't be handled by an untrained crew. She's too delicate. On her first voyage, with officers and crew accustomed to handling large liners, more than three hours were required to dock her here. We almost came to grief."

Raynal felt no one understood the seriousness of the situation. Broadside to the current, the *Normandie* could be carried into the piers and ships downstream—an 83,000-ton battering ram.

Weldon smiled. "The U.S. Navy has had some experience in handling large ships, Mr. Raynal."

"Not ships like this one," Raynal insisted. "She's so sensitive. She heels well past twenty degrees in a high speed turn. Just the draining of one boiler can give her a list."

Weldon interrupted him. "Mr. Raynal, the characteristics of this ship have been under study for some time. I'm sure the captain, the admiral are well aware of these matters. No doubt your expertise could be put to good use. But it's simply impossible. I'm sorry."

Raynal's men were arriving. Several stood behind Weldon, awaiting their assignments. To his embarrassment, Raynal suddenly found himself close to tears. "I only want to prevent something terrible from happening. . . ."

"I can understand your attachment to the ship, your

wish to contribute," Weldon said. "But there are other ships. You've done remarkable work here. You can be assured that all the authorities aboard have noticed. I'm sure the shipyard would be happy to secure your services in a permanent position. If you're eager to get back to sea, the merchant marine needs experienced officers. A waiver probably could be granted on the requisites for citizenship. I'd be glad to provide you with my recommendation."

Automatically, Raynal thanked him. Weldon moved away.

Turning to his men, Raynal soon got the work started. But throughout the morning, the conversation with Weldon lingered heavily in his mind.

He had no intention of spending the war in a shipyard. Nor did he plan to sail with the American merchant marine. After the *Normandie*, he doubted that he would be able to bear to serve in any other ship.

By midmorning, he had made his decision. The Americans would need his help. And they would get it.

When the *Normandie* sailed Saturday, he would be aboard—as a stowaway.

Shortly before noon, Raynal was standing in the open doorway between the Grand Salon and the Smoking Room, examining furniture and logging each piece as it was removed from the ship. The area was crowded. Numerous crews were at work. With the cold weather, more and more workers took advantage of the ship's interior warmth, walking to and from their worksites by passing through the Smoking Room, Salon, and Main Entrance Hall. Raynal had just completed his inspection of a row of leather chairs and was waiting for the stevedores to remove them. He glanced at a group of workers entering the Salon, realized they were not from his crew, and was turning away when he saw a familiar face.

For a moment, he could not recall where he had seen the

man before. But as their gazes met and locked, Raynal saw recognition in the man's eyes.

Not until the man had crossed the Grand Salon and disappeared into the starboard passageway did Raynal remember. The man was the one he had seen with a woman on the stringpiece, months before, studying the *Normandie* as if his life depended upon it.

Raynal ran after him, picking his way through the construction debris in the Grand Salon. By the time he reached the starboard passageway, the man had disappeared into the stream of workers.

Mattresses were piled high against the inside wall of the passageway. Hurrying forward, Raynal occasionally leaped into the air in an effort to catch a glimpse of the man.

He traveled a third of the way to the bow, searching, before accepting the fact that he had lost him.

Raynal then ran to the inspector's office and the phone. He dialed FBI headquarters in Foley Square and soon had Special Agent Halbouty on the line.

"I just saw the man you're interested in," Raynal said. He described the sighting, and the way the man disappeared into the crowd of workers. "He's on board the *Normandie* right now," he added. "But there are three thousand workers on board. I don't know how we'll find him again."

Halbouty's response was immediate.

"Alert your security people. Give them a full description. I'll be there with help in ten minutes. And don't worry. We'll find him."

19

Aboard the *Normandie*, Pier 88, New York City

As Bonham moved forward through the crew's quarters on D Deck, the din around him increased to ear-shattering levels. The tumult of the rivet guns, hammers, compressed-air-driven wrenches and drills, the yells of the construction men remained constant. The air held the stench of grease, machinery, and burning metal. As he stepped over a tangle of firehose, Bonham winced at the sudden sharp pain in his side, a souvenir of his beating. He glanced into the door of the open compartment.

He caught a brief glimpse of Von Beck among the dozen men still at work along the far wall.

He had managed to keep Von Beck in sight most of the morning. Now, with the approach of the noon hour, he felt he should move closer. Casually, he moved through the door and into the compartment.

More than a hundred workers from a dozen different crews were converting the room into a magazine for the forward three-inch guns. Von Beck and other pipefitters were installing a sprinkler system. Another crew was building safe storage racks for three-inch ammunition. Sheet metal workers were cutting through the ceiling to make way for a dumb waiter, which would deliver ammunition to the guns on the fo'c's'le above. Heavy, reinforced walls and a large metal door were being added in the interest of safety and security. Bonham walked slowly through the workers to a relatively out-of-the-way spot that gave him an unobscured view of Von Beck, and began his masquerade.

For three days he had roamed the ship with his clipboard and calm air of authority. Not once had his presence been questioned. He had flashed his credentials only to the guard on the pier. Once aboard, he had been accepted for what he pretended to be—an inspector from one of the multitude of contractors or government agencies involved in the conversion.

He now solemnly studied the sprinkler system, the ammunition racks, the reinforced bulkheads, and made elaborate notes while keeping Von Beck in view with his peripheral vision.

Through most of the morning, Von Beck had been working at a small machine, cutting and threading lengths of pipe. But now, as the other men put up their tools and searched for their coats and lunch boxes, he moved away and stood apart from the rest of the crew. Another pipefitter called out to Von Beck. Bonham could not hear what was said. Von Beck smiled, shook his head negatively, and said something back. The other man walked away.

Carrying their lunch boxes and coats, the workmen left in small groups, headed either for more comfortable facilities on the ship, or the restaurants and bars along Tenth and Eleventh avenues. Within two minutes, Bonham and Von Beck were left alone in the room. Bonham watched as Von Beck stripped off his leather machinist's apron and adjusted his clothing.

Bonham was uncertain what to do. He did not want to lose sight of Von Beck.

He was running out of time. On each of the last three days, he had called in sick to the Bureau, claiming he had fallen down a flight of stairs. Solicitous and as subtle as a Mack truck, Bullethead had inquired if he were receiving medical attention. Bonham had given him the name of the doctor who had treated him after the beating. Fortunately, the doctor had accepted Bonham's explanation about the flight of stairs. His injuries and contusions were compatible with the story that his fall had been broken by a metal railing. The doctor had wanted to check Bonham into a hospital. When Bonham balked, the doctor agreed to extensive bed rest.

Bonham had squandered those preciously gained days trailing Von Beck about the ship, sometimes losing him for hours at a time. Now, he no longer could afford to gamble.

Deliberately, he lingered for a moment, making notes, occasionally retracing his steps, pretending to re-examine some doubtful work. The other shipyard workers had left a profound silence in their wake.

He felt Von Beck's eyes upon him. Taking great care to remain oblivious, he slowly left the room, still writing on his clipboard. He walked to the end of the corridor, and waited.

Von Beck emerged a few minutes later and stood for a moment in the doorway, watching the corridor as if waiting for someone. Again, Bonham felt Von Beck's gaze upon him. Casually, he turned away. When he glanced back, Von Beck had disappeared.

Frantic, Bonham hurried down the corridor, pausing only briefly to glance into the compartment. It was empty.

He moved on forward, his mind racing through the possibilities.

He was now on a deck above the waterline. He was certain that whatever Von Beck was about to do would be done somewhere in the bottom of the ship.

When he reached the end of the corridor, he stepped into the stairwell, closed the door, and stood, listening.

For a full minute, the stairwell was silent. Then, faintly, Bonham heard a door close, far below.

314

Slipping off his shoes, Bonham hurried down the stairs in his stocking feet.

Each deck was labeled with a large, stenciled letter. Bonham had spent hours each night memorizing the insides of the ship. He now tried to recall the details.

F Deck housed the baggage room, a garage for the passengers' cars, and a stores hold. G Deck contained another, larger garage, and yet another freight compartment.

Below everything, running completely athwartships, was the hold, ringed by double-bottom compartments. Designed to give a corrugated reinforcement to the bow of the ship, the double bottoms extended aft as far as the engine rooms.

Bonham felt certain Von Beck was headed downward. Hurrying to the bottom of the stairwell, he stepped out into the hold, and gently eased the door closed behind him.

The large, cavernous space was dimly lit by a few strategically placed bulbs. Hundreds of wooden crates and cardboard boxes obscured his view.

At first Bonham could hear only the soft purr of the ventilators, bringing fresh air down from above. Then, from somewhere far up forward, he heard the screech of a bolt, freed from its rusty repose. A few seconds later came the unmistakable rasp of a socket wrench.

Still carrying his shoes, Bonham crossed the hold, clinging to the patches of semidarkness, hunkering low behind the crates and boxes. Easing forward, he approached close enough to see the source of the sounds.

Von Beck was unscrewing a bolt from the bulkhead. Puzzled, Bonham risked moving a few more feet forward. He remained mystified. He waited patiently while Von Beck laboriously removed four more rusted bolts, then lifted off a heavy metal plate.

At last Bonham understood.

The plate offered access into the double bottom. Once past the bulkhead, Von Beck was at the skin of the ship.

As Bonham watched, Von Beck shined a large flashlight

through the hole, examining the region beyond. He eased his body through the small opening, feet first, and disappeared.

Bonham drew his pistol. Cautiously, he approached the open hole.

20

Aboard the *Normandie*, Pier 88, New York City

Shortly after two o'clock in the afternoon, Lieutenant Hyman Roth completed his tour of the open decks and returned, half frozen, to the warmth of the Grand Salon. Although the temperature had climbed to thirty-one degrees from a morning low of sixteen, the vicious, twenty-six-knot wind out of the northwest had left Roth's cheeks and ears numb. He stood for a moment at the port side entrance to the Grand Salon, rubbing life back into his face, reassessing all he had learned from his inspection of the weather decks.

The drums of gasoline remained on the pier. While some of the debris had been removed from the ship's fantail, other piles had appeared on the fo'c's'le. Barrels of shavings and refuse were spotted throughout the ship. The paint locker on the Boat Deck immediately above the Grand Salon was filled with flammable material, poorly protected. The ship was surrounded by slush ice. If fireboats were needed, their access to the ship would be hampered.

And Lieutenant Malone had told him that a suspected saboteur was on board.

Although the FBI and security groups were hunting throughout the ship, Roth had a complete description and was conducting his own search. He had covered the weatherdecks, alert for a large man in work clothes with blondish hair, blue eyes, and ruddy, weathered skin.

Thus far, he had not seen anyone matching that description. And he knew he should be concentrating on his report. Time was running out. Already, word of the furor over his report had begun to trickle down from the inner circle of the admiral's staff. He was determined not to retreat. He now had new evidence to show that his report understated—rather than overstated—conditions on board the *Normandie*.

But he would need all the ammunition he could gather.

Roth unbuttoned his overcoat and began his inspection of the Grand Salon.

The ornate lighting fixtures of the Grand Salon had been removed, leaving the interior dim. Roth counted thirty men at work in the room. Others were passing through constantly. He saw none that matched the description of the suspected saboteur. Up forward, two sailors were playing the piano. One was attempting "Elmer's Tune," and making a mess of it. He switched to "The White Cliffs of Dover," with better results.

Three of the floor-based lighting stanchions had been removed. The fourth stood alone on the port side, in the after part of the room.

Roth examined the starboard bulkhead. The removal of the protective murals had left the raw plywood exposed. High overhead, wood once protected by fireproof ceiling panels also lay bare.

Roth sighed. The situation was the same throughout the upper decks. Although the *Normandie* had been designed as one of the most fireproof ships afloat, the stripping of her decorative veneer had turned her topside into a naval officer's nightmare. Amidship, from A Deck upward, she now was mostly wood.

The huge pile of kapok life preservers had been shifted from the starboard to the port side of the room to make way for the crews resurfacing the floor. The burlap bales now rose in disorderly fashion almost to the ceiling. Roth walked the length of the pile, counting his steps. He then paced off the width. He estimated that the life preservers covered an area seventy by eighty feet, stacked fifteen to twenty feet high.

A number of bales either had tumbled off or been tossed into the area between the main pile and the port side bulkhead. In passing through the room during the noon hour, Roth had seen a number of workers lounging on those bags. He thought he had smelled cigarette smoke.

The bags were still lying about in random profusion. Roth walked among them, searching for any evidence that the men had been smoking. He found none in the dimly lit area. He turned back to the main portion of the room and resumed his tour.

Forward on the port side, several rows of heavy leather overstuffed chairs awaited the movers. Roth walked by and admired them. A crew of six or eight joiners were at work with screwdrivers, laboriously removing carpet studs. In the center of the room, in the large section between the stanchions, eight carpenters were ripping parquet blocks from the dance floor. Roth lingered to watch them work. One man, on hands and knees, was tearing the blocks loose with a wrecking bar. The rasping screech of protest from the wood resounded throughout the room. Eight carpenters worked behind him, using claw hammers and smaller wrecking bars to remove the loosened wood. The work seemed to be progressing rapidly. Roth observed that the blocks were scattered in crude piles throughout that portion of the room, intermingled with scraps of carpeting.

The sailor on the piano switched to the newest song on the Hit Parade, "Blues in the Night." Roth walked toward the rear of the salon, where two men were laying linoleum.

319

Roth watched them work for a few minutes before he heard the bustle of activity behind him.

A crew was preparing to take down the last floor-based lighting stanchion. Acetylene and oxygen tanks had been brought into the room, and a chain gang was rigging ropes to the top of the fixture. Roth had wondered how the stanchions had been removed. From his background in engineering, he felt confident the steel structures weighed almost half a ton.

He walked over to see how it was done.

Lester Simpson pulled his tanks up to the last stanchion, arranged the hoses and torch, and let his irritation be known. "Come on! Let's get these things out of the way!"

The chain gang started tossing the burlap bags aside. But for each bale they picked up, another tumbled down from the stack.

Simpson shook his head in disgust. The day had deteriorated into a series of frustrations. Throughout most of the morning he had worked in the incinerator room, cutting lengths of angle iron for supporting uprights, and steel plates for a new bulkhead.

The trouble had begun when his snapper, Wallace Hagan, ordered him into the Grand Salon to burn off the stanchions.

The job was a bitch. Each stanchion was a little more than eight feet high. Hagan had explained that he was to burn the metal off about three and a half feet from the floor.

A hot air vent at the base of each stanchion complicated matters. But the big problem was the complete lack of organization. Everyone in the room was getting in each other's way.

The first two burnings had gone comparatively well. He had completed both before noon.

After lunch, everything began to go wrong. After he had

320

toppled the forward stanchion on the port side, Hagan had sent him to the bandstand to remove a smaller light fixture. But the band platform blocked his access to the metal. He had wasted almost an hour in his attempt, before telling Hagan that it was impossible.

Now, the life preservers were in the way.

Simpson patiently waited for the chain gang to finish moving the bags. Hagan saw the inactivity and came over to Simpson. "What's the holdup?"

Hagan was known as a hot-tempered driver of men. Simpson did not want to cross him without reason. The chain gang had now cleared an area three or four feet wide around the base of the stanchion. "We had to get those things out of the way."

Hagan pointed to the stanchion. "Get on with it."

Simpson shrugged. He did not see a fire watch, but they were never around when needed. Simpson waited until the chain gang attached their three guide ropes and put in place the metal shield that blocked hot metal and sparks. While his helpers arranged their hand-held asbestos shields, he dumped a bucket of water on the floor to cool any molten metal that dripped. He turned on the acetylene and ignited the torch. He lowered his goggles and fine-tuned his flame, slowly adding oxygen until he had a point four inches long, tapering into a white-hot tip. He gave the nod to the men holding the metal and asbestos shields, and began his work.

With a skill developed through many such jobs, he held the torch steady, moving it slowly as his jet of flame melted the steel, driving the white-hot liquid before it.

He paid no attention to the molten metal and sparks. Through the dark goggles, with his eyes adjusted to the white-hot flame and metal, he could not see them well. He left the responsibility to his helpers.

The burning took more than a half hour. By the time Simpson reached the last support, he was sweating profusely. The heat of the room was almost unbearable. The

321

air from the vents at his feet seemed to come from a furnace.

Simpson straightened a moment to rest his back. He then gave the signal to his chain gang that he was starting the last cut.

He burned more than three quarters of the way through the last support before the stanchion began to move. He applied another few seconds of heat, and the stanchion started to fall. He stepped back and raised his goggles.

As the three ropes took the strain, the weight became too much for his helpers. Shouting a warning, the chain gang lost control. The heavy stanchion slammed to the floor, missing the bags of life preservers positioned to cushion its fall. The crash reverberated throughout the room. The chain gang laughed, chiding each other for not holding onto the ropes.

His helpers removed the metal shield, which had been crushed by the falling stanchion. They moved in close with the asbestos sheets.

Simpson lowered his goggles and resumed his position to cut through the last bit of metal. He brought the steel to a white heat.

He had just started the cut when a voice cried out in unmistakable panic.

"Fire!"

Simpson stepped back, shut off his torch, and raised his goggles.

As he watched helplessly, a sheet of blue flame raced up the side of the pile of burlap bags.

Simpson stood for a moment, puzzled. His torch had been directed away from those bags. Sparks from the burning would not have been blown toward them. How had the fire started?

The flames seemed to glide along, spreading rapidly. Simpson ran to the bags and tried to beat out the fire with his hands. All around him, men were yelling.

Simpson reached for a bucket of water. In the excitement, someone had kicked it over.

Several men were now throwing the burning bales away from the pile.

Frantically, Simpson joined them.

Roth was walking away, heading for the portside entrance, when he heard the shout behind him. He turned.

Blue flame no more than six inches high was dancing along the surfaces of the burlap bags in an area ten or twelve feet square. As he stood, frozen, a large ball of fire seemed to shoot up through the pile, erupting at its crest.

A sailor rushed by. Roth reached out and grabbed him. "Go turn in the alarm!" he ordered.

"Aye, aye, sir," the sailor said, saluting.

Foolishly, Roth returned the salute. The sailor ran out the door.

Roth rushed for the fire hose he had seen lying on the floor. Searching desperately, he found it buried beneath the bales of life preservers the chain gang had thrown down from the stack. With the help of several workmen, he freed the nozzle.

He turned and yelled at a group of men milling in the doorway.

"Water!"

No one seemed to understand. A carpenter put his hand on Roth's shoulder and shouted. "I'll go turn it on!"

Roth held the useless hose as the fire continued to spread with alarming speed. The entire pile of life preservers was ablaze. With a burst of superheated air, flames shot up through the midst of the stack, soaring to the ceiling.

One of the chain gang was still on top of the pile, throwing down burning bales. Roth saw with horror that the man's clothing was on fire. He shouted for him to come down. Someone pulled the man off the stack. Others rolled him on the floor to put out the flames.

After an eternity, the hose in Roth's hands burped a bucket or two of water. He braced himself for full pressure, but it never came. The hose remained limp. The fire now was licking steadily against the ceiling.

"It's those fucking bales!" someone yelled, pointing. Roth turned to look. At least a dozen bags lay across the hose, blocking the water.

Roth held the nozzle while the workmen threw the burning bags to one side. At last, water spurted from the hose.

But something was still wrong. The water came without pressure. The stream from the nozzle reached out no more than ten or twelve feet. Across the room, another hose had been brought in through a window. Roth saw they were having no better luck.

The room was filling with black, choking smoke.

With a growing sense of helplessness, Roth advanced on the fire. He was amazed at the heat generated by the burning bales.

His piddling stream of water came back into his face as live steam, searing his skin.

Roth retreated, only vaguely aware of the burns, the searing pain in his lungs. He remembered the bedding stacked in the corridor, all along the Promenade Deck. Hundreds, perhaps thousands of mattresses were only a few feet away.

He dropped the useless hose and staggered toward the exit. He had just stepped into the corridor when the acetylene and oxygen tanks exploded.

Comforting hands seized Roth. He was half carried through blinding smoke to a gangway. He fought off his rescuers. There were so many things to be done.

He plunged back into the smoke, located petty officers and issued orders, even though he knew he had no authority.

He was attempting to organize another firefighting team when he simply collapsed. He tried, but he could not make his legs work.

Someone picked him up and again carried him to the gangway.

Fire trucks and ambulances were arriving on the pier, sirens screaming. Roth was placed on a gurney and wheeled toward an ambulance.

"I'm all right!" he protested.

A doctor knelt beside him. "We'll be the judge of that," he said.

At the moment, Roth did not feel up to a protest. He allowed himself to be loaded into the ambulance.

He could not resist a brief wave of satisfaction. Now he would not need to defend his report. The disaster he had predicted was happening.

21

Aboard the *Normandie*, Pier 88, New York City

On the suggestion of FBI Special Agent Halbouty, Maurice Raynal had taken up station by the elevators on the Promenade Deck, just forward of the Grand Salon, so he could monitor workers boarding and leaving the ship and search for the suspected saboteur. He was standing by the starboard bulkhead, watching the constant stream of workers, when a Coast Guardsman ran past, yelling "Fire!" Startled, Raynal turned to look into the Grand Salon. A sheet of flames was racing across the pile of burlap bags. Beyond, a huge cloud of black smoke was billowing toward him.

Raynal's first thoughts were of the ventilator intakes on the Boat Deck over the Grand Salon, and the three thousand men aboard.

Unless something were done immediately, the ship would quickly fill with smoke, trapping most of the men below decks.

Raynal ran forward, making his way past the theater, up past the children's playroom and florist's shop to the Sun Deck and the bridge.

He threw the two fire-alarm switches designed to ring clangers throughout the ship. The switches also were connected to a ship-to-shore fire alarm box under contract with the American District Telegraph Company.

Nothing happened.

Frantically, Raynal worked the switches back and forth. Still nothing happened.

He could only conclude that the switches had been disconnected.

He turned and ran back through the ship and down to the distribution room on D Deck. He yelled to the Coast Guardsman on duty. "Turn off the ventilators!"

The sailor was frantic. He seemed glad to have someone giving orders.

Power to the ventilators was halted.

Raynal realized that while racing about the ship, he had not seen a single fireman. He grabbed the Coast Guardsman's arm. "Where's your fire brigade?"

"They've been moved down to A Deck," the sailor said. "They don't have a phone down there!"

The fire had now been burning more than ten minutes. And as far as Raynal could determine, no alarm had been sounded.

He reached for the sailor's shoulders and shook him. "Send a runner to get them!"

He ran back to the Promenade Deck, and to the rail. A giant plume of smoke now rose into the air, driven southeastward by the strong wind off the Hudson. Below, Raynal saw a policeman near the bow. Yelling, he attracted the officer's attention.

"Turn in the fire alarm!" he shouted.

The policeman nodded, turned, and trotted off in the direction of the fire alarm box at the head of the pier.

Raynal looked back forward. Smoke was no longer sweeping into the downtake ventilators. But he knew the order had been given too late. He was certain that the engine spaces were full of smoke, probably abandoned.

At last the public address system came to life. Some sort of word, muffled and indistinct, was piped throughout the ship. Raynal only heard the one word, "Fire."

He saw that more gangplanks would be needed for the thousands of workmen evacuating the ship. The arriving firemen would need as many access routes as possible for their hoses. Moving through the smoke collecting volunteers, he directed the rigging of the extra gangplanks.

Workmen were streaming up from below, coughing, gagging, vomiting. Many were injured. Raynal carried several off the ship.

He guided the first firemen aboard, and told them how to reach the fire.

Within minutes, great streams of water were playing onto the ship from fireboats, from shore.

But the massive pall of smoke grew thicker and much blacker.

Raynal knew the flames had reached the thousands of mattresses stored in the passageways along the Promenade Deck.

And as he watched the streams of water begin to play on the ship, Raynal suddenly understood what was about to happen.

If the engine room had been abandoned—as he suspected—dwindling pressure in the boilers would sustain the ship's electrical power no more than fifteen or twenty minutes.

The Horowitz system—an intricate storm drain arrangement—needed power to operate. No other facility existed to remove water from the upper decks.

A fire captain stood on the Promenade Deck just forward of Raynal, directing the streams of water arcing onto the ship from the pier.

Raynal ran to him and grabbed his shoulder. "Let her burn!" he yelled above the din. "You're going to sink her!"

The fireman looked at Raynal as if he were crazy. He

placed a massive hand in the middle of Raynal's chest and shoved. "Get off the ship!" he shouted. "That's an order!"

Raynal turned away, confused and desperate. He would never make them understand. The danger was too complicated to be explained easily. He had to find someone who knew ships, and the fate of so many ships that had burned at their piers.

He plunged back into the smoke, hunting for Commander Weldon, anyone of authority.

He tried to reach the inspector's office, but was forced back by flames. The distribution room had been abandoned. No one Raynal encountered seemed to know who was in charge of the ship, or who was directing the evacuation.

Raynal staggered back onto the Promenade Deck, fighting for breath. He looked forward toward the bow of the ship. Fire engines and ambulances now blocked the pier and Twelfth Avenue. The New York City Fire Department was well organized. Great streams of water were pouring onto the ship from every direction.

Already the *Normandie* was taking on a definite list to port.

With sickening certainty, Raynal knew the ship was doomed.

22

Aboard the *Normandie*, Pier 88, New York City

In the reflected glow of his flashlight, Von Beck re-checked his figures. His conclusions remained valid. A shaped-charge on the outer wall, a shear-charge on the cross-beam support, and a cratering blast on the inner hull —all exploded simultaneously by Primacord—would put a hole in the side of the ship at least six meters across.

He could safely assume that certain conditions would exist by the time the *Normandie* reached the open sea. During the last six weeks, fifteen ships had been torpedoed off the East Coast. The Americans would be using the superior speed of the *Normandie* in an effort to evade U-boats. At thirty knots, the forward rush of the ship, combined with her 83,000 tons of dead weight, would act as a massive pump, filling the hold within a minute. He doubted that the next watertight bulkhead aft would be able to withstand the pressure. But to make certain, he would place a series of charges along the steel framing.

The destruction of that watertight bulkhead would send the cold water of the North Atlantic pouring into the engine spaces at tremendous pressure. The boilers would explode.

When that happened, with two-fifths of the lower decks rapidly taking water, the ship would have only minutes to live.

Von Beck remained concerned over having been seen by the French officer. He was certain that the man was suspicious. But he had shoved the worry to the back of his mind. With three thousand workers on board, the odds on encountering the Frenchman again were slight.

He climbed high on the outer hull. With a piece of chalk, he marked the spot where he would place the shaped charge. Moving across to the steel braces, he measured and marked the proper placement for the most effective shear action.

He carefully calculated the lengths of Primacord that would be needed. He then knelt by the inner hull and chalked the base for the cratering charge. He was standing motionless, braced against the steel plates, when he felt a faint tremor run through the ship. The vibration was barely perceptible. Only an experienced naval man would have noticed. But it told Von Beck that a major disruption had occurred somewhere on the ship.

He considered the possibilities. A head-on collision with a large tugboat a few frames forward might cause such a quiver. The wind might have tumbled one of the big cranes onto the deck. He glanced at his watch. Slack tide came at 1:51 P.M.—more than thirty minutes ago. Portions of the hull were aground. With the start of flood tide, the ship might have shifted slightly in its berth.

None of the explanations satisfied him. His instinct, honed by thousands of hours afloat, told him that he had heard a distant explosion, reverberating through the ship's ventilation system.

Quickly, he reassembled his gear. He was stuffing his tools into his canvas bag when he smelled the first whiff of smoke.

His first thought was of O'Neill and his Irish patriots. Instantly furious, he scurried across the steel beams toward

331

the access hole. Apparently the bastards had not waited. All his work would now be useless.

Bonham stood frozen in total quandary. Von Beck was scooting across the I-beams toward him. Thick black smoke was cascading out through the ventilators, rapidly filling the hold. Behind him, a speaker came to life. The brief message was muffled in echoes. Bonham caught only one word—fire.

He could not decide if he should move in to make his arrest, or if he should step back into the darkness, allow Von Beck to emerge, and follow him topside.

He could not shake the idea that Von Beck was somehow responsible for the fire. But that possibility was not essential to make an arrest. He now had more than enough evidence—the plastique stored in the warehouse, the meetings with the IRA leader, the many reconnaisance visits to the *Normandie*, and now chalk marks clearly designed for the placement of explosives.

The smoke was growing thicker.

He had to get off the ship.

And he could not leave Von Beck behind.

Von Beck was now only a few feet away. Bonham aimed his revolver through the hole and shouted.

"Freeze! FBI! You're under arrest!"

Von Beck halted in mid-stride. He looked up, his eyes wide with disbelief.

Bonham and Von Beck were standing motionless, staring at each other, when the lights went out.

With uncanny presence of mind, Von Beck switched off his flashlight.

They were left in total darkness.

Bonham took up station at the hole.

The long stalemate began.

23

St. Luke's Place, Greenwich Village, New York City

As she left the apartment, heading for Sixth and Houston to hail a taxi, Rachael saw the heavy pall of smoke sweeping across Manhattan, driven by the strong northwest wind. The fire apparently was uptown, over toward the Hudson River. Framed against the bright blue winter sky, the dense black cloud almost hid the skyscrapers to the north. An acrid odor clung to the air. Despite the cold, shopkeepers and pedestrians stood on the sidewalks, staring uptown, discussing the phenomenon. She could hear the wails of many sirens in the distance. Some seemed to approach, then fade away toward the East River.

Rachael walked on, absorbed in her own misery. She did not for a moment suspect that the fire concerned her.

She had never wanted her father more in her life. Never before had she so needed his comfort, his wisdom.

She was not at all certain of what she was about to do. And she had no one to advise her.

Even in her present state of mind, she no longer held illusions. With America at war, she was a spy for the enemy. Despite what the FBI agent had said, her voluntary surrender probably would not mitigate her punishment. She fully expected the death sentence.

The prospect did not bother her. She no longer cared.

But as yet, Von Beck had committed no criminal act. She would make that fact plain to the authorities. As an illegal alien, he no doubt would be interned, safe, for the duration of the war.

The thought gave her some satisfaction.

Two taxis waited at Sixth and Houston, their motors running, the exhausts raising plumes of vapor. The driver of the front cab turned in his seat and helped Rachael with the door. Thoroughly chilled from the wind, she was grateful for the warmth of the heater.

"The federal building on Foley Square, please," she said.

The driver nodded, hit the flag on the meter, and roared into the intersection. Rachael settled back in the seat, strangely relieved that her decision had been made.

As they approached the square, six ambulances passed, one behind the other, sirens howling. Two fire trucks came from the opposite direction, heading uptown. Rachael remembered the pall of smoke.

"Could you tell me what's happening?" she asked.

The driver waited until he was past an intersection before answering. "Big fire on the piers, lady. Know the liner *Normandie?* It's burning. Lots of people hurt already."

Rachael sat stunned. Her first, overwhelming concern was for Von Beck. She was rendered momentarily helpless by her sudden fear for him. She made several efforts before she could speak. "How do you know?"

The driver seemed strangely animated. "The radio. They're calling it a major disaster." He pointed to the disappearing ambulances. "They're taking people to hospitals in Brooklyn, all over. They're saying there's still some men trapped in it." He braked for a light. "I was in the Times Square subway wreck in twenty-eight. I wouldn't want to go through anything like that again, I'll tell you."

Rachael regained her voice. "Take me there!"

The driver looked in his rearview mirror to gauge her seriousness. He pulled toward the curb and braked to a stop.

"Are you all right, lady?"

"Yes. Take me there. Please!"

He shook his head. "Lady, I can't take you up there. It's a mess. The West Side Highway's closed at Twenty-third. Eleventh and Twelfth avenues are blocked off. They've got hundreds of cops all over Midtown, turning away all traffic except ambulances and fire trucks."

"I *must* go there!" Rachael said. "My husband is on board the *Normandie!*"

The lie worked. The driver thought for a moment. "I might be able to get you up to Forty-sixth, maybe even Forty-eighth. You'd have to walk over from about Sixth."

Rachael pleaded. "If you could, I would be so grateful!"

The driver put the taxi in gear, circled the block, and headed uptown. Leaning forward, Rachael saw that the smoke had grown even thicker, forming a broad band across mid-Manhattan.

Traffic increased dramatically above Thirty-second Street. Her driver weaved expertly through the snarls, frequently resorting to his horn. A civilian wearing a tin hat, armband, and gas mask kit was directing traffic at one intersection.

Her driver laughed. "Lookit," he said. "One of the mayor's commandos."

"I beg your pardon?"

"Office of Civilian Defense. An air raid warden, for Christ's sake!"

All westbound traffic was halted above Forty-second Street, the intersections almost completely blocked. Her driver aggressively took advantage of every small opening. At Forty-eighth, he pulled to the curb. She gave him a ten-dollar bill and left the cab, not waiting for change.

The wind had turned much colder. The sky was now overcast. Near the river, still six long blocks away, Rachael could see a gigantic, towering plume of smoke and many flashing red lights. With her face snuggled deep into her upturned collar, she started walking toward the piers, occasionally running until her breath came in short, painful gasps.

She remembered the many afternoons she had walked with Von Beck back to Broadway from the piers. She had considered the distance only a pleasant stroll. Now the blocks seemed endless.

By the time she reached Tenth Avenue, she was pushing her way through crowds. At Eleventh, Negro soldiers with fixed bayonets were attempting to keep pedestrians behind ropes strung across the intersection. There was trouble. Some youths ducked under the ropes and ran across the street, trying to join the larger crowd near Twelfth Avenue. The soldiers chased the white youths, punching at them with rifle butts. Around her, the crowd was yelling angrily at the soldiers.

While attention was diverted, Rachael slipped under the rope and dashed for the opposite curb. She heard the soldiers shout. She ran on without looking back, not stopping for breath until she had plunged into the crowd beyond.

Slowly, she pushed her way through to the rope barrier at Twelfth Avenue where she stood motionless for several minutes, numbed by the icy wind and her first full view of the burning *Normandie*.

The ship listed several degrees to port. Flames poured from her Promenade Deck—the Winter Garden, the Grand Salon, the Smoking Room. Great streams of water arced onto the fire, pumped from three fireboats close to the ship's port side. Smaller streams of water rose from the pier. A long ladder reached from the elevated highway to the bow of the ship. As Rachael watched, two shipyard workers inched along the ladder, making their way to safety. Each time the ladder swayed, the crowd gasped. Rachael became so engrossed in the drama that momentarily she even forgot the freezing cold.

Slowly, the two men reached the overhead highway and no longer could be seen from below.

Hundreds of men were milling around the ship. Rachael searched among them in vain for Von Beck's familiar build. A constant stream of shipyard workers flowed from the pier. No where did she see Von Beck.

Her view was partially blocked by more than a dozen fire trucks. Ambulances were arriving and departing constantly, sirens wailing.

The whole scene resembled a Hollywood costume production. The entire waterfront was awash with uniforms— policemen, firemen, the black soldiers with their leggings and bayonets, the Civilian Defense wardens with their tin hats, arm bands, and gas-mask kits, immaculate, well-groomed matrons in Red Cross uniforms, nurses, sailors, priests, doctors, Catholic nuns. In front of the pier, smartly uniformed women were dispensing coffee and doughnuts from a Red Cross truck.

Rachael wondered how they all had arrived so quickly. Around her, the spectators were talking animatedly, laughing, enjoying the excitement. Beyond the *Normandie* and the fire boats she could see another huge crowd on the Jersey shore. Two small planes circled low overhead.

As an ambulance pulled away, Rachael saw a row of stretcher cases. Doctors and nurses moved among them. Rachael caught a glimpse of an injured man she thought might be Von Beck.

Only vaguely aware of her movements, Rachael slipped under the rope and started across Twelfth Avenue, running toward the stretchers. She reached the middle of the street before a black soldier grabbed her arm.

"Miss! Nobody goes across this street without a pass."

Rachael struggled, pointing. "I see my husband over there!"

But as she said it, she saw that the man was not Von Beck.

The soldier roughly shoved her back toward the barrier. "Can't help it, Miss. Nobody goes beyond this point without a pass. Captain's orders."

He held the rope for her, then went back to his post.

Shivering uncontrollably, Rachael stood and watched the *Normandie* burn. Soon the flames were no longer visible. Only an occasional flicker could be seen behind the windows on the Promenade Deck. But the towering plume of smoke and steam had increased. Great cascades of water now poured from the ship's rail. The list seemed more pronounced.

More Negro troops arrived, marching in formation. A white officer shouted orders. The soldiers lined up in a solid row of bayonets and advanced.

With only an occasional scuffle, the crowd retreated. To Rachael's left, a heavy-set man protested loudly, explaining that he was a photographer from the *New York Daily News*. The white officer came and, after a heated argument, confiscated the man's large camera. The angry photographer was led away.

Maintaining steady pressure, the soldiers pushed the crowds back to Eleventh Avenue.

There Rachael took up her vigil. Her hands, face and feet were numb from the cold. But she was determined. She would wait until she saw Von Beck, if she turned to a block of ice.

24

Pier 88, Hudson River, New York City

Von Beck did not dare show the luminous dial of his watch and he had no way of knowing, but he was certain that more than two hours had passed. In all that time he had not moved, except to shift his weight occasionally to relieve the cramping in his legs.

The FBI man still guarded the hole. In the quiet of the hold, Von Beck could hear his breath, the faint rustle of clothing.

During his long wait, Von Beck had reconstructed the probable sequence of events on the ship.

After the outbreak of fire somewhere topside—probably on either the Sun, Boat, or Promenade Deck—the *Normandie*'s highly efficient ventilation system had sucked fumes and smoke into the interior of the ship. Someone had shut down the electrical generators in order to kill power to the ventilators.

From his extensive studies of the ship, Von Beck was aware of certain hazards that might not be of general knowledge. To protect the *Normandie*'s weak plumbing system, the fire mains ordinarily were maintained at a low pressure. Normally, on the sounding of the fire alarm, the pressure was raised by increasing the power to the pumps.

When the generators shut down, pressure in the fire ship's fire mains was reduced to zero. The ship now was totally dependent on the New York City Fire Department.

This fact no doubt accounted for the growing list to port. Land-based firefighters tended to battle flames with all the water available. Tons upon tons of water probably were cascading onto the upper decks, adding tremendous weight high above the ship's center of gravity.

From time to time he heard distant noises. Some he recognized. He could imagine the scene on the pier, the giant hawsers stretched tight, pulling bollards loose from the docks and slamming them into the side of the ship. He had heard hammering. The Navy was probably attempting to flood the starboard ballast tanks by knocking a hole in the hull.

Standing on a crossbeam in the darkness, Von Beck estimated that the ship already was canted over at least fifteen degrees.

He also knew other secrets about the *Normandie* not widely advertised. The ship had virtually no thwartship watertight integrity on the upper decks. Unhampered, all water entering the ship could accumulate at the lowest point. The Horowitz system—serving as the ship's storm sewer—was power driven. No other facilities existed for the release of large quantities of impounded water topside. With the electrical generators silenced, most of the water would remain on the upper decks, gathering in the direction of the list, well above the center of gravity.

The loss of power would have prevented the closing of fireproof doors throughout the ship. Early firefighters also would have encountered another difficulty. All fire connections on board were undergoing change from French fittings to American standard. Both types of connections and hoses were scattered throughout the ship. In some areas, valves had been closed, shutting off the fire mains while the work was done.

For a time, Von Beck wondered why the ship had not already capsized. Then he understood.

With the early return of flood tide, the *Normandie* still had very little water under her keel. She was flat-bottomed. She now was held from further list by the fact that the port side of her hull was resting on the bottom. When the tide reached full flood—sometime after midnight—the ship would float completely free and capsize.

The thought moved Von Beck to action. Turning his head so his voice would echo and be diffused, he spoke into the darkness.

"If you're interested in living, friend, you'd better get off this ship. She may not stay afloat much longer."

The disembodied voice came out of the darkness, calm and confident. "After you, Von Beck. I'll be right behind you. Just turn on your flashlight and come on out."

Surprised to hear his name, Von Beck wondered why only one agent had been sent to make the arrest.

"What's *your* name?" he asked.

The hesitation was brief. "Bonham."

The man who had visited Rachael! How long had he been onto them? Why was he apparently acting alone?

"Well, Bonham, you seem to have gotten yourself in a pickle," Von Beck said. "You have me, but you don't have me. You can't get me out, and I'm not coming out. Every minute you stay, you're putting your life in further jeopardy."

"You better be thinking about your own fucking life," Bonham said. "I'm not leaving without you."

Von Beck spent the next half hour analyzing his plight. He concluded that he had to get off the ship. He either had to trick or fight his way past the fanatic holding the gun. And he had only his few tools as weapons.

Moving cautiously, he felt the beams overhead, trying to remember their placement in relation to the hole. Careful not to make the slightest noise, he unwound his fifty-foot measuring tape from its reel.

Feeling his way in the darkness, he tied each end to an

341

overhead beam, then constructed a cat's cradle for his big five-cell flashlight.

Silently, he guided the flashlight through its arc, testing, making certain he had gauged its path correctly.

He picked up his heavy socket wrench. He stepped to one side, switched on the flashlight, and hurled it into its carefully planned arc.

Blinded by the sudden light hurling at him out of the darkness, Bonham fired. He was raising his gun for a second shot when the socket wrench sailed through the hole and hit him squarely between the eyes.

Stunned, he dropped to one knee. And in that instant Von Beck was upon him, going for the gun.

Bonham tried to swing the pistol clear. Von Beck seized his wrist. Straining, they grappled and fell to the steel deck.

The flashlight still swung in and out of the hole, casting eerie shadows. Bonham made an effort to twist away. But Von Beck was strong, and Bonham had not yet fully recovered from his beating.

With sickening frustration, he felt his muscles giving way. Von Beck was slamming Bonham's hand relentlessly against the steel deck. Pain shot up his arm. He tried to hold onto the pistol, but Von Beck battered it out of his hand.

They rolled across the deck, pounding at each other's faces. Von Beck then drove a forearm into Bonham's nose and spun free.

Bonham staggered to his feet. Through pain and swirling stars he saw Von Beck crawling for the gun. Bonham took two quick steps and kicked the revolver. It went skidding across the deck and disappeared into the darkness.

They fought by the glow of the flashlight, now almost motionless just inside the hole. Von Beck had the advantage of weight and strength. But Bonham had the edge of experience in barroom brawling. He knew the trick of dropping below Von Beck's haymakers, countering with solid, straight punches. Taking only an occasional blow to the top of his head, Bonham flailed away at Von Beck's face, breaking his nose, closing his left eye.

Von Beck seemed groggy. But in his weakened condition, Bonham could not finish him off. Growing overconfident, he swung a haymaker and missed. Von Beck lowered his shoulder and charged, driving Bonham back into wooden crates. Von Beck held Bonham there, ramming his shoulder into Bonham's stomach and chest time after time.

The pain on top of Bonham's earlier injuries was excruciating. Von Beck stepped back and hit him with two solid, roundhouse blows. Dazed, Bonham fell to his hands and knees. Von Beck kicked him full in the face and sent him sprawling.

When his head cleared, Bonham saw Von Beck running, flashlight in hand, toward the distant stairwell. Bonham reached for a wooden crate and pulled himself erect. Von Beck was almost to the door, taking all light with him.

Bonham plunged after him. As the light disappeared, Bonham kept the spot fixed in his mind and ran on through the darkness, not slowing until he was certain he was about to collide with the wall.

With the disorienting slant of the deck, he had veered several feet to the left. Frantically, he searched for the door, wasting precious seconds.

By the time he entered the stairwell, Von Beck was two decks above, still clattering upward. Bonham raced after him, taking the stairs two at a time.

The lingering smoke grew heavier as Bonham fought his way upward. Von Beck left the stairwell at A Deck, and again Bonham was in complete darkness. Recklessly, guided only by the handrails, he climbed to A Deck and fumbled his way through the door.

Von Beck was far down the corridor, running.

Bonham's long legs gave him an advantage, despite the

disturbing cant of the ship. Running at top speed, he managed to close some of the distance as Von Beck moved aft through a maze of corridors and passageways.

Bonham was only a few steps behind when Von Beck again disappeared into a stairwell.

They raced up four levels. Von Beck exited on the Boat Deck. Bonham plunged through the door after him.

He emerged into blinding, choking smoke. Six paces from the door he was disoriented, unable even to see Von Beck's flashlight. His ears were assaulted by the roar of a waterfall.

Choking, his hands outstretched, Bonham searched through the smoke, hunting for Von Beck.

He was exhausted, his lungs burning for air, when he saw the faint glow of the flashlight in the gloom.

He took Von Beck totally by surprise. Putting his full strength behind a blow, he caught Von Beck solidly on the side of the head. He aimed at the soft bones of the temple. The punch landed two inches too high.

Von Beck went down. Bonham tripped over him. His chin hit the deck. Before he could recover, Von Beck was on him, hammering at his face.

Bonham grappled, trying to throw Von Beck off balance. Bonham held his grip as they tumbled, end over end, down a long flight of stairs. When they hit bottom, the shock of the ice-cold water was paralyzing. Von Beck slipped from his grasp.

Bonham surfaced in panic. He was relieved to find the water less than waist deep. The smoke was much thinner at this lower level. Faint traces of daylight penetrated the haze. Bonham lowered his head and breathed much-needed oxygen. When he looked up, Von Beck was wading for the stairs.

Again, Bonham went after him.

They fought at the foot of the grand staircase. The slant of the deck, the slippery footing allowed no margin for finesse. They stood toe to toe, slugging.

With growing elation, Bonham saw that he was winning. Von Beck's blows grew weaker, more erratic. At last, Von Beck swung, missed, and lost his footing. As he slid toward the deeper water along the port bulkhead, Bonham followed.

Von Beck disappeared under water. Bonham did not realize he had been tricked until Von Beck grabbed his ankles.

Caught by surprise, Bonham took water into his lungs as he suddenly plunged beneath the surface. He fought his way back to air, strangling. Von Beck landed two stunning punches to his head, then shoved him back under water.

Bonham struggled desperately for air. Von Beck held him in an unyielding grip. He tried in vain to reach Von Beck's genitals, any vulnerable spot.

Slowly, his consciousness faded.

Von Beck reeled away from Bonham, pushing his way through the frigid water toward the grand staircase. He glanced back. Bonham was floating on the surface, sliding toward deeper water.

The grand staircase was in shambles, the bulkheads and ceiling charred. Using the handrails, Von Beck struggled upward, stumbling over twists of broken and abandoned fire hose.

The icy water had left him numb from the waist down. Blood still poured from his smashed nose. He had lost several teeth, sheered off at the gumline. His right eye was swelled shut. He suspected that his left cheekbone might be broken. And he had splintered the knuckles of his right hand against Bonham's hard head. The pain radiating up his arm was excruciating.

He had never fought so hard in his life. Bonham's persistence had been astounding.

He reached the top of the grand staircase. A few feet away lay the Boat Deck promenade, and safety.

Von Beck paused, and glanced back. He could not see through the gloomy, smoke-filled interior. But he remembered the last time he had seen Bonham, sliding into deeper water.

He knew the memory would stay with him the rest of his life—along with countless other such memories.

With a sob of anguish, he turned back and plunged down the staircase. He again went into the water, searching frantically. Great icy streams from the fireboats spattered through the shattered windows and raced down the stairway, forming vast whirlpools. Von Beck pushed his way into the maelstrom, making wide sweeps under the water with his hands.

He found Bonham against the port bulkhead. Ducking under the water, he managed to get his shoulder under Bonham's middle. Using the wall, he pulled himself erect.

Painfully, step by step, he inched his way through the water to the grand staircase.

Carrying Bonham, leaning heavily on the handrails, he floundered upward. Twice he fell in complete exhaustion, certain he would never make it. But each time he gained enough strength to go on.

Bracing Bonham against the wall of the grand staircase, Von Beck got his shoulder under him, pushed his way erect, and resumed his climb.

An eternity later, he emerged from the Grill Room onto the open Boat Deck. A shout went up from the pier as they were spotted. Within minutes, two firemen were at Von Beck's side. One knelt beside Bonham.

"He's in a bad way," he said. He looked at Von Beck. "Good God! What happened to you two guys? You fall down an elevator shaft?"

"Something like that," Von Beck said.

A breeches buoy had been rigged to the pier. Bonham was lowered first. By the time Von Beck reached the pier, a doctor was working over Bonham.

Despite his protests, Von Beck was loaded onto a

346

stretcher and carried to the stringpiece, where several injured men awaited ambulances.

The icy air over his broken teeth, the pain from his smashed nose had revived him. His wet clothing had frozen, painfully scratching his skin. He badly wanted the warmth of a hospital bed. But he knew he could not take the risk.

Attention was diverted as Bonham was loaded into an ambulance.

Quickly, Von Beck rolled off his stretcher and hurried across Twelfth Avenue.

He was halfway to Eleventh when Rachael came running toward him out of the crowd and buried herself in his arms.

25

Pier 88, New York City

By 6 P.M. the fire was out, at least officially. The flotilla of fireboats continued to pour water on smoldering pockets, but most of the engine crews rolled up their hoses and departed.

The work of attempting to save the ship began.

Naval officers, civilian inspectors and shipyard officials streamed back aboard to explore the possibilities. After rigging lights from shore, firemen fanned out through the interior of the ship, extinguishing minor but stubborn flames. Two Special Agents from the FBI went aboard and, with considerable difficulty, made their way to the origin of the fire to gather evidence.

On the pier, two Red Cross movable kitchens arrived and dispensed sandwiches and hot coffee to the hundreds of military men, firemen, and shipyard workers who would labor far into the night.

By 9 P.M., authorities first began to suspect that the battle might be hopeless.

The list had reached twenty degrees.

Lieutenant Hyman Roth stood in the terminal building,

waiting for the admiral to arrive. He had resisted three separate efforts to take him back to the hospital. His face and hands were badly burned, but he felt he still could make a contribution.

For the last three hours he had assisted the admiral's staff in assembling damage reports. One by one, the inspectors and shipyard officials had returned from tours of the ship to offer their descriptions and recommendations. From these reports, the staff had gathered an excellent understanding of the ship's plight.

The Promenade Deck from the Grill Room forward to the main bridge was gutted. The 1,100 bales of life preservers in the Grand Salon, the 2,200 mattresses in the corridors and Winter Garden had burned with tremendous heat. Water had pooled in the portside staterooms and along the promenade walk. This collection of water on the upper decks extended one third the length of the ship.

Every effort to remove the water had failed. The New York City Fire Department had brought aboard twenty basement pumps, each with a capacity of 250 gallons a minute. The pumps did not have any perceptible effect in lowering the water. An effort was made to use the fireboats to suck the water back into the river. The hoses would not reach.

Robins Dry Dock and Repair Company welders attempted to cut holes in the port side. The water put out their torches. Navy crewmen managed to knock holes in the starboard side of the hull. Five wing tanks were flooded, providing some counterbalancing. The list to port was slowed only for a brief time. Large cargo doors remained partially open on the port side. Efforts had been made to close them, but their hydraulic rams required the ship's power.

The inspectors offered a few glimmers of hope. Damage to the ship was limited. For instance, the theater firewall proved its worth. The theater was unharmed. Smoke damage throughout the ship was minimal. Only small amounts of water had seeped down stairwells onto C and D Decks. The Main Entrance Hall, the huge First-Class Dining Room were dry. The ship's boilers, turboalternators, and electric propulsion motors were unaffected.

The ship had been saved at a tremendous cost. Two hundred and twenty-nine officers and men of the U.S. Navy and Coast Guard, 283 shipyard workers and more than 200 firemen had been treated for injuries.

One man had died.

For three solid hours, ambulances had streamed onto the pier, taking away the injured.

That the ship remained afloat, relatively unharmed, seemed to be a miracle.

Now, an even bigger miracle was needed.

Admiral Adolphus Andrews arrived a few minutes after nine. He strode into the terminal, accompanied by the flurry that always surrounds flag rank. Escorted to the long table where his staff had compiled the damage reports, he listened to their analysis in silence, his expression grave.

Hyman Roth stood on the periphery of the group as the admiral studied the charts and figures. After a few minutes, Andrews glanced at his watch.

"Mayor La Guardia and Fire Commissioner Walsh will join us in a moment for a tour of the ship," he announced. "Afterward, we'll discuss a course of action."

As he moved away from the table, he noticed Roth and halted in midstride. "Lieutenant, have those burns had attention?"

"Yes, sir," Roth said, embarrassed.

"They look pretty bad. You sure you're all right?"

"I'm fine, sir."

The admiral grunted. "We don't need more casualties around here, now. You get that looked after."

"Aye aye, sir," Roth said.

"I've heard about your performance today, Lieutenant," Andrews said. "Excellent work."

350

"Thank you, sir," Roth managed to stammer.

The admiral swept past him, followed by his retinue. Roth was aware of the brief, puzzled glances from the admiral's staff. Barthelmess fell into step with Roth as they followed the group toward the front of the terminal.

"You feel up to this?" he asked.

"Of course," Roth said.

"You don't have to do it, you know. You've done your bit. The admiral was quite impressed. If nothing else, there'll be a Letter of Commendation stuck in your file."

"Frankly, I thought I made a bust of it," Roth said. "We should have been able to put the fire out in the first two minutes."

"Be that as it may," Barthelmess said. "The evacuation of the ship was what grabbed the admiral. Your quick action in stationing men with flashlights at the intersection of corridors was a brilliant bit of thinking. It's amazing, when you think about it. Three thousand men, most of them unfamiliar with the ship, got off through those passageways filled with smoke, with all lights and power off. And only one man lost."

"The night's not over," Roth pointed out.

Mayor La Guardia and Commissioner Patrick J. Walsh had just arrived. The admiral was introducing his staff.

"This is Captain Clayton Simmers of the Materiel Office. He has charge of thirty or more conversions in the Third District. Lieutenant Commander Victor Weldon. He is liaison to the contractors in conversion of the *Normandie*. Captain R. G. Coman, who is to assume command of the *Normandie* on completion of the conversion. Mr. Henry Wood, senior naval inspector. . . ."

As each man was introduced, he stepped forward and shook hands with the mayor. In keeping with his rank, Roth was the last of the inspection party to be presented.

Short and rotund, the mayor wore a heavy raincoat with a corduroy collar and fireman's boots. He seemed impatient.

When the introductions were completed, Admiral Andrews and Mayor La Guardia led the way across the gang-plank, onto the *Normandie.*

The emergency lighting had turned the Main Entrance Hall into a vast, shadowy cavern. Aides and junior officers carried electric lanterns, illuminating the various aspects of the ship as each was discussed by the admiral and the mayor. Roth and Barthelmess hung back, allowing the senior officers to go ahead.

The Entrance Hall and Main Dining room were dry. Not until they entered the stairwells did they encounter water. Leaning against the list, sloshing through pools accumulated on the landings, they worked their way down three decks to the engine spaces.

During the last half hour, enough water had reached the boiler rooms to put the level as high as the gratings. But there was nothing that could not be fixed with a few buckets and swabs.

"I'm amazed she's in such good shape," Admiral Andrews said. "She's hardly touched below D Deck."

Captain Simmers of the Navy Materiel Office agreed. "If we can keep her from capsizing, I can have her ready for sea by Friday."

The admiral seemed dubious. "Friday?"

Simmers nodded. "Most all damage is confined to the top three decks. We can strip out the burned bulkheads and put in new plywood. The rest of the outfitting can wait until she's through with sea trials in Boston."

"*If* we can save her," the admiral said. "The question is, what's to be done? Commander Weldon, are you still opposed to scuttling?"

Weldon hesitated. "I've made further inquiries since we last talked, Admiral. The far side of the slip was dredged deeper for the *Queen Mary,* and the bottom is uneven. There's a rocky ledge on the starboard side, and the bottom slopes to port. The consensus is that scuttling would only increase the hazard of her flipping."

"Scuttling is out of the question," Commissioner Walsh said.

352

The admiral fixed Walsh with a steady stare. "Why?"

"Valves are open on some of the fuel tanks. We can't have that oil flowing out into the river."

"I fail to see the point," Andrews said. "The same hazard exists if she capsizes."

"*If* she capsizes," Mayor La Guardia said. "I agree with the commissioner, Admiral. There's no use subjecting ourselves to that risk unless absolutely necessary. If the oil were carried downstream, into the other piers, the whole waterfront could go up in flames."

Andrews noticed the expression on Weldon's face. "Was there something else you wanted to say, Commander?"

"Yes, sir. I've talked to the Frenchmen on board. They told me the seacocks are very difficult to reach, and their effects delicate. The valves would have to be opened in a very controlled sequence to prevent capsizing."

The admiral seemed to grasp the problem immediately. Unless opened by experts—and under ideal conditions—the seacocks could only compound the danger.

"Well, that's out, then," Andrews said. He turned to Captain Coman. "This is asking a lot of a crew that has just reported aboard. But the machinery is in good shape. If we got up steam, do you suppose that with the help of enough tugs, we could back her out of the slip, take her downstream, and ease her aground on a soft mudbank?"

Coman considered his answer carefully. "The risk would be high, Admiral. My understanding is that the ship's bridge is inoperative. We would have to shift the conn to after steering. At night, with a totally untrained crew. . . ."

"There's something else, Admiral," Simmers interrupted. "The screws were disconnected to test the propulsion motors. Only one propeller is still attached to the drive shaft."

Andrews glanced at Coman. "Can you do it with one screw, Captain?"

The joke snapped the tension. The excessive laughter of relief swept the group. Andrews turned back to Simmers.

"How long would it take to reconnect the screws?"

"Five hours, Admiral."

Andrews did not answer. Everyone knew that the ship's crisis would come in less time.

The admiral sighed. "How much water is aboard. Has anyone made estimates?"

Commissioner Walsh pulled a slip of paper from his pocket. "We had thirty-five streams of water on the ship for three hours. That would be roughly eight hundred and forty thousand gallons. I calculate that less than three percent remained aboard."

Andrews thought for a moment. "Only six hundred tons?"

"That's my estimate," Walsh said.

The engine room was silent as all considered the problem. In the context of ship loading, six hundred tons seemed almost insignificant. But that weight was heavily fulcrumed by the *Normandie*'s flaring sides, her high center of gravity.

"And no pumps," the Admiral said.

"We've scoured the whole East Coast," Simmers said. "There are simply none of that size available." He glanced at Walsh. "But we could stop putting water on her."

"The fire is still smoldering," La Guardia said. "We've got to keep putting water on it."

"Water that's destroying the ship, Mister Mayor," Andrews said. "I understand that fighting the fire is your chief concern. But the responsibility for the preservation of the ship is mine. I formally request that you turn off the water."

"It's flowing over the rail as fast as we're putting it aboard," Walsh said. "The decks are full, the level constant. At this point, we're not adding more weight."

"I'm afraid we are," Simmers said. "Ice is forming on the side of the ship."

"As long as fire exists, we've got to keep it wet down," La Guardia insisted. "The commissioner is right."

Andrews looked at La Guardia for a long moment. "Mis-

354

ter Mayor, if this ship capsizes, you're going to have one hell of a mess on your front doorstep. No ship of this size has ever been refloated. Such a salvage operation staggers the imagination. If she had to be cut up for scrap, it would take months, years. And you'd have your two biggest terminals out of operation. I'd hate to take that responsibility."

Andrews and La Guardia exchanged stares.

Captain Simmers spoke. "May I suggest a compromise, Admiral. Suppose the mayor turns the water off until indication is seen that the fire is rekindling."

Andrews nodded abruptly. "That would be satisfactory."

La Guardia's hesitation was brief. "I'll send word to the fireboats," he said.

Barthelmess touched Roth's arm. "Could I talk to you a minute, Hyman?"

They waited until the inspection party moved away. Barthelmess checked to be sure they were out of earshot before he turned back to Roth. He seemed hesitant, and slightly embarrassed.

"What I mentioned earlier, about the Letter of Commendation, that came straight from the admiral," he said. "It wouldn't surprise me if you didn't earn another stripe this afternoon."

Roth was puzzled by Barthelmess's manner. "Thank you for telling me," he said.

"It was the admiral's suggestion," Barthelmess said. "And there's one other thing he asked me to mention."

Roth waited. Barthelmess seemed to have trouble finding words.

"About your report. You never made it. Understand?"

Roth stared at him. "But this just proves that everything in the report is true!"

"Exactly," Barthelmess said. "If this ship capsizes,

there will be a stink that won't stop. There'll be investigations by both houses of Congress, boards of inquiry, Naval Intelligence, the FBI, everyone. And if your report caused a flap with the Third Naval District staff *before* the fire, think what it will do in Washington *after* the fire. You don't want that, Roth. The admiral doesn't want it. The Navy doesn't want it.''

Roth did not answer.

Barthelmess clapped him on the shoulder. ''Just think about that extra stripe, Hyman.''

He turned and walked away. After a moment, Roth followed.

Three hours later, Admiral Andrews led a smaller inspection party through the ship.

The list had increased to forty degrees.

On completion of the tour, the admiral gathered his staff in the Main Entrance Hall.

''Get everyone off the ship,'' he said. ''She's going to go. There's nothing more we can do.''

26

Pier 88, Hudson River, New York City

The *Normandie* lay bathed in the eerie glow of flood-lights jury-rigged on the pier. Ice now sheathed her port side. Her list was past forty degrees. The fireboats, the tugs had withdrawn from the ice-filled slip. Remaining hawsers strained, cracked, and parted with the finality of cannon fire. A tall crane slid across her fo'c's'le, tumbled over the side, and disappeared beneath the floating cakes of ice. A few minutes after 1 A.M. the first gangway, stretched to its limits, pulled from the pier and fell with a tremendous clatter. The second followed a few minutes later. The final gangway dropped at 1:42 A.M., severing the *Normandie*'s last association with shore.

Her death rattles began.

Maurice Raynal stood on the stringpiece and listened, making no effort to stop the tears rolling down his cheeks. During his career, he had heard many legends of the sea. He remembered the story of the *Leviathan*'s last voyage en route to the scrap yard. With uncanny premonition, the ship had fought the crew every step of the way, putting everyone on edge. The last night out, the ship's foghorn of

357

its own volition had wailed for hours in mortal anguish, almost making basket cases of the whole crew.

He also remembered the survivors' descriptions of the unearthly sounds that came from the *Titanic* before she took her fatal plunge.

Raynal knew he was witnessing such a legend.

For minutes at a time there was only the hum of the generators for the emergency lights. Then a strident cacophony would erupt as vital gear from throughout the ship ripped loose, skidded across the inner decks, and slammed into bulkheads.

The mortal symphony seemed to last forever. With each sound, Raynal felt as if something vital were being torn from his own heart.

Added to his agony was his suspicion that the *Normandie* had been sacrificed as a pawn in some vast game he did not understand.

Too many factors were beyond explanation. The series of mistakes appeared to have been orchestrated—the kapok life preservers and mattresses stored in close proximity while the fire hoses, couplings, and alarm system were in the disarray of change, while the ship's screws were disconnected. The fire had seemed to spread with extraordinary speed. Instead of merely shutting down the ventilators, someone had ordered the boiler rooms abandoned, shutting off the ship's power with undue haste, reducing water pressure. None of the fireproof doors had closed. Cargo ports had remained open.

The *Normandie* had always been such a lucky ship. Such a string of unfortunate coincidences was inconceivable.

The temperature had dropped to nineteen degrees. A twenty-knot wind came from across the river, pushing the cake ice into the slip, piling it against the *Normandie*. Raynal huddled in the lee of the Cunard terminal, waiting for the inevitable.

Boats, tools, air tanks, hundreds of items of loose gear continued to tumble from the ship.

358

The end seemed near.

Raynal could see the mayor, Navy officers, and shipyard authorities waiting on the stringpiece near the Transatlantique terminal. Only a small crowd of spectators watched from Twelfth Avenue. From time to time the admiral and mayor spent a few minutes in the warmth of the admiral's car.

Shortly after 2 A.M., the sounds from the ship ceased. She hung at an incredible angle, as if dreading the plunge into the frigid mud and water. Only the drone of the generators, the engine of a passing car on the overhead highway marred the silence of the night. All conversation ceased.

At 2:45 A.M., with a tremendous sigh, the *Normandie* slowly rolled. Her high prow for a moment seemed to be searching in vain for support as the bow moved northward to the center of the slip. As she turned gently onto her side, her stern snuggled under the Transatlantique pier, nudging concrete out of the way. Her massive funnels stopped just inches short of the water. The mast missed the Cunard pier by only ten yards.

A peaceful ripple spread across the water and ice.

Then all was still.

Raynal stood for a moment as the terrible sight burned indelibly into his memory.

He then turned and walked away, heading for the Seamen's Church Institute in Lower Manhattan. There he would spend the night.

His decision had been made.

He was not a great admirer of Charles De Gaulle. But there was no choice. Tomorrow he would seek passage to England for enlistment with the Free French.

27

Bellevue Hospital, New York City

Bonham awoke to the ringing of bells, the strong smell of ether and disinfectant. He lay in the darkened room, staring at the dull gray ceiling, methodically assembling the disorder of sensations sweeping through his head. Sharp pain knifed across his heavily taped chest with each breath. Two ribs broken, possibly more. His face hurt. Experimenting through gentle movement, he ascertained that his nose and upper lip were bruised, swollen out of proportion. Cautiously exploring with his tongue, he found no teeth missing. His head throbbed with each heartbeat. After a time, he determined that some of the bells were ringing in his head, and others outside in the hospital corridor. Not until he moved, searching his pillow for a bell cord to summon a nurse, did he see the man sitting in the shadows at the corner of the room.

Bonham and the man exchanged glares in silence. At last, Bonham again moved to search his pillow for a bell cord. He found none.

"How long have I been here?" he asked. His mouth was dry. He was surprised by the weakness of his own voice.

The man continued to stare without answering.

Bonham tried again. "Who the fuck are you?"

The man did not offer the slightest indication that he had heard.

"Can you talk?" Bonham asked.

With a sigh, the man shifted his weight. "I'm not to converse with you," he said. "Those are my orders."

Bonham attempted to reach the nightstand at the head of his bed. A wave of dizziness rolled him back in a paroxysm of pain.

"Would you mind getting me a glass of water?" he asked.

The man did not move. "I'm not a nurse," he said.

"Well kiss my ass, then," Bonham said.

He lost interest for a time, wafting back and forth from vivid, technicolor dreams to his bland, drab hospital room. Reality and hallucination interfused. For a time he slept. When he again awoke, daylight had arrived and the room was filled with men in dark suits. Eight of them were gathered around his bed, gazing down at him steadily, impassionately. All seemed stamped out by the same cookie cutter. Each was in his late twenties or early thirties, solidly built, athletic, and of extremely serious demeanor.

"He's awake," someone said, speaking to the man standing by Bonham's right shoulder. He seemed to be the stud duck of the outfit.

Bonham waited warily, still sifting the nightmare images of sleep from harsh fact. He was familiar enough with procedure to know that he was in custody.

But he also knew that not even his defection from the Bureau would have instigated such an impressive show of force. Two or three Special Agents, perhaps accompanied by a stenographer, would have been sent for his initial interrogation.

Not eight investigators.

Who the fuck were these people?

Did they think *he* burned their goddamned ship?

A squat, no-nonsense nurse pushed her way through and approached Bonham's bed, a hypodermic needle poised. "If you gentlemen will excuse me. . . ."

The stud duck thrust out a hand, palm outward. "That can wait," he snapped. "We must talk with Mr. Bonham. He needs a clear head."

The nurse was not intimidated. Her frown of disapproval deepened. "The doctor——"

"The doctor will tell you that we are not to be disturbed," the man said. "Please be so good as to wait until we are through here."

The nurse hesitated briefly. She glanced at Bonham, then at the stud duck. "We'll see," she said. She turned and marched out.

The stud duck leaned over Bonham. At his signal, a microphone was shoved forward, and Bonham heard the whir of a wire recorder.

"Mr. Bonham, we are here to ask you a few questions," stud duck said.

"Credentials," Bonham said.

"I beg your pardon?"

Painfully, Bonham pushed himself higher on the pillow. "Names, credentials. I want to know who the fuck I'm talking to."

Stud duck looked at Bonham for a moment. He then reached into his shirt pocket and pulled out a leather case. "All right," he said. He held the badge and credentials out for Bonham to read. Bonham checked them carefully.

They identified the man as Albert J. Sykes, Special Agent for the Federal Bureau of Investigation. Bonham managed to hide his surprise. He had been certain the men were not from the Bureau. The credentials seemed authentic. But something nagged for several seconds in the back of Bonham's drug-clouded mind before he grasped what was wrong.

"Good try," he said. "But that number's too low."

"I beg your pardon?"

"The badge number. If you had a number that low, you'd be an old fart."

Sykes nodded. "Very good," he said. "Not many men would have noticed. That's my father's badge. He served with the Director in Chicago, back in the old days. I came into the Bureau after his retirement. By special order, the Director assigned me my father's old number. Does that answer your question?"

Bonham had heard of similar instances. But he remained uncertain. "All of you," he said. "I want to see everybody's credentials."

"Shit," Sykes said. But he moved aside and, one by one, his seven assistants came to the head of the bed and thrust out his folder for Bonham's inspection. Bonham studied each carefully, comparing each photograph with the man's face.

"Satisfied?" Sykes asked.

A trace of doubt remained, but Bonham could think of nothing else to do. He nodded assent.

Sykes gestured for the wire recorder to be rewound. Then they started anew.

Bonham went through the preliminaries of name and vital statistics automatically, thinking ahead, wondering how to handle what was to come.

Sykes paused before delivering the first significant question. "What were you doing aboard the *Normandie?*"

"Tailing," Bonham said, determined to make Sykes work every step of the way.

"Tailing whom?"

"A suspect."

Sykes sighed. "Who was the suspect?"

"I don't know his name. He identified himself usually as either Walther Von Beck or Walter Beck."

"You're a real suspicious fellow, aren't you? Preoccupied with names. Was this an assigned case?"

That was the big one. Bonham met it head-on. "No."

"So you took it on yourself to tail this man? Without an assignment?"

"I did it on my own time," Bonham said.

Sykes snorted. "You have a backlog of assignments a foot thick. You were working on this almost around the clock. What on earth possessed you?"

Bonham's effort to shrug was hampered by the tape on his torso. "I knew he was up to something," he said.

Sykes leaned forward again. "Did it ever occur to you that you might be fucking up an on-going investigation?"

"I checked the case files," Bonham said.

Again, Sykes sighed. "For your information, all investigations don't make it into the general file. Some are retained in the Director's personal file."

Bonham did not answer. He was trying to determine where the questioning was headed. Nothing made sense. If he had blundered into an on-going investigation, they could have halted him at any time with a word. He remained certain the Bureau had not been investigating Von Beck.

"Okay," Sykes said, "let's have it. From beginning to end. I want to know every fucking thing you did. Every move you, Von Beck made. I want to know what happened aboard that ship. Take your time. Tell me every detail."

Bonham lay silent, thinking. He now held little hope that he would be retained by the Bureau. Sykes was right about his backlog of assigned cases. He had gone off on his own, attempting the big score, solo. The Bureau was a team effort—one of the most tightly knit organizations in existence. No one in the Bureau's hierarchy would condone his actions.

He concluded that he had only one chance. He could safely assume that Sykes's special squad of investigators were well-ensconced, no doubt working out of Washington, under the direct orders of J. Edgar Hoover.

If he could demonstrate to Hoover that he had acted in the best interests of the Bureau, that he had exhibited initiative and exceptional abilities, his job might yet be saved by the one man who had that power.

He motioned Sykes into a chair. Fighting back pain, he pushed himself higher on the bed, until his back was resting against the headboard. After several deep breaths, he began to talk.

He described his initial theory that Hitler would send more spies into the country, his search through the Bureau files for methods, dates, names, his relentless examination of each person on his list of 161 suspicious refugees.

Sykes listened silently, but with an expression that grew increasingly incredulous. As Bonham described his tracing of Rachael Moser, his first encounter with Von Beck, his growing suspicions as to Von Beck's background, Sykes at last interrupted in exasperation.

"If you thought they were spies, why didn't you take your evidence to your superiors in the Bureau? What in God's name made you think you could conduct a major investigation alone?"

Bonham paused. He knew that his job might hinge on the proper answer to the question.

"I didn't have enough facts," he said. "My supervisors were busy men. I couldn't approach them with vague evidence that did not meet the Bureau's standards."

Sykes raised his eyebrows and rolled his gaze to the ceiling. Someone laughed.

"Okay. Suppose I buy that," Sykes said. "What strange process of reasoning led you to tackle Von Beck on board the *Normandie?* Why didn't you back off, call for help?"

Again, Bonham hesitated. He felt that if he could convey the quandary of that moment, he could convince them he had made the right decision.

"I followed him on board about noon," he said. "He mingled for a time with some workers in the Grand Salon. I kept him under close surveillance, but from a distance. He was acting strangely, glancing around, moving in a suspicious manner, frequently stopping to look behind him. When he reached the stairwell, he picked up a tool kit, and went down into the ship. I knew he was up to something.

And from the way he was acting, I was certain that he would soon do whatever it was he was going to do."

Bonham paused, aware that he was not creating the mood he wished. He took a deep breath and plunged on.

"He went to hell and gone below decks—way down below the engine spaces, clear to the bottom of the ship. There were little compartments, hatches leading down, huge tanks . . . it was like a maze. It was dark, with only a small bulb here and there.

"And then, when the heavy smoke started coming through the vents and word was passed about the fire, Von Beck went crazy. He began shouting in German, and started out of the hole—coming right at me. I was suspicious that he had something to do with the fire. I certainly felt that he should be held for questioning. So I stepped out, and shouted to him that he was under arrest."

He described the fight, the last glimpse he had of the Grand Salon filled with smoke, water cascading down from above.

Sykes listened until the end. He took out a small notebook, scribbled a few lines, and ripped out a page. He handed it to an aide, who read it, then hurried out the door. Sykes turned back and pointed a finger at Bonham's chest.

"You will remain here until you are ready to be moved. You will have no visitors. You will be permitted to respond to the doctor's questions concerning your medical condition, but you will communicate with no one else. Not the man on duty, the nurses, no one. Understand me?"

Bonham wanted to ask if he were under arrest, if charges were pending. He knew that merely by asking the questions, he would be implying that he assumed charges were justified. But he could not face day after day of wondering.

"What's going to happen now?" he asked.

Sykes gave him a long, sober stare.

"God knows," he said.

He then turned and walked from the room. His aides followed without looking back.

Two days later Sykes was back. He came into Bonham's room shortly after daylight.

"Get dressed," he said. "You're taking a trip."

This time Sykes had only two aides trailing behind him. One carried a suitcase Bonham recognized as his own, from a closet shelf in his apartment. He opened his mouth to protest, but abandoned the effort as useless.

No doubt they had gone over every inch of his apartment.

Bonham rose from his bed and dressed, rejecting Sykes's tentative attempts to help. Movement was still painful, but during the last two days Bonham had spent longer and longer intervals sitting on the edge of his bed, walking up and down his room. He found that despite the heavy wrapping on his chest, his best suit was now loose-fitting. In less than a week, he had lost more than ten pounds.

Sykes paced impatiently as Bonham dressed and painfully worked with his tie, trying to straighten the knot with his swollen hands.

"That's good enough," Sykes said. He nodded to an assistant. "Let's go."

Bonham did not move. "Where are we going?" he asked. "I have the right to know."

Sykes considered the question a moment, then answered with one word. "Washington."

Sykes and his aides formed a phalanx around Bonham. At the elevator, another aide held the door as nurses, doctors, and hospital visitors gaped. When they emerged on the ground floor, other aides provided escort through the lobby, out the front door, and down the marble steps to a waiting limousine.

The trip, creeping through Philadelphia and Baltimore, and observing the wartime speed limit of 35 m.p.h., took more than eight hours. They did not arrive in Washington until after three in the afternoon. Even then, the driver took

367

a circuitous route, driving almost as far east as the Capitol before turning north to Pennsylvania Avenue. Bonham assumed the driver would exit left by the National Archives to deposit his passengers at the entrance to the Federal Bureau of Investigation on Ninth Street, where he would be interrogated.

But the car did not slow. The driver continued down Pennsylvania Avenue.

"What . . . ?" Bonham leaned forward, wondering if he had mistaken the intersection.

Sykes pulled him back into the plush seat. "Bonham, for once in your life, just sit back, enjoy the ride, and keep your goddamn mouth shut. Today you are to listen, not talk."

Bonham watched speechless as the limousine continued westward for six more blocks to the White House, entering at the East Gate. A small platoon of men waited at the east portico.

Bonham was ushered through a bewildering array of halls and doors. Somewhere along the way Sykes disappeared. At last, Bonham was left alone in a small, oddly shaped room, hardly more than a closet. From another room came the soft sounds of a radio. Someone was giving a speech. Bonham waited patiently in an uncomfortable, spindly chair until a tall, graying man entered.

He studied Bonham for several seconds. "Do you know who I am?" he asked.

The face was familiar. But Bonham knew better than to guess. "No, sir," he said.

"No matter. I'm Harry Hopkins, special assistant to the President." He sat facing Bonham, paused, and stared at the carpet for a long moment, frowning. He rubbed his stomach, as if he might be in pain. He was thin and gaunt. Deep lines of worry creased his face. He did not look well.

Bonham sat silent and awed. Hopkins was the President's trouble-shooter. In recent months, he had been to London for a conference with Churchill, to Moscow to talk with Stalin.

Bonham did not know what to say, so he waited. After a time, Hopkins looked up.

"I'm here to apprise you of certain facts. You have created an extraordinary, unique problem for us. The decision has been made that it requires an extraordinary, unique solution. Do you follow me?"

Bonham tried, but he could make no sense of that. "Not entirely, sir," he said.

Hopkins frowned and made another effort. "Let me put it this way. Through no fault of your own, you have stumbled onto a situation that involves national security. Frankly, there has been a great deal of discussion on how best to handle this. At this juncture, the most attractive alternative is to take you into our confidence, to depend on your proven character and abilities. Now, do you follow me?"

Bonham did not. But he felt he might be appearing dense. "I think so, sir."

"Good. Now, first and most importantly, your activities concerning the *Normandie* must never, ever come to light. Not in any way. Do we have your word on that?"

"Of course," Bonham said automatically. Then, in a flash of blinding intuition, he understood.

"You knew about Von Beck all along."

Hopkins nodded abruptly. But he made no further explanation.

Thoughts were sweeping through Bonham's head too fast to assimilate. "If you didn't interfere, then you *wanted* Von Beck to succeed."

Hopkins was silent for a long, brooding interval. "Let's just say that for various logical reasons—a series of developments—the *Normandie* was not as essential to our government as generally assumed."

Bonham sat staring at Hopkins, unable to put his questions into words. Anticipating them, Hopkins effectively halted further discussion.

"You are here today because your persistence, resourcefulness, and energy won admiration in high places," Hop-

369

kins said. "What you have learned about the *Normandie* must never become public knowledge, not now, or even to history. The President wishes to speak with you, to ascertain that you understand. If you should ever attempt to make this meeting known to the public, all will be denied. And no record will exist to support your claim."

Bonham hardly heard the warning. His mind was locked on the word *president*. Only at that moment did he realize that the voice he had heard was not a radio, but President Roosevelt dictating to his secretary in the next room.

Hopkins glanced at his watch. "We're late," he said. "We shouldn't keep the President waiting."

As Bonham and Hopkins stepped through the doorway, President Roosevelt glanced up at the interruption, and held out a palm of restraint to Hopkins, the long cigarette holder as effective as a conductor's baton. The gesture stopped Hopkins in midstride. Never missing a syllable, Roosevelt continued his dictation to a young woman seated to the right of his desk.

Like most Americans, Bonham was vaguely aware that Roosevelt had been crippled by infantile paralysis. But newsreels, newspaper photographs, even political cartoons always tastefully ignored the fact. Neither crutches nor wheelchair were ever in evidence. The President always was portrayed either seated, or standing at a podium after his hidden braces were securely locked in place. Bonham's first impression was one of shock that the President was, indeed, severely crippled.

Roosevelt sat in an armless wheelchair beside his desk, his shrunken legs hidden under a laprobe. His broad shoulders were covered by a dark shawl. At first glance, from behind, the President could have been mistaken for an elderly lady, tucked away in a nursing home.

But that first impression was quickly dispelled by the sheer magnetism of the man's presence. His slightest gesture conveyed power under taut control. The familiar voice exuded unbounded confidence. There was strength in every movement of his leonine head, command in his orchestration of voice, gestures, and expression.

"Let's send a note to Sam and Carl," he said to his secretary. "Ask them over for breakfast in the morning to discuss the Soviet Lend Lease appropriation. You know what to say. And track down Henry Stimson. Set up an appointment with him tomorrow morning. Tell him we must have the Pacific War Council organized for an April first meeting."

Bonham assumed that "Sam and Carl" were Congressional giants Sam Rayburn and Carl Vinson. Apparently the secretary knew. She did not ask.

The President dismissed her. "Thank you, that will be all for now." He beamed his well-known smile at her for a moment, then abruptly wheeled his chair to face Bonham and Hopkins.

"Gentlemen! Gentlemen! Sorry to keep you waiting! But I wanted to get these details out of the way so we could talk!" He turned his charm full on Bonham. "So this is the young man who led us on such a merry chase."

He held out a hand. Bonham crossed the Oval Office and shook hands with the President. The grip was firm, effortless.

Roosevelt gestured Bonham and Hopkins toward the couch by a small fireplace, and maneuvered his chair closer. "How do you feel now, young man? We hear you had a close call."

Without thought, Bonham touched the bruise on his cheek. "Yes, sir. But I'm all right now, sir."

Bonham and Hopkins sat on the couch, facing the President, who still had his full attention on Bonham.

"I'm happy to hear you're feeling better. I assume Harry has filled you in on the situation."

Hopkins had not. But Bonham sensed that this was not the time to ask questions. "Yes, sir," he said.

"I know all this is most unusual. But you can trust Harry. He handed out eight and a half billion dollars, you know, under the Works Progress Administration, without the hint of a scandal. Nothing like it in the history of this country, or the Democratic Party, for that matter. Harry's my answer to people who say there isn't an honest man in Washington."

Roosevelt laughed heartily at his own joke. Hopkins shifted uneasily, his solemnity intact. Not knowing what else to do, Bonham smiled politely.

Turning serious, Roosevelt toyed with his cigarette holder for a moment. "I assume we can depend on your discretion in this whole matter."

"Of course, Mr. President."

"Excellent!" Roosevelt glanced at Hopkins, then back at Bonham. "That leaves only the question of what to do with you, now that you've stumbled onto some state secrets. We can't very well send you back to work under people not privileged to those secrets, can we?"

Bonham's last lingering hope faded. His job with the Bureau apparently was lost.

The President smiled. "If this were some other country —Nazi Germany, Russia—the solution would be simple. We could just shoot you. Fortunately or unfortunately, we haven't reached that point in the United States, at least not yet. So that leaves us with the problem. . . ."

Roosevelt turned to Hopkins. "Why don't you send this young man over to Bill Donovan? I think Bonham is exactly the type of man Bill needs for his new outfit."

A vague bell sounded in the recesses of Bonham's memory. Somewhere, he had seen a news item. "Public relations?" he asked.

Roosevelt threw back his head and roared with laughter. Even Hopkins allowed the ghost of a smile.

"There's a bit more to it than that," Roosevelt said. "We'll let Donovan explain it to you. But I can assure you the job seems much more suited to your talents than the

Bureau. Edgar likes people over there who follow the rules, sharp young men who never question the way things are done. Donovan likes people who take the bull by the horns and use their own initiative. You seem more Donovan's type. How about giving it a try?''

"I'm ready to serve wherever needed, Mr. President," Bonham said.

"Well answered." Roosevelt turned to Hopkins. "Send Mr. Bonham to Donovan with my warmest recommendations. Also, send a note to Edgar. He may give us a bit of trouble. But make it plain to him that we are petitioning for Mr. Bonham's release from the Bureau for a presidential assignment. Edgar's a good soldier. I doubt he'll delve into it."

Hopkins nodded and rose from the couch. Bonham scrambled to his feet. Roosevelt held out his hand.

"Good-bye, and good luck," he said. "I'm confident that you'll have a long, brilliant career."

Bonham shook his hand. "Thank you, Mr. President."

Roosevelt's grip tightened. "To the contrary, Mr. Bonham. I thank you. And when you are introduced to your new job, I think you'll see why."

28

Wolfsschanze, East Prussia

On the long, tedious flight from Berlin, Oberst Erwin von Lahousen wondered many times why he had agreed to make the trip.

Loyalty, even to Admiral Canaris, had its limits.

Canaris remained silent and morose throughout the journey. Lahousen did not intrude. The Abwehr now was fighting for its very life. Their interview with the Führer might decide its continued existence.

The admiral's dismissal as chief of Abwehr had been completely unexpected, and devastating. The message from the Führer had said only that Canaris was relieved of duty, and was to relinquish his post to Leopold Burkner. Canaris, every member of the Abwehr staff had been stunned. Not until several hours later did they piece together what had happened.

Sturmbannführer Walther Schellenberg had stumbled across the questionable activities of an Abwehr agent in Tangier. He also had discovered that the agent was a full-blooded Jew.

The overly ambitious Schellenberg had informed

Reichführer SS Heinrich Himmler, who was ever eager to receive any information detrimental to Canaris. With the able assistance of Reich Protector Reinhart Heydrich, Himmler had built into the SS agencies that were in direct competition with the Abwehr. Himmler had approached Hitler several times with a plan to absorb the Abwehr into his SS operations.

Armed with Schellenberg's dossier on Canaris, Himmler again had broached the subject with Hitler, taunting the Führer with the fact that his military intelligence section was permeated with Jews. He revived the long-dormant case concerning the five hundred Jews from Holland sent by Canaris to "infiltrate" South America. Affronted, Hitler had summoned Oberkommando Keitel and demanded an explanation. When Keitel pleaded ignorance, Hitler went into one of his celebrated rages, and ordered Keitel to dismiss Canaris.

Lahousen suspected that Canaris was hurt most of all by the fact that Keitel had not offered one word of defense on the admiral's behalf.

And now Canaris and Lahousen were going over Keitel's head, direct to the Führer.

As they approached the gate to the compound, Canaris leaned over and placed a hand on Lahousen's knee. "I'm grateful enough for your company, Erwin. You don't have to go in with me, you know."

Lahousen already had thought it through. The admiral was woefully ignorant of so many details concerning his own command. He would need support. "There might be questions that I could answer," he said.

Canaris nodded acknowledgment. "We will tell him about the *Normandie*," he said. "That should put him in a good mood."

They were received by the Führer's military adjutant, Oberst Gerhard Engel, who offered no words of encouragement. The adjutant was blunt.

"This is a very bad time, Admiral," he said. "So much

has happened in the last few days. Couldn't your visit wait?''

"I think not," Canaris said. "The longer it's postponed, the more painful it'll be for all concerned. I'm well aware of the entire situation."

Engel's raised eyebrows eloquently conveyed that he was deferring to rank against his own wishes. "I'll tell the Führer you are here."

As they waited, Lahousen was conscious of sidelong glances from members of the headquarters staff. Bad news traveled fast, especially in the upper echelons of the Reich.

The adjutant returned. "The Führer will see you, briefly. As you may know, he is to leave tonight for Berlin."

The Führer's schedule had been of vital concern to Canaris in planning the trip. Two days before, Dr. Fritz Todt, minister of armament, had been killed in a plane crash at Rastenberg airfield. He was to be given a state funeral in Berlin, and the Führer would be departing within hours on his special train.

Lahousen was now accustomed to the spartan furnishings at Wolfsschanze. As they were ushered into the apartment, he gave his full attention to the Führer.

Hitler received them standing, stiff, unsmiling, formal. He did not ask them to be seated. Lahousen instantly saw confirmation of the reports that the Führer had regained a measure of his health. Although his skin was still unnaturally white, his posture was more erect, and the mystic luster had returned to his eyes.

He glanced briefly at Lahousen—the aloof, detached, analytical study a lion would give a stray house cat—before turning back to Canaris.

"Herr Admiral, my decision has been made," he said. "I don't see that our meeting will serve any useful purpose."

Canaris remained unfazed. "*Mein Führer,* I'm here only to assure you of my complete loyalty. I'm ready to serve the Reich where most needed."

Lahousen remembered that Canaris always had said that the Führer could not be pushed into changing his mind. He only could be led.

Hitler seemed only slightly mollified by the admiral's words. "Herr Admiral, I was shown conclusive proof that Jews are used in confidential positions throughout the Abwehr. This practice cannot be tolerated!"

Canaris nodded, agreeing. "It's lamentable," he said. "Perhaps I acted unwisely. As we have discussed before, *Mein Führer*, the gathering of intelligence is an unsavory trade, and those who follow it have many motives. We obtain valuable information from those who are not guided as much from their love of Germany as from their hatred of the Communists. Some are romantics. A few are adventurers, seeking excitement. Many love the intrigue, the sense of power. And there are the Jews, with their capitalistic avarice. As you have said, *Mein Führer*, it's most unsavory."

Hitler did not answer. But he was listening. Encouraged, Canaris went on.

"We have brought you the most wonderful news, *Mein Führer*. Word has just been received. The *Normandie* has been destroyed."

For once, the Führer's fabled memory failed him. He looked at Canaris, uncomprehending. "The what?" he asked.

The admiral's poise remained intact. "The ship, *Mein Führer*," he said. "The French liner. We have burned her at her pier in New York. She capsized. She is a total loss."

Hitler began snapping his fingers in agitation. "You have interrupted my grief to tell me this?" His arms began to pump in rhythm. His voice rose. "With all that I have on my mind, you bring me this! With our armies retreating from Moscow! All our combat divisions down to one-third strength! Von Rundstedt refusing to hold the line at Rostov! When I have had to dismiss my generals and take personal command of the armies! When the British have taken Tobruk! When my Minister of Armaments lies dead! You have flown here from Berlin to tell me a ship has been sunk!"

"No, *Mein Führer*," Canaris said soothingly. "We are here only to offer our condolences, to assure you of our continued loyalty in this sad hour."

"But you mentioned the ship!"

"Only to make a point, *Mein Führer*," Canaris said. "You see, the *Normandie* was sunk by a hero of the Reich, a U-boat Kapitän who wears the Knight's Cross. I have known him since he was a child, and I can assure you that he would much rather be at sea with his comrades, in combat, than in the repugnant work of sabotage. But in these dark days we must all accept our assignments where we serve best. He did not complain, not even when ordered to work with a Jewish woman interested only in the money we paid her. Together, they sank the ship. It was a small but necessary victory. As you have said many times, *Mein Führer*, 'Our leaders must demand of themselves the sacrifice of overcoming their scruples.' "

Lahousen's blood chilled at the admiral's audacity. The Abwehr had not received a single word from Von Beck. The Jewish woman's reports had ceased abruptly almost a month ago. News of the loss of the *Normandie* had come from commercial radio in America. Although Canaris had sent a message to Minister of Propaganda Joseph Goebbels claiming successful sabotage by the Abwehr, no one knew for certain if Von Beck was involved. And few people dared to quote the Führer's words back to him for their own purpose—especially a phrase referring to the Final Solution.

Hitler did not answer. He fixed Canaris with his aloof, analytical stare.

"My only regret in leaving the Abwehr is that I would have liked to conduct a thorough investigation into Dr. Todt's death," Canaris went on, matter-of-factly. "I understand his plane exploded on takeoff, only seven hundred meters from the end of the runway. I find the circumstances most suspicious."

Canaris waited. Hitler continued to study him in silence.

At last Hitler spoke. "I, too, share your suspicions," he said. He paused, as if considering the ramifications of his decision. "I will order Oberkommando Keitel to reinstate you. A military tribunal will investigate Dr. Todt's death. You will provide every assistance."

"*Jawohl, Mein Führer,*" Canaris said.

Hitler reached to shake hands, signaling the end of the meeting. He ushered them to the door.

A few minutes later, they stood at the entance to the log and cement building, awaiting their car.

The night had turned cold. Light, powdery snow was falling, but had not yet covered the ground. Beyond the compound fence, the concertina barbed wire, and the mine fields, lights played eerily on the distant trees.

Canaris adjusted his hat and turned up his coat collar. "War is a most singular business," he said. "No other human endeavor demands more, or offers so little in return." He was silent for a moment. "Let me know the minute we hear anything from Von Beck."

Lahousen promised to do so.

The admiral's words hung heavy on his mind. Reflecting on the scene in Hitler's apartment, Lahousen was struck by a certainty: Canaris had made too many enemies among those who courted Hitler's favor. No matter what happened, the admiral's days were numbered.

Already subtle signs were in the air. He and the admiral had not been invited to ride back to Berlin with Hitler on the *Führersonderzug*. The train would be filled with ambitious men.

Lahousen knew he should make preparations to survive without the protection of the admiral. Perhaps he should volunteer for duty on the Russian front, where he would be beyond the reach of the Byzantine maneuverings within the Führer's court.

He followed Canaris out to the car for the ride back to the airport and the flight back to Berlin.

He might yet salvage some honor out of the war.

EPILOGUE

OCTOBER 1981

Nose broken at last interrogation. My time is up. Was not a traitor. Did my duty as a German. If you survive remember me to my wife.

> Admiral Wilhelm Canaris
> Final tap-code message to man in next cell,
> Flossenburg Prison, Germany
> April 9, 1945

29

Puerto Vallarta, Mexico

The setting sun had disappeared beneath the sea. To the west, the sky was resplendent with varying hues of red, spectacularly arrayed against the deepening blue of the ocean, the white sands of the beach. Behind Bonham, the seacliffs rose to dramatic heights. As he walked northward, seabirds swooped and circled around him, crying out against the approaching night. In the surf, a few swimmers persisted against the evening chill of the breeze from seaward. Shouting and splashing, they remained oblivious to Bonham's passage. Only a small Mexican boy, poking at a crab with a stick, turned to gaze curiously at the tall, lean Gringo in a three-piece business suit walking along the beach, carrying a briefcase, his Gucci loafers soaked by an unexpected wave from the incoming tide.

Bonham ignored the boy's stare. He was accustomed to appearing conspicuous, even ridiculous in foreign lands.

Favoring his bad leg against the pull of the soft sand, he walked on northward. At last, he reached the wooden stairway leading up from the beach.

He stopped for a moment, savoring the view.

The hotel stood on a shelf of the cliff, its wings spread to the sheer rock face on each side. Paths leading to the rooms were lined with bougainvillea, flowering yucca, roses and cacti of multitudinous blooms. Below the hotel itself, on a rock promontory, a dozen or more guests already were at dinner under Japanese lanterns. The surf failed to drown the distant, mournful ballad of a Mexican tenor, strolling with a string band among the diners.

Seldom during his entire life had Bonham experienced such total peacefulness. He stood for several minutes, savoring the setting, dreading what he had to do. Then, with a last glance to seaward, he shifted his briefcase to his other hand and started slowly up the wooden steps. At each landing he paused, battling a growing reluctance to take the final step of a long journey.

By the time he reached the top of the stairs, darkness had descended along the face of the cliff. Only a hint of twilight remained in the western sky. Overhead, a full moon had blossomed into silvery radiance, bathing the leaves of the trees around the terrace.

Lingering in the shadows, Bonham studied the diners—a sprinkling of American tourists, a young Japanese couple, a few wealthy Mexicans. He did not see a single face he recognized. He walked on toward the well-lighted hotel lobby, again regretting the compulsion that had brought him to Mexico.

Across from the registration desk, a television set was tuned to a soccer game in Mexico City. Six or eight young Mexican males were following the action, cheering each time their favorite team made a spectacular play.

"Could I help you, sir?" asked the desk clerk.

"I would like a room," he said. "Preferably facing the sea. Ground floor, if possible. I have a bad leg."

The desk clerk was a Mexican with a square face, a strong jaw, and a handsome moustache. He resembled Burt Reynolds. When he smiled, the similarity was unsettling—and obviously well cultivated. Bonham had no doubt he cut a wide swath among the women.

"You have reservations, of course," the clerk asked, smiling.

"No."

The desk clerk raised his eyebrows, suggesting disbelief that anyone came to Puerto Vallarta without reservations. He fished through a card file.

Bonham waited.

As last, the clerk held up a card. "Fortunately, we have had a cancellation. I believe we can accommodate you, sir." He gestured to the registration pad.

Bonham filled out the form with practiced ease.

"Your luggage?"

Bonham handed him the claim check. "It's at the airport. Please send for it."

He turned and followed the bellhop out the bougainvillea-lined path.

The room was small but pleasant, heavily decorated with native ceramics, weavings, and paintings. The large front window overlooked the bay. Bonham gave the bellboy a twenty-dollar bill.

"Bring me a bottle of good scotch, some soda, and keep the change."

The bellboy's grin conveyed the collapse of every house rule.

Bonham's leg was throbbing. He eased off his shoes and stretched full length on the bed until the bellboy returned with a bottle of Cutty Sark. Bonham poured a drink, turned out the room lights, and lay in the darkness, watching the diners on the patio, the shimmer of moonlight on the sea.

Slowly, he drank himself to sleep.

Most of the overnight guests were at breakfast when the owner of the hotel walked down from his suite for toast and coffee on the terrace. For a time he lingered, savoring the view. He did not go up to his office until almost nine.

When the overnight reports from the desk were brought to him more than an hour later, he was pleased to find bookings at a hundred percent of capacity. He wandered down to the desk, where Alfredo had just arrived for work.

"A full house," he said. "I thought there were cancellations."

Alfredo toyed with his moustache. "Only three," he said. "We had some late arrivals."

The owner of the hotel examined the register to see if any of the unexpected guests were regulars, deserving of special attention. A family by the name of Fitzgerald from Houston. He remembered them from two, maybe three years past. A petroleum engineer, an attractive wife, and two lovely young daughters. He would make a point of buying the Fitzgeralds a convivial drink. Rafael Gonzales and wife from Mexico City. He did not remember them. The third name, H. S. Bonham, seemed vaguely familiar. He thought back through the years before he remembered why.

For the moment, he discounted the possibility that it could be the same Bonham. But the remote chance was too worrisome to dismiss, and nagged at him through the morning. Toward noon, he took up station outside the cantina, at a table that gave him a view of the guests arriving for lunch and of those on their way to and from the beach.

When Bonham appeared, on his way to the terrace, the owner of the hotel felt the full shock of recognition. He remembered all too well the tall, lanky build, the hard, ropy muscles, the peculiar set of his mouth and jaw. Any remaining doubt vanished as their eyes met. Bonham stopped in midstride, blocking the walk. The moment seemed interminable, until at last Bonham seemed to become aware of other hotel guests behind him and moved on to give them passage. With only the trace of a limp, Bonham followed the maitre d' to a far table and sat facing the sea.

Shaken, the owner of the hotel rose and walked back into the lobby.

His mind was in turmoil. Why had Bonham tracked them down—after more than four decades?

All of the fears and uncertainties of their early days in Mexico returned with a rush. For years, they had remained suspicious of all Americans. They had dreaded every Mexican election, fearful with each new administration that bribed officials would become unbribed and their residency papers worthless. The arrival of each baby had revived the problem of citizenship, the threat of exposure. During the first decade they had remained concerned that their hard work in founding the hotel might be wiped out overnight through legal problems, perhaps even deportation.

But those terrible times had passed. The hotel had prospered. Now their three sons were grown and out on their own. He and his wife had been enjoying their security, their relatively new freedom.

Had he become overconfident?

Was Bonham a threat to everything they had accomplished, everything that gave their lives meaning?

He found his wife in the laundry room, instructing the two new maids on their duties. He waited until she had finished, then put his arm around her and took her into the hall where they could talk.

"Remember Bonham?" he asked.

She looked at him, not comprehending.

"He's here," he said. "He checked into one-eleven yesterday evening."

He saw the fear come into her eyes as she grasped the situation. "What does he want?"

"I don't know," he said. "I haven't talked with him."

She reached for his arm. "What can he do?"

"Nothing, probably," he said. "I'm sure the statutes of limitations have long expired for anything we've done."

In truth, he was not so certain. The penalties seemed to depend on time and circumstance more than on tradition. He recalled that the thirty-three German spies arrested by the United States before the war had received an average sentence of eighteen years. Most had been paroled after the war. But the foolish Leutnant Werner Kappe and his men had fared far worse. Disaster occurred, just as Admiral Canaris had predicted. Landed by submarines on Long Island and the coast of Florida, the eight saboteurs had been captured within days, tried, and given the death sentence. Six were executed. Only two survived the war.

"What will you do?" his wife asked.

He smiled, conveying confidence he did not feel. "What else can I do?" he said. "I'll talk to him."

He followed Bonham into the cantina, walking up to the bar just as Bonham was arranging himself on a stool.

"Mr. Bonham, I believe," he said. "Permit me to buy you a drink."

Bonham turned and looked at him for a long moment. "Why not?" he said.

The owner of the hotel signaled for Pedro to bring Bonham's drink, then escorted Bonham to a corner table where they sat, facing the sea. "I thought I recognized you this morning," he said. "But I wasn't sure until I checked the register."

If Bonham recognized the lie, he gave no hint. He seemed to be sharing the difficulty of finding their way into a relationship. He hesitated before answering. "I heard several years ago that you were down here," he said. He gestured toward the terrace. "Nice place."

The owner of the hotel watched Bonham's eyes, seeking any clue as to what was in his mind. "Thank you," he said. "We're in the midst of a long-term project. We may add another story to each wing."

Bonham seemed not to have heard. He appeared distracted, wary. "I've heard you have three grown sons," he said.

The hotel owner did not answer for a moment, wondering what lay behind the remark. Bonham obviously had gone to considerable trouble to find him, investigate his background. He spoke with a casualness he did not feel. "Almost a grandfather," he said.

388

Again, Bonham seemed preoccupied with his own thoughts, engrossed in some inner struggle. At last, he apparently arrived at a resolution. He looked up, his face serious and intent.

"Look, I want to know. Why did you come back for me, that day on the *Normandie?*"

Walther Von Beck shrugged. "I don't know," he said. "It just seemed the thing to do, at the time."

Bonham hesitated, as if he might explore the question further. Instead, he put out his hand.

"Anyway, I came down here to thank you. It just seemed shitty to let it go by without thanking you for what you did."

Suddenly Von Beck understood. Bonham apparently was plagued by the same unanswered questions that had always troubled him.

Bonham had come to Mexico to tie up loose ends.

Von Beck reached for Bonham's hand. "Why don't you come up tonight for dinner?" he said. "We'll open a bottle, and talk about old times."

Bonham sat in Von Beck's study, satiated with superb food, fully relaxed from the dinner wine and Courvoisier. The room was almost entirely lined with books—Shakespeare, Goethe, Conrad, Tolstoy, a wealth of classics. One wall was filled with histories and biographies of World War II in several languages, along with scores of volumes on the Central Intelligence Agency, contemporary United States politics, and economic theories. The books were not merely decorative. They had the well-worn aspect of considerable use.

The opposite wall was covered with photographs—Von Beck as a cadet at Flensburg, Von Beck posed on the gratings with his U-boat crew, Von Beck and Rachael supervising the building and operation of the hotel, Von Beck and his growing family, Von Beck and Rachael greeting various Hollywood stars and heads of state.

And over the mantelpiece hung a large painting of the liner *Normandie*.

Bonham had not been so relaxed in years. The huge leather chair was comfortable. In the cantina below, the tenor was singing "La Peregrina," a haunting love ballad.

Rachael had seemed wary of Bonham at first, but now appeared totally at ease. Even after forty years, Bonham would have been able to pick her out of a crowd of a thousand. She remained petite and childlike, her skin dark-tanned but smooth and unblemished, her posture erect, regal. The gray in her gamin-cut hair could have been mistaken for the frosted style of a much-younger woman. She now sat on the floor, her head and shoulders resting against Von Beck's thigh.

The years also had brought little change to Von Beck. He was lighter by fifteen or twenty pounds. His face was thinner, perhaps even a bit more handsome in full maturity.

Talk throughout the evening mostly had concerned anecdotes connected with the Von Beck children, with the operation of the hotel.

"It's been a good life," Von Beck said. "I'm glad we didn't try to go back to Europe. Fortunately, Rachael had some resources." He smiled. "But then you knew about that, didn't you?"

Bonham nodded.

"That was a start. We designed and built the hotel. It was touch and go for a while. We were too far off the beaten path. But a few years ago Hollywood made a movie down here. We had all we could handle, for a time."

Bonham made complimentary noises about the hotel.

"Rachael did the decoration, the furnishings," Von Beck said. "All local labor, all native crafts. I think she did a marvelous job."

Bonham nodded his agreement. His room was decorated with ornate tapestries woven by Indians. Even the ashtrays were ceramic, fired in native ovens.

The long evening had left Bonham loose and unusually

uninhibited. His gaze was resting on a well-known, scholarly biography of Canaris across the room. Something jogged in his memory—something from long ago.

"You knew Canaris, didn't you?"

Von Beck looked at him in surprise. "How did you know that?"

Bonham remembered. "I ran across your name in the OSS files. That was the first I knew you had been in U-boats. The report said you'd been relieved of command on direct orders from Canaris, and assigned to the Abwehr."

"That was true," Von Beck said. "Canaris and my father were close friends."

"What was he like?"

As Von Beck considered his answer, his gaze flicked to his extensive library, confirming Bonham's suspicion the volumes were well read.

"He was a strange man," Von Beck said cautiously. "I don't think anyone ever knew exactly what was in his mind. I suppose you know he plotted against Hitler from the first, and that he was hanged at Flossenburg Prison just before the end of the war. But he apparently wasn't involved in the attempt to assassinate Hitler at Wolfsschanze. He was innocent of the crime for which he was hanged."

"I saw him once, from a distance, in Spain," Bonham said. "I was there with Wild Bill Donovan, who met with him. Canaris was trying to arrange a deal. He and his group would seize Hitler, make peace with Britain and the United States, and continue the war against Russia while we continued the war against Japan. As soon as they got wind of it, Roosevelt and Churchill sent word to us to break off the talks. But I've thought since, maybe we should have listened to him."

Von Beck shook his head. "I'm not sure Canaris could have upheld his end of the bargain. His influence disintegrated steadily throughout the war."

"I've wondered. How did he keep his job so long?"

"You have to understand Germany, as it was," Von Beck said. "He was a patriot. No one—not even the Nazi inner circle—could ever forget what he represented. I think a part of him approved of Hitler as a political expediency, while another part of him saw and understood the terrible things that were happening." He gestured toward the bookcases. "I don't think the people on this side of the Atlantic understand yet what happened in Germany. If Hitler had died—or been murdered—at the time of the Anschluss in 1938, no doubt he would have been ranked as one of the greatest leaders in European history, greater even than Bismarck, for Hitler was the first to unify all German-speaking peoples."

"He was a monster," Rachael snapped.

"No, that is my point," Von Beck said. "If we merely dismiss Hitler as insane, then we absolve him of all responsibility for his actions. If we insist that he led the Germans into a mass insanity, we absolve all Germans of blame for what happened. This I'm not prepared to do."

"I was in Vienna during the Anschluss," Rachael said. "That was an insanity."

Von Beck sighed. "We have lived through terrible times," he said. "More people were murdered in our generation than in all the rest of human history put together. That's a terrible burden to bear. And because it *is* a part of our experience, I think we of all people should be able to recognize that the same conditions prevail today." Again, he glanced toward his books. "It is a fatal flaw that man may not survive."

Bonham remained silent. He had been in Vietnam, Chile, Lebanon, the Bay of Pigs, Nicaragua, other places. He had seen many things he could not discuss. Not with anyone.

Von Beck raised his glass and smiled in an attempt to lighten the moment. "So, we've retreated from it all—found our own little paradise." His hand moved to cover Rachael's. "Now the past—all that happened—seems like

392

a bad dream." He paused for a moment. "I understand you remained in government work. Are you now retired?"

"Retired once again," Bonham said. "I've been called back several times, for some job or other."

They talked for a while of less significant things. Von Beck mentioned that they had a boat. He invited Bonham to spend some time with them, and promised they would put the boat to use.

At last, Bonham felt the proper moment had arrived to broach the subject that had brought him to Mexico.

"I've been admiring that painting of the *Normandie*," he said.

Both Von Beck and Rachael laughed. "Thank you," Von Beck said.

Bonham understood. "You painted it?"

"The only remnant of my short-lived artistic career. I learned that as a painter, I'm a good draftsman." He looked up at the painting. "That's the only instance where I felt I managed to achieve something of what I saw in my mind's eye."

Bonham hesitated over his next remark. He hardly knew where to begin.

"There were so many unanswered questions. I've gone through all the FBI files—more than two thousand pages —the Senate committee report, the House Naval Affairs investigation, the New York Fire Department study, the U.S. Navy Board of Inquiry proceedings, the Maritime Commission Report. . . ."

Von Beck nodded. "I've managed to obtain most of them."

"On the day of the fire, I thought it was you," Bonham said. "Later, I reconstructed what you were doing. But I still wonder. Who did it?"

Von Beck did not answer for a moment. "At the time, I blamed the Irish. Now, I simply don't know."

Bonham had been uncertain as to how much he should reveal. He now made his decision.

"Something happened to me immediately afterward," he said. "Something that I've never told anyone. . . ."

Von Beck and Rachael listened enrapt as he described his trip to Washington, his briefing by Harry Hopkins, his meeting with Roosevelt.

"No one put it into exact words," he concluded. "But Hopkins implied that the government was happy to see the last of the *Normandie*. They apparently had me under surveillance. They knew every move I made. So they must have known about you. And probably about O'Neill."

Von Beck and Rachael honored Bonham's account with a long, meditative silence. Von Beck seemed stunned.

"That's a new thought to me," he said. "But it may make sense."

"How?"

"Let's look at it from Roosevelt's perspective. At that time, America's relationship with France was very complex. De Gaulle was in England, demanding that all dealings with the French underground be conducted through him. For Churchill and Roosevelt, he was a pain in the ass. The Vichy government was collaborationist. Anti-British sentiment was high in France, especially after the British Navy sank the French fleet. If the *Normandie* had been put to work, De Gaulle's position would have been enhanced. He was demanding full participation in strategy sessions for the invasion of Europe."

"There also was criticism in Congress over the seizure of the *Normandie*," Bonham said. "There was a widespread belief that since France was not a belligerent, the laws of seizure might not have been applicable."

"The *Normandie* would have been difficult to operate," Von Beck went on. "France and Germany used the metric system for machinery, armament, plumbing. Special tools and dies would have been needed to keep the *Normandie* and all of her auxiliary engines in repair. And she was topheavy. If you remember, the reports estimated that only six hundred tons of water remained aboard and caused her to turn turtle. Fifteen thousand troops would have weighed more than twice that. If the *Normandie* had been loaded with American soldiers, and they crowded to the rail at departure, the ship would have capsized."

"Surely they knew about that danger much earlier," Bonham argued.

"I'm not so certain. It was a well-kept secret during the *Normandie*'s career at sea. She was sadly lacking in water-tight integrity below decks. She was beautiful, but ex-tremely vulnerable. Somewhere in the reports, there is mention that she was being rushed into service to speed troops to the relief of General Stilwell in Burma. I think everything came to a head. First, they didn't have troops available to send. And as time for sailing approached, the Navy was horrified at the prospect of taking her out in her condition. Yet, that early in the war, they couldn't admit that so many mistakes had been made. But they saw a way for the *Normandie* to make a contribution."

"By burning?"

Von Beck paused to refill Bonham's glass. "You were aboard her. You saw conditions that probably existed in every shipyard and factory in the country. No security. Carelessness. Malingering. Confusion. There were strikes, slowdowns. The country wasn't into the war mentally, and Roosevelt knew it. The U-boats were using the lights of East Coast cities to silhouette tankers and freighters, and the cities were resisting efforts to impose a brown-out. Maybe Roosevelt felt it was time to wake them up. The burning of the *Normandie* brought the war home to Amer-icans as nothing else could have done, short of an air raid. If you remember, the newspapers called it a second Pearl Harbor."

Bonham thought of Hopkins' cryptic words, Roosevelt's jovial mood. He also thought of the many clandestine plots during his long career with the CIA.

"You really believe the government did it?" he asked.

"It certainly wasn't I," Von Beck said. "And I'm fairly

certain it wasn't O'Neill. After what you've told me, I tend to think the United States government is perhaps the most plausible candidate. But of course there is one other possibility."

"What?"

Von Beck smiled. "It truly could have been an accident."

ACKNOWLEDGMENT

I wish to thank most especially Michael Korda, who not only conceived the original story but also provided invaluable constructive criticism throughout the writing, and my agent, Aaron M. Priest, for his initial and continuing enthusiasm for the project. Also, Joseph M. Myers, former Special Agent of the FBI, for his guidance through a maze of more than two thousand documents obtained from the FBI files under the Freedom of Information Act, concerning the sinking of the *Normandie;* Milt Hopwood, who was serving as a commissioned officer in the Office of Naval Intelligence, Third Naval District, at the time of the sinking of the *Normandie,* and who provided an eloquent description of New York City during those dark days, and Harvey Ardman, who has compiled the first comprehensive book on the *Normandie* and her career, soon to be published by Harper & Row, and who generously shared his exhaustive research.